PRAISE FOR ED~~~~~~~~~~~~~~~~
LEGAL SUSPENSE

DIARY OF A SERIAL KILLER

"The legal thriller equivalent of a James Bond flick."
—*Publishers Weekly*

"Gaffney packs this story with humor, suspense, a great plot and wonderful characters.... Gaffney has boundless talent and his plotting knows no limits."
—*Mystery News*

"Another complex, fast-paced legal thriller for defense attorneys Zack and Terry... Ed Gaffney does it again and has developed a complex, compelling and thoroughly engrossing story that draws you into the mind of the killer.... Readers who enjoy a fast-paced, stress-inducing ride will really enjoy this novel."
—freshfiction.com

"Starts off... with a heart-stopping scene... The remainder of the book lives up to the opening."
—*Mystery Lovers Bookshop News*

SUFFERING FOOLS

"A legal 'thriller' that does not take itself too seriously... Funny... Moves along swiftly with a nice degree of suspense."
—*Deadly Pleasures*

"This is a meticulously plotted, fascinating glimpse at the real justice system. A first-rate, fascinating mystery packed with false leads and a quixotic ending." —*Romantic Times*

PREMEDITATED MURDER

"Great characters in a gripping story, wild twists, and—surprise—big laughs! I love this book!"
—*New York Times* bestselling author
Suzanne Brockmann

"[A] unique thriller filled with intrigue and nonstop action." —*Romantic Times*

"A deep legal thriller . . . Ed Gaffney writes a fabulous tale that grips readers from the moment Judge Cottonwood shows his bench bias and never slows down until the confrontation with number seven."
—*Midwest Book Review*

"Full to the brim with thrills, spills and chills . . . electric, tingling fare." —*Los Angeles Times*

Also by Ed Gaffney

PREMEDITATED MURDER

SUFFERING FOOLS

DIARY OF A SERIAL KILLER

ENEMY COMBATANT

Ed Gaffney

A Dell Book

ENEMY COMBATANT
A Dell Book / March 2008

Published by Bantam Dell
A Division of Random House, Inc.
New York, New York

This is a work of fiction. Names, characters, places, and
incidents either are the product of the author's imagination or
are used fictitiously. Any resemblance to actual persons, living
or dead, events, or locales is entirely coincidental.

All rights reserved
Copyright © 2008 by Edward B. Gaffney
Cover photograph © 2008 by Greg Pease/Getty Images
Cover design by Jamie S. Warren Youll

If you purchased this book without a cover, you should be
aware that this book is stolen property. It was reported as
"unsold and destroyed" to the publisher, and neither the author nor the publisher has received any payment for this
"stripped book."

Dell is a registered trademark of Random House, Inc., and the
colophon is a trademark of Random House, Inc.

ISBN 978-0-440-24374-8

Printed in the United States of America
Published simultaneously in Canada

www.bantamdell.com

OPM   10 9 8 7 6 5 4 3 2 1

This book is dedicated
To Suz—
To Melanie and Jason—
To Bernard and Mary—
To Grace, Mary Anne, Eileen, Bernadette,
    Steve, John, and Beth—
And to Eric, Bill and Jodie, and everyone
    in the Tribe.
Thank you for choosing me.

ACKNOWLEDGMENTS

Thanks to Kate Miciak and the team at Bantam Dell for their expert work. Continuing thanks to my agent, Steve Axelrod. Thanks to Eric Ruben for the research, and for his creative inspiration. Thanks to the brave first-draft readers: Steve Axelrod, Deede Bergeron, Lee Brockmann, Suz Brockmann, Scott Lutz, and Patricia McMahon. And thanks always to Suz, whose hard work has done so much good for so many.

PROLOGUE

MY PROPERTY LAW professor, J. Keenan Bowles, used to get angry with me whenever I used the phrase "with all due respect," because he thought it was code for "you don't know what you're talking about." He also loved to say that peace was nothing more than a state of mutual cowardice.

And my best friend, Cliff Redhorse, recently told me that according to traditional Navajo teachings, my arrest for murder in the middle of the Juan Gomez terrorism trial was merely the universe trying to put itself back into balance.

With all due respect, Professor Bowles and the Navajos don't know what they're talking about.

The only thing that was out of balance on the first day of the Gomez trial was me. I was exhausted because a cold front had rolled through central Arizona the night before, and Dad can't sleep through thunderstorms.

Right up until his stroke, my father, Henley Carpenter, had been the top assistant district attorney in Maricopa County. He prosecuted all the big criminal cases in Phoenix. He was a quick-thinking, fast-talking, high-energy lawyer in a town where everything seemed to run about two speeds slower than he did.

But by the time that Juan Abdullah Gomez was charged with plotting the infamous Denver Tunnel Bombing, my father had been retired for years, and I was taking care of him in my parents' house up on Payson's Ridge. The injury to Dad's brain had left him unable to speak, unable to move around without a wheelchair, occasionally forgetful, and terrified of electrical storms. So I spent most of that night with him in the living room, listening to *Barry White's Greatest Hits*—my father's favorite CD.

We have never discovered where Dad got his taste in music.

Anyway, from about midnight to a little after four in the morning, over the background of an alarmingly deep voice musically seducing dozens of sensuous women, I reassured my father that despite the intermittent flashes of blinding light and air-cracking explosions that rattled our windows for hours, we were completely safe, and everything was going to be all right.

Less than a week would pass before I realized just how pathetically wrong I was on both counts.

To this day, my naivety embarrasses me, depresses me, and really pisses me off.

I should probably apologize in advance for my tone. Until recently, I did not consider myself to be an angry person. In fact, before the Gomez trial, I would have told you that I had big plans for a very bright future. I saw the world as a treasure chest of promise, a complicated but beautiful origami of unfolding opportunities. The perfect day was one filled with discoveries.

My favorite word used to be *threshold*.

I don't have a favorite word anymore.

A perfect day for me now consists of a few chores, a bit of writing, and spending time with the remaining members of my family. I have been told that after a while, my feelings of betrayal and suspicion will pass, and my old self will reemerge, but I'm afraid that I have developed some rather severe trust issues. I wouldn't be surprised to learn that my old self was long gone, and hadn't left a forwarding address.

I guess we'll see.

ONE

IT WAS A FLUKE that I was in the courtroom at all.

The Juan Gomez trial was sensational by any standard, but for the scandal-starved Southwest, this trial was a thrill-seeker's ambrosia, and the good folks of Arizona were dying for a taste. Phoenix Superior Courtroom Number One-B was jammed with the curious and the vengeful as the trial opened on that fateful June 5. The defendant was being prosecuted for plotting two attacks: one in Houston, which, thank God, had been thwarted in the planning stage, and the one in Denver on that terrible May morning that killed one hundred thirteen people, and injured three hundred twenty-eight more. Gomez was the biggest terrorist suspect to be tried in the U.S. since Timothy McVeigh and Zacarias Moussaoui.

The only reason I got to see the trial in the first place was because Sarge, the chief court officer, had saved a seat for me.

Sarge was a former Marine, and the most physically

intimidating sixty-five-year-old man I knew. He had started as a court officer at around the same time my dad began his career as an A.D.A. As a child, whenever I accompanied my father to the courthouse, I would always spend a considerable amount of time staring at Sarge's terrifying but mesmerizing flattop haircut. It didn't hurt that he'd sneak me some Reese's Pieces every time he saw me.

My weakness for junk food dried up around the time I became a lawyer myself, but Sarge's affection for my family never did. And he knew that on the fifth day of every June—except for 1995, when my mother's appendix demanded an immediate detour to Phoenix General—my parents, my older brother, Dale, and I would attend whatever criminal trial was taking place at the superior courthouse.

It is the one family ritual I continue to honor even after everything that happened. But more about that later.

At the time of the Gomez trial, Sarge was well aware that my mom and Dale were no longer alive, so it was a real long shot that my father would have the energy to endure the wall-to-wall mob sure to make life in the wheelchair even harder than it already was. But that didn't stop the big court officer from saving a place for us anyway, just in case.

And so the stage was set for my spectacular and ill-advised pratfall into the unique limelight reserved for mass murderers.

I was in the third row, shoehorned between reporters from *USA Today* on my left and *The New York Times* on my right. All the big press outlets had swept into town like an Old Testament plague when it was announced that Gomez would be tried here in Phoenix. Fifty of the nearly three hundred seats in the gallery were reserved for them. They complained—hundreds of them were shut out—but they weren't the only ones clamoring for a firsthand view of terrorist justice, Arizona-style. Thousands of ordinary citizens competed for the remaining opportunities to witness what Governor—and current senatorial candidate—Atlee Hamilton had promised would be a demonstration of "good old-fashioned American West jurisprudence," whatever that was supposed to mean. And in a particularly opportunistic move, even for someone as publicity-hungry as Hamilton, he had pledged to attend a portion of every day of the trial.

One thing that was definitely not old-fashioned, however, was the trial's television coverage. That entire aspect of the case was being managed by the new, federally run Judicial Broadcasting System. The idea was to balance the public's right to view criminal trials with the limitations of space by setting up a single camera in the courtroom. That source would then provide a live video and audio feed of the proceedings to any television network or station that requested it.

And according to what I've heard, the system worked very well. Tens of millions watched as Judge Rhonda Klay presided over jury selection on that historic opening day of the trial.

I was sorry to see that Judge Klay had been assigned to the case—not because she was one of the meanest judges in Arizona, but because she was one of the worst.

The trouble was not that the small, lizardlike woman lacked the brains for the job. It was, instead, that Rhonda Klay used her considerable intelligence to twist the rules to make it almost impossible for any defendant to get a fair trial.

I realize that last statement sounds like it was written by a defense attorney, and, well, it was. But for several years before the Gomez fiasco, aside from a handful of very mediocre trial performances, I had made my living almost exclusively as a court-appointed criminal appeals attorney. It was my duty to review trial transcripts, and to spot judges who didn't follow the rules. I was pretty good at it, too. Usually, when I found a problem, it was because a judge didn't know or understand the relevant legal principle.

What made Judge Klay unique was that she knew and understood *all* the relevant legal principles. She just slithered her way around and through them so that virtually all her criminal trials ended in guilty verdicts. Often in ways that were not ethical.

Or at least they *seemed* not ethical. No one could prove anything, of course.

For example, the pool of potential jurors for the Gomez trial looked almost exclusively Anglo. Considering that the defendant was Hispanic, and that about one quarter of the population of Arizona is Hispanic, anyone in Gomez's position might well have wondered how twelve individuals culled from an all-white group of people could comprise a jury of his peers.

And anyone in Judge Klay's position might well have been concerned, or at least puzzled, at the unusual racial composition of the jury pool.

But the woman with the slicked-back hair and the skinny nose, seated at the head of the courtroom, looked like everything was just dandy. She knew that potential jurors were supposed to be randomly divided into different groups for different cases behind closed doors, by officials sworn to act in accordance with evenhanded rules. So she also knew that it was virtually impossible to prove that she'd tampered with the selection process to ensure a racial imbalance favorable to the prosecution.

Why was I so sure that Judge Klay had stacked the deck? Because in every one of the major criminal cases that she presided over where the defendant was Hispanic, the jury pool was always disproportionately Anglo. You do the math.

From her perch behind the bench, the judge glanced at the assistant district attorney. Then she turned and smiled in the direction of the defense table, and said in her pinched soprano, "There being no objections to the jury pool, the defendant may exercise his first round of peremptory challenges."

It was a classic Rhonda Klay move—cheat, and dare anyone to call her on it. What was a lawyer supposed to do? Accuse her of manipulating the composition of the jury without any proof?

And then, a surprise. *This* defendant did.

Or at least he tried to. At the judge's words, the short, brown-skinned man with the curly beard and the wire-rimmed glasses began whispering intently to his lawyer, stabbing his finger at the potential juror pool, then pointing to himself, then shaking his head. Finally he motioned to his lawyer with both hands, as if urging him to stand up and say something.

But Gomez's lawyer did neither. Which, sadly, was *not* a surprise. Because Gomez was being represented by Silent Steve Temilow, another disgrace to the criminal bar. Temilow didn't belong in the courtroom for any number of reasons, high on the list being that he couldn't lawyer himself out of a bad parking ticket. But Judge Klay had appointed Temilow to the case because Gomez had complained twice during the five months he'd awaited trial that he wasn't being represented adequately.

It wasn't particularly unusual for indigent defendants in capital cases to doubt that the same government that was trying to have them executed was going to provide them with an attorney who was really going to do battle for them. And Gomez was not exactly your run-of-the-mill indigent defendant in a capital case. Because he was suspected of a terrorist attack, he was treated by the government when he was first arrested as an "enemy combatant," which is another way of saying that he was held for the better part of six months without the most basic of civil rights, and regularly tortured for information about future terrorist attacks.

So it was hardly a shock when it was reported that after meeting his first lawyer, Gomez couldn't bring himself to trust the man, and promptly requested another one.

Gomez's complaint about Attorney Number Two—a decent lawyer named Bruno Smithson—was that after months on the case, the attorney refused to do anything except advise Gomez to plead guilty and thereby hope to avoid execution. Bruno actually called me twice while he was on the case. The first time, it was because he couldn't figure out a way to convince his client Gomez that they needed a lot of time to prepare. Gomez thought they should go to trial four days after Bruno was appointed.

The second call, several weeks later, was much more serious. Gomez was insisting that he was innocent, and refused to plead guilty. The problem with that was Bruno had never seen such an airtight case. Gomez had clear connections to the man who actually detonated the Denver bomb, as well as file cabinets full of other thoroughly damning evidence found when the government had searched Gomez's home. Bruno couldn't accept that it was in Gomez's best interests to force a trial, and their inability to get over that disagreement led to his dismissal.

Enter Silent Steve Temilow, the human doormat.

Now Gomez's gesticulations were getting more exaggerated, so the lawyer with the thinning hair and the prominent Adam's apple appeared to take yet another tack—to pretend that the heated whispers and the flailing arms of the man on his left were nothing more than the products of a curious phantasm, best ignored. Stiffly, Steve shuffled through some papers on the table before him, ignoring his client and clearly stalling.

Judge Klay preferred a more direct approach to the situation. "Mr. Gomez, kindly control yourself—this is a court of law. And Mr. Temilow? Is there a problem? May we have the defendant's first set of peremptory challenges, please?"

There would, however, be no denying Juan Gomez. As Temilow rose to address the judge, the defendant rose, too, unwilling to let his attorney off the hook. His increasingly insistent body language demanded eye contact. But Silent Steve soldiered on, bravely disregarding his client's sleeve-tugging and table-banging by repeatedly adjusting his glasses, and by adopting a robotic posture. His neck, shoulders, and upper body were so rigidly held he seemed almost physically incapable of turning and acknowledging the desperate pantomime taking place to his left.

Staring ahead at Judge Klay, he finally spoke. "Um, Your Honor, I'd first like to personally apologize, and to apologize on behalf of the defendant as well, both to you and to the ladies and gentlemen of the jury pool for, well, for any impropriety that may have taken place over the last few minutes at the defense table."

Gomez looked dumbfounded. Could this get any worse? The answer, incredibly, was yes.

"And with further apologies for any delay, and for any inconvenience caused by such delay, I would like now to address the court's inquiry regarding the composition of the jury."

As he realized that his attorney was finally, *finally* going to confront the extremely non-Hispanic-looking elephant in the room, Gomez seemed to relax a bit. The expression on his face became somewhat expectant. That expression would soon disappear.

Temilow continued. "First, Your Honor, the defense specifically waives any objection to the composition of the jury pool, it being well understood that the process by which these candidates were selected as potential jurors for this case was a random one."

When Gomez processed this capitulation, he began shaking his head back and forth, looking at the judge, and pointing at Temilow, in silent, negative commentary.

The lawyer twisted his body so that although he was still facing the judge, his back was now fully to his client. He seemed to hope that by maneuvering Gomez out of his field of view he might make the distracting little man disappear from the courtroom entirely. "And further, Your Honor, the defendant will also waive all peremptory challenges. The defendant is confident that any member of the community will render a fair and just verdict in this case."

It was at that point that Gomez could no longer restrain himself. "Oh, no," he said, continuing to shake his head, but now raising his shackled hands above his head as if Temilow had just scored a touchdown for the wrong team. "No, no, no. I am not waiving anything. And I am not apologizing for nothing, neither. I am firing this man. Right now. I want a new lawyer, Judge. This one is not working for *me*. He is waiving everything, and apologizing, and he is not listening to me at all. I ain't waiving nothing. I want a new lawyer."

With the exception of the frenetic scratching of reporters' pens and pencils against paper, the courtroom became deathly silent. Gomez lowered his hands, and just stood there, as if not quite sure what to do next. Then, abruptly, he sat down, and declared, "That's it. I'm done, Your Honor. I need a new lawyer."

Apparently, it was time for someone else to talk.

Yet it was not clear that poor Steve Temilow was up to the task. He had managed to keep his back to the defendant for the entire tirade, but Gomez had failed to dematerialize. Worse, the unpleasant fellow had added a sound track to his heretofore silent performance.

So Temilow did what he did best—he hoisted a white flag.

"Um, Your Honor, if I might attempt to address the court. With deepest personal apologies, of course, for the unusual nature of this situation. . . ."

However, Judge Klay was not so easily assuaged. "Your apology is not accepted, Mr. Temilow," she snapped, glaring at the defendant. "I rather think that it is Mr. Gomez who needs to address this court. Mr. Gomez?"

The defendant rose from his seat before speaking. "Yes, Judge?"

"Am I to understand that despite the fact you stand trial for multiple counts of murder and for conspiracy to commit murder as well as a number of other extremely serious crimes, you wish for me to discharge Mr. Temilow from the case?"

"Well, Your Honor, I don't know about no discharge. All I want is a new lawyer. This one ain't doing nothing for me. He sounds like all he wants to do is give up, but I didn't do nothing wrong, so I don't want him representing me."

The judge took a deep breath. She glanced over the

defendant's head at the courtroom crowded with people, reporters, a television camera, the governor and his wife, even those members of the victims' families who had made the trip down to see this fiend get what was coming to him. Then she looked at the prosecutor. Of course I don't know exactly what was going on in Rhonda Klay's mind at that moment, but I would have bet you a stack of pancakes that she was thinking there was no way in the world she was going to be shown up in her courtroom, in front of millions of Americans, on the first day of the slam-dunk trial of a mass-murdering terrorist.

She looked down at some papers that were laid out in front of her on the bench, and then she looked back up at the defendant with her coal black eyes, a clever smile squeezing her narrow face. I knew, right then, that whatever the judge was going to say, it was going to be bad news for Mr. Gomez.

"Very well, sir. Here is my ruling. You are entitled to have an attorney appointed to represent you, and according to the case file, you have had not just one, but *three* lawyers assigned to your case. And you have chosen to find fault with each one of the three."

She slapped the file shut, rather melodramatically, I thought, and then gave her ruling in a clipped staccato. "I find that this is nothing more than a pattern of behavior designed to delay the trial. You have had ample time to prepare, and ample representation. I will not indulge your behavior any further. Here are your choices, Mr. Gomez. You will either withdraw your request to have Attorney Temilow removed from the case and accept him as your lawyer, or you will proceed without any representation at all, and serve as your own attorney for the remainder of the proceedings."

It didn't take a legal expert to analyze that pair of options. There was no way in the world that Juan Gomez, shipping manager for Desert Furniture Warehouse, could possibly defend himself in a multiple murder trial before Judge Klay. And using Steve Temilow on a case like this was like trying to stop a freight train with a butterfly net.

But to Gomez's credit, he did not back down. "Your Honor, you talk about a choice, but that ain't no choice. I don't want Mr. Temilow as my lawyer, and I don't want to represent myself. All I'm asking for is an attorney that will stand up for me here. They are saying I did this terrible thing, but I didn't do it. I need someone who will tell that to the jury."

While this exchange took place, Steve Temilow was standing off to the side of the defense table, looking less like the attorney of record, and more like an overdressed spectator at a sporting event who had mistakenly walked out onto the field of play.

And the ball was in Judge Klay's court, so to speak, which Her Honor did not like one bit. It came whizzing back at the defendant with quite a bit of attitude. "Sir, you have heard my ruling." Pulling back the sleeve of her robe, the judge took a look at the watch she was wearing. "If you do not withdraw your request that I discharge Mr. Temilow from the case in the next fifteen seconds, I *will* discharge him. Consider your decision carefully. You now have . . . eleven more seconds."

It was at that very moment that some long-winded fool from the gallery jumped out of his seat, and shouted, "Your Honor, that's the most outrageous thing I've ever heard in nearly ten years of practicing law! You know full well that there has been no attempt to delay these proceedings—the record will reflect that while represented by his second attorney, the defendant filed at least three separate requests for a speedy trial.

Hardly the kind of thing one does when one wants to drag his feet. Not to mention the fact that Mr. Gomez spent more time being held without an attorney, and *tortured* by the *United States of America*—six months, thank you very much—than the five months he spent between the time he was finally put in the criminal justice system and the beginning of this trial.

"Fifteen-second countdowns belong on television game shows, not in this courtroom—or in any other American courtroom—especially in a trial which is so important. A man's life is at stake here, not to mention the fact that this is supposed to be about finding some kind of justice for the hundreds and hundreds killed and injured in Denver last year. If the case against Mr. Gomez is as strong as everyone seems to believe, then it will not be long before he suffers the consequences he so richly deserves. But, for the record, the court's response to the defendant's perfectly reasonable reaction to Mr. Temilow's behavior today is nothing short of shocking. And because the defendant's attorney seems incapable of doing so, I emphatically and strenuously object."

Less than two and one half minutes later, I was appointed as the fourth and final attorney for Juan Abdullah Gomez.

Because, as you must have surmised by now, that long-winded fool was me.

TWO

THERE IS A RITE of passage that every young attorney must face after he or she makes the decision to represent criminal defendants. Mine was that cold moment eight years ago, when Uncle Fred, at Thanksgiving dinner, took the mashed potatoes from me and asked in front of the entire family, "So, Tom, why in the world would you want to represent murderers and rapists? Especially considering what your father does for a living."

I should have been ready for it, but I was not. I was thinking about the turkey my mom had made, and how different my cousin Brittany looked without her braces, and whether her older brother, Drew, was a compulsive gambler.

And as the Detroit Lions kicked off, en route to their annual holiday thrashing, twenty-three pairs of eyes turned toward me, Mr. Big Shot Who Had Just Passed The Arizona Bar And Who Wanted To Represent Murderers And Rapists.

I froze. Uncle Fred. When I was thirteen and wanted

to try out for the middle-school baseball team, he was the guy who had hit ground balls to me. And now he had just turned into this gray-haired, scowling inquisitor. He knew that I was a good person, that I would never hurt anyone intentionally. Shoot—I used to baby-sit all the time for his kids before he and Aunt Jane moved to Los Angeles.

But here he sat, putting me on the spot, implying I had some kind of affection for violent, dangerous felons. He blinked at me from behind his thick black glasses. He wasn't smiling.

The silence grew.

Suddenly, from the head of the table, my father spoke. "Okay, Fred. You got me. I admit it. It was my fault."

Everyone turned to face the lifetime prosecutor.

"I was the one who encouraged Tom to go into criminal defense. Because the system only works when law enforcement and civil liberties are balanced by both prosecutors *and* defense attorneys. We need good, honest defense lawyers, Fred. They help make our civilization one of the most advanced in history. They're the reason we don't have to worry about secret police breaking down our doors in the middle of the night."

My father paused, as if to let Uncle Fred speak. But we all knew that there would be no reply. Henley Carpenter had no patience for shallow thinking, and in fifteen seconds my dad had revealed Uncle Fred's attack to be based on nothing more than that.

Then he continued, "Of course I was a little disappointed when Tom said, 'The heck with the Constitution, Dad. I'm going into the toughest and least popular job in law because I just *love* murderers and rapists.' But, what are you going to do? Can you please pass the gravy, Heather?"

And with that, Thanksgiving was back.

I mention that story only because I want to make it very clear that my outburst in Judge Klay's courtroom had nothing to do with any warm feeling that I had for Mr. Gomez. As far as I was concerned, he was as loathsome a character as any I'd ever met in my life, and I had absolutely no desire to have any association with him whatsoever.

It was just that I truly cared about how criminal trials were run, and what Judge Klay was doing was so contrary to everything that I had been taught, both at law school and by my father, that I simply couldn't sit there without saying something.

The last thing in the world I was thinking about as I was shooting my mouth off like that was getting appointed to the Juan Gomez case.

And then suddenly, I was watching the situation unravel right in front of my eyes as if I weren't the tall, dark-haired idiot standing in the third row of the gallery.

The defendant was saying, "Him, Judge. That's what I'm talking about. I want *this* man to be my lawyer. I want someone who will object to this bullshit."

The prosecutor was looking back and forth between me and the judge, finally saying, "Your Honor, I object. I object to this entire situation."

Sarge, who had risen from his station on the far right of the courtroom, was unreadable. All I could see was that it looked like he had gotten his bright white uniform shirt newly starched for the big trial.

But finally my attention returned to Judge Klay, where another nasty little smile was twitching its way onto her face. She pulled her beady stare away from the defendant and fixed it on me. "Attorney Carpenter, isn't it? Thomas Carpenter? Please approach the bench, sir. Immediately."

As I squeezed past the *USA Today* reporter, I felt him put something in my hand and heard him whisper, "We'll pay for an exclusive." The television camera had swung around, and was now tracking my progress as I clumsily made my way over the people sitting between me and the aisle. I would learn later that three million viewers watched me accidentally step on the right foot of Governor Hamilton's wife, Eulalia.

Yet even during my unceremonious catapult onto one of the biggest stages in American criminal justice, I wasn't thinking about Juan Gomez, or press coverage, or Mrs. Hamilton's sore toes.

I was thinking that Judge Klay was going to throw me in jail for contempt. And while, of course, it was going to be bad enough to be humiliated like that on national television, what was worse was that it was going to happen on a Tuesday.

For the past three years, I had had an arrangement with my sister-in-law, Amy. On Tuesdays, Thursdays, and Saturdays, she and her daughter—my five-year-old niece, Erica—would come over to my parents' place on Payson's Ridge. On Saturdays, Amy would cook. On Tuesdays and Thursdays, it was up to me.

And on this particular Tuesday, I had promised Erica that I would discuss with her—in detail—my impressions of her truly outstanding performance as the big green turtle in the Oak Canyon Elementary School kindergarten musical.

Before I arrived at the trial that day, I had stopped to attend the only public performance of *Our Earth, Our Home*. Since Erica's mother was a fourth-grade teacher at the school, and her dad, my brother Dale, had died in Afghanistan before she was even born, I always felt an obligation to show up for Erica whenever I could at school plays, athletic contests, dance recitals, whatever would normally have been attended by a father. It just seemed like something an uncle should do under the circumstances.

It was the second such event that I witnessed—Erica's first soccer game; she was four, and no one came close to scoring a goal—which transformed completely my sense of obligation into a feeling of anticipation and delight. I loved my niece, and I really loved watching her grow up.

So that morning I'd stood with pride at the back of a small auditorium filled with an army of video-recorder-wielding stay-at-home moms, while forty-four five-year-olds dramatically costumed as various flora and fauna sang songs honoring the environment.

I realize that I was not an objective observer, but I am confident of my opinion that Erica was by far the most talented of the four-legged creatures in her class.

By this I mean no disrespect to the other members of the vertebrate family. I am merely commenting on Erica's ability to carry a tune, and the other cast members' rather nonchalant attitude toward such mundane considerations as melody or pitch. Not to mention the red-haired giraffe who obviously felt comfortable only when his index finger was snugly inserted into his left nostril.

Yet despite its imperfections, the entire experience was quite moving. These feelings are not unusual for me, and I have been gently teased about them by Erica's mom, Amy, especially on those occasions when I get a little emotional at school concerts. I understand that as a single mother, Amy needs to look at the world in a very practical way. And I respect her choice to view elementary school musicals as a bunch of kids running around in funny-looking outfits, singing vaguely recognizable songs with almost no regard for the desperate accompaniment of a single, completely overmatched, upright piano.

But I know the voice of God when I hear it.

Before I reached Judge Klay's bench, however, she quite effectively derailed my train of thought about dinner and Erica's chorus. I was standing immediately to Steve Temilow's left, a few feet from the defense table, when the mean little woman changed my life forever. "You can stop right there, Attorney Carpenter." She signed a piece of paper, thrust it at her clerk, a nice guy named Manny Estrada, and turned back to face us. "Mr. Temilow, thank you for your service. Effective immediately, you are discharged from this case. You may file your withdrawal of appearance with the clerk." I heard a flurry of murmurs behind me. Five reporters had gotten up from their seats and were scuttling toward the exits. Most of the others were writing as fast as they could move their pens.

The judge continued. "Mr. Carpenter. Normally I am loath to reward the kind of outburst you just favored us with, but your presence here has given me a unique opportunity to solve several problems at once. I am hereby appointing you as attorney of record for the defendant in this case. Please file your notice of appearance with the clerk immediately. After the prosecutor exercises his challenges to the jury, we will be ready for opening statements. I suggest you take a moment to confer with your client and review Mr. Temilow's files."

You probably know by now that I have an excellent memory. Remember when I told you a little while ago that about a quarter of Arizona's population was Hispanic? If I had wanted to, I could have said that twenty-five *point three* percent of Arizona's population was

Hispanic. How do I know this? I remember it from reading it in a magazine last year. The *Southwest Law Journal*. I'm pretty sure it was in the August issue.

This is not a sign of intelligence, nor is it anything that I can claim credit for. It's just something that I was born with. I seem to automatically retain a great deal of what I've read and experienced. When I was a kid, I got a kick out of reading almanacs, especially when I found that I could remember most of the sports records. It helped in both college and in law school—I went through accelerated programs at each. And when I became an adult, I could be counted on to recall, with considerable accuracy, conversations and events—at least important ones—for years.

But try as I might, I cannot remember anything about what transpired next at Juan Gomez's trial. It was like any flow of intelligent thought in my mind had become instantly blocked by a massive dam of panic.

One minute I was watching the biggest trial in the country from the courtroom gallery, and the next I was on the verge of giving the opening statement for a defendant accused of murdering one hundred thirteen people in a terrorist attack.

The transcript of the case indicates that I raised some protest to the judge's actions, but there was no question that she had the authority to appoint me. I was a member of the bar, and I was on the list of attorneys who would accept appointments to cases such as Mr. Gomez's murder trial. I managed to stammer out an objection or two, but for the most part, I sounded like I felt—completely stunned.

The transcript then reflects that the prosecutor challenged two of the jurors. Both were immediately replaced with acceptable substitutes. It reveals that the judge next spoke to the fourteen jurors for a few moments about their responsibilities.

And I have absolutely no memory of any of that, either. For all I know, the first five minutes of my appointment to the case of *Arizona* v. *Juan Abdullah Gomez* featured a courtroom full of dancing flamingoes doing an encore from *Our Earth, Our Home*.

What I do remember is that in the moments before the prosecutor's opening statement, I was desperately looking through the files that Steve Temilow had left on the defense table, hoping to find a concise description of Gomez's planned defense against the charges. Unfortunately, this strategy consisted of little more than my fumbling vainly through piles and piles of unfamiliar and unhelpful folders and documents while my new client was thrusting pieces of paper in front of me on which he had written things like *I didn't do this. You got to believe me when I tell you I didn't do this.* And *Why would I blow up Denver??? I never even been to Denver.*

To be fair to Mr. Gomez and to Steve Temilow's filing system, even if I had found what I was looking for, it would have been impossible for me to do anything useful with it. My brain was going a hundred miles an hour, in about fifty-three different directions.

It turns out that none of that mattered, because soon after the prosecutor began to speak, my attention was completely committed to him. He was a stocky, rather short man, with salt-and-pepper hair and a mustache. In another era, you might have expected to see him with pince-nez and a pocket watch. His name was Preston Varick. He'd started as a prosecutor in Chicago, but moved to Phoenix over ten years ago. My dad never particularly liked A.D.A. Varick, but even Henley would have admitted he sure was good in that opening.

"Ladies and gentlemen of the jury, May sixteenth

of last year was supposed to be a very joyful day for twenty-seven-year-old Jill Henniker. You see, Jill had an appointment to see her obstetrician that day, because she suspected that after almost a year of trying, she and her husband, Daniel, were finally expecting their first child.

"But Jill Henniker never made it to that appointment.

"May sixteenth was also supposed to be a very happy day for fifty-eight-year-old Rodrigo Vargas. Mr. Vargas was retiring after thirty years of employment at the Denver Department of Public Works, and it was his last day on the job. A big celebration had been planned.

"But Rodrigo Vargas didn't make it to the party. The special photograph and plaque signed by all of his coworkers—all the people Rodrigo touched in three decades of service—was never presented.

"Over four hundred people did not get to where they were going in Denver on that May sixteenth, because they were viciously attacked. Jill Henniker and Rodrigo Vargas didn't get to where they were going because they were two of the one hundred thirteen who were murdered in that attack.

"You will hear testimony from experts who will describe the assault that was carried out on that day—the meticulous planning, the careful choices made to maximize the deaths and the suffering of the victims.

"The Marion C. Perkins Tunnel runs under an outcropping of rock for about one quarter mile along Interstate 25, approximately four miles north of downtown Denver. Two lanes of traffic run north in the easternmost of the two tunnel tubes.

"On May sixteenth of last year, at eight forty-three in the morning, traffic in the northbound tube was fairly heavy, but flowing at or near the speed limit of fifty miles per hour.

"A man named Esteban Cruz approached the tunnel from the south, driving a tanker filled with approximately eight thousand gallons of gasoline. When Mr. Cruz was about one thousand feet from the entrance of the tunnel, he activated a small device that had been installed on the tanker's dashboard, opening a hole in the underside of the storage compartment, allowing gasoline to begin spilling onto the roadway at a rate of several dozens of gallons per second.

"As Mr. Cruz approached the tunnel in the left lane he began to slow down, and as he actually entered the tunnel, he positioned his truck so that it occupied parts of both the left and the right northbound lanes. Now remember—he was spilling vast quantities of fuel all over the road as he did this.

"His actions created a tremendous backup of cars behind him as he slowly went into the tunnel. By the time that Esteban Cruz reached his predetermined destination, about halfway into the tunnel, there was a traffic jam comprised of cars, buses, and trucks extending almost one half mile behind him. Many of these vehicles were now positioned over the gasoline Mr. Cruz had just spilled.

"And then, Mr. Cruz abruptly swung his tanker truck over to the right. And then, just as abruptly, he veered hard left. He pulled the front of his tanker across both lanes of traffic, effectively blocking all travel in the tube.

"At that moment, he activated a second device that had been installed in his tanker. The device detonated an explosive charge in the fuel compartment of the truck.

"The resulting blast was phenomenal. The fuel in the truck burst into flames, immediately engulfing the trapped vehicles in the tunnel in flame, causing many of them to explode into fireballs, creating a chain of explosions both north and south in the tunnel, involving dozens of vehicles, including a commuter bus, killing and maiming first dozens, and then hundreds of people.

"But perhaps the most devastating—the sickest— part of this horrendous plot was that the fire from the exploded tanker truck also ignited the long and deadly trail of gasoline that Mr. Cruz had spilled in the tunnel and on nearly an eighth of a mile of the interstate leading to the tunnel. Two hundred forty-six cars, trucks, and buses had come to a stop by that time, gridlocked into position by the traffic jam that the tanker had created. All two hundred and forty-six vehicles idling on a road that had been doused with a highly flammable liquid. And as that gasoline burst into flames beneath the undercarriages of those vehicles, all two hundred and forty-six burst into flame. Some exploded into fatal infernos, some crippling and maiming the trapped and panicked drivers and passengers victimized by this unspeakable horror."

By this stage in the prosecutor's opening, it seemed that the entire world had gone still. Preston Varick had the jury—shoot, he had the whole courtroom—in the palm of his hand.

As the defendant's attorney, I knew that I was supposed to be analyzing the statements the prosecutor was making for compliance with the rules of procedure— not to mention preparing my own opening statement— but I was completely taken in by this description of the atrocity in Denver. Of course the tragedy had been reported endlessly and thoroughly in the press, and of course everyone was intimately familiar with what had happened. But there was something about hearing it in a courtroom filled with the victims, their family members, the man accused of planning it, and the jury chosen to decide his fate. . . . I was riveted.

And then Varick shifted the focus of his address to my client. He described the investigation into the attack, the discovery of Cruz's involvement, the connection between Cruz and Gomez, and finally, the raid on Gomez's apartment, and all of the evidence which directly implicated him in the planning of the devastation in the Marion C. Perkins Tunnel, and in the conspiracy to generate another.

"I will not go over each and every one of the hundreds of crimes charged against this defendant, this man to whom our government has affixed the label 'enemy combatant.' It is not necessary at this moment. But there will come a time, at the end of this trial, when you will know, beyond a reasonable doubt, that this man is responsible for all of them. And at that time, I will confidently ask you to render verdicts of guilty on each and every count of each and every crime—conspiracy, assault with intent to commit murder, and the murder of one hundred and thirteen people—including Rodrigo Vargas, who never got to his retirement party, and young Jill Henniker, who never got to hold her first child in her arms. Thank you."

No one made a sound in the courtroom as Varick returned to his seat behind the prosecution table. And then the air stirred, as if everyone in attendance suddenly remembered to exhale. The jury, fourteen people ranging in age from twenty to sixty-four, looked deadly serious. The spectators in the gallery behind me began to murmur. And I again started to sift through the papers on the defense table, looking for some miracle, I suppose, when Juan Gomez whispered something in my ear. With hindsight, I know now that what he probably said was, "Don't forget to say I'm innocent." Unfortunately, what I heard was, "Don't forget that Sadie M. is a saint."

This miscommunication was, I suppose, unavoidable. Mr. Gomez couldn't possibly have known that I have suffered from partial hearing loss since birth.

It isn't really that big a deal. Since I was a kid, I've always been able to compensate, usually quite simply by paying very close attention when someone spoke to me. Sometimes I wore the new, small hearing aids that fit right into my ear, as I was doing at the Gomez trial. But even with the aids, certain background noises, like those of the hum of the gallery and the rustling sound of the documents in my hands, tended to mask parts of human speech, especially when whispered.

Any confusion over my new client's message was short-lived, however. Because long before I was anywhere near ready, Judge Rhonda Klay turned to me and said, "Mr. Carpenter? Your opening statement, please."

THREE

ON AN EARLY—summer evening in 1989, when I was just twelve years old, my father came into my room as I was doing my homework, and said, "Hey, Tommy, I want to show you something."

Despite my parents' countless requests for me to sit at my desk, I was still doing my homework on my bed. My math book, my backpack, tons of worksheets, and the latest issue of *Sports Illustrated* were scattered all over the bedspread.

Dad was holding in his hand a picture that he had cut out of a magazine. The photo was taken at some distance, from an upper-story window behind and to the right of the person who was the centerpiece of the image—a solitary man standing in the middle of a road. He was dressed in a white shirt and dark pants, and seemed to be holding a briefcase of some kind in his left hand. And it also looked like he might have been leaning forward at the waist, just a little bit.

But what made the photograph so extraordinary was

that the man wasn't just standing in the middle of the road.

He was single-handedly facing down a row of oncoming tanks.

In a place I'd never heard of before, called Tiananmen Square.

My father came to believe that photograph was the single most important one taken in the twentieth century. He said anytime I needed to be reminded about personal strength, about the power of one individual, about how to behave in times of adversity—at those moments when it seemed that I was faced with my own line of approaching tanks—I should remember that picture.

Thereafter, the date on which that remarkable act of bravery took place became something of a family holiday for us. At Henley's insistence, over the next several years, on June 5, our family all attended a criminal trial together, because, as my father explained, our system of criminal justice was one of our country's best ways of ensuring that there would never be a Tiananmen Square in America.

So on that June 5, as I rose from my seat behind the defense table in Phoenix Superior Courtroom Number One-B, and faced the Juan Gomez jury, I thought of my father, and I thought of that anonymous Chinese man standing in the center of the road—that symbol of individual courage.

And then I started to speak, and totally screwed it up.

The problem, of course, was that I barely knew anything I needed to know to be the defendant's trial attorney. Thanks to the news media and the prosecutor's opening, I knew all about the Denver Tunnel Bombing, and I had a general sense of the evidence against the defendant.

But I had no idea what the defense was.

Except, of course, that Sadie M. was a saint.

So, foolishly, I attempted to employ a strategy which has been turned to by legal professionals for centuries. I opened my mouth, and made a noise like a lawyer.

"If it please the court, ladies and gentlemen of the jury, my name is Tom Carpenter, and I represent the defendant in this case, Juan Gomez."

And so began one of the most embarrassing oratorical journeys of my professional life.

Sure, I had had almost no sleep the night before, and I was still reeling from my surprise appointment by Judge Klay. But *come on*. Any lawyer worth a box of cheap business cards knows that defense attorneys don't have to make opening statements at the beginning of the trial. So what was I doing?

My strategy, such as it was, went something like this. I had no clue of what the jury thought of my rather unorthodox entry into the case. But first impressions in criminal trials were vital. By making an opening statement, I thought I would give myself a chance to reintroduce myself to the most important people in the room in a more positive light.

It wasn't long before that strategy became problematic.

"The defense in this case is not that the Denver Tunnel Bombing was not a tragedy. There is no question of the unspeakable violence and destruction that took place on that day.

"The defense is also not that law enforcement officials did not find evidence of plans for the Denver Bombing in the defendant's apartment."

When Dale and I were just kids, my parents took us

to Flagstaff one winter. My dad thought it would be fun for us all to learn how to ski. The most vivid memory I have, aside from when we were returning home and Dale fell down the stairs outside the lodge and broke his wrist, was the first time I started down the hill under my own power. At the beginning, there was exhilaration—I was *flying* down the slope. And then exhilaration was replaced by terror, because short of a fatal collision with a tree, I had no idea how I was going to *stop*.

As I paused and looked at Juan Gomez to consider my next line, that terror came rushing back. I had started my opening statement without any notion how I was going to end it. And the hill I was flying down that day was thick with some very large trees.

First of all, for reasons that I am at a loss to explain, I seemed strangely committed to using only sentences loaded with double negatives. That's always risky—it's easy to get mixed up and say precisely what you *don't* want to say. But more important, by telling the jury all about what the defense was *not,* I was making an implied promise that very soon, possibly preceded by a trumpet fanfare of some kind or perhaps a shower of confetti and balloons, I would reveal to them what the defense actually *was.*

It was quite rash of me to make that promise, of course, since I didn't have the faintest idea what the defense actually was.

Back when he was advising Gomez to plead guilty, Bruno Smithson had informed me that the case against the defendant was airtight. And nothing I had been able to absorb in my frantic rush through Steve Temilow's files had led me to believe otherwise.

The truth was that as I was preparing to tell the jury about Mr. Gomez's defense, it was my professional opinion that Mr. Gomez had *no* defense. And as I came to that realization, my brain chugged to a disgruntled halt. It was tired, it was pretty peeved at Judge Klay, and frankly, it wanted nothing more to do with the no-win situation I had dragged it into.

Incredibly, however, my mouth kept going. "Sometimes, however, when a tragedy such as this occurs, there is a natural tendency to assign responsibility, to attach blame, especially to the person who at first blush seems like he or she might be the cause of the tragedy."

My brain, having abdicated responsibility, looked on with anticipation. The last time my mouth had flown solo was two years earlier, when I got a little drunk at a cousin's wedding—maybe it was more than a little drunk—and declared that I thought my sister-in-law, Amy, was hotter than any bikini-babe supermodel centerfold I'd ever seen. It was true, but it really wasn't appropriate for me to have said it. Especially at that volume.

"And so, naturally, because there is a great deal of evidence that Mr. Gomez was responsible for planning the Denver Tunnel Bombing, he was accused of the crime."

The jury might not have known that at the very moment I said those words, I smashed face-first into the trunk of an oak. But thanks to my prolonged silence, they figured it out. I simply had nothing else to say. My opening statement had become the oratorical equivalent of walking my client to the edge of a cliff, and then shoving him off.

I am not sure exactly how long I stood there, silent, wondering what was going to happen next. But then, miraculously, my brain, perhaps out of pity, rejoined the team, and I managed to stammer out something.

"But even though it might have been natural to accuse Mr. Gomez of these crimes, in this situation, it was wrong."

That got some of the jurors' attention.

"It was wrong because you will see, as this trial unfolds, that Mr. Gomez is innocent."

That sounded pretty good, and since I really couldn't think of anything else, I said, "Thank you," and sat down.

With a little perspective, I can now say with a good degree of assurance that the opening statement for the defense in the Juan Gomez trial was the worst I've ever heard. The prosecutor had spoken for nearly twenty minutes, painting an emotional, vivid picture of loss at the hands of almost unfathomable evil and violence. And then he promised to share with the jury the mountains of evidence which established that to see the face of that evil, all you had to do was to look into the eyes of Juan Gomez.

And I countered with exactly nine sentences—if you count *Thank you* as a sentence—lasting one minute and thirty-two seconds. Eighteen of those seconds spanning a very long and awkward silence. And in those nine sentences, all I managed to say was this: There sure is a lot of evidence against Mr. Gomez, but don't worry—my guy's innocent.

It was not exactly my best work.

Mercifully, it was late enough in the afternoon for Judge Klay to recess the case and send us all home. I made hasty plans to speak with Gomez before the beginning of the following day's proceedings, and then my client was taken away by Sarge and another court officer, to be transported back to the jail where he was being held during the trial.

It took me a few minutes to gather up the papers and files scattered all over the defense table. Naturally, I hadn't brought a briefcase with me that day, so I had to track down Clerk Estrada in his office to borrow one for the evening. By the time I finally returned to the courtroom and filled the leather bag for my trip home, I was the only one there.

I welcomed the change. For the first time in hours, I felt like I had a chance to think quietly about what I was going to do, rather than just make things up on the fly. I was anxious to talk to some friends, like Cliff, and Amy and Erica. I needed a little sanity. I even had a chance at making it home in time to handle dinner.

I left the courtroom, walked down the deserted hallway, and headed for the front entrance. That was the closest one to the garage on Second Street, where I had parked.

But when I exited the courthouse, my plans instantly changed.

Because I had not counted on the dozens of microphones, the wall of television cameras, and the countless reporters who started shouting questions at me as soon as I opened the doors.

So much for getting to dinner on time.

I have seen video footage of my first press conference, and although it might be difficult to believe, I was worse there than I was in court.

What makes everything so much more pathetic is that I didn't have to stay on those steps and say anything to those people. I could have just walked around them, gotten into my truck, and driven home.

Instead, I stood there, as if anchored to the spot by my ever-burgeoning stupidity. How hard could answering a few questions be?

Apparently, pretty hard.

A good example of my efforts was the one endlessly replayed on untold millions of television screens and computer monitors during those early days of the trial.

The question posed to me was, "After provoking the judge into assigning you to the case, what did you hope to accomplish next?"

Did I deny provoking the judge? Did I take issue with the implication that I was actually attempting to manipulate the judge into putting me on the case? Did I ignore the question as one that probably could not be answered without making myself look—incredible as it might seem—even less capable than I already did?

Astonishingly, I did none of those things. My choice? To blurt out the following: "Well, I wasn't really trying to accomplish anything."

What a masterstroke. I could have responded in a manner which established that I had no personal agenda when I spoke out in the courtroom against what I believed was a blatant and serious injustice. But instead, I managed to utter a single sentence which admitted to both indifference and incompetence in the most important criminal case in years.

Finally, after twelve minutes and thirty-five seconds of the most stupefying and inept performance in the annals of public relations, a voice from the back of the crowd shouted out what was to be the last question of the press conference. "Mr. Carpenter, do you have any comment on the opinion of KFXT legal expert Conrad Thurry that Mr. Gomez would have been better off representing himself than having you appointed as his lawyer?"

That one broke the spell.

Because even though I knew that Conrad Thurry was a pretty harmless blowhard, the tiny part of my brain that was still functioning realized that I needed to stop talking and leave. I wasn't doing my client, or myself, any good here at all.

So I smiled, said, "Thank you," and walked away.

Of course that didn't stop the reporters. A dozen of them followed me all the way to the Second Street Garage, yelling things, trying to get some reaction from me. There were even a couple of guys in front of me, walking backward with cameras on their shoulders, filming footage right up until I reached my pickup truck.

But I was tired, and I was hungry, and I had an hour's drive ahead of me. This time I kept my mouth shut. I got in my truck, and headed home.

Just as I reached the entrance ramp to the interstate, my cell phone rang. It was Cliff Redhorse. Thank God. Cliff wasn't a litigator, but he was my best friend, and a very bright, excellent attorney. I really valued his thoughts on strategy. And even in those situations that looked darkest, he always had something upbeat to say.

That day he started the conversation with: "Dude, you're going to get beat worse than Custer."

FOUR

I'M A CRIMINAL appeals attorney. I'm used to losing.

In fact, I suppose you could argue that I should be happy when I lose. Because theoretically, every time one of my appeals fails, it simply confirms that the system has worked—a criminal defendant was convicted as a result of a constitutionally sound and fair trial.

I have always had a hard time maintaining that kind of perspective. My competitive streak made losing hard. And so even though I knew that Juan Gomez was a hopeless cause, I really didn't need to hear my best friend tell me that I was going to get beat—

"—like a disco cowbell."

"So you were watching? Great."

"Watching? Dude. Everyone in the state saw you tear Judge Gila Monster a new one. Nice tie, by the way. And *really* nice opening statement." I could hear the smile in Cliff's voice. This wouldn't be the last time I heard about that debacle.

"Yeah. Thanks. My finest hour. So what do you know about Judge Klay?"

"Other than she's a rule-breaking bee-yotch... Ouch!" Cliff's wife, Iris, was a ferociously intelligent computer engineer. She was also very funny, and loved Cliff to death. But she was extremely politically correct, and spent hours on her weekend current events podcast, railing against the use of certain words. Iris was also a brutal arm-smacker. Cliff directed his next comments to her. "I can't help it. She told my stupid pothead cousin Benny that he would spare everyone a lot of trouble if he pleaded guilty to simple possession of the joint the cops found in his pocket, so he did. And then she gave him two years plus six years probation on and after."

I had never heard of Benny before.

"I'm not kidding," Cliff continued, clearly speaking for the benefit of both me and his wife. "Until last year, it was the largest sentence for a first-time-possession offense in the history of the state. The woman is nasty."

That was bad news. Not that there was any doubt about the death sentence Juan Gomez would receive when he was convicted. Cliff's story just backed up my impression of Rhonda Klay. She had no business leaning on a defendant to plead guilty—

Cliff interrupted my thoughts—he was speaking quickly now, directly to me. "Dude. I don't have a cousin named Benny. I was just trying to make Iris feel guilty for—uh oh. She heard me. I am so busted." And then, in a patently lame imitation of a television sitcom husband, he said, "Hi, sweetie."

I hear something like this go back and forth between Cliff and Iris at least once or twice a month. Cliff constantly made up stuff—some of it really outrageous— just to see who would believe him. And he was a fantastic card player thanks to his ability to bluff. But away from the poker table, Iris was generally not amused.

"Seriously, I read this article," he continued, "and Rhonda Klay is a bad one." He cleared his throat, and spoke to me again, in an obviously stilted manner. "Apparently, Judge Klay is an extremely unpleasant woman about whom others have said many bad things using foul language." He took a breath. "Like bee-yotch. Ouch. Shit! Ouch. Don't *do* that."

When Cliff and Iris finally got themselves straightened out, he volunteered to check online to see if there was anything about Judge Klay—anything *real* about Judge Klay—that might be useful. I didn't have much hope, but at this point, I didn't have much of anything else, either.

After I hung up, I called Amy to ask what she and Erica wanted for dinner. Even though Tuesday was technically my night to cook, I guess I should confess all that really meant was that I stopped on the way home and picked up a take-out meal from their choice of restaurant.

But instead of a normal greeting, the phone was answered by Amy and Erica in tandem. My niece and sister-in-law did a surprisingly good imitation of a very excited, extremely high-pitched, two-girl fan club. "Oooh, Attorney Tom Carpenter, you're *so* cute!" And then they burst into shrieks of delighted laughter.

Yes, they had seen it too.

I waited for the hysteria to fade before I attempted to turn the conversation to more practical matters, but Amy spoke first. Her voice was clear, and clean, and always made me think of music. "Come straight home, Tom, okay? We've got a surprise for you."

"But what about dinner? Making a spectacle of myself on national television always makes me hungry. What goes with humiliation?"

"You're exaggerating. You were great. And we've got dinner all handled. Erica's play was today, my birthday is next week, and when we saw you on TV this afternoon"—Erica squealed in the background for punctuation—"we decided we needed to celebrate immediately. So we already ordered from Freddy's. They'll deliver, and it will be here soon."

"What about Dad?"

"Henley's having chicken soup."

"Wait a minute. Freddy's doesn't deliver."

"It does for famous television star lawyers," Amy responded gleefully. "Freddy says nice tie, by the way."

"Oh, my God. Is there anyone who *wasn't* watching?"

"I don't think so. Henley almost broke his chair hitting the bell."

My father's bell was one of the many brilliant attachments that Iris, Cliff's wife, installed when she modified Henley's wheelchair to include a computer keyboard with a monitor and a mirror so that what he typed we all could see, too. My father's dominant right hand had curled into a permanent fist. He used his left to type messages, but it was a painstakingly slow process. So Iris hooked up a bell that Henley could trigger just by hitting it. One ring meant *yes*. Two or more meant whatever he wanted it to mean.

"God. I hope I didn't embarrass him."

"Stop. Focus on the pizza. And get home soon."

Among the thousands of things that I love about Amy, one of them is her uncanny ability to know when I need a pizza from Freddy's. For some reason—Amy thinks it's got something to do with how the water affects the crust, but believe me, it goes way beyond that—

most Arizona pizza is virtually inedible. It's like a large, round, tasteless cracker, smeared over with tomato soup and flecked with tiny bits of nasty, unmelted cheese.

But against all odds, Freddy Sanchez, born and raised halfway between Silver City and Payson, Arizona, decided not to follow his three brothers into the family construction business. Instead, he taught himself how to make pizza. And not just any pizza. A pizza that would win awards if Freddy ever found the time or the inclination to enter a contest. The dough is soft at the edges, but firm at the center, the sauce is delicious, and the cheese is decadently gooey, rich, sweet, and plentiful.

The only reason I don't eat it every day of my life is because Freddy's place is out of the way for us, there's always a long wait, and my father can't have pizza anymore.

After explaining to Amy why she was the greatest sister-in-law ever, I spent the last twenty minutes of the drive home trying to focus on the pizza. But my thoughts kept getting hijacked by a mean-spirited judge who looked a lot like a reptile.

Back when I was in elementary school, my parents bought their place on Payson's Ridge. Most of the money came from my mother's inheritance—my grandfather had made a ton of money in the stock market. The house started as a secluded cabin on a mesquite-and-pine-covered mountaintop, far enough away from the city to make my mom—a country girl—comfortable, but close enough to the city for Henley to get to work in under an hour.

Over the years, my parents had remodeled the old cabin into the beautiful lodge I approached in my truck.

Henley was in his wheelchair when he greeted me at the door with a left-handed high five. He had already programmed his computer to play Marvin Gaye's "Let's Get It On," his favorite celebration song. Erica launched herself into my arms as soon as I cleared Henley's chair, and before I even had a chance to lower the towheaded bundle of energy to the floor, Freddy rang the doorbell with the pizzas.

Amy and Erica had decorated the dining room with brightly colored construction paper posters saying *Happy Birthday Amy, Happy Television Trial Tom,* and *Happy "Our Earth Our Home" Erica.* An hour ago I was being devoured publicly by media piranhas. Here, I was in much more tranquil waters.

Dinner was predictably fabulous. And Amy had made herself a chocolate birthday cake, so dessert was just as good.

It was later that I resumed my streak of doing and saying everything wrong.

Henley and Erica were playing a final game of checkers in the living room, while Amy and I put the plates in the dishwasher. A few minutes before we were done, I excused myself to retrieve a birthday present I had gotten for her the week before.

I did not share my mother's knack for buying perfect gifts. In fact, whatever gene had been responsible for my mom's talent must have mutated fairly severely before taking up residence in yours truly. Because no matter how much time I spent shopping, I always seemed to end up buying something at the last minute which was astonishingly lame. Or appallingly inappropriate. For years, my father proudly wore the ugliest sweaters and ties imaginable, solely because I gave them to him, believing, insanely, that they would look good when he wore them.

But I refused to quit trying. Especially when it came to Amy. Fate had been so cruel to her—leaving her a widow and a single mother before she was even thirty years old—there was no way I was ever going to let her think she was walking in this world without someone by her side.

And if that meant regularly buying her birthday and Christmas presents that she would never use, well, I had come to peace with that. Her closet might be full of junk, but darn it, she would know that she was loved.

That particular birthday, however, I somewhat out-did myself. For no concrete reason I could articulate, I had come to the stunningly inaccurate conclusion that it wouldn't be long before Amy finally decided to move on with her romantic life, get beyond the loss of Dale, and start to see other men. And thus, my birthday strategy was formed. I was going to get Amy a present to help her find a new husband.

Looking back, I realize how inane that sounds. But at the time, I truly believed it was a terrific idea.

I was well aware that Amy seemed to attract a disproportionate amount of light, and that when she smiled it was impossible to look at anything else. Yet I still managed to determine I could do something to increase her allure. My mission was fueled by the knowledge that Amy looked unbearably good wearing clothes that were the same color as her gorgeous blue-green eyes, and that she had the greatest neck and shoulders that any woman ever had in the history of the planet Earth.

So I bought her this turquoise-ish green blouse I'd seen displayed in a store window as I was walking to lunch one day. It was a light pullover with a kind of wide neck that I was sure would look absolutely devastating on her.

As I brought it into the kitchen, she saw that I was carrying a gift-wrapped box, straightened from the dishwasher, smiled her luminous smile, and said what she always said: "You didn't have to get me a present, Tom. You know I don't need anything." But she opened the box anyway, and as she did, I explained about her neck and shoulders, and the color of her eyes, and how I thought that when the time was right, she'd find a guy who probably wouldn't ever *replace* Dale, but instead someone who might keep her from being lonely. Someone she would want to share the rest of her life with. And I told her that when she found that guy, she should wear that shirt for him, because if she did, she would be completely irresistible, and it would totally seal the deal.

Naturally, I was wrong. The strange look on her face made it very clear that she totally hated it. Oh, she thanked me, and said that it was beautiful and all of the things you're supposed to say when someone gives you a shirt that you'll never wear for as long as you are choosing your own clothing. Happily, Erica came in at just the right moment to say that she had finished her game with Henley. Amy quietly put the shirt back in its package, and I knew that was the last time I'd ever see or hear about it. It was a little disappointing, but I was a seasoned veteran of bad gift-giving. Maybe next year I'd get it right.

After Amy and Erica went home, I helped Henley get ready for bed. His right side was so useless that dressing and undressing himself was no longer an option. Even using the toilet was occasionally an adventure.

When he was finally settled in with his latest audio book—a wildly popular romance novel by a best-selling author—I sat down at my computer, and started banging out motions for the next day at trial.

It was important work, but I was so tired that I wasn't sure I was going to be able to get it all done before I just dropped from exhaustion.

But then Cliff called. I picked up the phone, and everything changed.

"Dude," he said. "I got something on Judge Klay."

FIVE

I STAYED UP most of the night preparing motions and doing what research I could on the case, so I only got three uneasy hours of sleep. I was awakened before the alarm by a nightmare—I was standing on a stage before tens of thousands of people, dressed in a lobster costume, and I couldn't remember the words to the national anthem.

I needed to be alert, despite the fact that my average hours of rest over the past couple of nights was now two. So as I drove in to the courthouse, I had a couple of extra coffees.

By the time I met Juan Gomez before that day's proceedings began, I was not only alert—I had an unusually rapid pulse, sweaty feet, and a disquieting feeling that my entire body was vibrating.

Sarge led me to the small cell where Juan Gomez was being held. My client looked less agitated than he did yesterday. He was dressed, as he would be for the entire trial, in a green, prison-issue jumpsuit. Unlike the typical criminal defendant, his hands and ankles remained shackled, even when inside his cell.

Gomez seemed convinced that the only way he could be sure that I would truly fight for him was if he proved to me that he was innocent. To that end, he handed me three things through the bars of the courthouse holding cell confining him: a badly creased photo of himself standing next to a woman and a boy, a "Certificate of Merit" from Desert Furniture Warehouse, and a leaflet, on which was printed some general statements about Islam, including "Islam is a peaceful religion."

"That's my wife and son," he said, pointing at the picture. "My *ex*-wife. She left when they took me away. She and Emilio are in Ecuador now. They were afraid . . ." He took a shaky breath. "Anyway, I didn't do this thing, man. I don't know how this happened. I always did my job—you see that certificate? They only give that to the best employees, man. And then one day . . ." His voice broke.

We didn't have a lot of time, so I tried to redirect the conversation. There was no way he was going to convince me of anything in the few minutes we had before the trial started. "Can you tell me something that might help me understand how this happened? Do you know anything about the evidence—"

"I was *tortured*, man," he said, his voice thick with emotion. "That's what I know about. When they call you an enemy combatant, it doesn't matter if they're right or if they're wrong. They do whatever they want. They drowned me, again and again. Cuffed my hands behind my back, and they pushed my head into a filled bathtub, and they held it there. One time I breathed so much water that I passed out. They woke me up by pushing on my stomach to get the water out of my lungs. Then they just stood around me and laughed while I was lying there, coughing and choking and cry-ing and throwing up. I got so scared that every time they took me from my cell I pissed myself." By this point in the story, tears were running down his cheeks. "And I confessed to *everything* to make them stop. Everything, man. Anything they wanted, I agreed to it, because I couldn't take it. But they kept drowning me. And I didn't do nothing wrong. I didn't do nothing wrong."

I am categorically against torture. But in terms of trial strategy, what Juan Gomez said that morning was virtually useless to me. As cold as it sounds, pleas of in-nocence are not particularly helpful to criminal de-fense attorneys.

So ten minutes later, as I entered the courtroom, I felt no better equipped than the day before, with the exception of the motions I had prepared with Cliff's help the previous evening, and the briefcase in which I carried them. I took my seat at the defense table to my client's right. Both of us had calmed down somewhat since our meeting—his eyes were dry, and I was not nearly as jumpy.

One bit of good news was that my motions needed to be presented to the court before the jury came into the courtroom. I wasn't sure how Judge Klay was going to react to my requests, and I really didn't want the jury's already unfavorable opinion of me to be further damaged by things she might say to me.

As was the case yesterday, the rest of the room was packed with spectators, the press, the governor and his wife, and those survivors of the Denver attack who were not going to testify. It was all too easy to recognize them—many were scarred from the burns they'd suf-fered. And according to what Cliff reported later that day, the Judicial Broadcasting System television camera was working just fine. He was watching from the moment the judge entered, and Sarge announced that court was in session. I rose, offered the originals of my motions to Clerk Estrada, and gave copies to A.D.A. Varick.

The clerk made some notations, and then handed the motions to Judge Klay, who made a bit of a show as she flipped through them, one at a time, harumphing occasionally, and once, outright laughing.

Finally, she looked up, and said, "All right, Mr. Carpenter, I have had a chance to take a look at your filings this morning. I'll hear you, beginning with your Motion to Continue."

In criminal trial practice, these kinds of motions were commonplace. Typically, judges allowed the attorneys to make brief, boring arguments, after which the judges made the rulings they intended to make in the first place. I rose, buttoned my suit jacket, and said, "Your Honor, as you well know, I was just appointed to this case yesterday. Given the magnitude and the severity of the charges—"

The woman didn't even let me finish my second sentence. "The magnitude and the severity of the charges have not changed since yesterday, Mr. Carpenter. The motion is denied. This trial is not about you, sir. It is about your client. He was the one who chose to dismiss his prior attorney. He cannot now claim that his new attorney is not prepared."

"But Mr. Gomez isn't complaining—"

"The motion is denied, sir. Please proceed to your next motion." The judge lifted up a document and read the title aloud: "Motion for Mistrial, or in the Alternative, for a New Jury." She lowered the document. "On what grounds do you think the defendant is entitled to another jury, Mr. Carpenter?"

It took me a minute to shift gears so quickly. I expected Judge Klay to be creepy and unpleasant, but I really had not expected the vehemence and speed with which she blew off that first motion.

But I wasn't about to let that happen on the issue of the jury's race. Judge Klay had been playing dirty for too long. So I said firmly, "Not one of these people—" as I dramatically turned and pointed to the jury box to make my point. But, of course, the jury hadn't been called into the courtroom yet. Someone behind me snickered. Oops. Caffeine: One. Me: Zero.

I lowered my finger somewhat anticlimactically, and turned back to the judge. "Not one of the jury members is Hispanic. The record will reflect that the defendant, Juan Gomez, is of Hispanic descent. His surname, his skin color, his family history, even the accent with which he speaks English, make this obvious.

"Yesterday, when the jury was impaneled, from my vantage point, there were three, possibly four, persons of Hispanic descent in the entire eighty-five-person jury pool. Since none of those individuals ended up on the final jury—"

Once again, Judge Klay interrupted. It didn't look like she was even going to bother involving A.D.A. Varick in the conversation this morning. She was going to oppose my motions all by herself. "Do you have any evidence—other than your personal assessment, which, as I remember, was made from the courtroom gallery— of the racial composition of the jury pool?"

Part of being a defense lawyer is being willing to ask for things that you know you aren't going to get. Decent judges simply deny those requests. But judges like Rhonda Klay make you pay for asking.

"No, Your Honor. The jury had already been selected

by the time I was appointed to the case, so all I can offer the court are my personal observations—"

"What is your racial background, Mr. Carpenter?"

"I'm Anglo. Anglo American."

"I see. And are you also an expert on identifying, by sight only, Hispanic Americans?"

"Well, I've lived in the Southwest for my entire life—"

"But you have no formal training or expertise in determining, by visual inspection alone, whether any particular person happens to be of Hispanic ancestry?"

She had me. But she was going to swat me around for a while before she finished me off.

"No, Your Honor."

"I see. So your motion for a mistrial, or for a new jury, or whatever this is, is based entirely on your informal, visual, non-expert assessment of the racial composition of the jury pool?"

Anyone familiar with criminal procedure knew the question was an invitation to suicide. I decided that as long as she was going to make this hard for me, I'd see if I could return the favor. "Actually, Your Honor, I was counting on the court to make findings of fact to support the motion, as it was in the best position to recognize the racial imbalance of the jury pool."

Judge Klay blinked. She probably had never faced a lawyer crazy enough to ask her, point-blank, to publicly acknowledge the kind of impropriety that she had been orchestrating for years.

A nasty smile settled itself across her face. "You would like me to make findings of fact. Very well," she said, sharply. "For the record, I find the following: *One.* The court assumes, and without evidence to the contrary, finds, that the jury pool was chosen randomly for this case, without any regard for its racial composition.

Two. The court finds that the jury pool's racial composition was *not* imbalanced, and to the extent that the racial composition of the jury pool did not mirror exactly the racial composition of the community, the difference resulted solely from the random selection process.

"Accordingly, the defendant's motion for a new jury is denied, and the motion for a mistrial is also denied." She slapped the motion down and grabbed another one. "Next. Motion for Prosecutor to Refrain from Referring to the Defendant as an 'Enemy Combatant.'" She looked up at me. "Why in the world shouldn't the prosecutor be allowed to refer to the defendant in the same terms that the federal government does?"

She was angry. Normally, I didn't like getting judges mad at me. But by that time on that particular morning, I was actually enjoying it. Maybe the caffeine had temporarily eroded my self-preservation instincts.

"That's just the point, Your Honor. The crimes alleged in this case are essentially acts of terrorism—"

"Mr. Carpenter." Her voice was metallic. "This is a state court. The crimes alleged are murder, conspiracy, assault with intent to commit murder, and several others, as you know. The indictments say nothing about terrorism."

"Technically that's right, Your Honor. But if this trial is truly going to be a test of whether the defendant is guilty or innocent of these crimes, it doesn't seem fair for the jury to be repeatedly given the message by the prosecutor that the U.S. government has already decided that he is guilty."

"But that, of course, is not what the designation 'enemy combatant' means, is it, sir? 'Enemy combatant' is merely a procedural designation attached to certain individuals in order to indicate to authorities the procedures to follow while such individuals are in custody. Mr. Gomez is now a criminal defendant. Would you also like me to refrain from calling him a 'defendant,' Mr. Carpenter?"

She was really worked up now. Her black eyes were shining with a dark intensity, and her voice, although still under control, was strained. As much as I hate to admit it, I realized at that moment that my ability to push her buttons might actually work to my advantage. I don't know if I would have done it with a less despicable judge, but for better or worse, I chose a button, and I pushed.

"As a matter of fact I would, Your Honor. The prejudice inherent—"

But Judge Klay wasn't about to listen to me spout my personal beliefs about how the justice system is tilted toward conviction. She tried to cut me off before I could really stoke her fire. "I'm sorry, Mr. Carpenter. The term is what it is. The jury has been instructed already that the defendant is presumed to be innocent until proven guilty, and they will be so instructed several more times before they decide this case. The motion is denied. There is no prejudice to Mr. Gomez if the prosecutor refers to him as an enemy combatant, or as a defendant. Whether you like it or not, he is both."

I waited for a moment, to lull her into believing that I had given up. And then I lit what I knew to be a very short fuse.

"With all due respect, Your Honor, there is precedent for my motion. There have been cases where the court has precluded the prosecutor from using the term 'victim' to describe the complaining witness, where to do so would be to essentially validate and/or endorse the prosecution's version of the facts—"

Judge Klay jumped at the bait. She smacked her

hand down on the bench and shouted, "Are you for one minute suggesting that the hundred and thirteen people that died in Denver last May were not victims? You should be very careful, Mr. Carpenter, about how you defend your client. I will not tolerate disrespect of any kind in my court, especially toward the hundreds and hundreds of victims of that awful attack."

No matter how much I disliked Judge Klay, and no matter how much I disliked losing, there was absolutely no way in the world I was going to exhibit any disrespect for the victims of the Denver Tunnel Bombing. For weeks after the catastrophe, my heart broke every time I thought of their suffering. A month after the explosion, my sister-in-law's fourth-grade class held a bake sale to raise money to help buy a wheelchair for a ten-year-old who had suffered nerve damage in the disaster. I bought a cupcake for five hundred dollars.

My argument that morning had merely been meant to keep the prosecutor from sending an unfair message to the jury.

But Judge Klay had leapt to the wrong conclusion, and the reporters behind me were stirring at her outburst. I decided to play it cool. "I meant no disrespect whatsoever, Your Honor," I said, "and I will, of course, take the court's warning to heart." Then I snapped back to business. "Please note my objection for the record to the court's denial of the first three of my motions."

The judge glared at me, but there was nothing more for her to say. I had lost, and I had accepted it. She snatched up the last of my motions. She held it in her hand, shaking it slightly, while looking me dead in the eye with a cold, black stare. I had always thought the woman looked like a lizard, but in that moment, you would have sworn that on a distant, twisted, dark, and diseased branch of her family tree there was coiled a snake. "And in this final motion, Mr. Carpenter, you seem to be asking for a hearing to support your motion to recuse me from this trial."

The gallery began to buzz. There was no denying that asking a judge for a hearing to support a motion to throw herself off a case—well, was a little out of the ordinary. The undercurrent of menace in the judge's tone added a layer of tension to the already highly charged atmosphere of the courtroom.

But Cliff had found something important. It was slimy, though, and ugly, and needed to be dragged out into the sunlight.

"Yes, Judge. As my motion indicates, I believe there are real concerns that Your Honor might have a conflict of interests—"

She interrupted again. "You truly believe I can't judge this case objectively?"

"Well, I think there is certainly enough information contained in the motion to warrant an evidentiary hearing in order to explore—"

"I disagree. I find that I am perfectly able to conduct myself and this trial in good faith, objectively, impartially, and in accordance with all applicable rules. The fact that I am a member of the board of directors of a corporation which has nothing to do with this trial is irrelevant. The motion is denied."

I couldn't just let it go at that.

"With all due respect, Your Honor, it seems that the most prudent course of action would be to have a hearing, so that the court could rest its ruling on an evidentiary foundation—"

"And I disagree," Judge Klay spat back. "The motion is denied, Mr. Carpenter, without a hearing. Because there is no need for a hearing. My findings are based on my own knowledge of myself, of this case, and of the situation to which you refer in your motion. There is no connection whatsoever between any aspect of my personal life and this trial." The judge looked over to Sarge, and said, "Mr. Gilvery, we will take a ten-minute recess. Then please have the jury brought in so we may begin testimony. Thank you."

And with that, she slithered off the bench.

I hurriedly scribbled something on a sheet of paper. I folded it with the copies of my motions, and stuck them all into my breast pocket.

And then I bolted out of the courtroom.

SIX

THE PHOENIX Superior Courthouse is a seven-story rectangular building in the center of the city. The first three floors hold the Superior Court's criminal and civil clerks' offices and several courtrooms and judges' offices. The cafeteria and law library take up the fourth floor. A small jail and several administrative offices are located on the fifth and sixth floors, and on the top floor, appropriately, is the highest court in the state—the Supreme Court of Arizona.

The main staircase and two elevators run through the center lobby of each floor, and auxiliary staircases are located at each end, alongside the building's men's and women's rooms.

When I got out of the courtroom, I turned right, toward the nearest end of the building. Three members of the press followed me down the hallway, asking questions, mostly about my reaction to the judge stomping all over my motions. One was still interested in whether I thought my client would be better off without me.

I tried to hurry, for two reasons. First, I didn't know how much time I actually had, and second, I wanted to make the news guys believe that I had to go to the bathroom.

Actually, thanks to all the coffee, I really *did* have to go to the bathroom. But that was going to have to wait.

Anyway, by the time I reached the end of the hallway, the reporters were still with me, still asking questions. When I reached the men's room door I turned to face them, and said, "I'm sorry. I really can't talk to you now. I've got to, you know, take care of some business before the recess is over."

One of the trio looked at me a little funny, but in the end, at least for a little while, my ploy worked. They started back toward the courtroom.

And as they were walking away from me, I turned toward the bathroom door. But instead of opening that one, I opened the door next to it. And then I started tearing my way up six flights of stairs. Because if Judge Klay wasn't going to take herself off the case, I was going to ask the Supreme Court of Arizona to do it.

To be completely honest, "tearing my way" was not exactly how I ascended the staircase. It would be more precise to say that I was moving as quickly as I could, considering that I had to walk up the steps while keeping my right shoulder pressed along the outside wall of the stairwell, and my eyes averted from anything to my left.

Unfortunately, the courthouse staircases wind around an open air shaft which extends the entire height of the building. That means that as you walk up the stairs, you can look over your left shoulder, all the way down to the bottom floor.

The problem wasn't that this is dangerous—bars have been installed to prevent prisoners from trying to escape by throwing themselves over the railing and down the shaft to freedom.

The problem was that I was terrified of heights. Anytime I encountered a view which indicated that I was more than a few feet above the ground I got severely dizzy. In technical terms, I suffered from vertigo.

So by the time I reached the seventh floor, I was breathing hard and perspiring freely—not just from the pace I kept on the stairs, but from the effort it took to convince myself, as I was mounting those steps, that I wasn't really within three or four feet of a sixty-foot plummet to the basement. I put my hands on my knees and tried to compose myself before I walked down the hallway to the Clerk's Office of the Supreme Court. It wasn't going to do anyone any good for me to walk in there, vomit, and then pass out.

When I finally made it through the imposing double doors, I withdrew the papers from my pocket and tried to look like I hadn't just spent the last three minutes in hand-to-hand combat with an irrational phobia. I approached Kendra Styles, one of the assistant clerks in that office.

"Good morning, Attorney Carpenter," she said, coming out from behind her desk to meet me at the counter. Kendra was a large, elegant African American woman who carried herself more like a seasoned ambassador than a state-court bureaucrat. "I thought you were on the Gomez trial . . ." And then she saw the fistful of papers I was holding, and sudden understanding washed over her face. "Oh. That's why you're here."

Most lawyers know that the Arizona Supreme Court is the highest appeals court in the state. But what many don't know is that according to the Arizona State Constitution, it is also the place where you request a writ if, in the middle of your trial, you have an emergency which requires an immediate ruling about the conduct of a trial judge.

"What have you got?" Kendra asked.

"A recusal motion," I responded. I handed her the papers, and she scanned the handwritten one first, and then the others. "We're in a short recess right now," I said, "so I was hoping that I could get this before the court as soon as possible."

"Chief Justice Bridges will hear the motion," Kendra said, looking up. She was all business. "I'll bring it to his clerk right after I call downstairs and tell them there's a stay on those proceedings." She hesitated. "You did intend to move for an immediate stay in the lower court pending this court's ruling on this matter, didn't you?"

I knew I'd forgotten something. Of course I wanted the Gomez trial to be put on hold while the Supreme Court considered my motion. "If I had thought of it, I would have," I admitted.

She smiled. "I'll take care of it," she said, picking up the phone. "No extra charge."

Two minutes and fifteen seconds later, a dozen reporters and three camera operators burst through the clerk's office door. Before I could even apologize to Kendra, they started pounding me with questions.

Moments later, four court officers materialized out of nowhere. They escorted the media hounds out. As they left, I felt a hand at my elbow. A fifth officer ushered me through the side door of a cavernous courtroom. At one end was a raised platform on which sat a dark wood structure, serving as the bench for the seven members of the Supreme Court of Arizona.

I had actually been in this courtroom several times before, in my role as an appeals attorney. But the high court heard criminal appellate arguments only during the last week of every month. At those times, the court-room was packed with lawyers waiting to be called, me-dia, court officers, clerks, the court reporter, and dozens of spectators.

There was something very different about the room now that I was the only person in it.

Motions like mine were argued before only one of the justices, and since the hearings weren't scheduled in advance, there were no spectators present. The podium where I stood was a full eight feet below the bench. The gold-leaf ceiling of the room was more than twenty feet high. I felt positively tiny—like a three-year-old en-tering a church for the first time.

After less than a minute, there was a sharp bang, and then a door opened behind the bench. A court offi-cer entered the room and shouted, "Court! All rise!" He was followed by a court reporter, and then by a young woman—probably the Chief Justice's clerk—holding a slim manila folder.

And then, very slowly, in shuffled Chief Justice Hugo Bridges.

Arizona became the forty-eighth state on February 14, 1912. The running joke in the bar association was that Justice Bridges didn't attend the ceremony be-cause his horse threw a shoe.

He really wasn't that old. But he looked every one of his eighty-seven years. With the exception of a few stubborn wisps of white hair on top of his head, and a narrow fringe around the base of his skull, he was en-tirely bald. He walked in a stoop, his face was weather-worn and deeply wrinkled, and impressive jowls hung down on both sides of his jaw.

He wore huge, bottle-thick black glasses, which ap-peared to work only intermittently—at some times, he seemed almost entirely blind, and at others, you'd swear he was able to read the fine print on a contract you were holding fifty feet away.

But any deterioration in the man's body had stopped short of his mind. Hugo Bridges had been the state's leading jurist for over three decades and, despite his age, he showed no signs of slowing down. He'd written some of the most influential and groundbreaking decisions in the state's history. He was a man of fierce integrity—sharp, fearless, and brilliant. In the handful of times I had appeared before the Supreme Court, he had always been the member of the panel of judges I feared most. He unerringly exposed and then relentlessly probed the weakest aspects of my arguments.

I tried not to think about that as I looked up from the podium and watched the old man move into position. He suffered from arthritis in his right knee as a result of a war injury, so it took him a while to get into his chair at the center of the massive bench. Once he was settled, he peered out at me and said in a rasp, "Good morning, Attorney Carpenter. Before we begin, I'd like to express once again the Court's best wishes for a speedy recovery for your father. Assistant District Attorney Carpenter was one of Arizona's best prosecutors. His appearances before this Court have been missed."

My dad always said that he had never felt more like a lawyer than on those rare occasions when he'd argued cases before Chief Justice Bridges.

He also said that on those same occasions he'd never felt more like he needed a change of underwear.

"Thank you, Your Honor," I replied. "I'm sure that my father will very much appreciate the Court's kind words."

But the Chief Justice had already turned his attention to the papers that his clerk had laid out before him on the bench. He picked up the single sheet I had presented to Kendra in the Clerk's Office and held it close to his face. Then he pulled it away, and glared at me. "Did you handwrite this?"

"Yes, Your Honor. I'm on trial downstairs, and an emergency situation arose—"

"I can't read this," he interrupted impatiently, turning to his young clerk, who was sitting next to the court reporter in front of the bench. "What does it say, Miranda?"

Miranda stood up, and read in a clear soprano from her copy of the motion. "Now comes the defendant, Juan Gomez, and pursuant to Article Six, Section Five, of the Arizona Constitution, moves this honorable court for an emergency Writ of Mandamus directing the immediate recusal of Judge Rhonda M. Klay from Superior Court Trial Number 4201, State of Arizona versus Juan Abdullah Gomez. As grounds therefor, the defendant states that Judge Klay has a conflict of interests which renders her involvement with the aforementioned trial—"

"Thank you, Miranda." Justice Bridges turned back to me. "I assume that you have already raised this issue with Judge . . . who is it?"

"Judge Klay, Your Honor," I responded. "Yes, I did. I included in my filings with the Court the motion that I presented to her this morning." My heart was thudding. I remember wishing that I'd had more sleep the night before. If I could coherently explain myself, I had a chance. As tough as Judge Bridges was, he was fair. But if my concentration slipped for even a moment, I was through, as was any chance for Juan Gomez to receive a fair trial before a reasonable judge.

The Chief Justice sifted through the papers before

him, and pulled up the relevant motion. He read through it quickly. "What did Judge Klay say?"

"Well, she said that the fact that she was on the Trentacorp board of directors did not support my position because the company had nothing to do with this case."

"She did not dispute your assertions regarding the corporation?"

"No, Your Honor. She simply said they weren't important. And then she said that she could decide the case impartially, so..." My mind wandered for a second. I was thinking about whether Judge Klay thought that she looked like a lizard. The effects of the caffeine were wearing off.

"So?" Justice Bridges glared at me.

I took a deep breath. Where was I? "So she denied the motion."

"And why is that wrong?"

"Because, Your Honor, there is a concrete and extremely important connection between the corporation at issue and Mr. Gomez's case. Trentacorp is a federal contractor that produces millions and millions of dollars of weapons, body armor, and other equipment specifically designed to combat terrorism. If Mr. Gomez is found guilty in this case, there will be a tremendous benefit to Trentacorp. President Richie, and many in his administration, especially Secretary of Defense Ivanov and Undersecretary of Defense Newton, have made numerous public statements indicating that as the incidents of terrorism increase, the amount of money the federal government needs to spend combating terrorism will increase. And—"

"What is your defense in this case, Mr. Carpenter?"

The seeming non sequitur caught me by surprise. "My defense?"

"Yes, Attorney Carpenter. Your defense. What is the theory of the defense in the case at issue? Arizona versus Juan Gomez. What is your defense?"

It was a good question. The same good question that had made my opening statement something of a mess. "Um, the defense is, uh, that..." Sadie M. was a saint? "The defense is that the defendant is innocent. He didn't do it."

"So, your defense is mistaken identity?"

I knew enough about Chief Justice Bridges to know that he never fooled around. If he was asking about my defense, it wasn't because he was merely curious. It was because it was relevant to his decision. But if I admitted that our defense was mistaken identity, Chief Justice Bridges would want me to tell him who we thought did do the crimes. Of course I had no idea. So I tried to dodge the question.

"Your Honor, I'm quite new to the case, and, well, I guess I don't feel entirely comfortable being too specific about the defense at this point."

The statement was true, but it came out sounding flippant. Like I didn't think the highest court in the state of Arizona had any right to poke around in my business.

The old man sat back in his chair. He looked at me steadily for just long enough for me to start thinking about that spare underwear my father used to mention. Then he leaned forward again, and spoke forcefully. "Forgive me for making you *uncomfortable*, Attorney Carpenter. My inquiry is designed solely to provide me with the information I require to rule on your motion. So I will ask you again: Is the defense in your case mistaken identity?"

At this point, I finally managed to come up with a useful thought, even though I still didn't understand why my trial strategy was so important to the Chief Justice. What I recognized was that Justice Bridges was way too smart for me to successfully dance around his questions. If I didn't lay it all out for him—as ugly as it might be—I didn't have a chance. "Your Honor, the only reason I'm hesitating is because claiming that we intend to argue mistaken identity to the jury seems to imply that I know more than I actually know. All I can confidently tell the court at this time is that the defense is that Mr. Gomez did not do these things. That he is innocent. That he was set up. I don't know who did it, I don't know why Mr. Gomez was set up, I don't know much of anything. I'm afraid that, at this very moment, I don't even know yet how I will present the defense."

The old judge pondered that little confession for a moment, then he nodded. "Am I to understand that you will not contest the fact that there *was* an attack in Denver last May?"

And then, suddenly, the dawn broke, and I finally stepped into the light. The reason my strategy mattered was because it was directly relevant to whether Judge Klay had a conflict of interests. If all I hoped to do at trial was claim that the government had arrested the wrong terrorist, I was basically admitting that the Denver Tunnel Bombing *was* a terrorist attack. In that event, whether Gomez won or lost the trial wouldn't have any effect on the financial health of Trentacorp. To agree that the bombing was the work of some terrorists—*any* terrorists—I would have already acknowledged that there was increased terrorism in the United States.

The only scenario under which Judge Klay would have a conflict of interests was if our defense was that the Denver attack *wasn't* an act of terrorism. Under those circumstances, Trentacorp—and Judge Klay—

would have a financial incentive to see that Mr. Gomez was found guilty. His guilt would *prove* the government's theory that Denver was a terrorist attack. And that, in turn, would justify ever increasing governmental expenditures on Trentacorp's products.

Am I to understand that you will not contest the fact that there was an attack in Denver last May? Now that I understood the thrust of Justice Bridge's questioning, I wasn't quite sure how to respond. So I went with the unadorned truth.

"All I can say to that, Your Honor, is that I don't know yet whether we will contest that the Denver Tunnel Bombing was a terrorist act. Almost everything I know about the case is what I've read in the papers and heard on the news. I've only had a chance to speak to my client for a few minutes up to this point—"

"Well, why didn't you ask for a continuance?" the old man snapped. "Why in heaven's name are you trying a case like this without proper preparation?"

"I did move for more time, Your Honor," I replied. "Just this morning." He fished around in the papers before him, scowling. "Judge Klay denied the motion."

His eyes were on the document he held. Then he looked up and sighed heavily. "Of course she did," he said, shaking his head in disgust. "So you claim the judge has a conflict of interests, because your defense might rely on a challenge to the government's position that this bombing was a terrorist act, and in that case, the judge has a clear financial interest in making certain the defendant would lose."

"That's correct, Your Honor."

Judge Bridges picked up a pen and began to write. "Assistant Clerk Styles has informed me that your trial has been stayed pending my ruling."

"That's right, Your Honor."

He nodded, but kept on writing. Moments later he put down his pen, tore a piece of paper from a legal pad, and handed it to his clerk, saying, "Type this up for me, please, and get it to Judge Klay's clerk immediately." Then he stood up, looked down at me, and said, "You better hurry back to your trial."

SEVEN

AS I LEFT THE courtroom I saw that the reporters—minus the cameramen—had been in the room all along. I just hadn't noticed them.

They all followed me into the hallway, and the barrage of questions started up again.

But this time when I ignored their inquiries and walked quickly to the end of the hall, there was no pretense. I went right into the bathroom. My bladder was about to burst.

I washed up in a hurry when I was done. I was afraid I didn't have time to take the elevator, so I started down the steps. Once again I tried to ignore the seemingly infinite chasm at the center of the stairwell as I descended, this time while being trailed by the shouting reporters.

I finally emerged into the first-floor hallway, breathing heavily, sweating prodigiously, my personal cadre of stalkers having witnessed every moment of my embarrassing phobia on the descent. But clearly, I had made it down in time. Dozens of people were creating quite a din in the hallway outside the courtroom, waiting until the intermission was over.

The scores of reporters who hadn't chased me up to the seventh floor began swarming, yelling questions at me as I approached the door. Sarge, thank God, had anticipated the crush. With the help of another court officer named Mike, he helped clear a path for me to make my way back into the room.

The clamor inside the courtroom was even more intense than in the hallway. The spectators in the gallery were talking as if they were at a noisy cocktail party. Sarge knew to speak loudly enough for me to hear him as he walked beside me to the front of the room and left me at the defense table. Unfortunately, all he said was, "I hope you know what you're doing, Tommy," before he disappeared through a side doorway, probably to bring Gomez back into the courtroom.

I knew the senior court officer well enough to know what he meant. It was damn risky trying to toss Judge Klay off the case.

It shouldn't have been. Judges are supposed to conduct all aspects of trials without taking the actions of the lawyers personally. Especially things like motions to recuse.

But Rhonda Klay did exactly the opposite, which is one of the reasons she was such a bad judge. If I lost this gamble, and Judge Klay stayed on the case, she would do everything she could to make my life a relentless festival of misery, and we all knew it.

I checked my watch. Almost ten minutes had passed from when I had left Chief Justice Bridges. Fatigue was beginning to creep up on me. I considered standing and walking around, just to keep myself alert.

But then a noise to my left caught my attention, and I turned to see Sarge leading Gomez into the courtroom. Judge Klay must have received Chief Justice Bridges's decision. There was no other reason to bring the defendant in.

Gomez was wearing his green prison jumpsuit, and as usual, his feet and hands were shackled. His eyes looked unnaturally large behind his glasses. He sat down next to me and asked urgently, "What's going on, man? What's the holdup?"

Under normal circumstances, keeping my clients informed of my actions in their case was easy. As an appeals lawyer, I was either doing legal research, writing their brief, or waiting for a decision on their case. Pretty much a predictable routine.

This was the first time I'd sprinted up six flights of stairs to try to throw a judge off a trial.

"I made a motion to have Judge Klay removed from the case," I told Gomez.

The defendant studied me in confusion. Or was it suspicion? "I know," he said. "She denied that motion this morning."

"No. I mean I went to another court to have *them* throw her off the case."

"Whoa. You went over Judge Klay's head? Damn." Gomez shook his head. "You got some balls, my friend. Great big balls. I just hope she don't screw you bad."

And on that jolly note, the door at the front of the courtroom opened up. First Manny Estrada, the clerk, emerged, carrying a file folder. Manny was followed by Sarge. Instantly, the room fell silent, and everyone got to their feet. I turned and saw the red light above the Judicial Broadcasting System camera blink on. This was it.

But no one called the case back into session. Manny stood behind his desk, set his folder down, and simply said, "Please be seated."

I was puzzled. Had Chief Justice Bridges changed his mind, and decided to rewrite his decision? How long would we have to wait?

Clerk Estrada began to speak.

"As you know, this trial is in recess. During that recess, an order has been issued out of the Supreme Court of Arizona. I would like to read a portion of that order now." He opened the folder on his desk, and withdrew a single sheet of paper.

"'In the matter of The State of Arizona versus Juan Abdullah Gomez, Superior Court Number 4201, it is hereby ordered that Superior Court Judge Rhonda M. Klay be and she hereby is recused, and the Administrative Judge of the Superior Court is hereby ordered to appoint a successor judge to preside over the trial forthwith. Pending such appointment, the aforementioned matter is to remain in recess.'

"And the order is signed by Chief Justice of the Supreme Court of Arizona, Hugo H. Bridges."

And without another word, Manny replaced the document, scooped up his folder, and walked back through the doorway, out of the courtroom.

The door hadn't even swung completely shut when the spell holding the courtroom silent was shattered. "Wait a minute!" I heard one reporter cry out. "So who's the new judge?"

But instead of answers, the question was met with a chorus of more questions. I couldn't understand a word of any of it.

And then Sarge was barking, "Quiet! *Quiet in the court!*"

It was like someone had hit the mute button. One minute, the place was buzzing like an angry beehive; the next, instant silence. Sarge stood in front of the clerk's table, facing the gallery. His big hands were slowly and rhythmically squeezing into and out of fists. He almost looked like he hoped someone would say something, so he could finally discover if grabbing a person by the throat really would pop their head right off.

"This case is in recess until at least tomorrow," he snarled. "The new judge will be reassigned sometime later today, and the announcement will be up on the court's Web site as soon as it happens, along with information about when the trial will be back in session.

"Until then, this courtroom is closed!" he shouted. "I'll expect it to be empty in five minutes." Then he followed Manny Estrada out through the door behind the witness stand.

The murmurs started up again the instant Sarge left the room, but before they got too loud, Sarge's partner, Mike, eased into the good-cop role as if the pair had been dealing with rowdy courtrooms like this for their whole lives. "All right, everybody. Clear the courtroom. That's it. Clear the court. Thank you." From the look of the way most people were moving, the place was going to be vacated long before Sarge's five-minute deadline.

I was stunned, and sat there, speechless.

My client, however, had much to say. He was pounding me on the back, shouting, "Holy shit, man, you're a good lawyer!" and, "You really got that nasty judge thrown off my case? Damn. So what's your next move?"

It was a perfectly legitimate question, yet I almost laughed. I had no answers for Juan Gomez. Up to that point in my professional life, I had prided myself on my preparation. I planned for every contingency I could imagine, feeling like that was part of my responsibility in representing my clients zealously.

But in this trial, I had absolutely no idea what my next move was. In the two days I'd worked on the

Gomez case, I'd spent more time flying by the seat of my pants than I had in all my years since law school.

And I had a feeling that my aerial stunts were just beginning.

One of the court officers arrived to take Gomez back to his holding cell. I followed them, both because it allowed me to leave the courtroom without having to fight my way through the mob that was noisily milling around in the hallway, and because it gave me a chance to explain to my client that I was pretty much making this all up as I went along.

The irony was that Gomez didn't believe me. For the first time in over a year, an attorney in the criminal justice system had done something that worked to his benefit, and he was firmly committed to believing that attorney was going to keep it up. He was elated.

As I left him there in the holding cell, I was much less confident than he.

I had other things to think about, though. I hadn't had breakfast, and I was starving. I decided to get something fast from the cafeteria before heading home. I figured that even if some reporters were lurking up there, I'd just grab something to go. I returned to the main corridor from a side door between the courtroom and the end of the building, which kept me from running into the small crowd of people who were still hovering at the courtroom entrance.

I'd gotten some grease on my hand when I leaned on Gomez's cell door as I was talking to him, so I headed for the bathroom to wash up.

The room was empty, which was fine with me. The fewer people I ran into, the sooner I'd be able to eat something and get home. I stepped over to the sinks on my right, turned on the faucet, and soaped up my hands.

My reflection did not look like one of a man who had, albeit unwittingly, taken the first steps along a path which would risk his life and, with it, the lives of everyone he loved.

Rather, it looked like one of a bleary-eyed thirty-year-old with a vague resemblance to Gregory Peck's less attractive brother on a bad hair day, wearing a dark gray suit and a blue tie with a coffee stain on it.

I looked away from my reflection, down again into the sink, and rinsed the soap off my hands. Then I cupped them together, collected some water, and splashed it onto my face.

It was refreshing, but for only about one, maybe two seconds. Because just as I reached out to turn off the water, I felt a presence behind me.

In retrospect, I bet I would have noticed the man coming into the bathroom before that moment if I hadn't been washing my hands. Splashing water masks most sounds even for people with perfectly normal hearing.

As it was, I paid no particular attention. Until I felt fingers close around my throat and heard a voice say, "Make one sound, and you will die right here."

EIGHT

FOR ABOUT A quarter of a second I caught sight in the mirror of a man wearing a blue ski mask. And then, before I could respond or even regain my balance, I was pulled into one of the toilet stalls.

I am not a small man. And although I have been described as gangly, I am by no means a weakling. One of the ways I pass time up at my father's house is to chop mesquite logs for the woodstove that he loves to sit near. My hands, and especially my shoulders and arms, are pretty darn strong.

And my survival instincts run very much against getting murdered in a bathroom, so I started to fight.

The struggle didn't last long, though, because my attacker now had my throat in the crook of his elbow like a vise. As soon as I grabbed at him, he choked off my air quite completely. I knew from my days as a high-school wrestler that I didn't have much time before I passed out, so I braced for one final effort to break his hold.

But in the split second before I made my last stand, my assailant released his grip on my throat slightly, and murmured, "Stop. I'm now holding a gun to your head." He spoke in a harsh whisper that sounded like it was intended to disguise his voice. I twisted slightly in his grip, and my temple bumped into something that sure felt like the muzzle of a weapon.

I've read books and seen movies where the hero is as cool and calm as a mountain lake while he's all tied up and the bad guy is sticking a gun in his face. "Weren't you scared?" coos the beautiful starlet, as she gently wipes the blood from our hero's bruised jaw.

"If he'd wanted to kill me, he would have done it right away," Captain Manly explains, squinting gallantly.

Here's a tip to those of you who haven't yet had the experience of being held at gunpoint: Bruce Willis dialogue is not what's racing through your brain as you stand there in a deserted bathroom, while the smell of disinfectant mixes unpleasantly with the sharp metallic odor of a deadly weapon less than an inch from your skull.

What *is* going through your mind? Well, you probably start wondering if you have any chance at grabbing the handgun before it blows a hole in your head, and then you nearly jump out of your shoes when you hear a voice come through a walkie-talkie of some kind, saying, *"Beta, this is Gamma. Cafeteria is clear. Over."*

And before I had a chance even to begin to try and process that, my gunman responded, "Roger that, Gamma. First-floor bathrooms are clear. Kappa is on five then seven. Go up to six—check everything. Including the women's rooms. Over."

And then Gamma—*Gamma,* for God's sake—shot back, *"Roger sixth floor. Out."*

I probably should have thanked the guy with his arm around my throat for so completely confusing me that I was momentarily distracted from the fact that I was one heartbeat away from death.

Who the hell were these people? And who were they looking for? It couldn't have been me—otherwise Mr. Gun At My Temple wouldn't have said that the first-floor bathrooms were clear.

But if I wasn't their target, why in the world had he grabbed me? Surely he'd seen me before I'd seen him. He could very easily just have walked out the door before I even noticed him, and then happily continued his search for whatever poor sap he, Kappa, and Gamma were so intent on finding.

As if he could hear my thoughts, the man behind me rasped directly into my ear. "Your life is in danger" was how he started.

"No kidding," I wheezed out in response. I was running on one hundred percent hormones and zero percent brain.

"Not from me, dumbshit," he said. His tone did not leave room for disagreement, so I said nothing, but I remember feeling that the gun pressing against my head was at least mildly inconsistent with his last statement.

"I'm the least of your problems," he continued. "Your ass is on fire because your little stunt with Judge Klay this morning has pissed off a lot of very powerful people in the prosecutor's office. And right down the street in the Arizona Statehouse. Not to mention Washington, D.C. They're *really* bullshit back there."

If this guy thought he was making things easier for me to understand, he was sadly mistaken. "I have no idea—"

"Listen up, Counselor," he snapped. "I'm almost out of time. This whole trial was put together very carefully. And Judge Klay was a major part of it. The case didn't just land in her lap accidentally. Big people have put a lot of effort into making sure Gomez fries for what happened in Denver, and Rhonda Klay was on the team. You stepped in some serious shit, my friend, when you managed to kick her out.

"So from now on, they see you as a real threat. You are going to be watched. You are going to be bugged. Everything you say and everything you do is going to be monitored. By the feds, the cops, people you can't even begin to imagine.

"You aren't safe. Your father, your sister-in-law, your niece—nobody is safe. You should be especially careful around this state cop Landry. He used to be in the army. He's going to be all over you, and he's a fucking freak. Watch out for him. That psychopath will do anything. So—"

My new benefactor was interrupted by one of his fellow Greek letters. *"Top floor is clear, heading for rendezvous point on one. Over."*

"Roger that, Kappa."

The walkie-talkie went silent, and he spoke to me. "I don't have much time," he said. "Put your right hand behind your back."

For a second I thought about resisting, but I did as he said. The threat of a bullet to the brain was quite effective. I felt and heard a handcuff click into place around my wrist. "Keep facing forward, but take a step back. I'm going to lock you to the pipe here"—there was a tug on my wrist, and another click—"and I'm putting the handcuff key in your shirt pocket." He did as he said. "It will take you about thirty seconds to get out of here after I leave. Do not tell anyone about this. *Anyone*, understand? If you do, I guarantee that within sixty minutes, you'll be lying on your face, with a bullet in the back of your head. And so will anyone within a hundred yards of you."

Then he patted me down, as if looking for weapons. Before I reminded him that normal people don't know how to smuggle guns into buildings guarded by metal detectors, he reached into my breast pocket and withdrew my cell phone. "I'll just leave this on the sink—I don't want you calling anybody for a minute or so."

It was all so insane, it was hard to decide whether I believed him. But I sure believed that pistol poking me in the face. I was so overwhelmed with everything that had happened to me over the last twenty-four hours that I couldn't think of a single thing to say.

Then I felt a ski mask come over my head, except the eye holes were missing. I couldn't see a thing.

"Leave the mask on until you hear the door close. Then take it off, and get out of here. They're going to make contact with you. Just do what they say and nothing will happen to you or your family. Stay smart. Keep being Gomez's lawyer, but don't do anything fancy, okay? Nothing unusual, nothing stupid. I'll be in touch. Don't worry. I'll let you know when it's time to make some noise."

And then, like it was nothing out of the ordinary, he just walked out of the stall. A second later, I heard the bathroom door open, then close.

He was right—it took me about a half a minute to pull the ski mask off and unlock the handcuffs from my wrist. I didn't rush out into the hallway after the guy, though. I knew he'd be gone.

And even if he were standing out there like an idiot in a courthouse hallway with a gun, what was I supposed to do? Talk him into voluntarily laying down his weapon? Less than sixty seconds ago he'd been a finger twitch from shooting my brains out. He didn't seem like the kind of person I was likely to convince to surrender.

I sat down on the toilet seat, locked the stall door, and took a second to try to bring my pulse rate down to something in the triple digits.

Just to clarify, when I said earlier that I was open to life's opportunities, I wasn't including the opportunity to be victimized by a nonsense-spouting thug in a courthouse lavatory.

Why would everyone involved in the Gomez case bother to conspire to fix a guilty verdict? The evidence against him was overwhelming. I hadn't had time to review it in detail, but I'd seen enough of Steve Temilow's files to know that they had video- and audiotapes of the defendant doing and saying some seriously incriminating things, many of them establishing a strong connection between Gomez and the suicide bomber who actually committed the Denver atrocity. And then there were the things found in Gomez's home—maps of Denver with the tunnel highlighted, photos of the tunnel, photos of fuel tankers, dozens of radical Islamic texts, and printouts of instructions from the Internet on how to make detonating devices.

Not to mention a newspaper article detailing the most heavily trafficked stretches of road in Houston, and a map of that city which had been highlighted to show exactly those spots identified in the article. And then there were printouts of train, bus, and airline schedules from Houston to Phoenix.

Sure, some of these things could be explained innocently, but taken all together, especially with the tapes, there was absolutely no way Gomez was getting off. The only thing I could think of was that the authorities were so afraid of some freak jury thing—like what happened in the O.J. case—that they had decided to cheat, just to make certain there was no chance Gomez would go free.

It didn't make a lot of sense, but it made more sense than what I could piece together about my own little personal encounter.

Question one was who was that nut with the gun? And exactly what the hell was he trying to do? Not to sound ungrateful, but did he really think he was doing me a favor by telling me that there was some crackpot conspiracy behind the trial? If everything he said was true, I was soon to be contacted by powerful people who were going to threaten to kill me and my family if I refused to represent Gomez without doing anything fancy, stupid, or unusual. Whatever that meant.

So how did getting threatened at gunpoint in a bathroom make that any less monstrous? Did my assailant think that I wouldn't take the conspirators' threat seriously if I didn't literally have a gun to my head?

But that couldn't have been it—the guy in the bathroom made it pretty clear that he was not part of the conspiracy.

Or at least he didn't want me to think he was.

Maybe this was the most sophisticated good cop/bad cop routine in the history of coercion. The bathroom man sticks a gun to my head and threatens my life, and he's the *nice* one. The message could be *Look out for the other lunatics out there. They're really out of control.*

I wasn't thinking clearly. I needed to get out of the bathroom and get some food, some air, and some rest. The artificial energy that my body had generated at the prospect of being on the wrong end of several violent felonies was oozing out of me fast. I was woozy from fear, hunger, and lack of sleep.

I got up, leaving behind the ski mask and the handcuffs still attached to the pipe above the toilet for somebody else to worry about. As promised, my cell phone rested on the edge of the sink. I dropped it into my pocket, and headed out into the hallway, still uncertain of what to do.

Sometimes, when I look back on my actions, they seem so naive. I knew I needed help—I just had no idea who I could turn to safely. Were all state cops a threat? Or was it just the one named Landry? And was he really a threat? Or was Beta's message intended to raise my suspicions about one of the cops that I really *could* trust?

I walked to the main lobby to take the elevator up to the cafeteria. Lunch would help me clear my head. I needed a plan.

The area outside the Gomez courtroom had cleared. There was only the normal lunchtime traffic in the hallway as I made my way toward the center of the building.

As I boarded the elevator and pressed the button for the fourth floor, I found myself hyper-alert, closely examining everyone who came into the cab with me. First was a young man and a young woman, both carrying heavy briefcases, and also heading to the fourth floor. They were obviously on their way to the library. The final two riders were older women who pressed the button for the fifth and sixth floors—probably administrative workers.

As the bell rang and the doors started to slide together, I caught sight of a pair of men standing next to each other in the corridor. Both wore dark pullover shirts and trousers. One was African American, and had a goatee. The other was white, and his head was shaved. Just before the doors closed completely, the white one smiled at me. Then he made a gun with his thumb and index finger, and shot me.

I knew that I was in no condition to think through this mess rationally, but it was hard to ignore the waves of paranoia that were beginning to wash up on the shores of my consciousness. As the briefcase couple and I exited the elevator, I found myself wondering if their heavy satchels contained weapons, and was greatly relieved when they turned left off the elevator, and really walked toward the library.

I decided that right after lunch, I had to go to the cops.

I freely admit that part of my decision came from watching countless victims in Hollywood blockbusters end up dangling from a frayed rope over a pit of crocodiles, or single-handedly trying to disarm a thermonuclear device with a thumbtack and a Q-Tip, all because they failed to get help from the police just because some bad guy told them not to.

By the time I reached the cafeteria, I was resolved. The man in the bathroom was just not credible. *Operation: Rig the Gomez Trial* was too far-fetched to start with, but to think that the nutcase in the bathroom knew about it, and took it upon himself to valiantly, albeit terrifyingly, "warn" me about it—for no apparent reason—defied all reason.

What I *was* convinced of, though, was that Beta was dangerous. I had no intention of recklessly ignoring his threats. But realistically, if I was careful about it, how would he ever know if I talked to the cops? I decided that right after lunch, I would drive directly from the courthouse to state police headquarters, go in there and tell them the whole story, right down to my encounter in the men's room. They'd protect me if I really needed it. What was the Greek Alphabet Squad going to do about that? Storm a police station?

I finally reached the lunch line at exactly three minutes before one o'clock, and I was so desperate to get something into my system quickly that I grabbed two sandwiches and two bottles of water, threw them on my tray, and almost sprinted to the cashier. Marge, a tiny, ancient woman with the whitest hair I'd ever seen in my life, rang me up. "Somebody's hungry today," she said.

I'd known Marge since my eighth birthday—the first time my father had brought me here for lunch. She'd given me an extra bag of potato chips that afternoon to celebrate. If Marge was a part of this conspiracy, the entire planet was doomed. "I missed breakfast," I admitted. "I don't think I've ever looked forward to chicken salad so much in my life."

I paid, picked up my tray, and headed to the first empty table I could find. But before I could get there, fate saved me my trip to the police, as a state trooper stepped right in front of me. Wearing not only his khaki uniform but an uncharacteristically big smile, the cop said, "Counselor, I'm glad I found you. I thought you might have already left, and I wanted to get a chance to speak with you before you took off. My name's Trooper Paul Landry."

NINE

I HAVEN'T HAD much luck with lying.

My limited experience started back in second grade, with my first, and probably biggest, whopper.

I was sitting at one of the five cool, short, round worktables in our classroom annex with Rocco Rufo, Billy Valparaiso, Lisa Perez, and another girl whose name I've forgotten. We had moved there from our regular desks because Ms. Jennings had told us we were going to have a special activity. But before we could begin, we had to sit quietly and wait for her, because she had to run out of the classroom for a minute and *she would be right back and no one had better make a single sound or there would be a severe punishment.*

After about thirty seconds of her absence, the power of that warning began to fade. After sixty seconds, it was all but forgotten. Any room full of seven-year-olds contains a tremendous quantity of kinetic energy. We were no exception.

At our table, Lisa and the other girl managed to remain astonishingly quiet, but the rest of us began a lively discussion about modern art. Specifically, Rocco's amazing ability to draw trucks.

In my eyes, although Rocco Rufo's creative talent was beyond dispute, the single most impressive thing about him was his unparalleled generosity. I'd personally seen him on at least two prior occasions give away, *for free*, cupcakes that his mother had packed for his lunch.

At that point in my life, those were the greatest humanitarian gestures I had ever witnessed.

Billy said something like, "Shoot, I can't even draw a stupid car," to which Rocco replied, "You want me to draw you a car? 'Cause I can draw cars, too."

Billy could say nothing but "Cool!"

Talking while Ms. Jennings was out of the room was one thing, but the unauthorized drawing of a car seemed like a pretty chancy undertaking to me. Rocco, however, was unfazed. He reached into the middle of the table and took the top sheet from the pile of laughably low-quality paper that our school seemed to love. But then he really went for broke. He grabbed a red marker from the forbidden cup.

On each of the five tables, next to the stack of cheap paper, Ms. Jennings had stationed a large plastic cup which contained supplies that only she was allowed to use. Scissors—the real kind—a glue stick, a ruler, a stapler, and several awesome-looking, but absolutely taboo, permanent markers.

In retrospect, putting prohibited items like that within easy reach of our eager, stubby little fingers and then walking out of the room was like dropping a freshly grilled hamburger in front of a puppy and telling him not to eat it.

My sister-in-law, Amy, has very high standards for public educators, and whenever she hears this part of the story, she suggests that Ms. Jennings was an incompetent ass.

In any event, Rocco's work was, as always, impeccable. The sports car he rendered for Billy was magnificent, complete with three dramatic rear fins, flames shooting from the oversized exhaust pipe curiously positioned in the center of the trunk, and, if I remember correctly, machine-gun turrets mounted above the headlights. He passed the drawing to Billy and returned the marker to the cup just before I saw the classroom doorknob turning.

The noise level was perilously high when the door swung open. To make matters undoubtedly worse, at the very moment that Ms. Jennings walked into the room, a futuristic-looking paper airplane glided gracefully past her left ear. Regrettably, that considerable aerodynamic accomplishment was lost on our teacher, as was readily apparent from the Armageddon-is-nigh look that had taken up residence on her face.

"Everyone back to your desks *immediately*!" she screeched, and suddenly the only sounds in the room were those of twenty-five chairs scraping across the floor, and fifty small feet scampering to what their owners hoped to be the safe haven of their desks.

"I leave you alone for the shortest amount of time imaginable, and I cannot believe..."

She abruptly halted what was ramping up to be a first-rate tirade, and the entire classroom was abruptly plunged into a very tense, vacuum-like silence. I knew it was dangerous, but I lifted my gaze from the broken screw on the left side of my desk to find out what had happened. Ms. Jennings was standing next to our now-deserted little round table, and looking down. Then, in a terrifyingly ominous tone, she asked quietly, "Who used the red marker?"

At first, I thought that Ms. Jennings must have been employing some sensory organ found only in teachers. There was no way she could know that Rocco had used the red marker. There simply was no evidence. Rocco had given the picture to Billy, and then put the marker back.

But then I noticed that our tabletop was badly stained with red ink. It must have bled through the crappy paper.

By now, several seconds had passed, and no one had responded to our teacher. Her head snapped up and she faced us again as if trembling on the verge of committing mass homicide.

"I said who used the red marker?" This time Ms. Jennings screamed the question so forcefully that her face was almost purple. "If the person responsible for this does not come forward immediately, this entire class will stay after school, and a serious notation will be made on everyone's permanent record."

In my tearful conversation with my parents later that evening as they put me to bed, I explained that they had told me always to think of the right thing to do, and then do it.

Confessing to the misdeed was the best I could come up with on the spur of that moment.

As far as I could see, the entire situation was poised to explode into any number of injustices. Why everyone in my class—including the twenty people not even sitting at the scene of the crime—should have been made to stay after school and to suffer a blot on their permanent record, was simply inconceivable to me.

The two girls at our table were completely innocent. And certainly Billy bore no blame. He hadn't suggested Rocco use the proscribed marker.

And that harm could come to Rocco for the latest in

an incredible string of selfless acts—first cupcakes, and then an original drawing of a fabulous car—seemed utterly intolerable.

That night, after I explained the many details of the profound dilemma I had faced, my father and mother went out of the room to talk. Then my dad came in and told me I should just try to go to sleep. It was going to take them some time to figure out the appropriate consequence.

At my high-school graduation ten years later, my dad told me they were still working on it.

On that second afternoon of the Gomez trial, I sat down at an empty cafeteria table with Trooper Landry. Beta—the man in the bathroom—had specifically warned me about him, and urged me to lie—at least by omission—in any dealings with the purportedly renegade cop. Whether I could pull that off convincingly was an extremely open question. But I wasn't buying Beta's story—at least not yet.

Landry had already eaten, and insisted that I have my lunch while he filled me in.

It turns out that the State Police Captain in charge of overseeing security at special public events had been keeping tabs on the Gomez trial from the start, and the captain had seen my ignominious effort on the courthouse steps as I left the courtroom at the end of day one. He thought I might appreciate knowing that he'd assigned Trooper Landry to the courthouse for the duration of the trial, to ensure that neither A.D.A. Varick nor I was overwhelmed by the media, or by other spectators, whether at the trial or otherwise.

"Funny you should say that," I said, taking a bite of my second sandwich. And just then, my cell phone rang. The only people who have my number are my family and Cliff, so I swallowed hastily, and then answered.

A voice spoke that I instantly recognized as the man who all too recently had held a weapon to my head. "Didn't you hear what I told you? Landry is *not* your friend. If you tell him anything about what happened with me, you won't make it home to your father alive. Nod your head and say, 'Of course.'"

I hesitated. I am not particularly good at following arbitrary directions, especially those given to me by people who have recently threatened my life. Landry was sitting across from me, smiling. If there was a doomsday plot and he was a part of it, Satan had done a great job casting him in this role. The man was the most unassuming state trooper I had ever seen in my life. It's not that Landry didn't look like a cop—it's just that he looked like he'd be everyone's first choice to visit the neighborhood kindergartens to teach the kids how to cross at the corner.

The voice on the phone continued. "Landry's phone is going to ring in ten seconds. Just stall. Stay on the line with me so I can keep trying to save your stupid ass."

I was totally confused. I believe all I managed to say was "Excuse me?"

The voice merely said, "Four, three, two, one," and one second later, exactly as promised, Landry's phone chirped. He checked the caller ID, excused himself, and then walked to another empty table, and took the call.

"How did you know his phone would ring?" I asked. "And how did you get this number?"

"Never mind that," my bathroom buddy replied. "If you don't start paying attention, you're gonna get whacked."

"You keep telling me that, but you're the only one who's ever held me at gunpoint. Why should I believe anything you say?" I was speaking quietly, looking around to be sure I wasn't overheard by the four women at the next table.

"Fine," the man said, obviously disgusted. "Don't believe me. You will soon enough. Just don't say anything to Landry. He's going to give you his phone number, and a special device—he'll call it a panic button. He'll tell you to keep it with you at all times, so you can call for help if you need it.

"But it's much more than that," Beta continued. "It's going to have a GPS chip in it, and a bug. If you carry that thing around with you, they'll know exactly where you are, and exactly what you're saying, twenty-four seven."

"How do you know—"

"He'll be hanging up in a second. Don't tell him anything. If you talk to him, your death is on you. Saving your butt was a long shot anyway. But I am not wrong. Do not trust him. Your life depends on it."

And then he hung up.

A second later Landry finished his call, and came back to the table. "So, you were saying?" he said, taking his seat again.

I knew I was being monitored—how else could my bathroom assailant know that I was on the verge of telling Landry what had happened? What I didn't know was whether spilling my guts to the cop was going to end up killing me, or whether I was just being played.

I decided to wait. If Landry ended the conversation without giving me the panic button, then I'd know the voice on the phone had lied. But if the cop gave me the device, then I'd hold off. I'd decide what to do later, after I'd had a chance to check it out.

"Yeah," I said. I had finished eating. "I was saying funny that you were assigned to keep us from being hassled by the press. I was wondering if you could get me out of the courthouse today without having to run that gauntlet on the front steps."

Technically, it was not a lie—I really was hoping to get to my truck without having to survive another grilling from the press. But it wasn't what I'd originally intended to say to the smiling officer.

"No problem. Follow me." We stood up, and headed together to the elevator and went down to the basement level.

We walked through a secure checkpoint manned by another state trooper and a court officer, and entered the private parking garage used by the judges and other court personnel. Then Landry gave me a quick ride in his cruiser to my truck, past the crowds of reporters still milling around the courthouse. By the time we reached my parking spot, Landry hadn't given me anything except an increased feeling that the man in the bathroom was a dangerous person that I needed protection from.

The last thing I needed was to be constantly looking over my shoulder as I fought my way through what was going to be an impossible trial. "I just wanted to let you know that I've had some pretty strange things happen to me these past couple of days," I began.

If Trooper Landry had realized that I was gearing up to unload on him the entire story of my curious incident in the lavatory, he never would have interrupted me. But he must have thought I was just making idle conversation about the courtroom events of the past twenty-four hours. So he jumped in, and changed my life forever.

"I hear you," Landry said with a toothy smile, as he reached into his pants pocket and withdrew a small device that looked a lot like a miniature garage door opener. "That's exactly why I want you to keep this with you at all times. It's called a panic button."

TEN

I MANAGED TO make it home that afternoon without getting whacked.

I still didn't know whether Landry was as trustworthy as he seemed to be, or whether paramilitary toilet boy was telling the truth, but I had decided to play it safe. I took the panic button from Landry, and said nothing about the assault.

As I climbed the ramp to the front entrance of our house, Liana Kaas, the woman who stays with my father when I have to go into the city for work, opened the door. She was a divorced woman in her forties with two kids, both living on their own, one in Mesa, and one out in California. Liana seemed to have boundless positive energy, and even managed to get Henley to do his therapy with the elastic exercise tubing he hated so much.

"He's napping," she reported, as I dropped my briefcase in the entryway. "Everything's fine, though the phone's been ringing like crazy since lunchtime. There must be thirty messages on the machine. And some file boxes from an attorney named Timilow or Temilow came for you. All of a sudden, you're a very popular person." She followed me into the kitchen, where I opened the fridge and got myself a beer as she gathered up her things. "Oh, and the cable guy was here. You're getting a free upgrade for the next sixty days. Some movie channel wants you to sign up, I guess. Henley was thrilled." She called out over her shoulder as she took off. "See you tomorrow morning."

I had been introduced to Liana about six months earlier by a friend of mine from the Payson Center Health Club named Joe Hextall. Joe had met Liana in the early days of his recovery from a stroke, and had only great things to say about her.

It was hard to believe that I'd actually shot some baskets with Joe only two days before. The wiry African American's recovery was coming along great, but his left side was still much weaker than his right. He was only thirty-five, though, and his prognosis was excellent.

"Why don't you overplay me?" he had asked, limping to the right as he always did. "You know I can't go left. Your sorry game needs all the help it can get."

"How about I take care of the defense, LeBron?" I replied. Joe looked a little like LeBron James. And the only thing bigger than his mouth was his heart. "The minute I overplay you right is the minute you suddenly discover you're all better, go past me on the left, and I'm standing there with my pants around my ankles."

"And how is that different from any other day?" he said, clanging an ugly heave off the front rim.

I remember standing there, watching Liana leave. I was thinking about an overloaded answering machine. I was thinking about defending a mass murderer. And I was wondering when I would next be able to enjoy the simple pleasures of playing basketball and pretending to be insulted by my friend Joe.

I spent the afternoon listening to phone messages from increasingly desperate journalists, looking at damning videotape of my client meeting with the Denver suicide bomber, and reading police reports and witness statements, vainly hoping to prepare myself for the next day. When I got thoroughly disheartened, I went outside and split some logs for Henley's woodstove.

After I showered and caught a quick nap, I drove over to Cliff and Iris's house and hung out with their dog, Wilbur, until they got home from work. We lived only twenty minutes away from each other, and I didn't want to use the phone. Until I figured out who I could trust, I had decided not to trust anyone. Cliff and Iris were surprised to see me parked in their driveway, but quickly understood what I needed, and agreed to come over later for dinner.

I had met the couple through Henley. He had prosecuted a case seven years ago against a pair of racist brothers who had taken exception to the fact that Cliff and Iris, who had been married only a few weeks earlier, had moved into their neighborhood. The essence of the problem was not only that Cliff was a full-blooded Navajo, but also that Iris's mother was Mexican, and her father was Jewish.

Henley took particular pleasure in going after people who were cruel, and what these idiots had done to Cliff and Iris certainly fit the bill. For weeks, the two newlyweds had endured battered mailboxes, pig's blood splattered on their front door, and even a burning cross on their lawn.

They knew the jerks who lived across the street were

doing the damage—a pair of brothers whose oversized pickup truck was liberally festooned with Confederate flag stickers and obnoxious slogans. The only two things more cluttered and filthy than the inside of that truck were the brothers' souls.

But Cliff and Iris couldn't prove anything. Until finally, the bastards went too far.

For their three-month anniversary, Cliff bought Iris a playful and friendly puppy named Wilbur that looked like a mix between a black Lab and a German shepherd. Less than a week after they'd gotten the dog, Iris returned home to find a small window in the kitchen door broken, the door unlocked, and the puppy missing. For hours that night, she and Cliff drove around the neighborhood, searching for the lost pet.

They gave up hope a little after dark and returned home, only to find little Wilbur cowering on their front stoop, tied by some rope to the handle of the front door.

The poor animal had obviously been abused—his ear was damaged, and he was limping.

But most shocking was the swastika that had been crudely shaved into the fur on his back.

Cliff was incensed, and wanted to storm across the street and call the cowards out, but Iris, who had been using their Polaroid camera to take pictures of the damage to the door and the injuries to Wilbur, stopped him. Because every time she aimed the camera at Wilbur, the dog flinched and tried to run away.

He was terrified of the camera. The creeps that had taken him and hurt him had obviously taken pictures of him, as well.

The couple waited until nearly dawn, when their evil neighbors were undoubtedly asleep or passed out from alcohol, and then they walked across the street to where the truck was parked. They shone a flashlight through the passenger-side window, and sure enough, right there on the car floor were pictures of one of the brothers holding Wilbur while the other shaved his back.

Cliff and Iris called the cops. Thanks to a restraining order and some quick work on Henley's part, the brothers found themselves in jail. Henley had really taken a liking to the young couple, and had introduced them to me, and we'd been friends ever since. We often got together for dinner and a game of hearts afterwards. My father "held" his cards in a stand that I had scavenged from an old board game, and played them with his good hand. Cliff was a terrific poker player—ruthlessly bluffing his way to win after win. But at hearts, Henley was just as good.

On this second night of the Gomez trial, however, Henley went to bed right after dinner. When I returned from saying good night, I found that Iris and Cliff had already gone into my bedroom to begin the counter-surveillance portion of the evening.

Iris was a small woman with light skin and dark features. Her energy and intensity belied the underlying sweetness to which Cliff was drawn immediately when they met in college. Although Iris really wanted to be a nationally famous political reporter, the one time her blog was mentioned on the Channel 7 local news was as close as she got. To earn a living, she worked in Mesa as a computer technician, saving the lives of countless college students whose hard drives crashed, or whose PCs were overloaded with software spies and viruses picked up from surfing the Web.

Although they shared the most tender of hearts, the images Cliff and Iris presented to the outside world were in sharp contrast. While Iris favored cargo pants and boots, Cliff dressed like he was the spokesman for

Navajo Gentlemen's Quarterly. He was a healthy, handsome real estate lawyer, and he wore the uniform of the young professional with aplomb. Yet his business persona was not a false one—he fully incorporated his laid-back, peaceful aura into his stylish image. It was a very successful combination.

That night, Iris had brought a bag of electronic gizmos along, and was now fishing through it. Assuming the worst, Cliff and I stood there with a pad and pen, trying to have a "normal," non-suspicious-sounding conversation, while communicating our real thoughts in writing.

As Iris laid out some power cords on the bed, Cliff said to me, "Nice work getting the Lizard Queen off the Gomez case. You rock."

"Yeah," I stammered. "I guess I was wondering if you could, uh, you know, help me with more motions. You know. For the trial."

Cliff rolled his eyes and wrote, *Dude. Not good banter much.*

It was ironic. I was normally comfortable speaking in front of a courtroom full of strangers, yet the presence of a tiny microphone in my own home made me feel intensely self-conscious. Cliff, on the other hand, was fine, despite the fact that he was so bad with crowds that he almost passed out when he and Iris said thank you to the fifty guests they had invited to their fifth-wedding-anniversary party.

By now, Iris had taken a palm-sized device out of her bag. It looked like a television remote control with a display, and she pointed it at the panic button that Landry had given to me earlier. Cliff said, "Work isn't too bad these days. I might be able to do some research." A series of red lights all came on at once on

Iris's device. She took the pad, and gesturing toward the panic button, she wrote, *This is definitely a bug*.

"Great," I said out loud, as the three of us moved back into the living room. On his way to bed, my father had put a Delphonics CD on the stereo. "La-la Means I Love You" was playing. If you didn't like seventies and eighties soul, you were going to have a hard time hanging with Henley.

"Want some more dessert?" I offered. But I sure wasn't feeling hungry. The bathroom attacker hadn't lied. The trooper *had* given me a bug. What the hell was going on?

"No thanks," Cliff said. "I'm pretty full. How about you, Iris?"

But before Iris had a chance to answer, I found myself pointing at the device that she still held in her hand as she walked through the doorway into the living room.

"Whoa," I said, involuntarily.

Cliff looked over at me, and said, "What?"

I pointed to the flashing red lights, which apparently indicated either that the machine was faulty, or that I had a bug in my living room. "I thought I saw something. Outside," I added hastily, in hopes that I didn't sound as ridiculously stilted as I felt.

By now, Iris was directing the device around the room, trying to isolate where the signal was coming from. She pointed it at the television, and then, as she got closer, at the cable box. She looked down at the device, and then up at me. "I'd like a little more coffee," she said, nodding vigorously. It looked like our cable company's trial upgrade had also come with a free listening device.

Suddenly the bathroom assailant was looking a little less like a crackpot. For several reasons, that did not comfort me.

Cliff, Iris, and I sat down and shared some small talk while scribbling notes back and forth on the pad. According to Iris, there was no way I'd be able to disable either listening device without alerting the people who'd placed them to the fact that I knew about them.

I also needed to assume that my phone lines were tapped. Iris swept the device over the phones in the kitchen, living room, and my bedroom and found nothing, but there was no telling whether they were being monitored from a remote location through the phone lines themselves.

As of that moment, I was certain that some potentially dangerous entity was eavesdropping on everything that was being said in my house.

The first thing I had to do was decide what I was going to do about the panic button. I didn't have any reason to believe that Landry would suspect I knew it was a bug, so theoretically, I could leave it home, and if he ever checked up on me, I could tell him I forgot it.

But I wasn't real confident in my ability to deceive the cop. I still didn't believe everything Beta the mugger had told me, but I now knew that Landry was the kind of law enforcement officer who didn't really care whether he broke the law himself. I feared that type of person might be better able to sniff out a lie than I would be able to tell one. Especially since the stakes were considerably more serious than my elementary school permanent record.

Before I went to bed I dug around in my closet for my old cell phone and plugged it into its charger. I had gotten a new one some time ago, because the old one couldn't maintain power for more than ten or twenty minutes of use. But I had held on to it, intending to give it to Henley for emergencies. Back then I was under the impression that Henley's recovery would be more robust than it turned out to be.

The next morning, I put the panic button in my briefcase. I thought it was a particularly astute compromise. If Landry approached me, I could show him I had it. But on the off chance that I needed to say something that I didn't want overheard, I could walk away from the bag before saying it. Iris had told me the range of the bug was no more than ten feet.

Next, I needed to get word to Amy before she and Erica came over to the house again. So on my way to work, I stopped at the convenience store along the way for some coffee, and before I got back into the car and within range of Landry's listening device, I called my sister-in-law on my old cell phone. If the state troopers and the cable guy were bugging me, I had no doubt that my current cell phone and my e-mail accounts were being watched, as well.

Amy was obviously running a little late, and every other thing she said was directed at Erica as they prepared to leave for school. But when I told her all that had happened the day before, and what Iris had found that night, Amy stopped talking to Erica, and in a quiet, tense voice, asked, "Are you telling me this is the end of the world?"

ELEVEN

AMY'S QUESTION was not as paranoid as it might have first appeared. She was merely referring to a code we had set up after we had seen a city disappear before our eyes.

The Hurricane Katrina crisis occurred when Erica was three years old. About a week after the floods wiped out New Orleans and ended or destroyed the lives of hundreds of thousands of its inhabitants, Amy and I set up our own private emergency procedure. We agreed that if either of us ever became aware of a situation that required immediate escape to safety, we would get a message to the other that the world was coming to an end. We would then both take off for a pre-designated rendezvous, where we would make specific plans in order to fend for ourselves.

And if we lost contact in the middle of a crisis, we were to call Cliff or Iris and communicate through them. They were constantly calling or text-messaging each other anyway, and they'd make sure Amy and I stayed in touch.

Even as I write this, I realize that Amy's reaction to the Gulf Coast disaster sounds a little extreme. But as the mother of a small child, Amy believed it was the only responsible thing to do. After all, from her perspective, the towers that fell on September 11 were only the first of a series of lethal dominoes that, for several years, had been regularly and brutally crashing down on her little family.

We didn't actually lose loved ones in the attacks on that cursed September day. Our personal tragedies began some months later, when death came to Dale on a distant battlefield.

My brother was a member of the Arizona National Guard when he and Amy were married on February 13, 2001. Two days after the attacks in New York, Pennsylvania, and Washington, on his seven-month wedding anniversary, Dale was called to active service. In October, he was assigned to an army base in California, and in November, he was on his way to Afghanistan.

By then, Amy was six months pregnant. That made Dale's deployment even more anxiety-filled for all of us. Amy moved in with my parents until Dale's expected return, to save money for when the baby came, and to feel a little less lonely.

Eight weeks later, when Amy was a month from giving birth, a phone call delivered devastating news: Dale was missing in action after a series of explosions destroyed his unit's position. I can still see Amy standing there that Saturday in my parents' living room, belly swollen, shoulders shaking, tears streaming from her reddened eyes. The memory breaks my heart. My father kept telling her that she needed to stay hopeful and strong, because Dale might just be lost, or injured. But somehow Amy knew that her husband was gone.

And she was right.

I happened to be visiting on the miserable Sunday morning when the two men wearing dress military uniforms rang my parents' doorbell.

Dale had died as a hero in a place with a name more suited for a children's bedtime story than for the demise of a young father-to-be: Tora Bora.

The only direct experience I have ever had with the military was on September 12, 2001, when I was told by a very rigid recruitment officer that my hearing loss made me ineligible for armed service. So I wasn't prepared, in the least, for all of the ceremony attached to my fallen brother and his funeral. Amy suddenly became the centerpiece of a series of rituals played out over the following days: the official visit from the two servicemen who notified Amy of Dale's death, the return of the flag-draped coffin containing those few fragments of Dale's body that were recovered—for some reason, I cannot stand to use the words "his remains"—the memorial service and then the funeral itself, with full military honors: twenty-one-gun salute, taps, presentation of the flag, the whole tragic business.

I found myself resenting the pomp. It seemed designed to distract me from the real issue—the loss of my big brother. The kid who cheerfully slept on the floor next to my bed when I was five because I was scared that there was a monster that was crawling around on its belly in my room. The golden boy with the flashy smile who taught me how to skateboard, and how to throw a curveball, and what to say to a pretty girl. The guy who never missed one of my high-school baseball games, no matter how bad we were. The only person I ever told about my crush on an up-and-coming country singer named Shania Twain.

My captain, my personal hero, the brother I blindly

followed with the certainty only a younger sibling can understand, had just disappeared from the planet.

I didn't want to remember Dale with pageantry. I didn't want to have to remember him at all.

And then a month later, like a final chord to Dale's personal symphony, I received his last correspondence. It began, "Greetings Captain Rootbeard. If you are reading this, then I must be dead." The salutation refers to a Halloween persona I chose at the age of five, thanks to some misinformation I had been given regarding a famous pirate whose name I mistakenly understood to be Blue Beer. I carry the letter with me to this day.

But almost as if it were mocking us, life went on as if Dale's death didn't matter. Dad kept prosecuting cases, I kept appealing them, and Mom kept going to Lamaze classes with Amy.

Much sooner than seemed possible, Erica was born. Predictably, Amy suffered terrible postpartum depression. There were days when she could barely get out of bed. My parents and I did what we could to help—we all took turns caring for Erica as Amy got back on her feet.

But of course Amy wasn't the only one suffering. I had never seen a person deteriorate faster than my mother did after she buried Dale. Try as she might, she never got over the death of her oldest. Her smile just never recovered its spark, even at the birth of her granddaughter. It was as if the only thing she could see when she looked at Erica was Dale's empty chair at the dining room table.

And before Erica had even reached her first birthday, my mother developed pneumonia. From what I could see, she never even fought the illness. No doctors would connect my mother's demise to Dale's, but I didn't need them to. Anyone who knew the woman knew that grief killed her.

Even though seven months separated the deaths of my mother and my brother, my mom's passing felt like it happened the day after we buried Dale. I remember feeling somewhat numb at her funeral—as if my soul hadn't recovered sufficiently to truly feel the void that had been left.

And then, the following year, my father suffered his stroke.

Amy was an only child whose parents had died in a car accident four years earlier—shortly after she'd begun teaching. The rapid succession of family catastrophes underscored a message that had already been seared into Amy's tender soul: The lives of your loved ones are treasures that can disappear in an instant.

So when Amy decided to put her own emergency plan into place in the aftermath of Katrina, I could hardly blame her.

I do blame myself, though. Because I was the one who failed to recognize the true potency of the venom that had just been injected into our lives. I was the one who failed to trigger the plan, until it was too late.

In retrospect, it's hard to believe I was so naive. After all, there I was, standing in a convenience store parking lot, so suspicious of my own government that I was afraid to speak to my sister-in-law on my own cell phone. Less than twenty-four hours earlier, I had been accosted in a men's room at gunpoint, and informed— also at gunpoint, thank you very much—that a group of very powerful people in my state and federal governments was illegally monitoring everything I did and said. And in case there was any doubt about that, less than twelve hours earlier, I had confirmed that at least one state policeman had planted a bug on me.

Yet how did I answer Amy when she asked if the world was coming to an end? With the ignorance of someone who really couldn't believe that the institutions in which he placed complete faith were actually no more trustworthy than the people who had been elected or appointed to run them. "No, I'm sure it's nothing like that. I've just got to see what's going on, try to figure out what to do next. Just to be safe, though, I think it's probably best if you and Erica stay away from the house for a few days—at least until the weekend. I bet things will be much clearer by then."

Although I had no idea what I was talking about, that last bit turned out to be pretty prophetic.

TWELVE

EVEN THOUGH Hugo Bridges had thrown Judge Klay off the case, much of the rest of his decision did not help the defendant's situation at all.

The Chief Justice specifically stated that any rulings made in the trial to that point were to remain in effect. That meant there would be no chance for a different jury, and I would not be allowed any extra time to prepare. So when I arrived at court and learned that Judge Lester Lomax had been assigned to the case, I headed for the courtroom, expecting that testimony would begin first thing that very morning.

But I had underestimated Judge Lomax. He had something he wanted to do first.

"All rise!" bellowed Sarge, as the judge entered the courtroom. Then there was the sound of several hundred people falling silent while rising to their feet. A thin, clean-shaven, silver-haired man wearing a long black robe took his seat at the front of the room. "Court is now in session," Sarge intoned. "Be seated."

I had read through the biographies of the possible

replacements for Judge Klay the night before. According to the Superior Court's official Web site, Lester Lomax was a graduate of UCLA Law School, and had served as a prosecutor for a few years in California before coming to Phoenix to join Bench, Barkley & Coogan, one of the largest and most prestigious firms in the city. At the age of forty-five he was appointed to the Juvenile Court Bench, and had moved to the Superior Court at fifty-two. He was now sixty-three years old.

But nothing I had read prepared me for what was to be the judge's first official act in the case. Before even acknowledging the defendant, either attorney, the television camera, or the several hundred people who were in the room with him, the judge turned to face the jury. He broke the expectant silence by clearing his throat, and then he began to speak.

"Good morning, ladies and gentlemen. My name is Lester Lomax. I am a Judge of the Superior Court, and I have been appointed to preside over this case from this point forward."

His voice was firm, but rich, and cordial. He wasn't trying to intimidate anyone, but he wasn't trying to ingratiate himself, either. He sounded like a man at ease with his position in life.

"Thanks to the kind cooperation of Judge Klay and the extraordinary efforts of our court reporter, I have been informed of the progress of this case to this point, and I can assure you that in a moment, you will be hearing the testimony of the state's first witness.

"Before we begin, however, there is a tradition that I honor at the beginning of each of my trials. Before the first witness is sworn, I ask the jury to join me in a moment of preparation for what is to come. Our civilization rests on the strong and able conscience of the people of this great nation, and on the respect that we accord the institution of this court. As a fellow citizen, I salute your contribution to our society, and as the presiding judge of this case, I welcome you to this noble and most important undertaking and responsibility."

In hindsight, the judge's message reads a little stiff, a little formal. You could even call it corny. But that isn't how it sounded when Judge Lomax said it. In that moment, we were all completely captivated.

He sat forward, placed his hands on the desk in front of him, and then said, "Ladies and gentlemen of the jury, please rise, and stand for a moment with me in silent contemplation of the task that we are about to undertake on behalf of our country."

And then he stood. The fourteen women and men in the jury box stood as well. And for the next several seconds, the judge made eye contact, in turn, with each of the jurors in the top row. The only three female jurors over fifty years old—who coincidentally occupied seats one, two, and three—the Arizona State University graduate student with the light-colored and sparse beard in seat four, the Asian American chef in seat five, the hotel maintenance worker with the nervous cough in seat six, and the surly, overweight construction project supervisor in seat seven.

Then the judge worked his way across the bottom row. Juror number eight was a pretty young woman who worked for the post office. Jurors nine and ten were the oldest members of the panel—a sixty-four-year-old retired electrical engineer, and a sixty-year-old taxi driver. Juror eleven was a math teacher at a public middle school; juror twelve was the youngest member of the group—a twenty-year-old part-time student at Phoenix Community College. Juror thirteen was a retired parole officer, and the last juror was a teller at the downtown branch of the First Bank of Arizona.

Judge Lomax spent no more than a second or two looking into the eyes of each of the fourteen, but in that half minute, the courtroom transformed itself from the previous day's cauldron of tabloid moments into something much more solemn and appropriate—a chamber dedicated to rendering justice in the aftermath of the monstrous violence that had killed or maimed hundreds.

"Thank you," the judge said simply, sitting and turning his attention to the prosecutor. "Mr. Varick, please call your first witness."

And we were off.

Preston Varick had many ways he could go with his case. There were hundreds of survivors of the disaster who were potentially able to testify. And the emergency response to the explosions and injuries and the subsequent investigation had been so vast that dozens of police, federal agents, firefighters, EMTs, doctors, and terrorism experts were also available to him.

It came down to how he wanted to tell the story. Varick stood up, and in a voice that always seemed a little higher pitched than I expected said, "I call Denver Police Officer Liam Kenney."

I have to admit that I was a little surprised—I had expected the assistant district attorney to begin with a parade of maimed burn victims to the stand. But Officer Kenney was a perfectly valid choice. He happened to be traveling on the interstate when the explosion occurred, and he was the first officer to respond.

And when Kenney came through the doors at the back of the courtroom and walked down the aisle toward us, I understood exactly why Varick had chosen him as his first witness.

It wasn't just that the witness was a cop—the job and the uniform lent every police officer's testimony a great deal of credibility. It was the man's face. Unlike so many police officers who seemed maniacally intent on portraying themselves as chest-beating drill sergeant types just dying to scream something into your face, Kenney seemed quite human. He was probably only in his mid to late thirties, average height and weight, and you could see the beginnings of what were to become jowls forming at his jawline. His eyes were peaceful, and somehow, sad. He carried himself confidently, yet without the swagger that so many in authority seem to adopt.

In short, he looked completely and unquestionably believable, and utterly sincere.

And as anyone who had ever seen a television or read a newspaper over the past thirteen months knew, he was also a bona fide hero.

He took his place on the witness stand, the clerk swore him in, and after the preliminaries were out of the way, Preston Varick began the real questioning.

"Were you on duty on the morning of May sixteenth, last year?"

"Yes, I was. I was on routine highway patrol on Interstate 25 when I heard the explosion."

Varick paused and glanced down at what must have been Kenney's report. "You heard the explosion?"

Kenney nodded. "I was still about a half mile away from the tunnel entrance. At the time, I didn't know what it was. It was just this hollow-sounding *boom*. Traffic was already slowing down, but I wasn't able to see anything unusual. So I called in to HQ to report the delay, and to check to see if the tunnel had reported trouble."

"I'm sorry? You expected trouble?"

The trooper smiled apologetically, and shook his head. "No. Nothing like what happened. What I meant was that when I saw the traffic backing up, I figured there must have been some kind of tie-up ahead. Usually, if there is an accident or any kind of breakdown in the tunnel, the guys in the tube put in a call so we can set up for the response."

"Could you explain that, Officer? 'Set up for the response'?"

"Yes, sir. Depending on what the situation is, we can provide immediate medical assistance until EMTs respond, or traffic control, or whatever might be needed."

The witness was both humble and professional. By this time, it was impossible to believe that anyone watching harbored the least suspicion about the truth of what Trooper Kenney was saying.

"And what happened as you were making this call to headquarters?"

Kenney took a deep breath. "By this time, I had come around a bend in the road, and the entrance of the tunnel was visible to me. I could see smoke coming out of the tube, and then I saw flames, and then..."

Kenney's voice cracked. He swallowed, blinked a few times, then said, "Sorry. I, uh, I saw smoke and flames." He sniffed. A tear ran down his cheek, which he wiped away quickly. "And then I saw a car explode at the entrance to the tunnel. And more flames and smoke. And then I saw a, um, coming out of the smoke..."

Kenney stopped again to compose himself. It's not often that you see a police officer break down on the witness stand. I don't mean to be cynical in the least when I say that by now, it was clear that Preston Varick had made an exceedingly good choice of opening witness.

The cop picked up his story. "A young woman was

running against traffic along the right shoulder." He swallowed. "But a line of flames was racing along the roadway from the tunnel, parallel to her. And just as she passed one of the vehicles that was standing still in the right lane, it caught fire, and exploded."

One of the jurors gasped. Number eight, the postal worker, was sitting back in her chair, covering her mouth with her hand. The expressions on the rest of their faces ranged from anguished to horrified.

"The woman who was running just, I don't know. She just disappeared right in front of my eyes. It was like she just vaporized."

Next to me, I heard Juan Gomez shift in his seat. I looked over at him. My client was crying.

"At that point, what did you do?" Preston asked.

The witness went on. By now, a curious emotional compromise seemed to have worked itself out within him. Tears continued to run down his cheeks, but his voice came under control. "I told the dispatcher that we had a major incident in the tunnel, with explosions and multiple serious injuries. Then I pulled off onto the right shoulder, turned on my emergency lights, and drove toward the entrance to the tunnel."

"You drove *toward* the tunnel?"

"Yes, sir."

He said it like it was the most natural thing in the world to plunge headlong into an ever-growing, life-threatening inferno. For me, it felt like I was in the presence of the spirit of the hundreds of police and fire-fighters who had run into the World Trade Center on September 11.

"And as you approached the tunnel, what else did you see?"

Kenney took a sip of water that had been offered to him by the clerk. "By that time, so much thick, black smoke was pouring out of the tunnel that it was impossible to see the entrance. I saw several other cars explode. It looked like the interstate itself was on fire, at least back from the tunnel to about the quarter-mile marker. I stopped my cruiser there, got out of my vehicle, and started banging on cars, telling people to evacuate their vehicles and run to safety."

Although Kenney stopped speaking at that moment, it didn't really look like he had completed his thought. His mouth remained open slightly, and his attention seemed to be focused on something beyond Preston Varick, possibly something at the back of the courtroom.

Varick filled the silence with another question. "And again, where were you by this time?"

Instead of answering immediately, Kenney continued to just sit there, staring off into the distance. Then he said, softly, "That's when I saw a little girl get out of a burning car three vehicles ahead, and start running toward me.

"She was on fire."

THIRTEEN

NO MATTER HOW many rules we try to impose on ourselves as we tinker with the machinery of criminal trials, we always run into the fact that we are human beings, not robots. Sometimes, rules don't anticipate what large groups of real people need to do when they are processing experiences like the one Officer Kenney was describing to us on that first day of testimony.

Technically, Assistant District Attorney Varick should have been guiding his witness through the series of events of that morning in small increments of time, instead of letting the testimony go on and on about the story of his actions that morning in Denver. Technically, when Kenney said things like, "I heard somebody say," or "I found out later," he should have been instructed to confine himself to telling us only those things that he did and that he saw, not what other people had said or concluded. But there was no way that Judge Lomax or Preston Varick was going to interrupt this witness from telling us what we all needed to hear.

And there was no way I was going to object, either.

"The little girl was on fire. She was screaming, and running with her arms extended, like if I could only pick her up, or something, I could help her. So I ran toward her, took her in my arms, and raced off the road toward the grassy area beyond the right shoulder."

To be honest, I cannot say with complete assurance that my choice to remain silent during Trooper Kenney's testimony was based entirely on a determination that it was the best thing for my client. In retrospect, I believe that it was. We all had seen and read the news reports of what had happened that day. Whether Varick used one witness or one hundred to tell the stories of courage and tragedy wouldn't have made a difference. If I had tried to get in the way by forcing the prosecutor to follow strict evidentiary protocol, it could have reflected badly on Mr. Gomez. It might have seemed like I was trying to prevent the truth from coming out.

"As soon as I reached the edge of the shoulder I dove into the field there, spinning so that my back would hit the ground first. That way, I didn't crush Sheniqua—it turned out she was an eight-year-old named Sheniqua—by falling on top of her."

Because of the arrangement of the courtroom, it was impossible for me to see anyone in the spectators' gallery without turning around in my seat. But even though I didn't see them, I could feel the steady gaze of the survivors of the attack who had made the trip to be at this trial, especially those who bore the scars of the burns that they had suffered. My clothes, my seat, in fact the entire defense table at which I sat with my client, grew slightly, but uncomfortably, warmer.

"I rolled over and over in the grass with Sheniqua in my arms. I was hoping to put out the fire. I don't know how long we were down there together. It seemed like a long time, but somebody told me later that it was only about fifteen or twenty seconds. Anyway, after we rolled around for a while, I stopped, and got up off of her. She was lying on her back in the grass, and her clothes were still smoking, but there were no more flames. She was coughing, and still crying a little. I didn't want to leave her, but I felt like I had to get back to the road to see if there was something else I could do.

"Anyway, I told her to wait there and that more help would be coming. Then I turned and started to run back toward the other cars, but I heard her call out after me, 'Mister!'"

I stole a quick look at the jury, and as I suspected, they were transfixed. Most of us had read of Liam Kenney's actions on that day, and we knew what was coming, but we were all engrossed.

"I stopped running and turned around. Sheniqua had gotten up, and was chasing after me. She was saying something about saving her little brother. Turns out her brother, Edwin, was in the car, too."

"The car that was already on fire when Sheniqua got out of it?" Preston's question was more to fill up the emptiness than anything else. We all knew that Officer Kenney wasn't finished telling us what had happened.

"Yeah. I told Sheniqua that I would try to get her brother, but only if she returned to the grass by the side of the road to wait for help—"

Varick interrupted. "By the way, Officer, what else was happening around you at this time?"

Kenney shook his head. "It was chaos," he answered. "The fuel that had spilled on the road had ignited, and cars all along that stretch were on fire, or exploding. People were abandoning their cars and running away from the tunnel, or off the sides of the road.

People were screaming and crying, and the smell . . . the smell was awful. Burning gasoline, burning cars . . ."

"Were you able to get back to Sheniqua's car?"

"I was," the cop answered. "But by now, it was fully ablaze. I didn't think it was possible that there was anyone alive inside. Flames were coming out of the open back right door that Sheniqua had used to escape, so I went around to the other side, figuring that's where her little brother might be.

"There was so much smoke inside the car, I couldn't tell anything from looking in the window. I tried to open the door, but it was locked. So I drew my service revolver, and smashed it against the window."

The hero cop made a noise like a laugh, but there was no humor in it. "Turns out that was a bad mistake, because when I broke the window, I created a draft, and all that did was give the fire more oxygen to work with. There was this roar, and the whole backseat area seemed to erupt into a bigger fire."

"Weren't you concerned that the fire would reach the gas tank and that the car would explode?"

By now, the tears had stopped falling from Liam Kenney's eyes. His gaze was clear, his voice strong. At that moment in my life, I had no idea of what he had gone through, so I couldn't imagine pushing through the emotions as he did to share his story with us. I remember thinking that if I had had to relive that experience in front of a room full of strangers, I would have started crying, and never stopped.

It's funny how experiences like Officer Kenney's change you, though.

"Yes, I knew, but as soon as I broke through that window, I also knew there was a young boy in that car. I had to get him out."

"And did you?"

"I had to pull my uniform sleeve over my fingers because it was so hot, but I managed to unlock the door and open it. Edwin was unconscious, but by some miracle, the fire hadn't yet reached his part of the backseat, so he wasn't burned. I knew I had to move fast, though, because the flames were coming toward him, and I didn't know when the car's gas tank would explode. So I decided to get him out of there by grabbing the entire car seat. But I couldn't get the damned thing unbuckled from the car." He cleared his throat. "Excuse the language."

Someone in the gallery let out a short, nervous laugh. As if the utterance of that mildest of oaths had the slightest impact.

"What happened next?"

"I tried to unbuckle him out of the car seat, but my eyes were stinging and watering so bad that I could hardly see anything. And I didn't have any kids at the time, so I was unfamiliar with the design of the locking mechanism. Long story short, I couldn't get him out of the car seat."

"What did you do?" Preston asked.

"I felt like I was just about out of time, so I took my penknife out, and I cut through the straps of the car seat, and pulled Edwin out. Like I said, he was unconscious, so I decided to give him mouth-to-mouth as I ran toward the field where I'd left Sheniqua. But just as I was about to blow the first lungful of air into him, the car exploded.

"The blast knocked me off my feet. But by that time, I was close enough to the edge of the shoulder that luckily I landed on the grass. I was able to hang on to Edwin, but this time, I couldn't control my fall, so I didn't land on my back. To protect him, I stuck my elbows out, and tried to use them as kind of shock absorbers. At first, though, when I got off of him, he was still completely out of it. I had no idea even if he was alive.

"I started CPR right there. By this time, Sheniqua had joined us, and was shouting things like, 'C'mon, Edwin! You got to breathe. C'mon!' I wasn't really paying attention, though. CPR is time-sensitive, and I had no idea whether Edwin had any chance of survival at all. All I knew was that I had to keep trying.

"And then, he coughed. And Sheniqua started screaming, and Edwin kept coughing. And then he started crying. Turns out the little guy was okay."

Because of my hearing issues, I can't be sure, but it seemed to me that at that moment, the entire courtroom exhaled with relief. But as most of us knew, Liam Kenney's story wasn't over quite yet.

Preston Varick helped bring it all home. "Who was driving Sheniqua and Edwin's car, Officer Kenney?"

"Her name was Karen Nielson," he responded. "She was their foster mother."

"So Sheniqua and Edwin were not living with their parents?"

For the first time since he'd taken the stand, the police officer's expression betrayed anger. "They had been abandoned two years earlier."

"Do you happen to know what happened to those children?" Varick asked. "After you rescued them from the fire?"

"Well, Sheniqua suffered first- and second-degree burns, but she has recovered almost completely. She has a few scars, but she'll be fine. And Edwin, well, we really don't know how this happened, but he just had some minor respiratory symptoms as a result of smoke inhalation. He's completely okay now."

"I take it that you've stayed in touch with these two

children." The question was obviously and shamelessly intended to set up an answer that would bring the emotional house down. But I didn't try to stop it. I wanted to hear the answer, too.

"Oh, yes," Officer Kenney replied. He finally allowed himself to smile. "I'm in very close touch with Sheniqua and Edwin. And so is my wife. Because ten months ago this Tuesday, we adopted them."

When you work in criminal law, you do not get a lot of opportunities to hear stories like Officer Kenney's. You also do not get many chances to hear a courtroom erupt in spontaneous applause. Sarge jumped to his feet, but Judge Lomax held up his hand. He had everything under control. He waited for a moment, then tapped his gavel gently on the bench. The room quieted down very quickly.

"I have nothing further, Your Honor," said the assistant district attorney.

Judge Lomax turned to me. "Cross-examination?"

Of course, there was nothing that this witness could do to help my client's cause. Officer Kenney's involvement in the Denver Tunnel Bombing had no connection to Juan Gomez in the least. He didn't know Gomez; he didn't see the tanker that started the blaze. He didn't even know the cause of the catastrophe until after he'd been taken to the hospital.

But just to emphasize that to the jury, I thought it might be good to ask a single question of the witness. I was as impressed and moved by his testimony as anyone, but in reality, it had virtually no bearing on whether Juan Gomez was guilty of anything. And my job, at the very minimum, was to ensure that when the inevitable guilty verdict was rendered, it was done so after the prosecution produced a reasonable amount of evidence to support it.

So I stood, and said, "Officer Kenney, have you ever had any dealings or involvement whatsoever with the defendant?"

My goal, of course, was to plant the idea in the jury's mind that this witness's testimony really didn't have anything to do with my client. So that when Preston Varick put his next overwhelmingly sympathetic witness on the stand, the jury might remember that no matter how moving or inspirational that witness was, testimony about the events of May 16 did not connect my client to guilt.

Because, of course, Officer Liam Kenney had never had any involvement with my client. So the answer to my question had to be no.

And then the witness blinked, looked quickly over at Juan Gomez and then back to me, and said, simply, "Yes."

FOURTEEN

THERE IS A RULE of thumb in litigation—
both civil and criminal—that young lawyers-in-training
learn in every law school in the land: Never ask a question of a witness to which you do not already know the answer.

I suppose that, technically, I broke that rule with Officer Kenney. To be fair, I had read his police reports regarding the Denver disaster, and he had never mentioned anything about Juan Gomez. Based on that, I believed that Kenney's answer to my question had to be no.

The problem actually arose as a result of the uncanny powers of recall possessed by Michelle Kenney, Liam's wife. The day before Officer Kenney left for Phoenix to testify, Michelle finally was able to put her finger on just what had been flitting around at the edges of her memory during the three weeks she had known that her husband was going to take the stand.

"A story about how we were going to adopt the kids ran in *Newsweek*," Officer Kenney explained to Varick on redirect examination. "For the next few weeks, we got tons of cards and letters from people all over the country." Then the witness reached into his pocket and pulled out a small envelope addressed to the Kenneys, care of the Denver Police Department. The postmark was Phoenix. "One of them was from Juan Gomez."

The envelope bore my client's return address label. The card itself was simple and quite tasteful. On the front was a watercolor painting of a saguaro. The inside was blank, except for a handwritten message in black pen:

> I will never forget the actions you took toward those children.

And it was signed Juan Abdullah Gomez.

For those of you not well versed in the Arizona rules governing evidence in criminal trials, statements made by the defendant, whether verbal or written, are always admissible.

And all prosecutors love them.

It's fascinating how even the most innocent-sounding communications get distorted through the lens of criminal accusations. So no matter what an individual says, when it is entered into evidence against him at a trial, inevitably it is viewed, somehow, as damning. Claims of innocence come off as attempts to wrongly deny responsibility. Claims of ignorance come off as disingenuous efforts to mislead authorities.

And in the case of Juan Gomez, a card expressing admiration and support of the selfless gesture of Liam and Michelle Kenney came off as a twisted threat.

I objected, of course, but Judge Lomax correctly admitted the card into evidence. My own stupid question on cross-examination had raised the issue—Preston Varick had every right to exploit it.

In the morning recess, my client took pains to explain himself.

"I didn't even think they were gonna get that card," he said, as the room emptied. "I read that magazine article. I just wanted them to know I thought it was great that they were adopting those two kids. But in here, they made it sound like I was, I don't know. Some kind of psycho."

My line of work has brought me into contact with plenty of people convicted of unutterable horrors. One of my clients murdered his pregnant wife and their three children, and then went to work the next day like nothing had happened. To look at him, you'd never have guessed that he was a killer. But you might have guessed that he was the manager of a local hotel. And you would have been right.

In my experience, you cannot distinguish people who commit atrocities from accountants or librarians or anybody else just by looking at their faces. So as I studied Juan Gomez after Officer Kenney's testimony, I wasn't particularly shaken by his outward appearance of decency. This man seemed to truly believe that he had been wrongly accused—that he was being misjudged. That didn't mean he was innocent, though.

But my interest in the card he'd sent was quite practical. "Have you written anything else to the Kenneys? Or to any of the other victims? I know it might not seem like much to you, but anytime the prosecution surprises me, the jury picks up on that. And when they do, they think that you are holding out on me. And that makes you look more guilty." I left out *if you could look more guilty*.

The truth was, Liam Kenney's testimony was just

the beginning. Preston Varick had any number of ways he could go from here. Pretty Cheryl Taylor was one of the four people who miraculously survived the explosion on the commuter bus. Cheryl could testify to the gruesome experience of watching her fellow passengers burst into flame. Or she could explain the challenges she now faced daily since her hands were amputated.

Tonya Romard could describe the screams she heard over her cell phone when the conversation with her fiancé about their honeymoon plans was interrupted when his little sports car erupted in flames.

Or James Wu could relate his gallantry as he dragged six people to safety before being overcome by smoke inhalation. And then he could describe his shock at watching three of them die before his eyes, and the post-traumatic stress disorder that has haunted him ever since.

No matter how many times I emphasized that these witnesses did not begin to establish who was responsible for causing the misery and death that day, the jury was going to want someone to blame. And they were going to look around the courtroom to see who was in the defendant's chair, and they were going to choose Juan Gomez.

"No, man. I didn't know anybody who was in the tunnel. I just wrote that card because of the article."

"Well, did you talk to anybody about it? Anybody in Denver?"

"Everybody was talking about it. You know. At work and stuff. But that was all here, in Phoenix. Of course I talked about it with my wife and my son." He paused. "That was before they left." Isabelle and Ernesto Gomez had fled the country shortly after Juan's arrest. He hadn't heard from them in months.

"My sister, she lives in Colorado Springs, you know. I talked to her about it on the phone a few times."

Colorado Springs was only forty-five minutes outside of Denver. "Did your sister know any of the victims?"

Gomez shifted in his seat. "No. Her boss was on the road when it happened, so he got stuck in all the traffic that day. And one of the ladies my sister works with at the library knew one of the people who died. But my sister didn't know any of the victims."

Sarge came past the table on his way back to his station. "Coupla minutes," he warned.

The noise from the gallery was increasing as people came back to their seats. I don't know why I turned around at that moment, but as I did, my attention was drawn to a man in dark clothing leaning against the far wall. Just before I was able to get a good look at his face, he turned away, and walked toward the exit at the back of the courtroom.

As he did, he passed Trooper Landry, who smiled broadly at me. I couldn't tell whether he was sending me a friendly—albeit disingenuous—salutation, or whether his expression was more malevolent. What was the etiquette for across-the-room, nonverbal greetings to crooked cops who have bugged you illegally?

I tried to smile back. I was not sure, however, that I achieved the desired expression. I was banking on the belief that Landry would chalk up any facial misfire not to my complete distrust of the man, but instead to the fact that I was already getting my tail rather sensationally kicked in this trial, and we hadn't even made it to lunch on the first day.

My attention was jolted back to business when Sarge announced that court was in session, and we learned that the next witness was the chief investigator for the Colorado State Police, Captain Oswald Francona.

Captain Francona was not a particularly large man, but he carried himself with authority. He had thick, dark, curly hair, which was beginning to turn gray, and a small scar on the left side of his chin.

Preston spent the rest of the morning and the first part of the afternoon establishing Francona's qualifications for the work he had been assigned to do in connection with the tunnel bombing. He had been through the police academy, and had taken an impressive number of courses in ballistics, in demolition and munitions, and in counterterrorism, as well as the departmental tests required to rise through the ranks from trooper all the way up to captain.

By the time his introduction to the jury was complete, there was no question in anyone's mind that this was a dedicated, highly trained law enforcement professional, well equipped to oversee the staggering investigation necessary in Denver.

It wasn't until late in the afternoon that his testimony began to address the specifics of what he'd found at the crime scene.

"Because of the number of victims requiring rescue or recovery, the fires and the resulting heat, smoke, and noxious fumes, etcetera, we were not actually able to get into the tunnel to begin our investigation until late on the seventeenth, over twenty-four hours after the initial explosion."

"Did you find the source of the fire?"

Varick was working from a large, three-ringed binder. His goal, apparently, was to follow up the emotional testimony of that morning with a more scientific, fact-based presentation.

At first blush, it seemed that by shifting away from

the effect of the blast on the people in and around the tunnel, Varick might be squandering the momentum that had been generated by the heroic story of Officer Kenney. But as the testimony began to play out, I saw that it made some sense. The jury needed to catch its breath. Varick knew that there would be plenty of tales of heartbreak and valor to come. He was just pacing it so the jury could endure them.

"Yes," the captain answered. "Fire inspectors discovered that a tanker truck containing—"

"Objection." I don't know whether Preston was expecting me to interrupt his witness. But he should have been. Whatever Oswald Francona was about to say was information told to him by others. A classic example of hearsay.

And while I was perfectly happy to allow Officer Kenney some leeway in telling his story, none of which directly affected my client, the cause of this catastrophe was what was ultimately going to be vitally important to Juan Gomez. I couldn't let the prosecution get away with presenting that part of their case without following the rules.

"Sustained."

The A.D.A. tried again. "When you investigated the tunnel on the afternoon of May seventeenth, what did you see?"

"I saw several burned vehicles in the tunnel, including dozens of cars, two commuter buses, and a tanker truck that had been carrying gasoline."

"And these vehicles were all burned?"

"Yes. In most cases, severely or completely burned. The windows were all broken, and in some cases, the damage was so extensive that the metal had actually warped from the extreme heat of the fire."

"And was the cause of the fire discovered?"

"Yes."

"What was that cause?"

I stood up again. "Objection."

Judge Lomax had been watching the witness, but now he turned toward Varick. "Sustained. May I see the attorneys at sidebar, please?"

Sidebar is the official term for the end of the judge's bench farthest from the jury box. It's where the lawyers and the judge meet to discuss issues during the trial that are not supposed to be overheard by jurors. I've always been struck by the sight of a judge, a court reporter, and any number of attorneys huddled together at one end of a very long table, whispering, carefully keeping the jurors—the very people who are going to make the ultimate decision in the case—in the dark.

Judge Lomax waited for the court reporter to get into place, and then spoke in a low voice to A.D.A. Varick. "Do you have any witnesses who can testify directly to the cause of the initial fire?"

"No, Your Honor," Varick replied. "Anyone who was in a position to see the tanker explode died."

"Well, then," the judge said. "You'll have to bring in someone to lay a foundation for the conclusion that the explosion of the tanker was the precipitating event."

"I know that, Your Honor." Preston seemed a little agitated. "It's just that defense counsel didn't raise one hearsay objection to the testimony of the first witness, and I simply believed that since he knows that we all know what happened, he was waiving hearsay objections in order to move the trial along. If I have to—"

"The reason I didn't object before—"

Judge Lomax quietly interrupted my interruption. "Keep your voice down, please." I looked over at the jury. They all were looking at me. The loud guy.

Sometimes I forget to whisper at sidebar, especially

when I get ticked off. For some reason, the idea that Preston Varick would assume that I was going to waive all objections for all witnesses got under my skin. The combination of that with my hearing loss made my voice a little strident under the circumstances. I tried again. Softer.

"The reason I didn't object before, Your Honor, was because Officer Kenney was testifying to facts that have no direct connection to my client."

"Plotting the explosion that set those kids on fire seems like a pretty direct connection to me."

I was beginning to see why Dad didn't like A.D.A. Varick. It was one thing to believe you knew the truth about everything, but it was quite another to expect that everyone involved in a criminal trial would accept that truth.

"That connection is the crux of the whole case," I whispered. "Officer Kenney's testimony didn't have anything to do with that. But when you get into the cause of the fire, you're getting into an area that might have a direct bearing on my client's guilt or innocence. And I can't just let that go in through hearsay testimony, or without a foundation."

"Fine," Varick said. "I'll bring in those experts next week."

"Have you got anything more for this witness?" Judge Lomax asked.

"Oh, yeah," Varick replied. "He's going to tie the defendant to the suicide bomber who started this whole thing. Esteban Cruz."

FIFTEEN

IN THE BRIEF time that I had been able to look through Steve Temilow's files, I had seen the information that had been gathered in the investigation into Esteban Cruz, and it was not good. Frankly, I wasn't sure that it made any difference, but Judge Lomax adjourned the trial for the day, before we got into that subject. The next day, Friday, promised to be somewhat arduous.

Before I left the courtroom, Sarge let me speak with Gomez. I had every expectation that he would be absolutely no help, and he didn't disappoint me.

"I got no ideas why they are even talking about Esteban Cruz," he said. My client's grammar might have been a little weak, but his meaning was certain as stone. He was adamant. There was absolutely no connection between him and Esteban Cruz, despite all of the evidence I had seen.

"What about your sister?" I asked. "Didn't you say she was from Colorado Springs?"

"So what?"

"So, Esteban Cruz lived between Denver and Colorado Springs," I said. "Is there any connection there?"

Gomez looked at me hard. "I thought you were on my side."

At the time, I didn't recognize the true absurdity of the situation. I had been assigned to represent the man accused of killing one hundred thirteen people in the worst terrorist attack on U.S. soil since 9/11. In a mere forty-eight hours, my work on his behalf had gotten me ridiculed on national television, assaulted and threatened at gunpoint, and illegally spied on by as yet unknown forces connected with any number of governmental law enforcement agencies.

And now he was questioning my loyalty.

"Of course I'm on your side," I said.

"Then stop trying to prove there's something between me and this crazy man who blew up that tunnel," he said.

A moment later, Sarge came over and took Gomez away.

Naturally, I had no desire to uncover a link damning my client. I was merely trying to piece together a better understanding of the situation in an effort to prepare myself for the following day's debacle. Contrary to what my behavior over the previous few days might imply, being an effective criminal defense attorney involves more than putting on a suit and tie and running up and down staircases.

But unbeknownst to me, that better understanding of the situation was going to have to wait until the coming weekend.

As I packed up my briefcase, I looked back into the gallery. It was entirely cleared out, except for Sarge's partner, Mike, who was standing by the doors, waiting for me to leave before locking up. I took a minute to enjoy the relative calm before moving toward the exit. I was looking forward to getting home, maybe chopping some wood for Henley's stove, doing some reading for the case, and getting a good night's rest.

But before that, I was going to have to run the media gauntlet. Undoubtedly, every reporter in the Western Hemisphere was waiting to ambush me on the courthouse steps. I wondered what they'd want to ask me today.

Mr. Carpenter, do you have any comment on the New York Times/CBS News *poll that shows ninety-six percent of Americans believe your client should be executed?*

Mr. Carpenter, if you win this case, do you think the United States will be a better place?

Mr. Carpenter, if your brother had survived the war against the very terrorists you are trying to defend, do you think he would be proud of you?

I knew it wasn't going to be that bad. My imagination was just running amok. Or at least loping around at a pretty good clip.

Still, I really didn't want to bother with that whole scene, so I took the elevator down to the basement, toward the exit that Trooper Landry had shown me yesterday.

The same Trooper Landry who was standing right in front of the doors when they slid open to let me out.

"Hey! Counselor! I was just coming up to see if you were still here! I was hoping to talk to you." He stepped aside to let me out of the elevator. "Going out through the garage? Great. Who needs those television nut jobs, huh?"

The perpetual smile that hung on the young policeman's face seemed less genuine today. I wasn't sure whether it was because I now knew that he had been lying—or at least misleading me—when he gave me that panic button and told me it was for my protection.

As we walked down the hall, he put his hand on my left shoulder. I managed not to flinch.

About a year after I met Cliff, we played on a softball team together, and as a result of colliding with Big Eddie Samson in right center field, I managed to break my collarbone in three places near where it connected to my left shoulder. The doctor said that it had healed stronger than it was before the break, but ever since that injury, it had never seemed the same. And Landry's hand resting up there felt very unpleasant.

"So, Counselor, how do you think it went today?"

I have to admit that for a second, I had no idea what he was talking about. It took me a moment to realize that he was inviting me to gossip about the case. And given what I'd learned about the cop, his motivation was anything but innocent.

Every interaction with Landry seemed to confirm the warning from Beta—the man in the bathroom. That was not particularly comforting for any number of reasons, chief among them the fact that I didn't want to be stalked by an amoral state trooper with an agenda I couldn't begin to guess. But I also was not anxious to learn that the paranoid ravings of the masked man who had accosted me two days earlier weren't paranoid at all.

"Oh, you know how it goes. It's hard to say. So much of this stuff was already reported on the news."

Landry didn't seem to notice that my answer was entirely nonresponsive. As if he were just waiting for me to finish speaking before it was his turn to talk, he said, "I was wondering whether you thought it was such a good idea to object to Captain Francona's testimony.

You know. When he started talking about what started the fire."

I looked over at him, and the smile was still in place. But now it looked more like the expression of an animal baring its teeth before striking its prey. A crazy person with a gun to my head had told me that Trooper Landry would illegally spy on me, and that he was ruthless. So far, he had gotten the bugging part right. I didn't want to test the rest of the prediction.

"It's always a judgment call," I said carefully. "I've got to represent my client's best interests, of course—"

"Of course," my genial companion chimed in. "You're a lawyer. You've got to watch out for your client's best interests."

"So I need to make sure the state follows the rules as it tries to prove its case."

Landry nodded, as if acknowledging something very important, and wise. "But everybody already knows that Cruz spilled the gas and blew up the truck to start the whole thing. I mean, unless this jury was living on Mars, they know what happened." He stopped walking. His hand was still on my shoulder, and it would have been awkward for me to go on without him, so I stopped as well, and turned to face him as he said, "Isn't it possible that it's not in *your* best interests to give the prosecution a hard time when all they're doing is telling a story we've already heard a hundred times in the news?"

It was not lost on me that Trooper Landry's free hand was very casually resting on his holstered service revolver. His words were cloaked in innocence, but his message was laced with threat. The abandoned basement corridor was suddenly ominous. We were still out of sight, and well out of earshot, of the personnel stationed at the courthouse exit.

I had to get out of there. I didn't know exactly what

was going on, but whatever it was, I didn't like it. I had been a lawyer long enough to know that confrontations with bad cops never went well.

"I hear you," I said. There was no need to fake the expression on my face. I was sure that it resembled that of a man considering some very serious information, because at that moment, that's exactly what I was. "You've got a point, there."

I just wasn't considering the information in the way Trooper Landry was hoping.

"Well," he said, breaking the mood, as we started to walk again toward the exit. "I bet you can't wait to get back home. How's your father doing, by the way?"

Any doubt that I was being threatened was rapidly disappearing into the ever-thickening cloud of insincerity that was enveloping us. I had never mentioned my father to Landry. Although it wasn't any particular secret that I lived with and cared for the man, it certainly wasn't something that I expected to discuss at my workplace with a relative stranger in our second conversation.

"Pretty well, I guess," I replied. About forty feet down the corridor we'd make a right turn, and we'd be at the exit. But the cop stopped me again.

"Hang on just a sec, Counselor. You know, everyone around here thinks the world of Henley Carpenter." It was getting harder and harder to pretend I believed anything that Landry said. All I needed was forty more feet, and this would be over. "Listen. We've been hearing some pretty scary things at headquarters. Nothing definite. Just enough to keep us on our toes."

And once again, I had returned to the state of almost total ignorance that I seemed destined to inhabit for the foreseeable future. What danger could Landry possibly be warning me of?

"I had a grandmother who had a stroke once, so I know how vulnerable people with partial paralysis can be. If you see or hear anything, and I mean anything, that you think seems out of the ordinary, especially around your house, use that panic button right away. You've still got it with you, don't you?"

I smiled and patted my briefcase. I tried to look confident, or at least reassured. I felt neither. "Right here," I confirmed. "And thanks. I will."

"Seriously," Landry persisted. "If anything happens to you or your father, I will feel personally responsible."

By now, I had managed to start moving again toward the exit. But the effect of Landry's words, whatever the intent, had been to usher Henley into the coils of terror that seemed to be closing around me with each second that passed in the cop's presence.

The idea that this thug would even *think* to whisper the vaguest threat involving my incapacitated father was so heinous that I instantly came to a complete stop. In fact, I was about a half a breath away from blowing up in his face when my brain mercifully sent me a reminder—a quick flash of déjà vu. Suddenly I was back in front of Judge Klay after blowing up in *her* face, and getting appointed to the trial which had led me, well, right here.

I chose my words with care, hoping to maintain whatever illusion remained that I trusted this man. "If anything happens to my father, I will come to you." I paused there. If he could be ambiguously threatening, then so could I. "And I will expect you to help me find whoever was responsible. And then, I'll do what I have to do."

If Landry was terrified by my little speech, he hid it well. He merely nodded, giving me a friendly pat on the arm as I left the building. "Understood," he said. "See you tomorrow, Counselor."

On my way home, the part of me that remained optimistic made a quick call to Amy on my old cell phone to make tentative plans for a picnic on Saturday with her and Erica if everything went well.

And the other part of me called Cliff to let him know I might need someplace safe for my father if everything didn't.

SIXTEEN

WHEN I GOT home that day, Henley was napping. The more exciting news was reported by Liana: He had spent the afternoon working on the manuscript of our book.

From the first time that my father took me to work with him, back when I was eight years old, I was fascinated with the drama of the courtroom. But that was before I went to law school and started studying the theories behind the rules that governed that drama. Then, my fascination began to wane.

Our system's method of establishing the truth behind a disputed event is to have twelve disinterested people get together and agree on it. That seems, on its face, to be reasonable. But in practice, how do we give these twelve people the information they need to make this vital determination? By sitting them in a box, talking to them in language that is centuries old, and forcing them to watch silently while two parties holding diametrical viewpoints—often based on financial considerations—verbally attack each other, and present testimony from pre-selected witnesses which will only support their position in the dispute.

And as if that weren't bad enough, we further handcuff the process by applying laughably complicated evidentiary rules which usually serve only to keep information from the decision-makers that they would probably love to have. They don't get to ask questions, they don't get to choose witnesses, they don't even get to decide what would be useful in making their decision.

Henley and I were talking about it one night, and decided right then and there that we would write a book—a father-son, prosecutor-defender volume which would turn the criminal justice system on its head, suggesting radical changes to criminal procedure, such as the mandatory sharing of information between parties, and allowing jurors to choose and question witnesses.

And oh, did we ever have big plans for the hearsay rule, thanks to the case of *Arizona* v. *Charles Jackson*.

Simply put, hearsay is a statement—spoken or written—made outside of the courtroom. And the general rule is that no witness can testify to hearsay, because the maker of the out-of-court statement isn't subject to cross-examination. But thanks to piecemeal analysis and badly outdated logic, the rule and its exceptions have become nothing more than ways for clever lawyers to block the jury from those facts which hurt their cause. The idea of getting at the underlying truth has all but been forgotten.

And in the case of Mr. Jackson, the hearsay rule helped put an innocent man in jail.

I didn't know that Charles Jackson was innocent when I was assigned to handle his appeal. His innocence was conclusively proven by a DNA test done after he'd served five years of his twenty-year sentence. Naturally, Charles had claimed that he and his father,

Henry, didn't commit the armed robbery that had left a local business nine hundred fifty-six dollars poorer and a grocery store clerk in a coma, but as I've mentioned before, I hear such claims from almost every one of my clients.

What stood out about Charles Jackson's trial was that the case contained absolutely no physical or direct evidence of guilt. The store's surveillance video showed that the robbers wore masks, and revealed only that both were black, and one had graying hair. Apparently the jury believed the two eyewitnesses who said they saw Charles and his father, two black men, one with graying hair, running quickly down the street, away from the store, at about the same time as the robbery.

So the verdict was guilty. Despite the fact that eyewitness testimony is notoriously inaccurate. Despite the fact that Charles and Henry had worked steadily, six days per week, for the eight years prior to the robbery, at Henry's auto repair shop, five blocks away from the store. Despite the fact that Charles testified that he and his father were at the shop late on the night of the robbery, working on a car that had to be ready the next day. Despite the fact that Henry Jackson had a badly arthritic hip, walked with a severe limp, and hadn't run anywhere, at any speed, for years.

But the thing that really made me nuts was that Henry's dying words were not allowed in as evidence, because of the hearsay rule.

See, the police were initially stumped by the robbery. They didn't have any suspects. And the eyewitnesses hadn't been able to identify anyone from the mug shots they had been shown.

But then, just by chance, an off-duty police officer pulled into Henry Jackson's shop to replace a headlight. Both Charles and his dad were working at the time, and when the officer saw two black men, one with graying hair, within five blocks of the robbery, he decided to bring the eyewitnesses down for a look.

One was eighty percent sure they were the pair he'd seen running away from the grocery store. The other was one hundred percent sure. And that was that.

The only reason Henry wasn't charged with the crime was because when the police came to arrest him, he got so upset he had a heart attack on the spot, and died right there.

But before dying, in the midst of the agony of a massive coronary, he tearfully pleaded with the police to believe him when he said that he and his son had nothing to do with the robbery. He confessed that the only crime he had ever committed was failing to report that he had accidentally broken the taillight of a parked car when he was learning to drive, fifty years ago.

And with that mea culpa, he left this earth.

At trial, the defendant's attorney argued that the statement should have been allowed into evidence. The prosecutor argued that it was hearsay. The defense lawyer countered that the "dying declaration" exception allowed out-of-court statements into evidence if made by people who knew they were dying. The theory behind the exception was that such statements are overwhelmingly likely to be true because of the circumstances under which they are made.

What the defense lawyer had forgotten was that the dying declaration exception applied only to statements identifying whoever it was that killed the person who made the statement. Nothing else.

To add insult to tragic injustice, the judge correctly mentioned in an aside that it was too bad the defense couldn't use Mr. Jackson's statement about the taillight, because there was an exception allowing *that* kind of hearsay as evidence, since the statement had the potential to get Mr. Jackson into trouble, either with the law, or financially.

Seriously. Look it up. It's in the rules of evidence.

That kind of nonsense drove my father and me crazy.

But Henley and I had only reached chapter three in our book when the stroke got him. We had been on hiatus ever since—one that I thought was permanent.

I closed the door quietly behind Liana as she left, and softly stepped into the living room. My father was asleep in his wheelchair. A legal pad was resting on a laptop desk that Henley occasionally used. I was surprised to see he had made some handwritten notes. My dad had all but given up writing, because his left hand was so slow and clumsy. I couldn't read what was written, but I didn't care. I was just happy he was getting back into it. It didn't matter to me if my father was stuck in a wheelchair for the rest of his life. I'd push or carry him wherever he needed to go, if it came to that. I just wanted him to still be able to do things that he loved. And he loved trying to make the legal system better.

I changed my clothes, grabbed a beer from the kitchen, and went out the back door to the pyramids of cut wood I stored about fifty yards from the rear of the house.

To me, this area was far more than just a bare patch of earth featuring tall stacks of split logs. When I stood on the far side of the piles of firewood, I was at the edge of the pine-and-mesquite-covered mountain that rose above our house. Dale, Henley, and I had cleared paths into the woods, and we'd spent many summer afternoons climbing up to the top of the hill. When the weather was good, you could see the entire valley. I remember regularly bringing my new binoculars up to

catch the setting sun as it hit the colorful rock forma-
tions next to the monastery on Goat Head.

Dale thought I was just up there to check out Suzie
Rios sunbathing by her parents' pool.

And while I freely admit that the valley's beauty was
undeniably enhanced by Suzie's outstanding bathing
suit collection, I still spent far more time at the base of
the hill, at the woodpile. It became my sanctuary, my
place of meditation.

And on that Thursday evening, while Henley napped,
I put down my beer, rolled into position one of the sec-
tions of mesquite trunk that I'd cut up earlier that year,
grabbed my ax, and got started.

There's a rhythm to the chopping of a good cord of
wood.

I position my right hand just below the blade, and
grasp the handle at the other end with my left hand. I
hoist the ax head high above my shoulders, slide my
right hand along the handle to where my left is anchored, and then I pull down hard, cutting into the
waiting log with a soul-satisfying *thunk*. Hoist, slide,
pull, *thunk*. Hoist, slide, pull, *thunk*.

I started chopping wood in high school, to try to
strengthen the muscles in my upper body. I was on the
baseball team, but I was skinny, and I didn't feel like I
had enough power to be any kind of a serious hitter. I
was wrong about a lot of things back then, including
the correlation between swinging an ax and swinging a
baseball bat. But even though the exercise bore limited
results on the baseball diamond, it wasn't long before I
began to find pleasure in the chore itself.

Over the years, I got really good at it. My strength
built steadily, and my eye-hand coordination became so
developed that not only could I bring the blade of the
ax down, in a full swing, onto a spot less than one inch

wide, but I could actually throw the ax as a weapon over a short distance.

On that Thursday evening, the last one I was to spend there chopping wood for my father, the physical effort in my arms, shoulders, and back morphed into spiritual relaxation. It wasn't long before the day had slid into that magical time, where just enough light still hovered in the air for chopping, but sounds seemed to be gently muffled by the slowly falling darkness. That time when it becomes easier to believe that life really can be lived one breath at a time. One moment, one glance, one kiss, one laugh at a time.

It's tempting to look back on the serenity of that evening as the calm before the storm. But I think rather that it was a combination of things: the happy surprise of Henley's return to our book, the realization that in only a couple of days, I'd be seeing Amy and Erica again, and the emergence of a fundamental belief that the Juan Gomez trial was only temporary. When it was over, I was going to return to my life. Until then, if I needed to move my father for his safety, I would. If I had to protect myself, I would.

Come what may, I would manage. I would endure.

Hoist, slide, pull, *thunk*.

I put down the ax, finished my beer, and went inside. It was time to make dinner, talk to Henley about the idea of taking him somewhere else if that became necessary, and prepare for tomorrow's testimony.

I have forgiven myself for many of the mistakes I made during that disastrous week, but I have yet to come to peace with what I did, and what I did not do, for Henley on that day. I am mortified that despite Landry's threats, I only vaguely warned Liana that I might need to come home early and take my father somewhere safe. I am aware that it would not have made a difference, but I am still ashamed that I did not act sooner to protect him.

Even now, with a full understanding of the evil that was to strike at my family's heart that day, I have to admit that Friday morning was one of the most beautiful I can remember. Everything around me seemed to be in perfect color and contrast as I drove in to Phoenix. The trees and three tiny, cottony clouds were sharply outlined against a peaceful blue heaven. The cool mountain air was touched by the gentlest breeze, and even as I made my way down through the warmer valley and into the less idyllic city, it was hard to lose that feeling of hope that had flowered in me the day before.

The first indication that the content of the day was going to be considerably different from its attractive packaging was the envelope bearing my name, peeking out from beneath the legal pad that I had left with a few books on the defense table the night before. I saw it as soon as I began to unload my briefcase. I struggled against the dread that was pushing its way into my breast, hoping it was a perfectly innocent note, possibly from the clerk or the court reporter, perhaps about an administrative detail that needed to be taken care of for the case.

It was a note, but it was neither innocent, nor about a minor issue. The small, single sheet of paper read,

> *Go to the location of our first conversation. There's something for you on the floor near the wall. You'll need it to know what to do. Use it.* DO NOT GO TO THE COPS. *You heard what Landry said yesterday. Your father's life depends on it.*

It was signed with the letter *B*. For Beta.

I resented it all. The feeling that in a matter of only four days, my world had transformed itself from someplace peaceful and safe to a place where tranquillity was regularly assaulted by fear and suspicion. The belief that going to work was little more than submitting myself to a fusillade of threats against my family. The knowledge that aside from Amy and Erica, Henley, Cliff and Iris, I could trust no one.

I placed the last file folder from my briefcase on the table, put the note in the case, closed it, and took it with me into the hallway. There were still a few minutes before the trial was to resume. I'd go to the bathroom, get whatever it was that Beta had left for me, and make it through the day.

One step at a time. One breath at a time.

One threat at a time.

I was a tall and athletic kid all through my childhood, so I never experienced the anxiety I've heard that children face when going to the bathroom in some of the tougher middle schools and high schools. On the rare occasions during my teens that I ran into something or someone unusual in a school bathroom, I never felt nervous.

But as I stood at the door to the men's room at the end of the hallway that Friday morning, fear flooded through me. I didn't expect to get jumped again, although I realized that was a possibility. I just couldn't imagine what I might have done or not done to deserve another pistol in the face.

But then again, I still didn't understand why I'd been threatened in the first place. And I still couldn't imagine why Landry had bugged me. Or how Beta knew about yesterday's veiled threat—if that's even what it was—against my father.

I was running out of time—I had to get back to the courtroom. Steeling myself for whatever I might face, I pushed through the door, just as Preston Varick was pulling it open. I was startled, naturally, as was he. "Morning," he said, rather gruffly I thought, as he hurried past me, before I even had a chance to respond.

I let the door swing closed behind me as I entered. The bathroom was empty, so I went over to the sink where I had been first accosted, and looked down at the floor near the wall. There was nothing there, except a discarded matchbook.

Had the note been wrong? *The location of our first conversation.* I eyed the stall I'd been dragged into. Technically, that was where our first conversation, such as it was, had taken place. I went in, closed the door, and looked down at the floor near the wall to the left of the toilet. There was nothing there. Nor was anything to the right of the toilet.

I couldn't see directly behind the toilet, so I bent down and reached around. Sure enough, I felt something that had been taped to the floor back there. It was one of those small manila envelopes. Inside was a smaller plastic sandwich bag, which contained what looked like a hearing aid.

You'll need it to know what to do. I took a good look at it. It was obviously designed to fit inside an ear canal, just like a hearing aid. Unless I was very wrong, this thing was a radio receiver of some kind. Beta wanted me to wear it instead of one of my hearing aids, so he could talk to me in the courtroom, during the trial.

Whether or not I was right, I certainly wasn't going to worry about it now. If it was a receiver, and Beta started to talk to me, I could always ignore him, unless what he was saying was actually useful.

And if it wasn't a receiver, what was the harm of using it to replace one of my aids? A slight reduction in my hearing, I supposed. I took the aid out of my left ear, placed it in my jacket pocket, and replaced it with the miniature receiver.

Later, Cliff would admonish me for failing to realize that it could have been a remote-controlled explosive device. While no doubt the high drama of an ear bomb would have been a perfect addition to the already mounting tension of the situation, I am happy to report that with all of the disastrous scenarios running through my mind as I headed back into the courtroom, having my head simply explode was not one of them.

My client was already seated at the defense table by the time I returned. Before I could say anything more than *"Good morning,"* a voice came through the tiny receiver and into my left ear.

"If you can hear this, fit down, sock free books in a pile in front of you, and then push them off to the side of the table."

The voice was unrecognizable—it was probably being processed by some electronic device, and it was soft. I suppose that a person with normal hearing might not have struggled with it, but I had to resist the urge to plug my ears with my fingers in order to make the words out more clearly. *Fit down, sock free books?*

No. *Sit* down. *Stack* three books.

I sat. I followed the instructions.

The voice said nothing more than *"Good."*

And then Sarge walked into the room, and bellowed, "Court's in session. All rise."

SEVENTEEN

CAPTAIN FRANCONA was back on the stand. The courtroom, as it had been since the beginning of the trial, was packed. The little red light on top of the Judicial Broadcasting System's television camera was on.

It was time to hear the official and formal version of the story behind the actions of the nation's most recent monster: Esteban Cruz.

"Captain Francona, can you describe for us what you saw when you were finally allowed to enter the tunnel?"

From the wording of the question, and the confident look of the witness, it was clear that A.D.A. Varick had spent some time preparing Captain Francona, instructing him on just what he could say in court without provoking me to object.

"Yes. I entered the tunnel from the north. As you might remember, traffic in that tube was traveling from south to north, so after the fire began, traffic backed up beyond the south end of the tunnel. But those vehicles that were not affected by the fire exited the north end of the tunnel."

"So was the north end of the tunnel clear?"

"Essentially, yes. The tunnel is approximately one quarter mile long, and the northern half of it was empty. However, even before I reached the first vehicles that had been damaged by the explosions and fire, I saw that smoke had left a sooty residue on the ceiling and the walls of the tunnel. And there was a strong smell of smoke in the air, as well."

Preston was standing with his hands clasped behind his back. He looked quite composed. "I see. When you did reach that part of the tunnel that contained burned vehicles, what did you find?"

The witness looked up, as if it would help him remember. I didn't get the sense that he was faking it, but on the other hand, it was hard to believe that he wasn't already one hundred percent sure of exactly what he was going to say.

"The first six vehicles I saw were five cars and a van. I was facing the south, so in the west lane—the lane to my right—there were three vehicles. All relatively small cars. The driver of each car had been burned to death in the driver's seat.

"The eastern lane, the one to my left, also had three vehicles. But only two were cars. The other one was a passenger van.

"Again, each of the vehicles had been badly damaged by fire and/or explosions. The windows were all broken in each. And again, the occupants of all three vehicles had been burned beyond recognition. In the two cars, there was just a driver. But besides the driver of the van, there were two other passengers. Both wheelchair-bound. The van was registered to a nonprofit organization which was funded in part by the city to provide transportation to disabled persons to doctors' appointments, therapy, that kind of thing."

The gruesome details of the tunnel bombing had been thoroughly hashed over by the media in the weeks and months following the disaster. It looked like Varick had chosen to deliver the testimony of the catastrophic human toll in small doses, rather than in a mind-numbing avalanche of corpses. I thought it was a smart move. Clearly, the jury was his to lose. There was no need to antagonize them, or appear to insult them, with redundant and ghastly detail.

"After your inspection of those six vehicles, what did you do next?"

"About one hundred feet to the south of those six vehicles was a destroyed fuel tanker truck, sitting in the middle of a scene of tremendous damage to the roadway running through the tunnel. Much of the pavement had been melted and/or exploded away, leaving a hole—actually, something like a shallow crater—in which the truck was lying.

"The walls of the tunnel at this point were also damaged—much of the tile had been blown away, revealing the concrete subsurface, which was also damaged. The walls and ceiling of the tunnel there were entirely black from the soot and the smoke generated by the fire and the explosion. The vehicle itself was lying on its side. It was entirely demolished."

"Were you able to ascertain the fate of the driver of the truck?"

The jury knew full well that Esteban Cruz was the driver of the truck, and that he was dead. If pressed, they probably could have drawn you a reasonable sketch of the man's unusually thin face, dark eyes, skinny mustache, and the oval birthmark on his cheek. But Varick knew that he had to play this straight, because unless he could formally and convincingly tie Cruz to Juan Gomez, his case would collapse.

"When I inspected the cab of the vehicle, I was unable to see any human remains. In fact, much of what was visible was difficult to identify, because the damage from the fire was so extensive. Anything that was plastic, or leather, or glass—in fact, anything that wasn't metal—seemed to have been burned away, or burned and melted into a condition that made it impossible to recognize."

Varick interrupted the Q and A at this point to introduce photos of the scene that Francona was discussing. The witness was doing a good job. His descriptions were apt. The annihilation of the tanker truck was astonishingly thorough.

"Given the condition of the truck after the explosion, can you tell the jury what you did to ascertain the owner and/or the driver of the truck?"

"We caught a break there," Francona replied. Unlike the devastatingly emotional story of Liam Kenney, this witness's testimony was gripping because everyone felt compelled to understand this horror. The firsthand account of the lead investigator somehow made us feel closer to that understanding. "Parts of the truck literally blew apart, and scattered all over the place. Lucky for us, one of the pieces of the truck that survived was its license plate. We found it embedded in the ceiling of the tunnel, approximately forty feet from the blast site."

"How were you able to determine that the license plate found was from the exploded tanker truck?"

The question was important, and Captain Francona was ready for it. "There is a video surveillance camera at the entrance to the tunnel," he said. "We reviewed the tape corresponding to the time immediately before the explosion, and we saw the tanker truck entering the tunnel. We were able to see the license plate from the tape, and verify our identification from the plate in the tunnel ceiling."

Varick now addressed the judge. "Your Honor, I'd like, at this time, to play what the parties have stipulated as Exhibit Sixteen, the surveillance tape recording of the moments before the explosion."

"Very well," said the judge.

At this point, Sarge dimmed the lights, and then, with a remote control, turned on a television monitor mounted in the upper right corner of the room. Then, using a second remote control, he started the tape.

The picture wasn't particularly high quality, and the camera was mounted low and aimed down and toward the tunnel entrance, so that you couldn't see much except a small piece of roadway and the lowest parts of vehicles just before they passed into the tunnel.

A second or two after the tape began to play, the rear end of what was obviously a fuel tanker came into view, bearing license plate number 2R–3309.

But more disturbing was the fact that once the truck passed from view, the roadway surface was soaked with what we all now knew to be gasoline.

And as if that weren't bad enough, some seconds later a cloud of black smoke emerged from the right side of the frame. And then the transmission ended.

Sarge stopped the tape, and brought the lights back up.

Varick then pulled a large plastic bag from a box sitting on his table. It contained a badly damaged license plate. It was partially melted, and so severely warped and dented that the first digit was impossible to discern. The remaining ones were R-3309. He handed it to Francona. "Are you familiar with the item that I have handed to you?"

The witness made a show of examining the exhibit, reading it, and then turning it over. "Yes," he said. "This is the license plate that exploded off the back of the tanker truck, and lodged itself into the tunnel ceiling, approximately forty feet away."

I was coming to appreciate Varick's efforts this morning. He could have already paraded God knows how many autopsy photos in front of the jury by this point. In any murder case, such exhibits were prosecution gold. They were undeniably relevant, and emotionally devastating. Every judge instructs juries to keep emotions out of their deliberations, and every lawyer knows that when the autopsy photos are admitted, it's virtually impossible for them to find the defendant not guilty. Those photos make them need to hold someone accountable for the violent death they had been made to witness.

But Varick chose instead, at least so far, to tell the prosecution's story without the typical tabloid gore. The jury was getting the facts they needed to perform their duty. This witness's testimony, supplemented by the photos of the scene and the ruined license plate, did an excellent job. There was no question in any of our minds how powerful the blast had been, and how hot the fire had burned on that tragic spring morning in Denver.

"Were you able to identify the owner of the truck based on the license plate identification?"

"Yes. The truck was registered to a business called Mountain Star Trucking Company. The owner's name was Samuel D'Amato."

"And without telling us of the content of any conversation you might have had with Mr. D'Amato, did you speak to him?"

I'm afraid that we all had me to thank for the awkwardness of that particular question. Because of my insistence on strict adherence to the rules of evidence on the previous day, Varick was bending over backward to be sure that his witness's testimony didn't contain hearsay—like the content of his conversation with the truck's owner.

"Yes, I spoke to him."

"And after that conversation, what was the next step you took in your investigation?"

"My next step was to apply for and to obtain a search warrant for the home of Esteban Cruz, 523 Smythe Place, in Dutton, Colorado."

One of the reasons my father and I were writing that book was to try to avoid the silly dance that Varick was doing with his witness. The jury, as well as virtually every one of the millions of viewers of the trial, knew that Francona had asked D'Amato who had been driving the truck that morning, and learned that it was Cruz. Then he asked where Cruz lived, and D'Amato checked his records, and gave the police captain the address.

But we couldn't hear that testimony, because, technically, it might have been hearsay—the words of an individual other than the one on the witness stand.

"Did you act on the warrant?"

Captain Francona had brought what looked like a copy of his police report with him to the stand, but as he had with all of the other questions to this point, he answered without consulting it.

"Yes, sir. Several officers and I arrived at the subject's home at approximately nine A.M. on May eighteenth. We knocked and announced that we were police officers, but no one answered. The front door to the home was unlocked, and we entered, again announcing our presence. But shortly after we gained entry, it was clear that no one was in the residence."

Judge Lomax interrupted at that point. "Before we get into what the police did or did not find in Mr. Cruz's home, I think it would be prudent for us to take the morning recess. Ten minutes."

He stood. Sarge shouted, "All rise," and we stood up as the judge and the jury left the room.

As we all sat down again, my client turned to me and asked, "So, how do you think it's going?"

"So far so good," I replied. "But that's only because they haven't started to talk about the evidence they have which links you to Cruz."

Gomez shook his head. His brown eyes were as earnest as any I'd ever seen. "I'm telling you, man, there ain't no evidence that links me to that psycho. I never seen him before in my life."

I had a box full of papers and tapes at home that contradicted my client's assertion, but I didn't see the point in belaboring what we both already knew.

Gomez wasn't quite ready to let it go, though. "You're ready to do something, though? You're not going to let them just get up there and say anything, are you? You're going to—I don't know. Object, say something about my rights, tell them I'm innocent?"

I had prepared a cross-examination for Captain Francona, based on a few areas of his testimony that I expected were going to be thin.

But frankly, it wasn't going to be much.

"I don't know exactly how damaging it will be to their case, but when it's my turn to ask questions, I promise you, I will . . ." To be honest, I didn't know quite how to finish the sentence. But then, Beta's words from the bathroom came back to me. "—Make some noise."

And then a tiny voice from the device lodged in my left ear said, *"Damn right you will."*

EIGHTEEN

IT DIDN'T TAKE long for the witness to recapture our attention.

"The first thing we found when we walked through the door was directly in front of us, right there in the entrance. I don't know what you'd call it. A display, or a shrine, maybe. It was this arrangement of a small table with a chair on either side of it. On top of the table was a Koran, lying open. On the chair to the left of the table, there were two pictures. One looked like it was a family portrait. There was a man and a woman, probably in their forties, with three children standing in front of them—two girls and a boy. The boy had a birthmark on his right cheek.

"The other picture was just of the boy, but as a young man, holding a certificate of some kind. In front of that photo was a driver's license, issued to Esteban Cruz. The person in the driver's license photo was the same person as the boy in the family portrait."

Preston introduced the two photos and the driver's license as exhibits, and they were passed through the

jury box. Everyone had seen the pictures before—
they'd been all over the news within a week of the blast.
But there was a difference when you held photos like
that in your hands. It made everything more real. And
much worse.

When the jury was finished with the exhibits, Preston
asked, "What was on the other chair?"

"It was a suicide note."

Cruz had printed his final letter from his computer
on plain white paper. He hadn't been one of the world's
great typists, or spellers, but the message was clear
enough. It read:

> *Allah is great.*
>
> *Today I am a marter. Today, I go to paradise.*
>
> *I do this for Allah. Praise always to him, the al-
mighty one.*
>
> *The Koran tells me to do this for the world. To
die for the world. Read it and you will see.*
>
> *I cry for you, my family. My mother and father. I
cry for you always. And my sisters. The wolrd will be
bettter this way. I die, and many infidels die in the
hottest fire.*
>
> *My truck is my prayer to Allah.*
>
> *Allah be praised.*

This note was also leaked to the press months ago,
so I was surprised to see two or three of the jurors react
visibly when they were reading it. The good-looking
postal worker seemed saddened—maybe from the realization that so much misery could be caused by just one
desperate person, or maybe from the loss of this man's
soul to the hatred that had scarred our country so
deeply. It was abundantly clear, though, that seeing this
letter made the taxi driver and the math teacher angry.

I have to admit, my feelings toward Esteban Cruz also leaned in that direction.

When the last of the jurors had viewed the suicide note, Preston returned to his questioning. "Did you say that the Koran that was out on the table between the two chairs was open?"

"Yes."

Varick handed the captain a leather-bound volume with a protruding bookmark. "Do you recognize this?"

The witness took the book from the prosecutor, examined it, opened it to the bookmarked page, and said, "Yes. This is the Koran that was sitting on the table in Esteban Cruz's home."

Preston nodded. "And the pages that are bookmarked? Do you recognize them?"

Francona looked at the book, and then back up at Varick. "Yes, sir. Those were the pages that the book had been left open to. Certain of the passages were highlighted."

"Would you read those highlighted portions aloud to us, please?"

Returning his attention to the book, the witness read, "'Make holy war on the unbelievers and the hypocrites; hell will be their home.'"

Varick let that sink in before his next question. "Did you find anything else of interest in your search of the premises?"

Captain Francona handed the Koran to the clerk, and looked back up at the A.D.A. "There was nothing else of particular interest in the entryway or in the living room. Just past the living room was a kitchen, which also was unremarkable. But there was an eat-in area at the end of the kitchen. There was a folding table set up there, with a couple of chairs. And on top of that table, we discovered a calendar, with the date May sixteenth circled in red."

And on it went. Next to the dramatically marked calendar were several flyers advertising various talks being given by a Muslim cleric named Maliq Al-Hazra, who apparently had been visiting Cruz's home mosque, in Colorado Springs, during the six months before the attack. The flyers weren't particularly high quality. Some of the language describing the topics of Al-Hazra's talks was unquestionably radical.

Cruz's checkbook indicated that he had cleaned out his bank account the day before the tunnel bombing and sent his remaining money to one of his sisters.

Although there wasn't much doubt that Esteban Cruz was the man who had been at the flashpoint of this tragedy, there was little to no evidence from this witness that connected him to my client.

Still, after the lunch break, when it was time for cross-examination, I felt the need to emphasize that fact to the jury. I knew that the bulk of the evidence linking Juan Gomez to Cruz had been found in Gomez's place. But I still felt it was important for the jury to realize that at least so far, the prosecution had established absolutely no connection between Juan Gomez and the catastrophic events in Denver.

I stood, buttoned my suit jacket, and faced the witness. "Captain Francona, in your search of the home of Esteban Cruz, did you come across the name 'Juan Gomez' anywhere?"

Intelligent witnesses, especially those on a mission to influence the outcome of a trial, often analyze the opposing attorney's strategy, and try to keep one step ahead of them. Unfortunately, Oswald Francona was such a witness. And he was pretty good at it, too.

"No, sir, I didn't. Of course, I didn't see anyone else's name anywhere in the apartment."

"I'm sorry," I responded. "I thought you said that you saw Maliq Al-Hazra's name on several flyers on the table next to the calendar."

The police captain smiled and nodded. "I apologize, Counselor. You're absolutely right. When you asked if I'd seen your client's name anywhere in the apartment, I thought you meant written anywhere by Mr. Cruz. But the answer would have been the same—I didn't see the name of Juan Gomez handwritten, printed, or typed, in the apartment."

Captain Francona wasn't just intelligent—he was obviously very experienced in testifying in criminal trials. In less than sixty seconds, he had managed to get quite a bit accomplished. First, he initially misinterpreted my question so that he could undermine my message to the jury. "Don't make too much of the fact that Juan Gomez's name wasn't anywhere in Cruz's apartment—no one else's name was in the apartment, either."

And then, when I called him on it, he managed to apologize in a way which made him out to be the good guy, and by implication, me the bad guy. I didn't take it personally. I knew that criminal trials weren't popularity contests. And I knew that I was in the middle of an unwinnable case. But to be fair to my client, I had to try. And so far, there really was no link between Esteban Cruz and Juan Gomez. It was my job to make sure the jury did not forget that.

"Okay. So the name Juan Gomez wasn't anywhere in Esteban Cruz's apartment. How about Mr. Gomez's phone number? Was that found anywhere?"

I knew that the answer was no. But I also knew that this witness wasn't going to just leave it at that.

"No. Actually, we didn't find an address book, or a phone book, or any list of any kind in the subject's apartment." The witness smiled. "I guess you could say the answer is similar to my first one. We didn't find your client's phone number, but we didn't find anyone else's phone number, either."

"I see. Well, how about evidence of travel by Mr. Cruz to Phoenix? Or even to Arizona? Did you find anything in the apartment to support the notion that Mr. Cruz had ever come to see Mr. Gomez?"

Again, Captain Francona merely smiled and shook his head. "No, sir. No credit card receipts for plane tickets to Phoenix, nothing like that."

I wasn't ready to let go. "How about a cell phone? Sometimes cell phones have phone books in their memory, or a list of recent calls. Did you find a cell phone that contained records that indicated any connection between my client and Esteban Cruz?"

"No cell phone was found, sir. If Mr. Cruz had one, we assumed that he had it with him on the truck when it exploded."

I nodded. But I was hoping to drive home the point to the jury in as thorough a way as I could. So I pushed forward. "Did you check Mr. Cruz's financial records? Did the bills he received for any phone service he might have had reveal any connection between Mr. Cruz and Mr. Gomez?"

The captain shifted in his seat. Finally, I had gotten into an area he wasn't completely prepared for.

"Well, in Mr. Cruz's trash, we did find a handful of recently paid bills. One of them was a cell phone bill. And there were no calls made to or from Phoenix, or Arizona."

"But you checked into the phone numbers that did appear on the bill, didn't you?"

"Yes."

"And there were only four different numbers that Mr. Cruz called, isn't that correct?"

The witness wasn't happy with me, but he was doing a good job hiding it from the jury. "That's correct."

"And wasn't one of those numbers for Mr. Cruz's parents' home line, and the other three numbers the cell phones of his mother and his two sisters?"

"Yes, that's right."

"So although you didn't find Mr. Cruz's cell phone, you did find a bill for his cell phone service for the period running from about six weeks before the attack to two weeks before the attack, and over that four-week time span, the records indicate that Mr. Cruz had no cell phone contact, whatsoever, with my client, the defendant, Juan Gomez?"

"That's right," the witness replied. "But of course, he might have bought disposable cell phones and contacted your client that way."

Up to that point in his testimony, the state police officer had seemed only interested in making sure that the jury kept in mind that just because my questions were steering them in one direction, there were plenty of other directions to work with.

His last effort along those lines sounded less like he was just making sure we had all the facts, and more like a gratuitous shot at me to make sure that the jury believed only his version of the facts.

In a trial where I felt like the opportunities to come out ahead were going to be very, very rare, I seized this one.

"But of course, you found no disposable cell phones in the apartment, nor any receipts indicating that Mr. Cruz had purchased any disposable cell phones."

The police captain knew he had to concede, and

when he finally did so, he did it quietly. "That's correct."

I didn't think I had anything else I could get out of Captain Francona, so I returned to my position behind the defense table, and prepared to excuse the witness.

Just then, the voice from the device in my ear said, *"Don't stop there, Counselor. It's time to make some noise."*

NINETEEN

I'VE USED HEARING aids since I was seven years old. And ever since then, I've been fully aware of the fact that the way the aids work is to amplify the sounds I'm hearing naturally. It never made sense to stick my finger into my ear to improve a hearing aid's performance.

So for the first few years I used the aids, I was confused when I saw television personalities occasionally put a finger in an ear. I had no idea they were trying to hear whatever the producer or director was communicating to them through their earpiece. I just thought they didn't know how to use their hearing aids.

When Beta began to speak to me through the earpiece, the first thing I wanted to do was to put my finger into my ear, so that the only thing I could hear through that passageway was the little voice from the tiny piece of plastic lodged in there.

Of course, that would have made me look spectacularly suspicious. Just like someone listening to a disembodied voice through a hearing device.

Happily, I managed to detour my hand just south of its original target, and before untold millions of viewers, I stood behind the defense table, and self-consciously scratched my left cheek. Rather than suspicious, I merely looked stupid.

"Ask him if he's familiar with the death of an unidentified individual which took place two days before the tunnel bombing in Greene County, Colorado, just north of Colorado Springs."

The only thing that I managed to do in response to this message was to stop scratching my cheek. Since no one else in the courtroom had heard what Beta had told me, it merely looked like after Captain Francona had answered my last question, I decided to return to the defense table, and stand there, intermittently attending to my itchy face.

"Mr. Carpenter," Judge Lomax said. "Do you have any further questions for this witness?"

"Ask him!" snarled Beta. *"Don't just stand there. Trust me. It'll make sense soon enough."*

I had no idea where Beta was going. I had no idea where anything was going. But even though I didn't understand the purpose of the question, I decided there was no harm in asking it.

Unfortunately, by that time, I had forgotten it.

"No . . . I mean yes, Your Honor," I said. "Yes. I have further questions." I turned to the witness. "Captain Francona, are you familiar with the death of an unidentified individual . . ." It was all I could remember.

Beta was disgusted with me. *"Jesus Christ. Which took place two days before the tunnel bombing in Greene County, Colorado, just north of Colorado Springs."*

The voice was crisp, and clear. Not particularly loud, though, which was a bit of a concern, because when it was speaking, I found myself freezing into a completely still position, as if that would minimize any ambient noise that might interfere with my ability to understand what was being said.

Cliff later said that I looked a little bit like a defective robot. Every once in a while, I would stand dead still, looking straight ahead, saying nothing. And then, all of a sudden, I would snap out of it, and start moving and speaking again.

"Which took place two days before the tunnel bombing in Greene County, Colorado, just north of Colorado Springs."

Varick was on his feet in no time. "Objection, Your Honor. Irrelevant."

Judge Lomax turned to me. "I assume that the relevance of this information will become apparent in a reasonable amount of time, Mr. Carpenter?"

I swallowed. I had absolutely no idea. "I believe so, Your Honor."

"Very well," the judge said. "Continue."

Now all eyes turned to the witness for his extremely anticlimactic answer. "No, I'm not familiar with any John Doe situation in Greene County two days before the tunnel blew," he said. "Of course, just because I didn't hear about it, doesn't mean there wasn't a John Doe up there."

That was fair enough. Unfortunately, as far as I could see, as A.D.A. Varick had pointed out, it was also completely irrelevant to this trial. I tried to stall by flipping over a page on the legal pad sitting in front of me on the table. I sensed that my client, sitting to my left, could see that it was blank. Finally, my cue came. "The body was autopsied by the medical examiner's office."

I was painfully aware of how much time had passed between the end of the witness's answer and my next question, so I started talking a little bit before my brain had completely formulated the appropriate question. "Um, the body was autopsied . . . so you are unaware of the fact that this unidentified individual, the corpse of this John Doe, was autopsied by the medical examiner's office?"

Captain Francona did not try to hide his confusion. "No, sir. Obviously, if I didn't know that there was a John Doe, I didn't know that he had been autopsied."

Even experienced courtroom lawyers occasionally look silly as they're conducting cross-examination. A witness takes a left turn when they're expecting a right, and suddenly, their entire line of inquiry, and sometimes their entire case, gets blindsided.

I was far from an experienced courtroom lawyer, and I was being fed my lines by a non-attorney, on the fly. "Silly" didn't begin to cover how I was looking at that moment.

"Ask him if he has Cruz's fingerprints."

I sighed, and considered telling the judge I was done. It sure sounded like Beta didn't have anything worth saying, and I really didn't feel like making a mockery out of the system I held so dear.

"Ask him, Counselor. In about two minutes, this whole thing is going to go nuclear. Innocent people's lives are on the line, and I can't save them without you. Just ask him about the damn fingerprints."

Judge Lomax was losing patience. "Mr. Carpenter?"

I came out from behind the table. "Sorry, Judge." I turned to the witness. "Sir, did Esteban Cruz have a criminal record, to your knowledge?"

Francona was caught off guard by my question, and blinked. "No. As a matter of fact, we checked that out after we spoke to his employer. But no. He wasn't in the state system, or the federal system. No warrants from other states, no arrests, nothing."

The voice in my ear began to say something, but I talked over it.

"I see. So then, you have no fingerprint records for Mr. Cruz?"

By this time, I had an inkling where this was going. I didn't believe it, and I didn't like it, but until I found out more, I was going to play along with Beta's theory.

"That's right. We had no fingerprint records."

I pressed on. "So then when you searched Cruz's apartment, you didn't dust for prints, correct?"

"That's correct," the witness responded. "We were not looking for evidence as to whether Mr. Cruz had been in his apartment. We were not looking for his fingerprints."

I was in something of a rhythm, even though I now knew I was going to end my time in the spotlight far before I achieved anything significant. "And naturally, you did not attempt to retrieve DNA samples from the apartment, correct?"

"That's correct. That's not why we were there."

"And because the tanker truck had been so thoroughly incinerated, there was no ability to take fingerprints or DNA samples from the inside of the driver's compartment, correct?"

Again, the witness confirmed my statement.

"There were no surveillance cameras pointed at vehicles entering the tunnel other than the one that recorded the tape we just recently viewed. Isn't that correct?"

"That's correct."

And with that, sadly, my rather modest mission was complete. I have to admit that I was disappointed. The secret earpiece and Beta's clandestine communications had suckered me—or at least the very naive and competitive part of me—into believing that I was about to uncover some pivotal fact, some vital information, that would have a significant impact on the trial. Instead, my elaborate cloak-and-dagger two-step with Beta the Bathroom Assailant had led only to the presentation of the most facile, transparent, and frankly, lame attempt to create reasonable doubt in the jurors' minds.

The argument was supposed to go like this: Ladies and gentlemen of the jury. In order to find my client guilty, you must find that he committed these crimes beyond a reasonable doubt. You have evidence that an unidentified individual died two days before the Denver Tunnel Bombing. An autopsy was done, fingerprints and DNA samples were taken. The prosecution wants you to believe that Esteban Cruz was the driver of the truck that caused the explosion in the tunnel, but they have no direct proof that he was the driver. And they have no DNA or fingerprints of Mr. Cruz, so we cannot rule out that he, in fact, was the John Doe who died two days before the bombing. Since there is a reasonable doubt that Esteban Cruz was responsible for the Denver Tunnel Bombing, you must find my client not guilty.

I took a deep breath, and returned to my place behind the defense table. "I have—"

"*Don't say anything yet,*" my invisible companion said. "*But go ahead and sit down.*"

I'm not sure why I rebelled at that point. Maybe I was just tired of being threatened, of following orders from someone I really didn't trust. Or maybe I was just frustrated with myself at believing the implication that something important was coming, when Beta so dramatically said, *It's time to make some noise.*

But I had had enough. I said, "I have nothing further, Your Honor," and I sat down.

As the judge thanked the witness, Beta said, *"I can't believe you did that, you idiot. Reach under the table. Get the envelope I taped there."*

Cliff said that even though the camera was located behind me, he could see that at that point, I was disgusted. I looked off to the left, shaking my head, and then I reached under the table.

One part of me didn't believe there would be anything there. The other part believed there would be an envelope, but that it would contain nothing of significance.

In a matter of seconds, I learned that neither part of me was right.

While Oswald Francona got up and left the witness stand, I awkwardly reached under the table and sure enough, I felt something taped there. I pulled the large manila envelope onto the table in front of me, removed the single sheet of paper contained within it, and immediately stood up.

"I apologize, Your Honor, but I have one more question of the witness." Judge Lomax looked at me hard. "With the court's indulgence," I added, somewhat meekly.

"Very well," he said, gravely. His tone indicated without much doubt that I had just used up whatever indulgences I was going to receive.

By this time, Captain Francona was halfway up the aisle of the courtroom, so it took him a minute to return to the witness stand.

"You are still under oath, sir," Judge Lomax reminded him.

And with that, I approached the witness, and handed him the piece of paper I'd received from Beta. Then I asked, "If Esteban Cruz truly was the driver of the gasoline truck that ignited the explosion in the Marion Perkins Tunnel in Denver, and his body was entirely cremated by the resulting fire, then how is it that he appears in this autopsy photo taken of his corpse two days *before* the Denver Tunnel Bombing?"

TWENTY

THE PICTURE was unambiguous. It was Esteban Cruz, right down to the oval birthmark, lying there, dead, on an autopsy slab. The photo had been certified by the Greene County Medical Examiner as taken on May 14, two full days before the Denver Tunnel Bombing.

Preston Varick was apoplectic. "Objection, Your Honor!" he shouted, jumping up from his seat. "I have never seen this picture, and I have no way of knowing of its authenticity. This entire thing is an outrageous stunt designed to confuse the jury and obfuscate the facts in this case."

I rather thought that was an overstatement, but I certainly could understand why Preston was so upset. Right there, in front of the jury and everyone watching television all over the country, reasonable doubt had just kicked open the door to the courtroom, and it looked like he was planning to stay, at least for a little while.

By now, the entire gallery was buzzing. Sarge got up

from his seat with a strange look on his face, just as Judge Lomax said, in a loud voice, "If this room is not silent immediately, I will instruct the court officers to clear the room."

That quieted everyone down.

Captain Francona was sitting there in the witness chair, staring at the photograph, apparently dumbstruck. Preston Varick was standing behind his table, in a state Amy likes to describe as "emotionally vibrant." Cliff told me later that it looked like if you had plucked the man you'd have heard a high E-flat.

And the jury was absolutely rapt. Most of their faces were frozen in shock. The grad student sat there with his mouth actually hanging open.

"I think this would be a good time to excuse the jury," Judge Lomax said, turning to them. "Ladies and gentlemen, I expect that this objection will require some discussion between myself and the attorneys. You are instructed not to speak about this latest development, nor about any other aspect of the trial, with anyone, including amongst yourselves."

Sarge called out, "All rise," and we stood up, as Mike led the jurors out of the room through a door near the end of the jury box.

When they had left, we all sat down. Except for A.D.A. Varick, who looked like he might not ever move again.

Judge Lomax turned to me, and said, "Mr. Carpenter. A.D.A. Varick has not seen this photograph before."

I stood. "That's right, Your Honor. I just learned today of the existence of this picture."

Preston made a noise of disbelief.

"I see," the judge continued. "Do you intend to enter it as an exhibit?"

"Yes, Your Honor."

"With the necessary foundation, I assume. Do you anticipate calling the medical examiner as a witness?"

Anytime a party wishes to introduce a photograph as evidence in a trial, they are required to present a foundation—that is, the testimony of an individual confirming that the photograph is a fair and accurate representation of what appears in the photograph.

"Yes, Your Honor, I do." Of course I hadn't, five minutes earlier. But now that I did, I had no idea how I was going to find him. Until the electronic voice in my ear said, "Damn right you intend to call him. I made sure he went into hiding, yesterday, but we can get him here if you need him."

To Beta, it sounded like placing people in hiding was a commonplace event. To me, the fact that a county official had to fear for his life as a result of his involvement in this case was the latest in a series of considerably alarming discoveries delivered by my electronic prompter.

"I have no idea who this mystery witness is," complained the assistant district attorney. "How can I possibly prepare my cross-examination if I don't know the first thing about the witnesses the defense intends to call? I again object to this entire line of questioning, Your Honor. Justice is not served by allowing the defense to pull off these last-minute tricks and theatrics to cloud a process so important to the hundreds and thousands of victims and survivors."

If anyone was being theatrical, I thought it was Preston himself. But I didn't think it was particularly seemly to point that out at the moment.

Judge Lomax looked back and forth between us, and then at the clock on the courtroom wall above the empty jury box. "It is now twenty minutes to four. I think that given the circumstances, we will all be best served by recessing until Monday morning. Mr. Carpenter, you will deliver the necessary information regarding this witness to Mr. Varick when we reconvene at that time. And, Mr. Varick, after you have finished presenting your case, if Mr. Carpenter calls the witness, I will make sure that you have adequate time to prepare your cross." He looked back at me, pointedly. "Is there anything else before we break today?"

I couldn't tell if the judge was prompting me. The only thing I could think of was a long shot, but I really couldn't see the downside of trying. "Yes, Your Honor. At this time, I'd like to move that the court dismiss the charges against Mr. Gomez, with prejudice."

"Oh, snap," said my client, sitting to my left.

"I don't know how or why it happened, but this entire case has been built against my client based, in large part, I believe, on the fact that a man named Esteban Cruz was the Denver Tunnel Bomber. We now know that Mr. Cruz was dead at least forty-eight hours before the bombing occurred."

Once again, the murmuring in the gallery behind me began to grow. Sarge stood up, and the judge looked out past us. The noise subsided.

Preston cut in before I had finished. "Judge, this is preposterous. He's as much as moving for a directed verdict before I've even had a chance to present our entire case against the defendant. I object."

Judge Lomax faced me. "Are you now moving for a directed verdict of not guilty, Mr. Carpenter?"

"No, Your Honor, I'm not. I'm moving for a dismissal of the charges against the defendant on grounds that the prosecution brought a case against my client when one of the fundamental facts supporting their theory of the case was false."

I was tiptoeing around an issue that was one of the

dirty little secrets of criminal law: prosecutorial misconduct.

Sometimes, in their zeal to convict defendants, prosecutors went too far. They coached witnesses to lie, they manufactured inculpatory evidence, they withheld exculpatory evidence. They did what they had to, in order to get the verdict they felt their job demanded.

On the rare occasions that such prosecutors were caught, courts had the power to dismiss the charges against the defendant, *irrespective of guilt*, as a sanction. It was a sort of punishment given to the district attorney's office.

The problem, of course, was that such sanctions were, in essence, the jurisprudential equivalent of cutting off your nose to spite your face. Most defendants got charged with crimes because they committed crimes. If courts dismissed charges against guilty defendants, it was, in effect, an attempt to address one injustice by creating another.

But as Juan Gomez's advocate, I had to leave those considerations to the judge. It was my job to make the motion, and let the chips fall wherever. To tell the truth, at the beginning of that day, I fully believed that Juan Gomez was deeply involved in the planning of the Denver Tunnel Bombing. At quarter to four that afternoon, I still thought so, but I was somewhat less certain. If the state could have gotten the Esteban Cruz thing wrong, couldn't they have gotten the case against my guy wrong, too?

"Are you claiming that the prosecution intentionally presented misleading testimony concerning Mr. Cruz's involvement in this matter?" Judge Lomax knew his stuff. He didn't have any authority to dismiss the case unless he found that the prosecution's misstep was intentional.

"No, Your Honor," I said.

"You should have said yes," Beta suggested.

"I don't have any knowledge of intent," I continued, drowning out the voice in my ear. "But this case has been developed after months of investigation. If the prosecution is so negligent in preparing its presentation of the facts that it misidentifies one of the key figures in its theory of the defendant's guilt, then it should be held accountable for such negligence."

Juan Gomez was getting into it. "Seriously," he said, under his breath.

The judge turned to Preston. "Mr. Varick?"

The assistant district attorney was barely keeping himself under control. He was palpably enraged. "I don't think I've ever heard anything so unprofessional in my entire career," he said, teeth clenched. "This defendant is a mass-murdering monster. And now his attorney has the gall to suggest that because of a so-called mistake—I have no idea whether that photograph is authentic or a fake, Your Honor, so I do not concede any mistake at all—his client should go scot-free. That is the most appalling request I've ever heard."

Judge Lomax made a notation on a piece of paper before him, and then looked back out at us. "I'm going to deny the defendant's motion to dismiss the charges at this time. There is no claim of intentional prosecutorial misconduct. But, Mr. Varick," he continued, "I'm quite disturbed at this development. Given the national tragedy underlying this case, it is paramount that we all conduct this trial in the most professional and transparent of manners. As you just mentioned, hundreds and thousands of victims and survivors are looking to this trial as a part of the long process of healing. Absence of truth will only prolong the suffering of the people and the country.

"Court is in recess until nine o'clock, Monday morning."

We all stood until the judge left the room. When the door closed behind him, the courtroom erupted in conversation. Juan Gomez patted me on the shoulder and said, "Good job, man. You're some lawyer. I like you. You're doing a great job." And then Mike led him away.

A.D.A. Varick packed his briefcase, then lifted it off the table, and looked up at the television camera. The red light was off. For the first time since I'd been assigned to the case, he came over to speak to me. His face was florid. A single droplet of sweat had run from his hairline down his left cheek. He was breathing audibly.

In short, he was furious.

"That was some stunt you just pulled, *Counselor*," he hissed, leaning on the last word as if it were an insult. "Remember who you're representing here, friend. I'd watch myself if I were you."

And before I could even think of a response, he turned on his heel, and stalked through the gallery, toward the exit.

But Varick's nasty outburst was just a pebble in the avalanche of thoughts and questions raining down on me. Who was Beta? Was that photo real? If it was, how did he get hold of it? And how did he get access to the courtroom to tape it to the bottom of my table and set me up with the earpiece?

I slowly packed up, and headed out of the courtroom. I was really looking forward to the weekend. I needed to get home and move my father to someplace safe. The veiled threats circling above my head like dark vultures had no place in his life.

Then I needed to find a way to get some distance

from this case. I'd contact Cliff, and Amy, and try to spend some time with them.

But just as I reached the door to the hallway, I heard one last thing come through my earpiece. It was a series of loud pops, like gunfire, then there was a crash, and then Beta shouted in my ear, *"Shit! They found me. You're on your own, Carpenter. Watch out for Landry."*

And then there was silence.

TWENTY-ONE

BETA'S FINAL communication added to my bewilderment. Were those pops really gunshots? And if he was being shot at, who was doing the shooting? Where were Kappa and Gamma? And when had I *not* been on my own in this mess?

I left the courtroom and turned toward the main lobby, intending to take the elevator down to the garage. Even if I happened to run into Landry down there, I didn't think he was going to do anything here in the courthouse. And I was willing to endure whatever he had to say if it kept me out of the media maelstrom sure to be hovering just outside the courthouse doors.

But the press had caught on to my games, and as soon as I emerged from the courtroom, they came at me from both sides. Landry was nowhere in sight. Before I knew it, I was literally surrounded by reporters shouting questions, sticking microphones in my face, and filming the whole chaotic mess.

For me, there was nothing to do but say, "Excuse me, please," and move slowly through them all toward the exit. I had no desire to answer any of their questions, despite Cliff's admonition to use my fifteen minutes of fame to drum up business for myself. I had learned from my first press conference that I wasn't at my best in front of a bank of microphones, and I was fine with that.

It took me about ten minutes to make my way through to the door, and another five to get down the steps without killing myself or the relentless film crews that swirled around me like large, technologically advanced pests. Finally, I made it to the sidewalk, followed only by one woman who kept shouting questions at me. It was possible that she thought I'd answer her in some kind of acknowledgment of her persistence.

If so, she learned that she was wrong as I entered my truck. I fired up the engine, and pulled out of the parking garage, leaving her there, writing something on a pad.

When I reached the highway, traffic was a little lighter than I expected, and I got about halfway to Payson's Ridge in only a half hour. I used the time to decompress—I was going to call Cliff and Amy, but I needed to stop and get out of range of Landry's bug before I did. Even if Beta hadn't shouted out that last warning about Landry, I still didn't trust anyone. I assumed that everything that was said over my phone lines was being listened to.

I pulled off at a truck stop in Black Creek Canyon, but before I had a chance to call, my own cell phone rang. I answered it, and the speaker on the other end didn't even bother to identify himself before he began speaking.

"I thought we had an understanding."

It was Landry.

"I'm sorry?"

"We spoke yesterday, and I thought I made it clear to you that if you gave the prosecution a hard time, it was going to be very difficult to protect your family. Especially your father."

His voice was cold.

"What are you saying?" I asked.

"I told you yesterday that threats were made, and that I feared for your disabled father, didn't I? And I told you that if you challenged evidence in this case that we all know is true, I didn't know what was going to happen."

I knew for a fact that Landry had not said that, but he didn't sound like he was interested in my memory of our conversation.

"Now you've really done it, Counselor. You've started something serious. Something I can't control, and something you sure as hell can't control. I'm sorry. I'm very sorry. But there's nothing I can do for you now. You're the one who decided to defend that scumbag terrorist, Gomez. And you stepped over the line today, and now you're gonna pay the price. Or I should say, your father is."

The hairs on the back of my neck were standing up. He wasn't sorry about anything. I started up my pickup and sped onto the entrance ramp to the highway. I had to get home immediately. I couldn't keep the anger out of my voice. "Are you threatening my father?"

The sadistic monster laughed. "I warned you again and again, and now *you're* taking a tone with *me*? Who do you think you're dealing with, Tom? You're not just talking to a state cop, stupid. This thing is so much bigger than you can imagine. I was right there for you, ready to help you get through it. But instead, what did you do? You ignored me. And now your father's gonna get hurt."

By now, I was going seventy-five. The speed limit was fifty-five, but I was probably fifteen minutes from home. I knew that if I got pulled over I wouldn't be able to help Henley, but I was afraid that if I didn't get there soon, it wasn't going to matter. "What did you do to him, you psychopath?"

Landry laughed again. He was enjoying this. "Let's just say it's a damn shame that the entire fire department was called away on a national security emergency about an hour ago. And that all the phone lines around your house are down. And that Henley's not in his wheelchair."

By now, so much adrenaline was pumping through my system that my teeth were chattering. I was going eighty-five, and I was still over ten minutes away. "If anything happens to him—"

"Oh, I remember," Landry interrupted. Then, in a mocking voice, he threw my own words back in my face. "If anything happens to your father, you're going to come looking for me. Good luck with that plan, tough guy."

I was going so fast I almost sailed right past my exit. I slammed on the brakes, and hit the ramp at sixty. I barely kept the truck on the road as it curved around to merge onto the state highway that would take me home.

"What have you done with Liana?" I asked, as I straightened out and pushed the speedometer back up over sixty-five. I was now on a two-lane road, speed limit forty.

"Don't worry about her," Landry said. "She got called away on an emergency of her own. You've got enough on your plate with your father. In fact, I'm gonna let you go now, 'cause you're going to be busy for a few days, taking care of the, you know, arrangements."

I didn't want to keep talking to him, but I didn't

want to give up the contact, either. Somehow, as long as I was on the phone with him, I felt like I had at least some input into the situation. Without that, I had nothing but my fear.

"Wait—" I said, but the connection went dead.

I needed to call Amy, but I was certain that even if I got rid of Landry's panic button/listening device, there was another bug planted somewhere in the truck. I didn't have time to stop. I had to get to my father.

When I reached the steepest part of the climb, near where we lived up at the top of Payson's Ridge, I had to slow down. The roads were so narrow that if I took them at more than forty-five, fifty at the most, I'd have run too great a risk of totaling the truck, and never making it to my father.

My imagination was a blur of horrendous possibilities, all featuring my incapacitated father as the victim of a homicidal maniac.

When my parents had lovingly chosen this remote hilltop, they, of course, had no idea that by isolating themselves so completely, they would be making it that much harder for me to get up there today. They were relying on what we all take for granted—fire and police departments that are not under the control of some crazed psycho who has the power to divert them from the community that really needs them.

Just before I made the last turn I tried to figure out who could possibly have enough power to make our entire emergency service support system disappear. But then I came around a curve in the road, and finally saw how bad it was.

From the bottom of the driveway, the trees were so thick that you couldn't actually see the house. But rising above the trees, against the beautiful blue sky, I saw something which made all of my catastrophic imaginings laughably benign.

A thick plume of black smoke, like the putrid exhaust from hell's darkest furnace.

Our house was on fire.

TWENTY-TWO

THE BUILDING was fully ablaze as I skidded to a stop at the end of the driveway and jumped out of my car. As Landry had promised, there was no sign of Liana, and no one else was there to help. No cops, no EMTs, no firefighters, no approaching sirens. I was on my own.

There was no way to know that my father was in there, but I had to assume he was. The van was in the driveway—also on fire. And it would have been difficult to transport him in any other vehicle.

The porch and front door were completely engaged in the fire. I couldn't possibly get in that way, so I ran around to the back of the house. All I could see through the windows was smoke and the flickering lights of flame. The building was a wood-framed structure. So much of the outside walls was engulfed in the fire that there was no obvious way in. And the metal bulkhead doors to the cellar were locked.

The blaze was throwing off a tremendous amount of

heat. It was hard just to stand within twenty-five feet of the place, much less run toward it.

And then I noticed that there was one spot, at the back of the house, near the kitchen, where it wasn't quite as hot. At first, I couldn't understand why, and then it came to me. The floor was tiled, the walls were tiled, and the countertops were granite. The fire probably hadn't spread into that area of our home yet.

With no training and less time, I determined to enter the house through the kitchen.

But the only way in was through the windows above the sink, and they were locked.

I ran to the woodpile, grabbed my ax, and ran back to the house. I heard a crash from inside, and then saw a flare of light through the window, which only served to illuminate just how dark it was in there. Smoke was everywhere. Even in the air outside the house it was tough to get a good breath.

I wondered how my father could possibly be alive if he was in there, but that didn't stop me from dragging our picnic table over to the house, climbing up, and breaking a window. Smoke began to pour out as I used the ax to clear away the shards of glass, and then I reached in to undo the lock. I didn't think to check if it was too hot to touch. Luckily, it wasn't.

I slid open the window, and shouted, "Dad! Henley! Are you in there?"

I listened intently through the crackle and the rushing of the air of the inferno for a response. There was nothing. Of course, it was too much to hope for. If by some miracle Henley was even alive, there was no way he could possibly be conscious with all of this smoke. I remember frantically shouting my father's name and at the same time recalling, with no small amount of self-loathing, that fifty to eighty percent of people who die in fires die from smoke inhalation, not from burns.

And then I heard it. A bell. And then it rang again. And then repeatedly—insistently.

Henley was ringing his bell.

You didn't need any special training in languages to translate that conversation:

ME: *Henley, are you in there?*
DAD: *Hell, yes. Get me out of here.*

Somehow, my father was *alive*.

In no time I had tossed the ax into the kitchen, climbed through the window, and tumbled into the sink. Later I would learn that I had cut both hands and one knee on the broken glass while scrambling in, but all I was thinking about, as I bent down to pick up my ax, was getting into the living room. That's where I thought I'd heard the bell.

There were, however, a few problems with that plan.

First, when I jumped down from the sink, the inside of the house was so hot, I was having trouble even orienting myself toward the living room. The skin on my face felt like it was going to burn right off. But more important, the smoke was so thick that even when I managed to force open my eyes, I could see almost nothing.

And then I made my biggest mistake—I inhaled.

Suddenly, the urge to cough overcame me, which led to more coughing, and more inhaling smoke. By now, my eyes were stinging so severely that they were tearing up. I had started partially deaf, but thanks to the fire, I was now mostly blind.

And choking.

It was only going to get worse, so I threw my arm

across my mouth and nose to protect my face from the heat. I was also hoping that it might provide some kind of filter for the smoke I was continuing to inhale, but I kept coughing. With every breath that I gasped, I felt like I was searing the inside of my chest.

I surged forward in the direction of the living room, my lungs inflamed, my eyes slit open but of almost no use at all, my left arm across my face, and my right hand holding the ax. The temperature was so high it felt like my entire body was getting badly sunburned all at once, especially those parts of my skin that weren't covered with clothing.

As I staggered forward, I also realized that I was getting dizzy from lack of oxygen. Every inhale was a lungful of hot smoke, every exhale a scorching cough.

I lost my balance, and fell forward onto my hands and knees. It was dumb luck that I didn't tumble onto the flaming Oriental rug that was about three feet to my right on the floor. Even though this part of the wood floor had not yet been immolated, it was still plenty hot.

Down on the ground I realized that the smoke was slightly less dense, and I thought I saw the wheel of Henley's chair. Unfortunately, though, it didn't seem to matter. All I was able to do was cough. I tried to crawl toward the chair, but my brain was so lacking in oxygen that the smallest increment of progress only led to more dizziness. I reached forward to grab the wheelchair and lost my balance so badly that I actually tipped over onto my side, my arm still extended pathetically.

Just then, I was startled by the sensation of someone grabbing my outstretched hand and pulling. Pulling hard. Actually dragging me.

And then whoever it was let go of my hand, and grabbed hold of my shirt, and pulled me even farther. And I was surprised to find my face in contact with something far less hot than the wood floor of the living room.

My sizzled brain couldn't make sense of it. I couldn't have been dragged onto the tile floor of the bathroom. I hadn't made it that far into the house. And I was heading away from the kitchen when I fell. There was no way I was on those tiles.

And then I felt a wet, rubbery thing being pushed into my coughing mouth, and I felt something cool and sweet. Real air. No smoke.

I couldn't understand it. But I didn't care. Between skull-racking coughs I gulped a breath of fresh air, and then another. And then the tube was withdrawn.

I tried to hold my breath until the tube came back, and when it did, I greedily sucked in more oxygen. My brain was slowly coming back on line, and I squinted my eyes open just enough to see that I was lying partially on the hearth, next to Henley, who was alternating the life-giving tube of fresh air between us. I scrambled forward until I was lying directly beside him.

How the hell was he doing this? Another breath, and the coughing subsided enough for me to take another quick look. He had fed a length of exercise tubing into the flue of the wood-burning stove, and out through the exhaust vent in the wall. We were breathing the outside air.

Landry, or whoever the thugs were that had done this, must have thrown Henley off of his chair and onto the ground, lit the place on fire, and then left him to die. He'd had the presence of mind to drag himself over to the one place in the house that was designed not to be flammable: the enlarged hearth around the wood-stove he loved so much.

As we got into a rhythm, trading the air supply back and forth, my mental faculties returned to me fully, and

I became acutely aware of how little time we had. The temperature was beyond dangerous, and the fire had done so much damage that now embers and small pieces of wood were falling down all around us. It was only a matter of time before the roof, ceiling, or floor collapsed.

I took a long hit from the oxygen, passed the tube to Henley, and wheezed, "We've got to get out of here. I'm going to carry you." I waited to inhale again until he passed the tube to me. As he held his breath, he grabbed my hand, and pulled it down toward his leg. I shifted my focus in that direction, and then I saw what Henley wanted me to see. Someone had handcuffed his ankle to his wheelchair.

I nodded, passed the tube back to him, and said, "Stay still. I'll take care of it."

I remained low, dragging myself along the hearth, pushing the ax in front of me, until I was close enough to get a good look. The way the restraint was used, the chain that linked the cuffs was resting on the floor. Perfect.

I got up onto my knees, pulled the ax over my head, and brought it down, hard, on the chain, breaking it cleanly.

Then I slithered back next to Henley, leaving the ax behind. I wouldn't be able to hold on to it while I was carrying Henley. He gave me the tube, and I inhaled fully. Then I returned it to him and said, "Take a good long breath, and hold it."

He did, then I took one more. And then he hooked his left arm around my neck, and I slid my arms underneath his shoulder blades and his knees, and hoisted him up.

At ground level, the smoke was almost bearable. Standing, it was so thick I was effectively blind. But I had a good breath of air filling my lungs, and my father was counting on me. I was going to get us out of here whatever it took.

Which, in this instance, meant plunging forward into the blinding black smoke.

Unfortunately, the fire had cut down my options. The front door and porch were engulfed in flame, as were the back door and deck. Henley's condition and the design of the house made it far too dangerous for me to drop him out of a window, and I obviously had no time to try to fashion a harness of some kind and lower him to the ground.

For a second, I thought about trying to get back outside the way I'd come in, but just then, a giant ceiling beam dropped down into the middle of the kitchen, cutting us off from that exit.

I could only think of one more way out. With the last of my strength and breath I stumbled into the hallway toward the back of the house, and opened the doorway on the right. The one that led to the basement.

I half expected to be greeted with a blast of hellish air, or even a curtain of fire, but it turned out that the blaze hadn't had a chance to do as much damage to this part of the house yet. The air was much cooler than it was in the living room, and it was also relatively smoke-free. As quickly as I could, I lumbered down the stairs with Henley in my arms. The stairway was narrow, though, and part of the way down, I slipped, and lurched to the side, banging Henley's paralyzed right arm and shoulder hard against the stone wall. He inhaled sharply.

Among the difficult realities I had come to discover after my father's hospitalization was that even if a stroke victim loses the ability to move certain parts of his body, those paralyzed limbs do not lose sensation. It's like the worst of both worlds. You can't move your arm, but it can still feel pain.

Of course, that quick breath Henley took as we smashed into the rocks was the most he'd ever complain. But I knew right then that if we managed to get out of this mess, I'd find a nasty bruise when I had a chance to inspect that shoulder.

When we finally made it to the bottom of the cellar steps, it became immediately clear that our situation was only temporarily improved. Already, the fire had burned through parts of the flooring above us, and glowing red embers were falling down around us. Smoke was beginning to poison the basement air.

Then, as if in a bad dream, flames dove down through a hole above us that had been created by the fire, and raced along one of the beams supporting the living room floor. Then there was a crash above us—probably some part of the second floor coming down into the first floor. It would only be a very short time before the house collapsed on top of us.

I ran over to the bulkhead, but I had to put Henley down for a minute to use both hands to unlock and push open the doors. The bright sunshine that poured through the opening into the basement seemed like it was coming from a different universe. But I didn't have time to admire it. I had to get Henley and get out.

I knelt down, and once again, Henley looped his good left arm around my neck. I slid one arm under his knees and the other around his back, and hoisted. I had just made it to the first step when another crash sounded from above, and then, a much bigger sound, a rumbling, crackling roar, came to my ears.

As fast as I could I struggled up the steps with my most valuable cargo, emerging from the bulkhead just as I heard a tremendous crash behind me in the basement. The house was beginning to fall in on itself. I ran away from the structure toward my woodpile, hoping to reach the trees beyond for some shelter.

The roaring continued, and I could have sworn that even though I was running away from the house, the temperature of the air on my neck and back was rising. Halfway to the woodpile I heard another huge crash, and finally, I lumbered past the chopped wood and into the thicket beyond, where I fell to my knees on some pine needles, and let my father down.

I turned back just in time to see the final section of the roof smash down onto the second floor, with a gigantic shower of sparks and flames, and then the entire structure collapsed into its center, as if being sucked down into Hades itself.

A wave of hot air passed over us, and then the air cooled slightly. We were well over one hundred feet away, partially blocked from the intense heat by the woodpile and some trees. I turned to Henley, who was pushing himself up to a sitting position with his good hand. As if anyone cared, he began wiping at a dirty smudge on his right sleeve where we'd crashed into the wall on the way down the basement stairs.

I took a deep breath. My chest still burned, and I was still coughing, but I was going to be fine. I turned to the inferno that had been my home. Still no fire department, no sirens, no response at all. Even though Henley and I had survived, it was abundantly clear that we were in some considerable trouble here.

I used my old cell phone to call Cliff, and make a plan.

When I was done, I called Amy. I said simply, "It's the end of the world."

Then I got Henley into the truck, and took off.

TWENTY-THREE

CACTUS CURT'S Steakhouse opened in 1977 as a tourist attraction, and over the next thirty years, evolved into one of the best restaurants for mesquite-grilled steak that I know, provided you respect the dress code.

To my niece Erica, Cactus Curt's was unsurpassed in every way. She gobbled up the food—steak, salad, and beans were the only things on the menu—but what she really loved was the ambiance.

To enforce the casual atmosphere of the place, the patrons all sit at picnic tables. And everyone on the waitstaff is equipped with scissors, because any customer wearing a necktie has it unceremoniously snipped off under the knot and the severed portion literally stapled to the walls, already festooned with thousands of prior transgressors.

And anyone ordering their steak well-done receives instead a boot on a plate when dinner is served.

Each time I went with Erica and Amy, I wore a garish tie, pretending to forget the consequences. Erica positively quivered with anticipation as the inescapable confrontation with the waitress approached, and howled with glee when the offending cravat was chopped off.

Then, I would order my steak well-done, solemnly explaining to my little niece that I had been told that the management had changed their policy, or that I had spoken to the maitre d', or that I read in the newspaper that the restaurant no longer embarrassed their diners by serving them a boot on a plate.

When I was inevitably proven wrong, my mock confusion and outrage simply heightened Erica's delight. And for the rest of the night, the sight of my artificially shortened neckwear would start her giggling again.

And all that took place *after* the Wild West show.

We always timed our arrival so that we'd get a good spot along Main Street, Cowboy Town, a faux Old West movie set constructed between the parking area and the restaurant. Twice per night, at five-thirty and six forty-five, a desperate shoot-out takes place between brave Sheriff Goodheart and the Barton Gang, five gun-toting outlaws led by Mad Bill Barton, the notorious ax-murderer.

And for twenty minutes or so, six stuntmen run up and down the street shooting at each other, in and out of the entrances to the saloon, the jail, and the general store, hiding behind hitching posts, dying dramatically in water troughs and haystacks, and generally making a lot of noise and kicking up a lot of dust.

The finale is the big showdown between the sheriff and Mad Bill, on the third-floor balcony of the Golden Palace Hotel. Mad Bill, wielding a six-shooter, lies in wait behind a rocking chair. When Sheriff Goodheart emerges from the hotel onto the balcony, Mad Bill shoots him!

The sheriff falls, but he isn't dead yet, so Mad Bill

aims again, but luckily for our hero, the bad guy is out of bullets. Not so luckily for our hero, as you will recall, Mad Bill is an ax-murderer, and his trusty and bloody weapon just happens to be right there under the rocking chair. He raises it above his head to finish the sheriff off, when, miraculously, the sheriff finds the strength to fire one last shot. Mad Bill's homicidal career comes to an unforgettable end as he crashes through the balcony railing, and falls spectacularly into the wagon conveniently located directly below him.

To Erica, this was entertainment of the highest order. It was so much fun for me to watch her during the show and at dinner that I had asked Amy's permission to bring her there every day of her life.

Amy has gently reminded me that one of the reasons the experience is special is because it isn't a daily event. I know that she's right, of course. I just love seeing the joy in Erica's eyes, and knowing that I had something to do with putting it there. So we only eat at Cactus Curt's on evenings that Erica and I have designated as "Humongously Big Occasions."

That Friday night, of course, Henley and I were going to Cactus Curt's Steakhouse for a much different reason than to enjoy the cowboy extravaganza.

As we headed into the foothills surrounding Scottsdale, I filled my father in on everything that had happened, and the plans I'd made with Cliff. I was driving pretty aggressively, because I wanted to make the six forty-five show. That was the one that always had the bigger crowd. I hadn't been followed, but I assumed that Landry and company would be able to track down my truck. I had to get another vehicle, quickly, and secretly.

I pulled into the huge parking area, parking as close as I could to the throng standing on Main Street. We waited for the show to end, and as the crowd poured into the parking area, I called Cliff, and let him know where we were. Then I got Henley out of the car, and carried him into the middle of the mob.

Despite the streams of people swirling all around us, Cliff found us in less than one minute. He looked at me carefully, and said, "You really okay? You look a little like garbage."

"That's funny. I feel great."

He nodded, and said quickly, "Three rows back on the left, five cars in." Then he handed Henley a manila envelope, said, "Call me when you get there," and then walked past us.

I waited about ten seconds, then turned around and, shielded by the mass of people still buzzing about the shoot-out they'd just seen, walked back three rows, and found the fifth car on the left, and smiled.

Cliff had gotten me a yellow Volkswagen beetle. A turbo.

I put Henley into the passenger seat, and headed to our next destination—my home at the southwestern edge of the San Luis Navajo Indian Reservation.

Not that I'd ever lived there. In fact, the last time I'd even laid eyes on the place was about four years ago, some months after Henley had his stroke.

I'd gotten the house as a result of an unusual case I'd worked on, thanks to Cliff, and won, thanks to the arrogance or incompetence of Governor Hamilton.

The story went like this. Cliff's cousin, Miles, was a car mechanic, and usually a law-abiding, responsible employee. But he was also an alcoholic, and one night he fell off the wagon with considerable gusto, managing to hot-wire and drive around a succession of cars for no reason he can remember. The end result was serious property damage to a pickup truck and four automobiles, including the last one Miles stole—a yellow Volkswagen beetle turbo—which ended up lodged in the bushes directly in front of the Copper City Police Station. Miraculously, no one was physically injured except Miles, who was found passed out in the driver's seat, with two broken ribs.

Once incarcerated for his night of multiple felonies, Miles became a model prisoner, and soon began employment in what the Arizona Correctional System called "The Industries." These were jobs, like making license plates, that were designed to provide inmates with the opportunity to make a small amount of money so that when they were ultimately released from prison, they would have some savings. They were only paid one dollar per hour when Miles started, but the state legislature voted a twenty-five-cents-per-hour raise during Miles's second year in jail.

Coincidentally, that was the first year that Atlee Hamilton took over as governor. The law had been signed by his predecessor mere days before he left office, and was to take effect four months later.

It isn't exactly clear whether Hamilton did it intentionally or through an oversight, but four months after the law was signed, he did not take the steps necessary to give the inmates the raise.

Fast-forward six more months. Miles, who had been looking forward to the additional money, had written several futile letters requesting his pay increase. He finally called Cliff, to ask if there was something he could do about it. Cliff contacted the prison authorities, who informed him that due to budgetary restrictions, the raise had been put on indefinite hold. Cliff came to me, and convinced me to help him bring a class-action suit to recover the lost wages.

Interestingly, the state agreed that since there were

no facts in dispute, there was no need for a trial. The case was to be decided by a judge on cross motions for summary judgment. And a year and a half after the raise was supposed to happen, Superior Court Judge Wilma Tuggert awarded damages to the class of plaintiffs in the amount of $765,000.

You'd be surprised how quickly twenty-five cents per hour builds up when you've got a few thousand people working twenty and thirty hours per week.

Cliff and I were awarded attorney's fees of $155,000, which we decided to use to buy a secluded vacation house on the reservation that we could time-share. I asked Cliff to keep it solely in his name, because despite the fact that I won more appeals than the typical attorney, I still lost my share. And one of the occupational hazards of practicing criminal law is having dissatisfied clients sue you. I thought it was prudent to keep my assets modest. Legally, the place was all Cliff's. But I'd bet my life—in fact, as I drove my father there, I realized that I was betting more than just my life—that Cliff would always honor our agreement to share it.

And the house would work perfectly as a temporary hideout—it was tucked away in a remote corner of a sparsely populated Indian reservation. No one would find us there.

After Henley's stroke, I did some work on the place, both to spruce it up, and so that he could get around if we ever got a chance to use it. I put a fresh coat of red paint on the front door, then I replaced a pane of glass in one of the windows that bordered it. I built a ramp from the entrance down to the driveway, widened some of the interior doorways, and even bought a smaller and lighter backup wheelchair, because some of the hallways were a little tight for his usual one.

As I drove the final stretch of dirt road up to the

house, I realized that extra chair was going to come in very handy, since Henley's usual one had been incinerated.

When I arrived at the house, I was happy to see that Amy and Erica were already there, sitting in their car, waiting for us.

We all made our way into the wood-and-stone house, which, thankfully, was in better shape than I'd remembered. Cliff and Iris had obviously done some work of their own on the place. All the lightbulbs worked; the spiderwebs were small enough so that even Erica felt comfortable clearing them out of the corners with a broom; there was hot and cold running water; and the refrigerator actually contained items we could use: a gallon of water, a six-pack of soda, four beers, a bottle of ketchup, and a jar of olives.

The kitchen cabinets had some canned goods, as well.

We certainly were not overstocked, but for an emergency, this was not bad.

I got Henley situated in his new chair, and while he and Erica explored the bedrooms, Amy came over to me in the living room and took off the heavy backpack she had been wearing over her black sweatshirt. I couldn't imagine what was in there. She had always impressed on me the urgency of leaving quickly in an emergency, and I had no idea what she'd managed to pack before taking off.

She handed the bag to me, and said, "I hope nine thousand dollars is enough."

TWENTY-FOUR

I ZIPPED OPEN the backpack to find it stuffed with newspapers.

But below three copies of that day's *Arizona Herald,* I found approximately seven hundred ten- and twenty-dollar bills.

I had forgotten entirely about the money.

When we made the original "end of the world" plan, we decided that on her way to the rendezvous, Amy would stop at a bank, and get as much cash as she could out of the savings account she'd created with the life insurance proceeds she'd received from Dale's death. Apparently, anyone withdrawing ten thousand dollars or more in cash had to fill out forms that Amy didn't have time for, so she settled on nine thousand.

I hefted the bag onto my shoulder. "Wow. You're the greatest survivalist ever. If you hadn't remembered to get this, we'd be on the lam with a total of about thirty-five dollars. No, wait. I bought a sandwich for lunch. Twenty-nine dollars. Thanks."

"I can't even imagine what you've been through. Cliff called me. How's Henley?"

"Well, other than the fact that his house burned down, and he had to save my life before I almost dislocated his shoulder on the way out, he seems great."

She peered at my face closely, her blue-green eyes intent as she inspected the cuts. Then she reached up and gently touched my forehead above my left eyebrow. "You sure you're all right?"

"Cliff asked me the same question. I feel fine. What's the matter? Don't I look okay?"

She shook her head slightly, grabbed me by the elbow, brought me into the bathroom, and turned on the light. "See for yourself," she said.

I checked the mirror, and said, "Oh." I did not look my best.

First of all, my hair—never a particularly strong suit for me—was ridiculous. It had arranged itself into a part greaser, part madman look. My face was extravagantly streaked with black smears of soot. I was also sporting two rather impressive-looking gashes—one on the left side of my forehead, the other on my right cheek.

I touched them, and couldn't feel a thing. Either they were superficial, or the nerves in my face had temporarily shut down.

"Maybe I'll clean up a little," I offered. But before Amy left the bathroom, I asked quietly, "Hey. What did you tell Erica?"

Amy checked to be sure that the little girl was out of earshot. "I said we were having a special, instant vacation with you and her grandfather, because there was a fire at your house. She's so smart that I'm not sure she entirely buys it, but she's certainly willing to play along."

Then Amy left me alone.

I washed my hands and face, only to find that there

were no towels in the bathroom, so I left, dripping water liberally. I found my way back into the kitchen, hoping to find paper towels or napkins. There, Amy seemed to be heating something on the stove, although for the life of me, I couldn't guess what it was. When she saw me, face and hands soaking wet, she said, "Wait right there," and hurried off toward one of the bedrooms. Then she returned with a towel and two large packets of ten-dollar bills in her hands, and gave them to me.

"What am I going to do with all of this money?" I said, putting it on the counter, and wiping my face with the towel. She had placed a can of corn and a can of beans in a pan of water, which she had brought to a boil. "And how did you have time to pack a towel?"

"When you told me you thought it would be best if Erica and I didn't come over for a few days, I packed a couple of bags, just in case," she said. "I've never heard you sound so worried in my life. And you need to put that money in your pockets."

So much for reassuring Amy that everything was going to be fine.

I stuffed the bills into my jeans just before Henley and Erica returned to the living room. The little girl took her grandfather's left hand. "Grandpa says that his shoulder doesn't hurt so bad," she reported. "And he doesn't have his bell here, so we made up a new system. Whenever he wants to say yes, he will squeeze my hand. Right, Grandpa?"

Henley smiled his crooked half-smile, and obviously squeezed his granddaughter's hand. She beamed, and enthusiastically reported, "He says, 'Yes!'"

Amy then announced that dinner was ready, and we all sat down around the table in the dining area. Along with the corn and the beans, Amy opened up a few cans of tuna fish. We ate on paper plates, with plastic forks that Cliff and Iris had left behind from their last visit.

I had no idea how hungry I was until we started. The canned vegetables and fish turned out to be the most delicious dinner I had ever eaten.

And as I sat there with the three most important people in my life, sharing some hard candies Amy had found for dessert, I was surprised at my emotional state. Because despite the fact that I had just seen my home burn to the ground and my father nearly murdered, at that moment, I felt incredibly lucky.

Bedtime for Henley was more difficult than usual.

He was fine with the new surroundings in general. The problem was that I had not yet outfitted the house with the special things needed by people with disabilities, like grab bars at the toilet and the tub, and an easier bed to get into and out of.

Fortunately, the second bathroom—the one at the end of the house by Henley's bedroom—was equipped with towels and soap. Henley was much cleaner than I was after the fire, so all he needed was a sponge bath. The bruise on his right shoulder looked painful, but fortunately, the skin wasn't broken.

Our biggest challenges involved the toilet and bed, where we had to get a little acrobatic. Thank God the stroke had left my dad's sense of humor intact.

By the time I finished dealing with Henley, Amy had begun Erica's nighttime ritual. Although the process usually took somewhere in the neighborhood of a half hour, for Amy, the payoff was well worth it. After putting on pajamas, getting a drink of water, reading a bedtime story, going to the bathroom and brushing teeth, and discussing what would happen tomorrow, the little girl always fell asleep quickly and easily, and slept deeply all through the night.

I grabbed the opportunity to take a shower.

Before getting undressed, I removed the hearing aid from my right ear, and the listening device Beta had given to me from my left, and put them both on the edge of the sink. Then I stripped off my clothes, which had been ruined by the fire.

The little nicks I'd gotten in the blaze had begun to make themselves known by that time. There were a few cuts on one knee and some on my hands to go with the two on my face. Curiously, I seemed to have been spared any burns, with the exception of one on my forearm and one on my neck. It looked like a couple of embers might have burned through my jacket and shirt without my notice. But none of that stopped me from enthusiastically blasting myself with the hot water spray.

As tired as I was, a feeling of freedom began to build in me as I stood there, washing the last of the fire's grease and soot from my body. I was convinced that I had survived the worst of this experience. I wasn't willing to risk my father's life to defend Juan Gomez. There were other lawyers in Arizona. Someone else would be appointed to represent him—probably someone else much more qualified than I was.

And I was also sure that even if Amy and I had to take our family on the run for a short while, until the trial had blown over, we'd manage to find somewhere safe.

Obviously, I had no idea what was yet to come.

After I dried off, I threw on an extra T-shirt and pair of jeans that I'd left in the house the last time I'd worked there—the time I'd finished the wheelchair ramp to the front door. I had fully anticipated future carpentry trips to the place, but they never came to pass.

Henley hadn't recovered as quickly or as aggressively as I'd hoped. As it became more and more obvious that he was going to need months, if not years, of rehabilitative therapy, and would spend the rest of his life in considerable discomfort, I felt somewhat selfish spending a lot of time away from him, messing around with a second home, when all of his needs were being met in the house on Payson's Ridge.

As I came out of the bathroom and sat back on the decadently luxurious couch Cliff, Iris, and I had picked out on the day after we closed on the house, I began to question my decision. The rich wood paneling on the walls, the exposed beams running across the ceiling, the skylight view of the blue-black night sky and the full moon, were all powerful reminders of how much I loved this place.

And then Amy walked in.

She had changed out of her getaway black sweatshirt, sweatpants, and sneakers. She was barefoot and in jeans now. And she was wearing the blue-green shirt I'd given to her earlier that week.

"Hey," I said, stupidly. "You're wearing the shirt. Wow."

She sat down on the couch next to me, and looked down. "I know. Is that okay?"

Okay didn't even begin to cover it. Everything I had imagined about how the shirt would look on Amy had been swept away by a dazzling reality. The color of her already gorgeous eyes was now so vibrant that it was hard to look elsewhere. But that neckline literally demanded my attention, and from there, it was a very short trip to a very dangerous area that I could not afford to visit with my gaze, however briefly.

Yet of course, I did.

She didn't look just amazing—she looked stunning. Like some Hollywood movie star from the era of the great beauties. Grace Kelly in *Rear Window*. Ingrid Bergman in *Casablanca*. "Um," I said. She even smelled perfect. "I thought...I didn't think...You like it? I mean, I didn't expect you to wear it."

Again, she looked down, and then back up at me.

And then she did smile, and I was lost.

"But you told me to wear it, remember? When I found the person that I wanted to share the rest of my life with? That's why I put it on."

I graduated near the top of my class at Arizona State University. I went on to Stanford Law School, where I edited the law review. So I understood very well what Amy was saying. It's just that I still felt a loyalty to the relationship between Amy and my brother, even though he had died five years earlier. That loyalty had never allowed for even the possibility of Amy and me becoming lovers. The following idiotic statement was its last stand. "I don't know...I wonder...Is it right...You really did put it on, didn't you?"

As I uttered this nonsense, Amy moved closer to me on the couch. When I finished speaking, she punctuated my message with a firm, moist kiss on the lips. Now I was paralyzed *and* breathless. Pulling away approximately one inch, she proceeded to administer the coup de grace with a husky whisper directly into my mouth. "And I can take it off, too."

Then she leaned back, and with a devastatingly sexy glint in her eye, she did.

TWENTY-FIVE

THE SAN LUIS Navajo Indian Reservation is a vast territory which, predictably, principally comprises some of the most inhospitable desert and mountain terrain in central Arizona. By law, such reservations are under the jurisdiction of the sovereign Indian nations to which they were given, and law enforcement is handled by tribal police.

When Cliff was going to law school, he had been one of the youngest people ever to serve on the tribal counsel. His family still lived on the reservation, and he still had close ties with many of the tribal police.

I had asked Cliff to alert the people he knew to our presence at the house, at least until we had a chance to make longer-term plans. And even though I was sure we hadn't been followed, I also asked that they keep an eye out for any unusual or suspicious individuals or vehicles in the area.

So when I woke up the following morning, beside the woman I had finally and unexpectedly allowed myself to fully love, I felt safe enough to lie there quietly. I knew that we had many important decisions ahead of us, and that danger was just an ambush away. But for those few, unblemished moments, I just listened to a mockingbird sing to the new day, and watched as the rising sun's rays sliced through a narrow gap in the curtains and lit a sliver of the far wall.

Then I heard a creak near the entrance to the bedroom, and before I could react, the knob turned and the door opened.

It was Erica, wearing her very pink pajamas. She saw me before she saw her mother, burst into a big smile, and ran toward the bed. I tried to shush her, but she had already committed to a big entrance. "Hi, Sleepybones!" she said boisterously, reaching up to give me a hug.

That woke Amy up, and she turned over to reveal a truly glorious case of bed head. When Erica spotted her, the little girl laughed with delight. "Hi, Mommy!" she said, scampering around to the other side of the bed. "Look at your hair!"

Everything was unfolding so rapidly that the awkward moment I'd expected hadn't had a chance to arise. Before I knew it, Amy had hoisted Erica onto the mattress, and the little girl was crawling into position on top of the covers, between her mom and me. She rolled over so that the tip of her nose was touching mine. "Are you going to wake up now?" she asked me. "Is it time for breakfast?" I was just about to answer when she rolled in the other direction, facing Amy. "Mommy, are you going to marry Tom?"

I usually rise after a good night's sleep with my mind firing at a pretty respectable rpm. But Erica's entrance made it clear that I was fated to spend this morning staring stupidly at the conversation's receding taillights. "You'd like that, wouldn't you?" Amy countered, pulling her arm out from under the covers to brush a strand of hair off Erica's forehead.

A second later, an excited "Yes!" issued forth from the coral-colored dynamo that was suddenly scrambling toward our legs. A moment later, Erica was standing at the foot of the bed.

"And I'd also like breakfast, too, Mommy."

I happened to know that there was precious little to eat in the house. Cliff and Iris had left a loaf of bread in the freezer, though, and there were some spices and condiments in the kitchen cabinets.

"Um, I was thinking about some extraordinary cinnamon sugar toast, myself," I said, rising up on one elbow.

Erica gasped with delight. "Extraordinary cinnamon sugar toast? What's that?" She jumped up and down and clapped a few times, and then said, "I have to go to the bathroom," and bolted out of the room before I could answer.

"You know she'll be back in here in about thirty seconds, wondering if your extraordinary special cinnamon sugar toast is ready." Amy looked up at me with a sleepy gaze as I got out of bed and put on my clothes. Her hair was still a tower of dishevelment, but the morning did nothing to dull her beautiful eyes.

"I've got to get Henley up," I said. "It's probably going to take a little more than thirty seconds." I tied my shoes and then looked back up at her. The dam holding back all of the emotions that had been welling up in my heart had been so thoroughly dismantled the night before that it was hard to remember it had ever been there. "You do realize that this changes everything."

Amy sat up. She was wearing an oversized T-shirt that Iris and Cliff had given her with the words "What Part of 'Love' Don't You Understand?" across the front.

"I don't mean the extraordinary cinnamon sugar toast," I added.

She reached her hand out toward me. I took it and she pulled me in for a quick, soft kiss. "I know you don't mean the toast," she said, quietly.

I realized right then that I wasn't ever going to get used to the feeling this woman put in my chest about every fifteen seconds. And I also realized that I never wanted to.

Henley was awake when I went in to see him, and ready for the new day. Despite the absence of his regular chair and the bars and other aids I had come to take for granted at the old place, we managed to get him through his toilet with less of a struggle than we'd had the night before. He happily joined Erica out in the living room for a bit of coloring while I began the best day of my life.

The cinnamon sugar toast was a spectacular success—Erica, Henley, and I had several pieces while Amy got showered. When she emerged, she made coffee while Henley and Erica returned to the crayons, and I got a turn in the bathroom.

We spent most of the rest of the day relaxing. Cliff and Iris stopped by with some provisions, including refills of Henley's prescriptions they'd picked up on the way, down in Winston. They stayed for a late lunch before heading off to Iris's office to do her Internet radio show. She broadcast for two hours every Saturday afternoon, and used every single one of the one hundred twenty minutes to blast what she saw as the racist, fascist, sexist oligarchy ruling our country. She included in that gang Governor Hamilton, whom she thought of as nothing more than an amoral, power-hungry authoritarian who would do anything to get ahead. Iris had a small but growing national audience, which included some fairly impressive political insiders with whom she regularly exchanged e-mails. But thanks to her connection with Cliff and his family and friends, she was huge in the local Navajo community. They especially appreciated her oft-repeated message that traditional Navajo society's philosophy of freedom with responsibility was far more egalitarian and democratic than anything found in modern-day America.

After Cliff and Iris left, Henley fell asleep, and Erica curled up with a puzzle book, leaving Amy and me sitting beside each other on the couch. Nobody's shirt came flying off in a dramatically erotic and romantic gesture. But trust me—just holding hands with Amy that afternoon with the promise of a future together was giving my heart a very respectable workout.

In rough outline, our plan was to wait for a few days before fleeing far to the east. We expected that Henley's and my disappearance, and the destruction of our house, was going to become a big news story. We didn't want to try to go on the run when our faces would be on every tabloid cable news show on the air.

That night, after a simple dinner of hot dogs and hamburgers that was nearly as delicious as the tuna and canned corn of the night before, we shared some ice cream and went to bed early. Amy thought it was best if she stayed with Erica that evening, which was just as well, as a thunderstorm rolled through, and I needed to spend much of the night with Henley.

The next day, Erica woke me up with a series of gentle taps on my shoulder, and a whispered question. "Don't you think this is a Morning of Special Significance?"

Decoded: *May we have pancakes for breakfast?*

When she was three, and proclaimed that her favorite food in the world was "canpakes," I first learned that Erica and I shared a deep and abiding regard for the flapjack. As my niece soon thereafter learned—and I say this with all due humility—I make an exceptional pancake. The two keys are to use real butter on the skillet, instead of oil or margarine, and to use seltzer water in the mix, instead of milk. The results for me have been consistently outstanding. Ever since, Erica and I have had an agreement, that on so-designated Mornings of Special Significance, like Christmas and the first day of school vacations, I would make my specialty for us all to share.

So as I arose that Sunday morning, I assured Erica that she was absolutely correct, and asked her to wait until her mother woke up, and then tell her that I was going to the store to pick up what I needed to make breakfast on this beautiful day.

Of course, as I left the cabin, I had no idea that was the last time I would ever see it.

TWENTY-SIX

THE MINUTE I stepped outside and saw the large blue pickup truck parked next to my rented VW, I considered my options. I could try to confront the danger immediately, or I could retreat indoors, and attempt to hold back the assault from within.

Before I could decide, the passenger door opened and a tall, smiling Native American sporting an impressive beer belly and an Arizona Diamondbacks baseball cap emerged. "You're Cliff's friend, right? He asked us to keep an eye on you and your family last night. He said he was coming by sometime this morning."

I introduced myself to the big guy, David West, one of the tribe's police officers, and to his brother, Jack, who was driving the truck. I told them I was on my way into Winston to get some things and that I'd be back in about an hour. Then I took off, significantly more grim than I'd been just fifteen minutes earlier.

It wasn't that I was ungrateful for the help. In fact, I felt much safer knowing that someone would be watching the place while I went into town.

It was just that an ugly reality was invading the little fantasy world that I had so eagerly inhabited since dinner two nights before. Normal people don't need Navajo tough guys in pickup trucks to keep an eye on their family while they go to the store for butter and seltzer water. And normal people do not think of the presence of an unfamiliar vehicle in their driveway as a mortal threat.

But as I drove the narrow, empty road down the scrub-pine-dotted hills, toward the desert valley scarred by dozens of yellow and brown arroyos, I found my mind drifting away from suspicion and threat, and instead, shuttling back and forth from a blissful future to survivor's guilt.

Amy and I had talked about moving to Virginia, or possibly North Carolina. We were going to buy a house in wooded hills, so Henley would feel at home. But we'd be close enough to the cities so that Erica could go to a good school, and Amy and I could find work.

We'd buy a dog, teach Erica how to swim in the ocean, maybe have a baby of our own. And on summer evenings, I'd chop wood for Henley's stove until it was time for dinner with my family.

The family that Dale should have had.

He'd died before Erica was even *born*.

I knew that beating myself up over the many injustices surrounding Dale's fate was not a particularly healthy train of thought to ride. But by succumbing to the passion that I felt for Amy, that was the ticket I had purchased.

I knew Dale wouldn't have disapproved of what we were doing. He was one of the most unselfish and practical people I ever knew. "What's the most important thing?" he'd ask, whenever I came to him with an ethical dilemma. Admittedly, my problems were considerably less thorny back when I was ten—I recall many seemed to revolve around denying or admitting to eating cookies before dinner. But if Dale's spirit could have spoken to me in the car that morning, he would have asked the same question. And the answer, of course, would have been Amy and Erica. Which made me feel a little better.

Until I turned on the radio and the song that was playing was "La Bamba," by Los Lobos. Dale loved that song. He didn't speak Spanish, so he had no idea what the words meant, but that didn't matter to him. He just loved it.

Thinking about my brother as a twelve-year-old kid phonetically singing along to Tex-Mex rock was not helping my frame of mind, so I changed the station on the radio, and forced myself to acknowledge my situation. Dale wasn't here anymore. Henley, Amy, and Erica were. And they needed me.

But however I managed, or failed to manage, my guilt, it was ridiculously naive of me to think that all we had to do was hide out for a few days and then move to a different part of the country to be safe. I'd been pulled into a dark hole where soulless things murdered without the slightest remorse. A simple cross-country driving trip was not going to solve our problems.

But I didn't know that then.

My destination that morning was Winston, Arizona, the center of commerce in the area. It was located just outside the reservation, and featured a grocery store/drugstore/department store, two gas stations, two bars, three small restaurants, and a post office.

Two major roads come into the town: one from the reservation, to the town's east, and one from the southwest, which ultimately leads to Scottsdale and Phoenix.

Since almost no one was on the road, it only took me about twenty-five minutes to get from our little hideout to the supermarket. The parking lot behind the store was almost empty as I pulled in.

As I walked around the store, gathering up what I needed for the pancakes, I kept hearing Dale's voice one aisle over. What made the experience that much more disquieting was that I knew it couldn't be Dale, and yet, as I paid more and more attention, it still sounded just like him.

I came out of the soda aisle with a bottle of seltzer water and turned down the cereal and breakfast foods aisle, fully expecting to run into whoever had a voice that was just like my brother's. But there was no one there.

And then the voice said something about having to finish up some work before starting on a long trip. It seemed to be coming from the front of the store, where the cash registers were located. And as much as I tried to doubt it, the timbre, the accent, the hint of gruffness—it all *really* sounded like Dale.

I grabbed a box of pancake mix and hurried to the checkout station. I had to see what this person looked like.

I moved toward the only store clerk who was at the cash registers that morning. But he was standing alone. The customer he had just rung up was leaving the store. All I could see was that he had light hair and stood about six feet tall.

The guy didn't just sound like Dale. From the back, he was a dead ringer for him, too.

But it was simply impossible that the man was my brother. Which was why I didn't chase after him.

We had buried Dale over five years ago. But my thoughts of him that morning, coupled with the eerily similar voice I kept hearing in the store, had somehow pushed the impossible into the realm of the possible. And I'm sure that sleeping with Amy had added an extra ingredient to my personal psychological stew.

I blinked a few times, trying to clear my head. The world of the living was challenging enough—I was going to have to keep my concentration if my family was going to have any chance of surviving over the next few weeks.

As I'd planned from the start, I paid for my purchases in cash, on the off chance that someone might be tracking my credit card purchases. I wanted to give the impression that I had disappeared not just from the Juan Gomez trial, but from the planet Earth, as well. At least for a little while.

When I exited the store, I saw that a beat-up old white minivan had parked near my car. Its plate number was 0A1E-82. I remember that specifically because the zero was shaped like a rectangle, and so if you looked at it quickly, the plate seemed to spell out DALE-82. At least it did to me. I wanted to look at that morning's omens as signs that my brother was with me somehow, but it was becoming hard not to see them as a series of subliminal messages from a conscience that was slowly becoming overwhelmed with guilt.

As I opened the door to my car, I noticed a large, late-model, black SUV, stopped at the intersection near the store's parking lot. I don't know what drew my attention to it—maybe because the image of a big, black Cadillac Escalade sandwiched between a white Toyota Prius and another little white car seemed funny. But then I noticed that in profile, the man in the passenger seat of the Escalade looked a bit like Paul Landry.

I distinctly remember thinking that I was going to need to take a nap after breakfast this morning, because my imagination was running way too hot. First, I heard Dale in the grocery store. And then, I saw Landry at a stoplight.

And then the man in the SUV turned to face me, and it became immediately clear that the problem that morning wasn't my imagination.

The problem was that the passenger in the Escalade *was* Paul Landry. Who was now pointing at me, and shouting at the driver of his car.

I jumped in my VW, and took off.

I knew that it was going to take the Caddy some time to extricate itself from between the two smaller cars, but I didn't have much of a head start. And I didn't have much of a choice as to direction. Because of the layout of the roads in Winston, I had to take the route back toward the reservation.

Traffic hadn't picked up at all, so I was able to speed down the road into the reservation. I was driving north on the main road along the western edge of the territory. To my left an occasional clearing revealed a terrifying vista showing just how close to the edge of a cliff I was traveling. About five miles ahead was the right turn which led farther up the mountains, and ultimately to our little cabin. If I could make it to that turn before Landry was in sight, I could disappear.

But a couple of miles before the turn, I noticed that the Escalade was behind me.

And it was gaining on me.

Rapidly.

Even though I was going as fast as I thought was prudent, given the condition and the location of the road, I sped up. My right turn toward the cabin was coming up soon, and I had to make a decision. I could head toward the house, and hope I could reach help from the two guys sitting in our driveway before I got caught. But that would bring the evil that was riding in that black car right to my family's doorstep.

Or I could drive past the turn, and lead them away from the house, taking my chances that I could outrun them.

It was only seconds before I had to choose. The turn was coming up so quickly that if I didn't slow down, there was no way I'd make it without rolling the car over.

I accelerated, and blew right through the intersection, as if I'd never been considering the turn. Thanks to the turbo, I was going eighty-five now. I looked into the mirror, expecting that over the past minute, I'd have put some distance between me and my pursuers.

But the Cadillac was relentless. It was now only about one hundred feet away.

The road we were on was a two-lane highway with a posted speed limit of fifty-five mph, mainly because it was relatively narrow. There were stretches with some significant curves, and from time to time, a cardiac-inducing drop-off presented itself to the left. I had to avoid looking in that direction. The last thing I needed was to try to race these murdering thugs while fighting a case of vertigo.

At the next straightaway, I floored the beetle's accelerator, popping it up to ninety before I had to back down a little to handle a fairly sharp bend to the left.

But still, the SUV was closing. Seventy feet. And then sixty.

It was at about that time that Landry's arm emerged from the passenger window, extending toward me with a gun in its hand. A moment later I heard a crack, and then another.

Good-bye, stomach-clenching fear. Hello, unbridled terror.

I wanted to dodge the bullets, but I was going too fast to swerve.

I pulled my gaze away from the rearview mirror and noticed that there was a turnoff to the right coming up. I had never been on that road, but I assumed that like the route that led to our place, it ran roughly east, up the foothills, into the heart of the reservation. Since I didn't seem to be able to outrun this big car, I decided I'd try to outmaneuver him. I slammed on the brakes, skidded down to about forty-five, and pulled the car into the turn.

A quick glance in the rearview mirror crushed my hope that the Escalade would take the turn too fast and flip over. It continued its pursuit with regrettable gusto.

The road we were now on was narrower and more winding than the first, so although our speed was significantly reduced, it was hard for the SUV to get a good shot at me. I knew that if Landry was capable of murdering a paralyzed man by burning down his home, he was certainly capable of killing me while I was driving.

About ninety seconds after I turned off the main road, a tight S-curve forced me to slow to under forty. Coming out of the last bend, I saw a large, abandoned roadside stand off to the right. I yanked the VW off the road onto the old blacktop parking area surrounding it, and flew around behind it. I was hoping they'd drive by and I could double back and get away.

It almost worked.

As the black car sped past, I backed up, turned around, pulled out of the parking area, and headed toward the main road. But before I reached it, the Escalade appeared again in the mirror.

I turned right with as much speed as I dared, and floored it, heading north again. I didn't want to go back toward our cabin. Even though I had managed to put a little more distance between me and Landry, I was going to have to keep the VW over ninety to have any chance of keeping him from getting close enough to get a shot off at me. There was no way I'd be able to keep that kind of speed up near a populated area.

As the road stretched out in front of me, I realized I was going to have to keep my eyes focused to the right. There was now a sheer cliff to the left. Even though there was a guardrail at the edge of the shoulder, the vista in that direction, dropping down hundreds of feet to the mesas below, was textbook vertigo material.

Five minutes into the chase, though, it didn't look like vertigo was going to be my primary problem.

Because no matter what I did, I couldn't shake the SUV. In fact, it was closing.

When I was a kid, I was always annoyed by car chases on television and in the movies. They all seemed so formulaic—the pursuing car, usually full of bad guys, would catch up to the hero's car, and then, idiotically, bang into it from behind. It seemed like such a stupid, futile gesture. There was no way they were going to hurt the hero by tapping him on the rear bumper. Inevitably, the hero would whip his car into some kind of remarkable spin, and the bad guys would go sailing off a cliff, or crashing into a pile of rocks and bursting into flames.

When the Cadillac finally caught me, and started ramming into the VW, my perspective on car chases underwent an immediate transformation.

Unless you've tried, you have no idea how difficult it is to maintain control of a car going ninety-five miles per hour when you are being bashed from behind by another car.

With someone shooting at you.

But I had no choice but to try to hang on, and to

keep going. I was unarmed, and completely alone. If I didn't escape, I was dead.

The first two times the SUV hit me, the VW got shoved forward, and I felt a slight tug on the wheel, but I kept the car on the road, moving fast.

It was the third time that got me.

I think it might have been because the contact point with the VW was at the left taillight rather than directly in the center of the rear bumper. But whatever the reason, the car lunged forward and lurched dangerously to the left, threatening to fly directly across the road, into and over the oncoming lane. And as fast as I was going at the time, the guardrail would not stop me from sailing off the cliff and diving hundreds of feet to my death.

I gripped the wheel tightly, and pulled back to the right. Instinctively, I had taken my foot off the accelerator pedal, so I was slowing down. But that was only relative—I was still going well over seventy-five. So as soon as I felt the car respond to the turn, I felt gravity pulling me against the door, as if it intended to flip the car over.

I reacted by yanking back on the wheel to the left.

While I swerved back and forth, desperately trying to keep my car on the road, and upright, the Caddy accelerated past me on the left. And just when I felt like I'd gotten control of the VW again, the big black vehicle pulled directly in front of me, cutting me off.

I slammed on the brakes and turned hard right. Although I locked up the tires and the steering, and sent the car into a spin over which I had absolutely no control, incredibly, I avoided the collision.

But what I also did was stall the engine. So that by the time the car finished its dramatic pirouette, it was now facing south, and going at exactly zero miles per hour.

I heard a door slam. Landry had left his car and was coming over to me. If I could just get the car moving, I had a chance.

What I needed was a wingman. A trusted buddy riding shotgun. Someone to magically appear in my passenger seat, ward off the threat that was coming, and give me a few extra seconds to escape.

What I needed was Dale.

But I was alone. Frantically, I grabbed for the key. Five seconds. That's all I would need, and I'd be on my way back down the road, away from Landry.

I turned the ignition. Three seconds.

The window to my right exploded, sending pebbles of broken glass all over the seat and the dashboard.

Two seconds. The car's engine strained to come back to life.

One second.

The car door opened, and Landry dropped down into the seat next to me just as the car's engine caught, and I shoved the gearshift into first.

But it was too late. With his right hand, Landry slammed the car door shut, and with his left, he stuck the barrel of a gun to my temple.

I closed my eyes. It was over. I was going to be executed in the Arizona desert, on my way home from the grocery store.

And then I heard the homicidal cop's familiar voice say, "Cheer up, Counselor. I'm not going to shoot you."

I opened my eyes. But before I could say anything, he continued.

"Not yet, anyway."

TWENTY-SEVEN

IN HIS FIRST letter home to me from Afghanistan, my brother Dale bemoaned the fact that so many of his fellow soldiers didn't use their heads for anything except a place to put their helmets. "We really need people with your brains in this fight, C.R.," was what he wrote. He alternated frequently between "Captain Rootbeard" and its abbreviation. "Nobody ever tries to think. All they want to do is shoot guns, or drop bombs. I always admired how you thought your way through problems."

I'm pretty sure that Dale's overgenerous description of my intellect was principally thanks to high-school chemistry.

I first became aware of the difference between our brains in my sophomore year in high school. Dale was a senior by then, and was taking chemistry—a class I'd had as a freshman. In and of itself, that was nothing particularly noteworthy. Students at our school had a lot of discretion about when they took certain courses.

Dale wasn't the only one to have put off chem until the last minute.

But as I witnessed my brother's daily interaction with the periodic table, valiantly battling with atomic weights and electron shells, I saw him bested by processes and theories that I had found quite easy to understand. Once I overheard him on the phone "explaining" the difference between oxygen and the inert gases to one of his football teammates. His stunningly simplistic and deeply inaccurate description virtually guaranteed the pair a failing grade on the following day's test. I volunteered to assist, and he enthusiastically accepted, leading to a B-minus on the exam.

After high school, Dale joined the R.O.T.C. at Arizona State, and became an officer in the army. I never got a chance to help him out academically again, but he never forgot how I pulled him back from the brink in high-school chem. Yet to me, Dale remained the role model. Especially when he met and married Amy. It was obvious to everyone that they would be a great couple, and great parents.

And then 9/11 came, and Dale went off to war. And he died.

"You gonna ask me why I don't kill you, or you gonna sit there like a silly little bitch," Landry said, poking me in the leg with the gun.

I blame myself for a lot that went wrong during that week of insanity around the Gomez trial. But I have never felt guilty about the fact that I couldn't speak for several moments upon Landry's invasion of my car.

I kept wondering how he found me. And whether he knew where Amy, Erica, and Henley were. Not to mention the shock I was still experiencing from his attempt to gun me down on a deserted road, and by the cold fact that he now held a pistol to my leg, and was apparently threatening to kill me.

I was unarmed, sitting in the driver's seat of an idling VW on a virtually deserted road in one of the least populated areas in the country. I was being held at gunpoint by a sociopath. I was completely on my own, with no hope of rescue. So I chose to believe what Dale had said about me—that I could think my way out of anything.

This time the cop didn't poke me in the leg with the gun. He hit me with it, hard. "Is that all you got for me? A stupid look on your ugly face, Attorney Carpenter?"

The trooper's trademark disarming smile had been replaced by something twisted—neither friendly nor pleasant. His eyes were bloodshot, and emotionally disconnected from his sick grin. It looked like he had been wearing a mask before, and what had been revealed was quite ugly.

"I don't get it," I said, feeling the bruise on my knee forming already. "Why are you doing this? What happened—"

He cut me off. "Shut up, little girl." His expression was devoid of all emotion except scorn. "You don't get answers. You have no idea what's important. And right now, what's important is that we've got Amy and Erica, and if you want us to keep them alive, you're going to need to give up your father."

I knew he must be lying. If he had really grabbed Amy and Erica, he would have had Henley, too. Even so, I didn't have to fake the terror in my voice.

"What?" I choked out.

Landry exhaled in disgust, and shook his head. Then, suddenly, he screamed in my ear. "I just told you, you deaf son of a bitch! We have Amy and Erica! If you want them to live, you need to tell us where your father is!"

"But why do you want Henley?" I asked. I really didn't care—I was just stalling. Landry's abuse and his mention of my niece and Amy were all I needed to turn my fear into resolve. I didn't have much hope for myself, in the long run. But I would be damned, and I mean that literally, if I let this monster get hold of my family.

"Didn't I just tell you that you don't get answers?" he screamed. "Where is your father?"

Just then, I figured out what I was going to do. I just needed a few more seconds to compose myself before acting. So I took a gamble that I could keep him talking. "Are you Beta?" I blurted.

I knew it wasn't true. But I thought this might be the kind of thing that would get Landry thinking.

As I had hoped, a subtle shift came over my captor's face. The exaggerated and patently false expression morphed into a leer. "So?" he answered, ambiguously.

My plan was to feign anger. I did a pretty good job. "So if you are Beta, what the hell are you doing shooting at me?" I asked.

"Uh, you know I can't confirm or deny that I'm Beta," Landry said, slyly.

Then I really let it rip. What I was actually doing was making my final calculations, but for Landry's sake, I yelled at the top of my lungs. "Well, whoever you are, you damn well know that you already burned down my house, and killed my father in the process."

As soon as the words left my mouth, I knew that I hadn't sold the lie. I saw the cop come to the same conclusion. And then, fast as a cobra strike, using a backhand motion, he whipped the pistol into my face, hitting me with a real good one in the forehead, above my right eye.

If you had felt the force of that blow, you would have

known that provoking this maniac to an immediate physical reprisal was not my plan. I was momentarily dazed, and blood began to pour down my face, dripping all over my shirt and pants. My eyebrow was the only thing keeping me from being blinded by the flow. I still have the scar.

The pain in my head had two features—a sharp, burning feeling where the cut had been inflicted, and a dull, growing ache that ringed my entire skull, like an instant migraine.

"How stupid do you think I am, punk?" Landry spat. "I saw the ax head next to the broken handcuffs. Why don't you stick to things like defending murderers?"

The comment about the ax shook me up. I had never even thought about the killers returning to the house to find Henley's remains. Then I realized that they'd probably assumed that Henley would die—they'd gone back to see if they could find my dead body. And I had entirely forgotten about the ax, but none of that really mattered now. I tried to adopt an expression of defeat as I turned to face the state trooper. The next three or four seconds were going to determine everything.

He was still sitting sideways on the passenger seat, facing me. Landry was a lefty, which is why he held the gun in that hand. His right hand rested on the dashboard, above the glove compartment.

My best chance was for him to think that I had lost all hope. I waited for the leering smirk to return to his face, and then I pulled the car into second gear, yanked up hard with my right hand while grabbing his left, pinning both to the windshield. Simultaneously, I slammed the car's accelerator to the floor, and popped the clutch. The tires spun madly before they finally grabbed the blacktop. The engine screamed insanely. And seconds later, we were tearing down the road.

TWENTY-EIGHT

"**WHERE DO YOU** think you're going, brainiac?" Landry shouted over the engine's roar. I was watching the road accelerate toward me, so I couldn't be sure, but I thought I heard amusement tingeing the cop's voice. The swirl of emotions that were storming through me included a healthy measure of anger, and his smug attitude only increased the dose. I concentrated on the muscles in my right hand, and I snaked my index finger over his, and squeezed down hard, forcing him to pull the trigger.

The gun discharged with a loud *bang,* shooting a hole in the windshield, surrounded by a large spider-web pattern of cracks.

Landry laughed.

"You can't call the cops, 'cause *I'm* the cops. You can't call the feds, 'cause you know they're in on this, too. So, what? You're gonna shoot your own car?" Landry sounded genuinely amused. "Hey—I've got an idea," he continued, in a mocking tone. "Why don't you run away? Oh, that's right. I'm sitting right next to you, asshole." More laughter. "I thought you were supposed to be smart."

I wanted him laughing. I wanted him gloating. I wanted him thinking about everything except what I was going to do to him.

The car's acceleration had pinned us both back against the seats. My right hand and Landry's left were still wrapped around the handle of the pistol, and pressing it up against the windshield.

We were heading back south on the main road of the reservation. The cliff now was to our right.

Landry was straining to bring the weapon down so he could point it at me again. And even though he was no weakling, I had the advantage.

The problem for my assailant was that my right hand was under his, and to pin the gun to the windshield, all I had to do was to pull upwards. He was trying to pull down against me, and I had plenty of upper-body strength. I was using my biceps against his triceps. It was no contest.

I squeezed against Landry's finger again, shooting off another round. Another explosion, another hole in the windshield. The pattern of cracks of the second one overlapped the first.

I was running out of time. I pulled against his finger again, and a third shot blew another hole through the glass. Up ahead, the road bent slightly to the left.

"If you're trying to empty the magazine, I got more bullets, you know," Landry taunted. Then he finally gave up trying to control the gun with just his left hand, and he twisted around so that he could get his right hand into the fray.

That was my cue. Squeezing off one more shot, blowing out more of the glass, and forming one more pattern of cracks in the windshield, I gripped the steering wheel tight in my left hand, keeping us headed straight, instead of bending with the road to the left. We were heading for the cliff.

Landry saw where I was directing us, and sneered. "You gonna jump the rail? I don't think you have the balls, Tommy girl."

I shot the pistol once more, praying that I had done enough damage.

Then I slammed on the brakes.

Centripetal force threw me forward, but my seat belt locked me in place instantly. Landry, however, had never put his seat belt on.

In fact, his weight was shifted as far forward as possible. He was sitting sideways, with both hands reaching up to control the gun which was pressed against the severely damaged windshield.

When the car's brakes locked up, Landry's body continued at its previous speed of about fifty miles per hour. His flight forward wasn't impeded at all. And thanks to the damage we'd inflicted onto the glass, he went sailing out of the car like the windshield wasn't even there in the first place.

The car had begun its skid on the shoulder of the road, and then had slid off onto the dirt, veering toward the guardrail that protected vehicles from going off the cliff. I had hoped that the cop would just fly right over the rail, but even if I'd had the time to check whether that's what happened, I couldn't risk the vertigo. As soon as he made his unconventional but emphatic exit from the car, I got off the brake, turned hard left, pulled the VW back onto the road, and fled.

It was hard driving at life-threatening speeds without much of a windshield. The tiniest specks of dust and sand—heck, even the wind itself—affected my eyes. I didn't care about the stinging so much. Shoot, over the past two days I'd been pistol-whipped and nearly burned to death. A little irritation to my corneas was nothing.

The problem was that my eyes reacted to the pain by watering. And I might even have been able to cope with that, except that the blood that was pouring from the cut over my right eye was now flowing into the eye it-self. In short, I was barely able to see. At sixty miles per hour, that posed a significant problem.

I was in the middle of trying to work out some kind of system, a wholly ineffective rotation of holding the bottom of my T-shirt to the cut on my head, followed by shielding my eyes with my hand while ducking down behind the remaining fragments of the windshield, when I saw Cliff's friends, David and Jack West, head-ing in the other direction in their pickup truck.

As we passed, I saw clearly that they noticed what had happened to my car. I couldn't afford to stop, but I did watch in the side mirror as they crested a small hill, and stopped their truck, pulling it across both lanes of the road. Then they both got out, with shotguns.

I felt better, but only slightly. I was able to slow down now. There was no way that Landry and his driver were going to be able to get past the West brothers without significant delay, if they even tried.

But I didn't know who else knew where I was. Or if I was being followed. The roads around the reservation were deserted, but somehow, Landry had found me. How many others were there?

I had to assume that I was still a target, and that anywhere I went I would be followed by whatever group Landry was a part of. I couldn't afford to go back to the cabin—I had to run from it. If I was being chased, I needed to lead whoever was following me away from my family.

I called Amy on my old phone. She answered on the first ring. "Hey, where are you?" she chided gently. "We're hungry!"

I was so caught up in the need for them to get out of there, and in my need to run in the other direction, that I didn't realize this might be the last chance I ever had to talk to her. All I did was say, "Amy, I have to be fast—I don't know if they're tracing this, and the phone's almost out of power. You need to get away from there as soon as possible. I was followed, and I'm afraid I'll bring them to you. Talk to, you know, those people who, you know. Get help from them." I was afraid to say Cliff and Iris's names out loud, even though I was sure that whoever was attacking me must have already known about them.

Amy was silent on the other end of the phone. "You aren't going back to the trial, are you?" she asked.

"No," I said. "They'll kill me there."

"I love you" was all she said.

My headache got suddenly much worse. I wanted to spend the rest of my life with this woman, and the only way I could make sure she would stay out of harm was to run away from her. "I love you, too," I replied. "Be safe. I'll find you."

"Run," Amy said. "Run fast." And then she hung up.

To be honest, I can't say that the sixty-five-mile-per-hour wind I was getting in the face was the only reason my eyes were stinging right at that moment. I was miserable. Virginia? North Carolina? I didn't even know what country Amy was going to.

But survival had to be our first priority. I couldn't risk her life, or Erica's or Henley's. I had to get far away from here, so that if they ever found me, there would be no chance that they could ever find my family.

In short, I needed to vanish. If only Uncle Louis had taught me that magic trick.

I met my mother's brother Louis just once, when he flew out to visit us from his home in Florida. I was ten years old.

What I remember most about my uncle's visit was the magic. Card tricks, disappearing foam balls, pieces of rope that got longer even when you cut them—he was a wizard. And every time he did a trick, he'd say or do something that I thought was intensely funny. I don't know if I ever laughed more than I did that weekend.

After he left, I asked my mother why Uncle Louis couldn't come more often, and I was told that it was because he lived so far away, and because it was so expensive. I was too young to press the point, but even then, I doubted that was the whole story.

I suspect now that it had to do with the fact that Uncle Louis was gay, and that my mother's family never accepted him for what he was—a very nice, very funny man, who enjoyed life perhaps more boisterously than others were comfortable with, and who died too young at a party in Miami.

But unfortunately my deceased uncle would provide no help that Sunday morning as I fled down the road. I was going to have to create my own disappearing act, and I was going to have to do it quick.

I had a bunch of money—probably two thousand dollars—but I was driving around in a car that couldn't possibly be more noticeable. A yellow VW beetle with a blown-out windshield.

But even if I wanted to walk into a used-car dealership with a fistful of cash, it was Sunday morning. Nothing was open.

I considered renting a car, but they always wanted a credit card to use as a deposit. I needed to minimize the chances that whoever was looking for me could track my movements by payments. They'd be on me before I could get twenty miles down the road.

But the VW was so conspicuous that the drivers of almost every one of the few cars I passed did a double take at the damage to the windshield. As soon as the cops put the word out, I was dead. I had to switch vehicles immediately.

Then, I caught one of the few breaks I was to get during this entire surreal week. Ten miles south of Winston was Restful Creek, one of the northernmost suburbs of Scottsdale. I happened to know that there was a rental car place there, because on a Friday, three years ago, when both Amy's car and my truck were in the shop, I'd loaned her Henley's van. But then, out of the blue, I'd needed to drive to Tucson for an emergency hearing in a case I was handling.

The owner of this dealership—Fred Feenie was his name—had been terrific. He'd sent his only other employee on a long drive out to give me a ride to their office, where I rented the car.

But as I approached Fred's place that Sunday morning, I had no intention of renting a car. In fact, I was hoping that they were closed. Because I had another plan.

When I'd rented the car from Fred, I was supposed to return it that evening. But I didn't get out of the hearing until six, and by the time I got back to Restful Creek, it was after ten that night. Over two hours after Fred closed.

I'd called Fred when I knew I wouldn't make the deadline, and he told me to just pull the car around to the lot behind the ancient adobe building he used for an office, leave the car unlocked, and leave the keys above the visor.

Seriously.

So that Sunday morning, I was banking on the fact that in the past three years, Fred Feenie hadn't installed a nighttime drop slot in his door.

And that someone had rented a car from him and returned it late Saturday night.

If I'd known how to hot-wire cars, I probably wouldn't have been operating with such a pathetic plan to get a different car, but I couldn't think of anything else. So I drove into downtown Restful Creek that quiet morning. I parked the VW next to a Dumpster behind a restaurant a few blocks from Feenie's place. I assumed that Fred was closed Sundays, and the earliest they'd discover the theft was Monday. By keeping the VW out of sight, I hoped to delay even further the suspicion that I was the one who'd stolen Fred's car.

I walked the rest of the way to the Feenie lot. There were six cars there—all acceptably nondescript. I chose a Dodge first, but the doors were locked, and my hopes plunged. I went one by one down the row, only to find they were all locked.

Until I reached the last one. A white Mitsubishi Galant. I was so sure it was locked, too, that when the door actually opened, I almost fell backward onto my rear end.

I took a quick look around before I entered the car, but there was no one in sight. In retrospect, it was a foolish gesture. It wouldn't have made any difference if I was being watched by the entire adult population of the town. I had to get a different car, and I had to get out of there immediately.

I hopped in, shut the door, and hoping that my luck hadn't run out, I pulled on the driver's-side sun visor.

Like a slot machine payoff, the keys jingled down into my lap.

It's funny how quickly one's perspective can change, especially under extreme circumstances. Here I was, in the middle of committing my first felony. Yet when those keys appeared, instead of guilt, I felt like it was Christmas morning.

I put the key in the ignition, started the car up, and drove out onto the street. A red light stopped me a block and a half from the rental lot. A quick check verified that the gas tank was full. And then when I looked up to adjust the angle of my rearview mirror, I got an unpleasant shock.

A state trooper had pulled in directly behind me.

My stomach did a sudden flip. Could he have seen me in Feenie's lot? Did he see me pull out of there on a Sunday morning, when the place was obviously closed? Had he spotted the wrecked VW, called it in, and was now looking for someone in the area fitting my description?

I knew that my cut-up and bloody face would raise anyone's suspicions, so I looked down, and turned on the radio. I flipped through station after station reminding me that God was watching me every time I sinned, finally settling on a country oldies station, which just happened to be playing a song about a cheating wife.

I flashed a glance back into the mirror, but the cop's strobe lights weren't on, and he wasn't signaling for me to pull over. In fact, when the light turned green, I pulled straight through the intersection, and he turned right.

I took a huge shaky breath in, and then I let it out. With any luck, Fred Feenie would be closed all day, and the car wouldn't be reported as stolen for another twenty-four hours. I had an entire day to put hundreds of miles behind me. By the time the authorities finally put two and two together, it wouldn't matter.

I followed the road south toward Scottsdale, then I connected with the loop highway around Phoenix. Twenty-five minutes later I merged onto I-10 east, heading for Tucson. My plan was to drive into New Mexico, and then find a road headed north. I had a vague plan to end up in Kansas City, or Chicago. I didn't think there was any chance Amy would go there.

After I'd driven for a while, I pulled off at a rest area. I really needed to stop the bleeding from the cut on my head. I'd been pressing my T-shirt against it, but that hadn't done the trick. I've since been told that what I really needed was stitches, but even if I'd realized that at the time, going to a hospital was out of the question. It would have been far too easy for the police to learn my location. I would have settled for some ice, but I was even afraid to pull into a truck stop. All I needed was for a well-intentioned clerk to call 911 to assist the accident victim who had just staggered in to buy a bag of ice, a cup of coffee, and a box of Fig Newtons, and I'd be sunk.

The rest area proved to be a reasonable, if crude, substitute.

I was able to find a parking spot between two campers that helped shield me and my car from view. And on my way to the bathroom, I saw a soda machine. I made a purchase—the first time I'd ever bought Mountain Dew for medicinal purposes—and brought it back to the car. The chilled aluminum can, combined with pressure from the part of my shirt that wasn't entirely blood-soaked, helped somewhat. About forty minutes later, the flow had weakened considerably. It was down to a very stubborn trickle from the edge of the cut nearest my eye, and I got back on the road.

At five minutes after three, about six hours from the time I'd left the cabin that morning, and somewhere south and east of Tucson, my cell phone rang.

The voice on the other end of the line spoke with no greeting, but I didn't need one. I recognized the voice. It was Beta.

And as if that weren't bad enough, he said, simply, "Tom. This is Dale. You need to turn around."

TWENTY-NINE

BETA WAS DALE? Impossible. I refused to believe it.

"Dale is dead," I said. "I have no idea who you are, but you aren't my brother. That's for damn sure."

There was a pause. "Fine. You don't want to believe me? I can understand that. But you better stop running away."

The big green sign I was passing as he spoke read NEW MEXICO BORDER—109 MILES. I don't know how he knew it, but I was most definitely running away. In fact, if I could have snapped my fingers and instantly transported myself anywhere, the sign would have read WELCOME TO OHIO. Unless he really was Dale. But that didn't make any sense. "What the hell is going on? Who are you?"

"I didn't tell you before because I was afraid you'd get distracted. This is much bigger than both of us, Tom. They're going to kill you if they can. The only way to stop them is to get back to the Gomez trial."

The more I heard, the less I believed. "That's a bunch of crap, and you know it."

"You know, if I were you, I'd probably think that if somebody tried to kill my father by burning down my house, that would be about as bad as it could get. I'd probably think it was a good idea to give up any involvement I had in the Juan Gomez trial, and get out of town, so there'd be no chance anyone would come after me or my father again."

So he knew about the arson. But the rest of it—the stuff about me running away—could well have been a guess. I checked my rearview mirror. There was only one car in sight, and it had entered the interstate only one exit back. It had never gotten close enough to me to know anything about my car other than its color. As far as I could tell, I was completely free of any tail.

Still, I played it cagey. "That doesn't mean that I bolted."

There was a pause, and then Beta, or Dale, or whoever he was, said, "That's true, but I can't think of another reason why you'd be heading east, on Interstate 10, about twenty miles outside of Tucson."

My gaze shot to the mirror again. The single car was still way back there. It had been joined by another car, but neither was anywhere near close enough to know that I was in Fred Feenie's white Mitsubishi a half mile ahead of them. And from what Iris had told me on the day she confirmed that Landry had bugged me, minutes had to pass before they could trace the location of a cell phone.

"How do you know that?" I snapped.

"Relax, Tom. I'm the only one who knows where you are." There was a slight delay. "And I know a lot more than that, too."

I really don't know what it was that gave it away. The

ominous pause, the tone of Beta's voice, or perhaps my recently acquired fluency in the language of threats, thanks to my introductory lesson in the men's room five days earlier. It's possible that a week prior to this conversation, I wouldn't have attached anything of importance to that last statement. But as soon as I heard it, I knew something bad was coming. I just didn't know how bad. "What's that supposed to mean?" I asked.

"Come on, Tom," Beta chided. "Do you really think Landry is the only one who knows how to start a fire?"

I was still very early in processing my anger and frustration at being forced to flee from my family. And as impossible as I knew it to be, I was now wrestling with the bizarre suggestion that my brother was alive, and apparently threatening me. My head still ached from the injury I'd received from Landry. I wasn't thinking clearly at all. "What are you saying? You're going to burn down my house again?"

I didn't hear anything for a second, and I thought that the cell phone signal might have given out. But then Beta cleared his throat, and said the words that still live in my nightmares to this day: "I'm not talking about Dad and Mom's house, Tom. I'm talking about the one Amy and Erica and Dad are staying in right now."

My mind was a hundred different places at once, most of them in conflict. Dale was one of the very few people who knew where Cliff's and my house was. But Dale would never threaten his own family's life. It couldn't be Dale.

So whoever this was had to be bluffing. There was absolutely no way he knew where we had gone to hide. And if he did, how did he find out? Were Cliff and Iris in on this? Impossible. But what about Cliff's friends, the West brothers? I'd never seen them before in my life. But if they were involved, then why did they take up a position on the road as I passed, clearly designed to assist me in escaping from whoever had shot up my car?

As far as I knew, that was the entire population of the people who knew where Amy and I had fled to. So I was willing to bet that Beta was playing his last card here. For whatever reason, he felt like he had to manipulate me back into that courtroom, and he knew there was nothing he could use to get me there except Amy and Erica. So he gambled with an empty threat, hoping I'd believe that he could get to them.

He lost.

"I don't know what kind of game you're playing," I said. "But Amy and Erica are fine, and the only way I know to keep them fine is to stay away from the Juan Gomez trial. Which is exactly what I intend to do."

The silence that followed this statement was even longer than the last one. Was I being traced? I didn't think it made any difference. He knew exactly where I was at the beginning of the phone call. If he was intending to kill me, then he'd do it. I'd take my chances.

But dragging Amy and Erica into this thing was not an option.

"Okay, Tom. Here's what I'm going to do. I'm going to tell you where Amy and Erica are. And I'm going to tell you what they're wearing. And I'm going to tell you what they're doing."

I still didn't believe he had them. I couldn't afford to believe it. The road whizzed by under my tires. The sky was blue, and its bright color contrasted sharply with the browns and yellows on the horizon. Amy and Erica had to be safe.

"Amy is wearing jeans and a blue-green pullover with a wide neckline," he began. I felt a squeezing in my chest. "She's walking out of the house with Erica, who is wearing a T-shirt and shorts. The T-shirt says 'Grandpa Rocks' on it. I bet Dad loves that. They're both carrying backpacks."

I eased up on the accelerator. Either he had them, or he had seen them before, and was just making up a good story. I was banking on the latter.

"Amy is talking to Dad—he's at the door in his wheelchair. Now she's going to her car, and I wonder if she'll—yeah, she sees it. I let the air out of her front tire. She realizes she's not going anywhere. Now she's looking around, but she doesn't see anything. And now she's grabbing Erica, and running inside. Smart girl."

He still hadn't described the hideout—so for all the detail in his story, it still might be a fabrication.

"And by the way, Tom, I love what you've done with the place. Wood and stone cabin on the southeast corner of the Navajo reservation, blue curtains in the windows on either side of the red front door, ramp leading down to the gravel parking area at the end of the driveway ... Should I go on?"

The headache I'd had five minutes earlier had been replaced by a blinding pain across my forehead, as if a steel band had been wrapped around my skull and drawn tight. There was a rest stop about a half mile down the road, and I pulled into it, parking at the first space I saw. I closed my eyes, and sat back against the headrest. I was at least four hours away. I refused to believe this creep on the phone was Dale. But at this point, it didn't really matter anymore. If I managed to get hold of Amy by phone to tell her to run, her car was disabled. If Beta—or Dale, God help me—wanted to do anything to them, there was nothing I could do to stop it.

"You okay there, Tom?"

The false sympathy sickened me, and I couldn't have hidden my disgust if I tried. "If you hurt any of them, I will spend the rest of my life hunting you down, and then I will kill you."

The jerk actually chuckled. "Whoa there, Tommy boy, easy does it." If the pseudo-concern was nauseating, the condescension was infuriating. "Everybody's fine, and nobody's going to hurt anybody, as long as you take care of your end of this. I gave up way too much for you to back out now. I'm sorry about this, but your family is my only leverage left. You run away, and I'll kill them right here and right now. But you turn that car around, meet me so I can give you what you need for tomorrow, finish up the Gomez trial, and I promise you, everything is going to be just fine."

Things were as far from "just fine" as they'd ever been in my life. But we both knew it was all about Amy and Erica—if they were really in danger, I was going to do whatever he wanted. "How do I know you haven't already done something to them?" I asked.

"Call them right now," he said. "You've still got your old phone with you, right? Call Amy while I'm on the phone with you."

"How did you know—"

"Never mind," he interrupted. "Just call her. And be quick about it. Make sure she's okay, and tell her you're okay, and then hang up. Anything else and I'll get nervous. Don't make me nervous, Tom."

I took a deep breath. The constant, implied intimidation was taking its toll.

I had a little more time on my old cell phone, and I used it to call Amy. She answered right away.

"Are you okay?" I asked, holding both phones up to my mouth so that Beta could hear me.

"Tom? What's the matter?"

"Nothing," I lied. "I just needed to check on you before I, uh, left the state."

"We're fine, but we have a flat tire, so I had to call triple A to fix it before we leave. They'll be here in a couple of hours. And you need to tell me what's the matter. I thought you couldn't call me. Tom—you're scaring me."

I was in a perfectly impossible situation, acting like a perfect idiot. In an attempt to assure myself that Amy was okay, I managed to frighten her into believing that she was not okay.

"I can't talk now," I said. "But I'll call you later. I'm okay. I promise."

And I hung up.

"Good job, Tom. See? I got no reason to hurt anybody. Just don't push me. Meet me at Cactus Curt's Steakhouse at six-thirty. Sit alone. I'll find you. And I swear—nothing's going to happen to Amy or Erica. Or Dad. Just finish this trial, and I'll be out of your lives forever."

"How do I know—" was all I managed to say, before the connection went dead.

I didn't believe him, but I was trapped. There was nothing for me to do but go back, and hope that if I died trying to finish the Gomez case, Beta would let my family live.

It was one of the low points of a very low week.

In hindsight, I should have been able to figure out an awful lot from that conversation, but my mind was spinning. It was all I could do to keep functioning, much less puzzle out what was happening to me, and who was behind it all.

I went into the rest area to go to the bathroom, and as I was washing up, I saw my reflection in the mirror, and flinched. The two gashes from the fire were nothing compared to the cut on my forehead from Landry, which was still oozing blood. The area around it was very red, and very tender. I was going to have a gigantic bruise there, very soon.

The blood that had run down my face had dried in black streaks, and I was able to wash that off. But there was nothing I could do about the blood that had dripped onto my shirt and pants, and the huge stains that darkened my shirt where I'd pulled it up to hold against the wound when it was bleeding freely.

I returned to the road. There was a barrier dividing the eastbound and westbound sides of the interstate, so I had to drive farther east until I reached an exit where I could turn around. As I rolled down the ramp, I realized that I was going to have to stop for gas. The only question was which was the least risky way to pay—by credit card at the pump, which could easily be traced, or by paying in cash, and potentially arousing suspicion in the clerk.

Then, suddenly, it became clear that it was in my best interest to use a credit card. *And* to go into the store and have the clerk see my face. Because I wanted Landry, and whoever else was trying to keep me away from the trial, to know I was way out here. This gas station was over a hundred miles from my confrontation with Landry. As far as they were concerned, I was going to keep going east on the interstate.

When they found out I was well on my way to New Mexico, there was no way they'd expect that what I was really doing was returning to the Phoenix area, because I was going to Cactus Curt's Steakhouse. Because tonight was a Humongously Big Occasion.

THIRTY

IT WAS SIX twenty-five when I reached the restaurant at Cactus Curt's.

I had stopped at one more rest area to clean up before I arrived, hoping that my appearance wouldn't be so distracting that management would call the authorities. I knew the crowd of people at the restaurant would be so big that if I didn't attract a lot of attention to myself, there was no way I'd be noticed.

But the cuts on my face and the outsized bloodstains on my shirt made that a pretty big if.

Even though my head wound had finally stopped bleeding, it still looked very ugly—a jagged black line in the center of a large dark red area above my right eyebrow. And my shirt couldn't have been more of a mess. If you didn't know better, you'd have thought I'd been shot several times in the stomach.

I decided to do what I could to minimize the chance that my appearance would attract attention. I parked, and headed right for the gift shop, which was squeezed between the restaurant itself and the Wild West store-front that was to host the shoot-out in a few minutes.

Amidst the forest of racks of shot glasses, coffee mugs, and refrigerator magnets, I found a large T-shirt with "Cactus Curt's" stenciled on the front. I also bought a Cactus Curt's baseball cap, and some large sunglasses. The woman at the cash register winced when she saw the cut, and asked me what had happened. I believe the words I uttered were "Oh, it's not as bad as it looks. I fell on a rock trying to save my dog from running across the road. He'll be okay."

I told you I was a bad liar.

I made it out of the shop without further mortification, and went right back to my car, where I switched T-shirts, and donned the cap and the glasses. I had to adjust the band of the cap to make it too large for my head, because it hurt just to wear it. But with the bill tilted down slightly, and the glasses, I looked less like a horror movie victim, and more like a tourist who didn't know that he looked like an idiot.

It was now after six-thirty, so I hurried out of the car, and started toward the restaurant entrance. I had to walk across the street where the six forty-five shoot-out was being set up. Employees had set up barricades on the side of the road opposite the wooden facade on which were painted the signs identifying the sheriff's office, the saloon, the hotel, and the general store. Doorways were cut into the facade to make the illusion that much more real. Additional atmosphere was achieved by the hitching posts, watering troughs, the stretch of wooden sidewalk, and the wagon stationed outside the hotel for Mad Bill's dramatic death plunge.

The right end of the facade abutted the gift shop, which was the first real building on the street. To the right of the shop was the restaurant, and that's where I went.

The entrance was a large archway, with a hostess positioned at the right side. She didn't give me a second glance as she led me to my table, which spared me the effort of coming up with another explanation for the welt on my head.

But I hadn't taken four steps into the restaurant when I recognized someone across the entrance. He didn't see me—he was in profile, and speaking on a cell phone. At first glance, I was unable to put a name to the face. But curiously, I was not concerned. Even though I couldn't immediately place the man, I knew that I knew him, and I knew that he wasn't a threat.

And then it came to me—it was Joe Hextall! My buddy from the gym. I hadn't recognized him because I'd never seen him except in workout shorts and a sweaty T-shirt. For a moment, I was oddly comforted by the knowledge that my old world still existed. That there were still pickup basketball games on Monday nights, and meaningless insults to pass back and forth. That there just might be somewhere to return to if I could ever find my way out of this nightmare that had grabbed hold of my life.

I almost called out to him, but then he turned, and reality slapped me down. It wasn't Joe Hextall. It was just somebody who looked like him. First Dale, and now Joe. My mind was obviously reacting to the stress of the past few days.

But even if the man in the restaurant had been Joe, I couldn't very well have brought him into the mess I was dealing with. There was no way to know whether I was even going to survive the night, much less through tomorrow. If Beta kept the pressure on, I was going to have to stay involved in the trial. And if I did that, it was only a matter of time before Landry and his homicidal gang killed me. For all I knew, they were here, waiting in ambush.

I followed the hostess to my table. The waitress came over quickly, and I placed an order that I knew wouldn't create any special attention.

The restaurant had several dining rooms. This was one of the larger ones, rectangular in shape. One of the long walls featured oversized windows, which looked out on the Western street scene. Behind the opposite wall was the kitchen. Patrons entered at either end, through doors on the shorter walls.

Outside, I heard the beginnings of the Wild West show. Each one of the explosions from the blanks the cowboys were firing made me jump. With today's attempted murder by Landry, the subsequent pistol-whipping, the grand theft auto, the six-plus-hour drive through the desert, and the latest in a series of death threats to the people I loved most in the world, not to mention the insane notion that my dead brother might somehow be involved in all of this, my nerves were pretty frayed.

I was expecting Beta, but I still didn't know what he looked like, unless, of course, he really was Dale, which I still refused to believe. All I knew was that I had reached such a desperate point that if I believed he'd been acting alone, I might have tried to kill him right there, and suffer the consequences. But if Beta had any brains at all—and clearly he did—he'd have someone keeping an eye on Amy, Erica, and Henley. If Beta didn't check in, the people I loved most would die.

But while I watched for Beta, I caught sight of someone else who looked familiar. Like Joe, he was an African American man in his thirties, but unlike Joe, he had a goatee. He was sitting beyond me, near the far exit.

And then he stood up, and looked past me, toward the nearer exit, the one on my left. I glanced over at what had captured his attention, and suddenly I remembered who he was.

Because what the African American man was looking at was his partner, the white man with the shaved head. These were the two men who had appeared in the courthouse lobby on the day Beta had first contacted me, in the men's room. They were Kappa and Gamma.

And they were coming toward me. One from each side. With guns in their hands.

I got up from the table immediately, with absolutely no idea what to do. The exit to my left was blocked by the bald guy. The one to the right was blocked by the black guy. I chose straight ahead, toward the wall opposite the windows. Toward the kitchen.

Either they hadn't expected that I'd try to escape that way, or they'd overlooked it, but they were caught off guard. I ran for the swinging double doors through which the cowboy-hat-wearing waitstaff passed regularly. I pushed open the door, and took a hard left. I didn't know if there was an exit to the right, but if there was, I figured Kappa and Gamma would expect me to go that way. And I'd seen a door to the kitchen from the entryway when I first spotted the man who wasn't Joe.

My hasty turn, however, almost resulted in a bad collision with a waitress carrying a tray full of plates and glasses. "Easy there, hon," the woman said, before she realized I didn't belong there. "Hey!" she called after me, as I bolted past stainless steel shelves filled with salads and salad dressing, and turned right to avoid a bank of ovens.

I have to admit that I didn't even consider making a stand in the kitchen despite the fact that it was literally full of weapons. If I had been a Hollywood hero, no doubt I would have thought to grab a pot of boiling water, climb up to the top of some shelves, and dump it on my unsuspecting pursuers. Or I would have found a closet full of cleavers and hacked my way to freedom through a fusillade of bullets. But my mind was on escape only. I was so convinced that I was going to be shot if I didn't get out of there immediately, that I just raced through the kitchen without even the briefest notion to stop and confront the two guys with guns who were chasing me.

The room was bigger than I expected, extending behind both the entryway and what had to be the gift shop. About ten seconds after I reached the kitchen I heard a crash from behind me, and I assumed that Kappa or Gamma had slammed into a waitress carrying a tray as they entered. I didn't turn around to check. I just hoped it gave me enough time to reach my car and drive off before I got killed.

I had to dodge shelves and carts positioned at various places, but I was moving generally in the direction of the end of the building that abutted the Wild West show facade. Finally I saw an exit sign in the back corner of the room, and after slaloming around two startled busboys I burst through the door into a small, square entryway.

There were two other doors leaving the six-foot-by-six-foot space. One was directly in front of me, straight across from the kitchen. I wasn't sure where that one led. But the other was on my right. I chose that one, because it had to lead outside—to the back of the restaurant building.

I burst through, and was immediately hit with the

smell of garbage and the sound of weapons firing. I recognized the gunplay from the Wild West show taking place on the other side of the wooden facade that was immediately to my left. The smell was coming from two huge Dumpsters, extending dozens of feet from the building, which were stationed about twenty feet to the right of the doorway, blocking an escape in that direction.

But as I turned to the left to run behind the length of the facade, I heard a bang that was louder than the others. In fact, it sounded like it came from right behind my head. I turned around and looked up, and saw a smoking hole in the door behind me. When I turned back around, I saw two men in cowboy hats running back and forth through the facade—obviously two of the stuntmen, pretending to come in and out of the saloon during the big gunfight.

But another smaller figure, one without a cowboy hat, between one and two hundred feet away, was running directly toward me. I didn't recognize the man without the hat, but I could see the gun he held in his outstretched arm.

And then he fired.

THIRTY-ONE

IN LESS THAN a second, my brain processed the situation.

If I ran to the left, I'd head straight for the short man without the cowboy hat, who was shooting at me.

The Dumpsters were blocking an immediate move to the right. I'd have to go forward several feet to pass the Dumpsters before I could veer right, and move away from him. Even if he didn't cut me off, by the time I reached the end of the Dumpsters, he'd have a great shot at me.

I pulled open the door and tore back into the building.

To my left was the door to the kitchen. In about five seconds, it would burst open, and Kappa and Gamma would pour through. I yanked open the door to the right, and ran.

I should have known where it went, but I was still surprised when I found myself on the wooden staircase that the stuntmen used to reach the third-story balcony outside the faux Golden Palace Hotel.

There was nothing to do but race up the stairs.

I had about a five-second head start, and the design of the staircase was in my favor. Rather than one long, straight flight up two stories, the carpenters had built a landing on the second floor. That way, my assailants wouldn't have a straight shot up a long flight of stairs at me. The flight from the second story to the third was directly over the flight from the first floor to the second. They could try to shoot me from below, through the treads, but they wouldn't be able to see me.

The problem with all of this, however, was that the staircase was outside the building. So my peripheral vision was able to pick up the fact that as I fled up the steps, I was rapidly getting higher and higher above the earth.

For those of you who are curious, you can literally be running for your life with a system full of adrenaline, and still get nauseated from vertigo.

At the first hint of sickness, I shut my eyes.

It sounds stupid, but it works. The dizziness and motion sickness come from the brain's inability to appropriately process the data it is receiving from your peripheral vision. And a flight of stairs offers extremely consistent footing. If you are climbing a staircase using a handrail, even without sight, you can be pretty confident you aren't going to trip on a tree root or stumble off a curb.

The difficulty of such an effort is increased, of course, when you are being chased by homicidal lunatics firing loaded weapons at you.

The sounds of the stunt gunfight were all around me as I climbed the steps, but the real bullets didn't start flying until I had turned the corner and headed up the second flight to the third story.

Of course I was slowed down by the fact that I had

to open my eyes to see where I was going, which meant that I had to shield myself from the view of the terrifying drop over the banister to the ground below.

Once on the steps to the third floor, though, a succession of thoughts raced through my brain, as the sounds of the real and blank cartridges exploded all around me.

First, I guessed that I had an advantage, since I had been to Cactus Curt's so often. I was hoping that the three others chasing me weren't familiar with what was to come, and that I could use my knowledge against them.

But right on the heels of that comforting thought was the realization that what I knew wasn't going to help me at all. Because what I knew was that I was being chased right into a dead end. The terrace on the third floor of the fake hotel on the fake street next to Cactus Curt's Steakhouse had one way in, and one way out.

And then, just before I burst through the door to the end of my pathetic escape attempt, the final, shining piece of information that kept me from losing all hope presented itself.

The ax.

I had forgotten the positively joyful news that Mad Bill Barton was an ax murderer! And waiting up on the veranda for the stuntman who played the murderous outlaw was my weapon of choice. Right under the rocking chair. I was so excited about the prospect of confronting and defeating my enemies that I distinctly remember thinking that things couldn't have worked out any better.

That, of course, was a ridiculous thought. Any number of things could have been better, including the substitution of a machine gun for the ax, or a sudden stairway collapse plunging Kappa, Gamma, and the short guy to their deaths.

I mention it only to illustrate just how overtaxed my brain was at the moment that I hit the door to the balcony and emerged onto it with my beautiful, if terribly violent and risky, and ultimately farcical, plan.

My strategy was the following. I was still about five to ten seconds ahead of my adversaries. That would give me enough time to reach the other end of the balcony, and get hold of the ax. I would attempt to cross back to the doorway before the first one emerged, but I was pretty sure I wouldn't have the time. So I was prepared to throw the ax—the distance was laughably short. I would strike whoever came through the door first with a fatal blow to the chest.

The fact that the doorway didn't allow more than one attacker through at a time was the key to the rest of the plan. As soon as the first of them fell, I'd pounce on the dropped gun, and as the next two came through the door, I'd shoot each, and then make my escape.

A further indication of just how much stress I was under at the time can be seen in the fact that my master plan completely ignored the fact that this entire operation was to take place on a third-floor balcony.

That oversight, so to speak, became abundantly clear as I crashed through the final doorway of my journey at Cactus Curt's. I distinctly remember making eye contact with a woman watching the Wild West show down on the opposite side of the street, behind the barricade. Surprise covered her face as I made the scene.

My hands covered mine, as I dropped to my knees, instantly and powerfully ill.

Fighting to ignore the nausea that was now rhythmically seizing my stomach, I turned my head away from the flimsy wooden railing that stood between me and a drop to my death, and I crawled forward. The stuntmen below continued their wild battle as the sound of footfalls on the steps to the balcony grew louder. I was only five feet from the rocking chair now, but when I reached it, there would be no time to approach the doorway before the throw. My aim was going to have to be true across the entire twelve feet of balcony.

For a frightening moment as I scampered forward I couldn't see the ax, but then, when I was about three feet from the rocker, I saw the butt end of the handle. When I finally got to the chair, I reached under it for the weapon.

The approaching sound of the three killers had just about made it to the top of the steps when I finally laid my hands on the ax, grabbed it, and spun on my knees to face the assault.

One of the effects of abnormal amounts of adrenaline on the human brain is to dramatically speed up reflexes and mental reactions. This often leads to a perception that time has slowed down.

I thought I had already been operating with a full hormonal load as I blasted through the kitchen and up the stairs, but as my assailants pushed open the door to the balcony, my endocrinologic system pumped whatever adrenaline it had left into my bloodstream, and everything went into slow motion.

For purely theatrical reasons, the doorway to the balcony had been installed in an otherwise foolish manner. From the perspective of the audience on the street, the opening was on the right end of the balcony, and the door swung out from the building. Worse still, the hinges were on the left side of the door, so that as it opened, the person entering the balcony couldn't see who was waiting for him on the other side of the door until he had stepped past it.

For the purpose of creating suspense, this was a perfect arrangement. As the door opened, the crowd had a clear view of both combatants. The nefarious Mad Bill Barton, waiting fiendishly on the left side of the balcony, and the brave Sheriff Goodheart in the open doorway. But the sheriff's view of the balcony itself was entirely blocked by the open door. So he suspected nothing as he strode foolishly forward into the dastardly ambush.

I was in Mad Bill's position, only instead of standing there with a pistol, loaded with blanks, I was kneeling there, with an ax.

A lightweight, plastic, visually accurate, but completely useless, stunt ax.

THIRTY-TWO

I SHOULD HAVE known the ax was phony, of course, but the thought had never crossed my mind.

But if an inability to develop well-engineered battle strategies is one of the disadvantages of having an adrenaline-soaked brain, one of the advantages is an ability to make a multitude of on-the-spot superficial and desperate plans. So as the door opened, my brilliant scheme to dispatch the first attacker onto the balcony with a mighty blow to the chest with a heavy, metal, wood-chopping blade underwent an immediate revision.

The bald guy was first through, and he led with his gun, firing rather indiscriminately, I thought. Fortunately, since I was on my knees, his aim was far too high.

I waited until he had cleared the open door before I made my move. Which was to scream like a deranged person, and throw the fake ax at him.

Thanks to all of my practice, my aim was terrific. The look on Baldy's face betrayed undiluted terror as he processed first the scream, and then the hurled blade heading directly for his shiny head. As far as he was concerned, the ax was quite real, and quite deadly. Just as I'd hoped, he reacted quickly and emphatically, retreating back off the balcony, and pulling the door closed behind him with a bang.

According to my brain's manic calculations, bad guy number one's disappearance would be only momentary. After getting over the shock of nearly having his skull cleaved by a flying ax, he would compose himself, and reenter the balcony. Although he would correctly reason that I probably did not have an arsenal of wood-cutting weapons out there, nonetheless, he would approach with more care the next time.

And that would give me the time I needed. Because part two of my newly devised plan for survival was not complicated.

All I had to do was to overcome my pathological fear of heights, walk over to the railing, and jump off the balcony.

I was only five years old when I first learned that I suffered from vertigo.

The precipitating event was a trip up some motel stairs in Williams, Arizona, about thirty miles west of Flagstaff. It was summer vacation, and we were on a family trip to the Grand Canyon.

Dad had a court appearance he couldn't avoid on the morning of the first day of the trip, so we didn't embark until after lunch. That was fine with Dale and me—we loved traveling at whatever time of day or night. Eating in new restaurants, sleeping in strange beds—these were exciting adventures for us.

We ate dinner at the Stagecoach Depot, my parents'

favorite restaurant in Flagstaff. I had steak, mashed potatoes, and corn, followed by an ice-cream sundae. It was a magnificent feast, and I fell asleep in the car soon after we got back on the road.

We pulled into the Iguana Inn at about ten that evening, and the only vacant room was on the second floor. My dad brought the two small suitcases up to the room, and my mom followed with Dale and me up the exterior stairway.

My mistake was to look down to the side as we ascended. There was a floodlight shining so that the metal bars of the railing were clearly illuminated, as was a wooden lattice that blocked off a storage area next to the ice machine at the end of the parking lot.

As I climbed the stairs, the vertical members of the railing seemed to move against the grid of the lattice below. Suddenly, I had a bad headache, and a strange, tight feeling in my stomach. I was fascinated by the curiously shifting pattern of the vertical bars against the wooden grid below, as well as the significant drop from the second floor down to the parking lot.

Within seconds I lost my balance. I stumbled forward onto my knees, and quite unceremoniously vomited my fabulous dinner all over the place.

So as I crawled toward the edge of the third-story balcony of the Golden Palace Hotel, I looked directly down at my hands, using all of my concentration to keep my stomach under control. In about one and one half seconds I was going to vault over the railing, hoping to land safely in the wagon below, escaping certain death at the hands of three professional killers. If I started vomiting, my chances of success were going to drop precipitously.

In the Wild West show, Mad Bill took his swan dive after crashing through the center portion of the railing.

Since I believed that I had the best chance of surviving the fall if I did exactly what the stuntman did, I crawled right to the middle of the railing, and stood, with eyes closed, trying to hold off the inevitable vertigo for as long as possible.

Even though time was moving slowly, I knew I could not delay. At any instant the door behind me was going to reopen, and Kappa or Gamma was going to come back out here and shoot me. I opened my eyes quickly, and made sure the wagon was below me. As I expected, I instantly lost my balance, and fell through the break-away railing.

For those aspiring to the position of Hollywood stunt performer, I can now report with great confidence that a thirty-foot dead drop into a wagon-sized landing pad is not as easy as it looks. And for those curious, several centuries ago, Sir Isaac Newton determined that the rate at which one falls when diving off a building accelerates at the rate of 9.8 meters per second per second.

However rapid and short-lived, my descent felt endless, and was anything but graceful. I flung the balsa wood railing piece into the street, kicked my legs and windmilled my arms ridiculously, and shouted, "Whoa!" all the way down, as if that would do anything. Miraculously, I managed to land flat on my back on the thick foam safety mattress in the back of the wagon, unhurt.

More miraculous than that, even as I was still bouncing around on the cushion, well before I had a chance to climb down from the wagon, it began to move. Then I heard Beta's voice, shouting, "Get out of there, Tom! Quick!"

For a moment, I lay there, absorbing the fact that Beta was definitely not Dale. In my heart, I'd known it wasn't possible. Dale was dead. And there was absolutely no way that he'd threaten me or anyone else in his family.

But a tiny, irrational part of me had held out hope that somehow, my big brother had come to save the day, that the threats I'd heard over the phone earlier that day were some kind of misunderstanding, that everything was going to be okay.

That irrational part of me had conveniently forgotten that two days ago, I'd slept with Dale's wife, but before I'd even had a chance to wrestle with the now-irrelevant implications of that, I looked up at the face of the large man with the shaved head pointing a gun at me, and understood the all-too-relevant implications of my current predicament. Beta was dragging the wagon away from the building facade, so my pursuers couldn't follow me down the same way I had taken. But as Baldy aimed his weapon, I realized that I was just lying there on my back, staring up at him, waiting to be shot.

I rolled over just as the report of his gun's discharge sounded. I didn't feel anything, so I kept rolling, right off the foam padding, over the edge of the wagon, onto the street.

Another gunshot rang out, and a puff of dust kicked up two feet to my left. I ran directly across the street and into the applauding crowd, who must have thought this was the strangest Wild West show they'd ever seen in their lives.

Beta was about five feet ahead of me, and I followed him, mostly because I couldn't think of anything else to do. We were in the parking lot, but rather than running down the open aisles, we were snaking our way around and between cars. I figured we were hoping to make ourselves tougher targets to hit, but I was pretty sure we had a good enough lead to get away. After all, we had left my three assailants at the top of the stairs.

They were going to have to descend both flights of steps, come through the facade, and then cross the street just to reach the beginning of the parking area.

"Hurry up!" Beta shouted over his shoulder, as he turned right and ran down a row of cars, stopping at a nondescript, white Chevy four-door. It was a rather stupid command, I thought. I was running for my life—did he really think I wasn't going as fast as I could?

He jumped into the driver's seat and started the engine, and moments later I climbed into the passenger seat. Before I had even closed the door he spun the tires. We flew down the aisle and were almost out of the parking area when I saw a black SUV pull out into the aisle about two hundred feet behind us. "I think they're following us," I said, moronically.

"No shit," Beta snapped, pulling hard on the wheel as we exited the lot.

I'd been to Cactus Curt's enough to know that the road to the parking area was long and narrow, with few, if any, turnoffs for miles, until you reached the state highway that ran down to Scottsdale, or farther up into the mountains.

Depending on how fast Beta's car was, we had a chance to escape if we could reach the highway.

"You ever shoot a gun?" Beta asked, pulling a weapon out from under his seat with his free hand and holding it out to me.

I took the pistol and cradled it in both hands. It was heavier than I'd expected. "No," I said, lamely. "Sorry."

Henley's line of work had given him a great respect for weapons, and when I was in high school, he revealed to me that he had considered obtaining a permit and keeping one at home for protection, because of his job as a prosecutor. But he decided that the risk of some accident was higher than the risk of being successfully attacked as a result of his job.

For myself, I'd never really given much thought to owning a weapon. Up until about a week ago, I had always felt quite safe. As I sat there, cradling Beta's pistol in my lap like a live grenade, I felt pitifully unprepared. I also felt angry that it should have come to this. I was living in Arizona, damn it. In the United States of America. Not in some godforsaken Third World country where ordinary citizens had to protect themselves against roving bands of commandos.

"No problem," he said, with a half-smile. "The shooting isn't the hard part. It's the hitting something that is."

If the banter was supposed to relax me, it failed. The SUV was gaining on us, and my heart was pounding so hard my teeth were chattering. Beta quickly instructed me in firing a pistol, showed me how to disengage the safety, explained how many rounds of ammunition were in the clip, and then the back window of the car exploded, throwing bits of glass all over the car. I ducked forward, completely uselessly, and then rolled down the passenger window.

"Aim low at first," Beta shouted over the roar of the air rushing past the speeding car, and the repeated *pops* from the gun being fired at us. He began to pull the Chevy back and forth across the road in an irregular pattern, hoping to make us a tougher target. "See if you can pick up where the bullets are hitting the road in front of their car. That might help you take out the windshield."

Neither of us had any delusions that I'd actually be able to hit a target as small as a human being while shooting from a swerving car. But we thought the windshield was a possibility. I disconnected my seat belt, and turned around in my seat. Because I was on the right side of the car, I was going to have to reach out of the window and fire the gun with my left hand, which made success that much less probable. But then I realized that they'd already shot out our rear window— there was no reason to hang out the side window and use my left hand. I could just turn around in my seat and use my right hand to shoot directly out the back.

I had to hook my left arm around my headrest so I didn't fly into Beta as he tried to shake the SUV. It looked like the short guy was in the passenger seat of their car, leaning out the window and firing at us.

"Try not to flinch when he shoots at you," Beta shouted. "It doesn't do anything except make it harder for you to get off a good shot."

That was easy for him to say. Every time the killer pointed his gun at us, I felt like diving to the floor. Instead, I wrapped both of my arms around the headrest and held the gun in both hands, which served both to stabilize me as Beta swerved, and to give me the illusion that I was protected, as the seat back stayed between me and my attacker. Taking aim, I fired. The recoil threw my hands upwards so violently that I banged them hard on the ceiling of the car. It felt like my left hand was going to be pretty badly bruised the following day.

That was and remains the only bullet I have ever fired in my life. To say that the results were dramatic would be an understatement. To say that I was lucky would be a preposterous understatement. If pressed, I would have to concede that there was a chance that at the moment I squeezed the trigger, my eyes were shut.

But whatever the case, virtually instantaneously with the discharge of my weapon, the SUV's windshield shattered, and that vehicle veered radically off the road to the left. Beta looked through the rearview mirror and laughed. "Holy shit!" he said, as we sped toward the state highway. We turned south when we reached it, heading toward Scottsdale. "Nice shot." And then, as if it were the most natural thing in the world, he announced, "Listen—I got hit—screwed up my back a little. I want to get down the road a few minutes and then stop." He leaned forward, and I could see a large blood-stain on his shirt around his left shoulder blade.

Before I could say anything, he pointed at my left hand and said, "Looks like I'm not the only one."

I'd been so focused on our improbable deliverance from disaster and then Beta's injury that I'd been ignoring the throbbing of my hand, assuming that the pain was simply the aftermath of slamming it against the ceiling so hard. But when I looked at it, I could see that I was bleeding pretty badly from the fleshy part of my palm, beneath the pinky.

As soon as I gave the injury my attention, it started to hurt pretty good. My new shirt was relatively blood-free to this point, so I used it to try to stop my hand from bleeding.

About five minutes farther south there was a rest area, and Beta pulled off the highway. He parked in the long shadows of the concession building, but as I went to open my door, he stopped me. "We better wait until sunset," he said. "If anybody sees us bleeding and calls for help, we're in trouble. You didn't kill all three of them back there. Somebody called somebody. We're not in the clear, yet."

The absence of color in Beta's face punctuated his statement nicely. He rested his head back, and closed his eyes. "When it's dark, run in to the bathroom and grab some paper towels. Maybe we can stop this bleeding. I'm gonna rest a second."

This was the second time that day I'd pulled into a

rest area to administer first aid to myself, and as I sat there, waiting for the summer sun to set, some of the nervous energy that I'd generated during the shoot-out and the chase started to transform itself into anger.

Sure, if Beta hadn't pulled the wagon away from the wall of the building over at Cactus Curt's, Baldy could have jumped down from the balcony, and I'd have been caught and murdered. And sure, he helped me escape by driving me away from there.

But he was the person who put me into the danger in the first place. He was the man who had pretended to be Dale, to try to manipulate me. If he hadn't threatened Amy and Erica and Henley, I never would have been near Cactus Curt's—I'd have been into New Mexico now, well on my way to Texas. In fact, if he hadn't grabbed me that day in the men's room, none of this would have happened.

But just before I was about to unload on him, Beta opened his eyes and turned to me. He looked awful. "Listen," he said, pushing himself up and opening the door. "I must have been hit worse than I thought, so I gotta get in there." And with that, he opened his door, stepped out of the car, and fell to the ground in a heap.

THIRTY-THREE

I JUMPED OUT of my door and ran around to the other side of the car. Beta was lying on his stomach, one arm trapped beneath him, the other stretched forward.

As soon as I bent down to turn him over, I saw the problem. The wound to his upper back was bad enough—but there was another injury, lower on his left side, beneath his rib cage, where the real trouble was. The bloodstain from that one was huge, and growing.

I checked the rest area quickly. The three cars that had been parked when we pulled in had left already. Two new ones had come in, and the drivers were still in the bathroom. But it was only a matter of time—no more than seconds—before they emerged. I had no idea how I was going to deal with the kindness of strangers. I had to get Beta up and into the car again.

I touched him on the right shoulder, and he flinched. "What?"

"You passed out," I told him. "You've got to get back into the car or somebody's going to see you." I have to admit that my concern was not solely for the fallen man. I had to keep myself hidden, or I was finished, too.

My one, very fresh, personal experience with bullet wounds led me to believe that what Beta did at that moment was rather extraordinary. As if by sheer dint of will, he forced himself into consciousness, pushed himself up onto his knees and right hand, and then, slowly, stood.

The driver's door was still open, and he reached for it, using it to steady himself as he lowered himself back onto the blood-soaked seat.

I closed the door, and spoke to him through the window. "I'm going in to get some paper towels and water. Are you going to be okay?"

He smiled grimly, gave me a thumbs-up, and said, "Never better."

I turned and hurried inside.

The throbbing in my hand reminded me that I had taken a bullet, too. Once in the bathroom, I ran it under cold water in hopes that I might slow the bleeding, and possibly dull the pain.

But all that the water did was to increase the flow of blood, and intensify the pain. Upon further inspection, the bullet had torn a considerable amount of flesh off the side of my hand, but as far as I could tell, it had missed the bone. I grabbed a bunch of paper towels, soaked some of them with the cold water, and raced back out to the car to help Beta.

My feelings toward the man were conflicted. He had threatened the lives of my loved ones, and then, hours later, he had saved my life. I think that as cynical and hardened as I'd become in those few days, I simply hadn't yet reached the point where I could just turn my back on a man suffering from gunshot wounds received in helping me escape my own death.

When I got there, Beta was sagging back against the headrest, his eyes closed. His face was ashen, and I had no idea if he was even conscious. But as soon as I opened the door, he turned to me and asked, "Got those towels?" Then he leaned forward, resting his forearms on the steering wheel.

I pulled up the base of his T-shirt to reveal the ugly wound under the left side of his rib cage. Red-black blood was pulsing from it at an alarming rate, despite the fact that there was already some clotting at the site of the injury.

"Press some wet cloths against it," Beta said, in a soft voice. "We've got to stop the bleeding."

I took four or five of the wet paper towels and gently pushed them up against the angry hole in his back. Beta gasped at the contact, but when I pulled away, he said, "No. Leave it. I'll hold it there. Get your hand to stop bleeding." And then he reached around with his left hand and took the already blood-soaked towels from me.

While he attended to his back, I returned my attention to my hand. I made a crude bandage out of a folded pair of the wet towels, and then wrapped several of the dry ones around it. I lowered the mess down to the car seat, and pressed down as hard as I could.

Beta cleared his throat and began to speak softly. "Your brother was a hell of a soldier."

"You knew Dale? You were in Afghanistan?"

"I only met him once. We wanted him. We only recruited from men in the field. Only the best soldiers. Intensely dedicated. Fearless. Driven. But he saw the danger in what we were doing. Way before I did. He turned us down cold."

I thought it was possible that Beta was delirious, but

whatever he could tell me about Dale I wanted to hear. "What do you mean, he saw the danger? What danger?"

Ignoring me, Beta went on. "I think he even talked about you. Yeah. Told me if I ever got in trouble with the law, I should call you because you were a hell of a lawyer." Then he laughed, as if there were something very funny about that. "Want to take my case?"

Beta let out a ragged breath, then continued. He spoke hesitantly, like someone barely awake, recalling a dream. "We were recruiting for something called the Foundation. When the man signs on, the Foundation arranges his so-called death. The family is notified that their fallen loved one was a hero, and that very little of his body was recovered. Usually, the Foundation cuts off a piece of your body and sends it home." He pointed to his right ear. "See?"

I peered down and saw that there was no lobe. God almighty.

"They ship the fragment back in case somebody wants to do a DNA test. That way, there's never any inquiry. The family deals with the funeral. That's just as well, because to sign up with the Foundation, the soldier has to accept that he is dead to his family. And vice versa."

"Why would anybody do that?"

Beta sighed. "You think you're making a sacrifice that needs to be made. To protect the country. And then, you're in the middle of Phoenix . . ." His voice trailed off.

I didn't like the sound of that. "What are you talking about?"

Beta didn't answer for a while. Then, out of the blue, he opened his car door and announced, "We have to leave here." He staggered out of the car.

"Wait a minute." I jumped out after him, and reached

him at the vehicle's trunk. "We can't go anywhere. You're still bleeding."

He was, and badly. The paper towel compress had done next to nothing. Blood had dripped down into his pants, and had begun to seep through.

"If we stay here, they'll find us," he told me. "You drive, and I'll tell you what you need to know."

It made sense. The three goons had followed us from the restaurant for long enough to get a description of our car, complete with license plate. Sitting at a rest stop within fifteen to twenty miles of our shoot-out was just plain stupid.

I went around to the driver's side, and sat down on the blood-drenched seat. I waited for Beta to join me, then I started up the engine and left the rest area.

The sun had set, and darkness was falling quickly, so I got off at the first exit. I wasn't familiar with this particular part of the state, but I figured I could drive around until I found a safe place to stash the car where we wouldn't be seen.

As I worked my way along the small county roads, I asked, "Who runs the Foundation?"

Beta took a deep breath. "Yeah. Well. They manage to keep that pretty buttoned down, but I can tell you this much. It runs at least as high up as Undersecretary of Defense Newton. I know he's in it, because that's where my latest orders originated."

"And what exactly *is* the Foundation? What do you do?"

"We're a secret subgroup of the military, dedicated to keeping America safe from terrorism, at any cost."

My limited understanding of the armed forces came from Dale's experience. I had never heard of such a thing. "I thought the military was already dedicated to keeping America safe from terrorism."

"At any cost," Beta repeated. "*Any* cost."

The man's voice was soft. It was getting a little hard for me to hear him. He was obviously badly weakened by his injuries. "Are you sure we shouldn't get you to a hospital or something?" I asked.

"By now, they'll have people covering every emergency room within thirty miles of Cactus Curt's. As soon as they get the call, one of the Foundation will be in our ER within five minutes. If you bring me to a hospital, they'll kill both of us."

"But if you bleed to death, what difference is it going to make?"

Beta ignored me. "The Foundation plays by its own rules. You know how the Constitution restricts military action? That doesn't apply to us. We go wherever we need to go, and do whatever we need to do. You'd be surprised how many people will obey authority. There aren't that many of us. We're just in the right places, and we know how to give orders."

That was an awful lot of ominous information. "So the Foundation operates outside the Constitution?"

"I told you our mission—to protect the country from terrorism, at any cost. Including the Constitution."

I knew he wasn't inviting a debate, so I refrained from the obvious inquiry about exactly what country would be protected if the Constitution was destroyed in the process. "And you're in the Foundation?"

"How do you think I know all this stuff?" Beta asked.

So Beta was part of a secret arm of the military that ignored the Constitution in order to secure the country from terrorism.

"What does all this have to do with me?" I asked. "Why am I so important? And why did you have to drag my family into it?"

When Beta didn't answer, I looked over and saw that

he had passed out again. He was slumped over to the right, exposing the wounds to his back. The one on the bottom was still bleeding.

I was torn. Beta obviously needed help, but if what he said was true, I'd be risking his life, as well as my own, if I brought him to a hospital. And even if I weren't driving, I wouldn't have the first idea of how to help, other than to try to stop the bleeding, which clearly hadn't worked so far.

As I drove farther down the road, Beta drifted in and out of consciousness, occasionally repeating something like, "Watch out, Tom—don't let them white you," or "They'll white you if they can." Either I wasn't hearing him clearly, or he was speaking nonsense.

After about ten minutes, I drove past a billboard that was lit well enough to illuminate Beta's face for a moment. His face was the color of chalk, and he had broken out in a sweat. Right then, I made a decision. I realized it was risky, but I couldn't ignore the man's deteriorating situation anymore. I pulled over onto the shoulder, well out of the range of the billboard's light, and killed the engine. The sky was overcast, and the road was dark. I hadn't seen a car in fifteen minutes.

I pulled out my old cell phone, but it had run out of power. I took Beta's cell phone off of the clip on his belt, and I dialed 911.

"Why are we stopping?" Beta asked, weakly. Then he opened his eyes, and saw me holding his cell phone. "Don't use that," he said, reaching up and pulling the phone away from my ear, and thumbing the off button. He checked the display, and laughed quietly, without a hint of humor. "Oh, well. It was over anyway."

He looked out of his window, then opened the door. "Where are you going?" I asked.

He bent down, and slid a small gun from an ankle

holster. Then he opened the door, and stepped out of the car. Through the open door he pointed it vaguely in my direction, and said, "Stay away from me. They've been monitoring my phone. They'll be coming, now. You've got to get out of here." He reached into the area behind his belt buckle, and brought his fingers to his lips. "I just put a cyanide capsule into my mouth," he told me. "That second shot to the back did it. I'm finished."

"I can take you to—"

"There's papers in the trunk that explain everything. I wrote it all down. Read it. Whatever you do. Read it. Make sure you get to the trial tomorrow and tell everyone what you know. But stay hidden until the trial. The Foundation will be after you. If they get to you before the trial, you're dead."

I wasn't willing to leave him there, though. He so clearly needed help. But he kept pointing the gun at me, and threatening me, every time I made a move to get out of the car.

During that two or three minutes he spoke, occasionally rapidly, sometimes haltingly. He apologized for trying to trick me into thinking that he was Dale. He admitted bugging my cell phone that first day in the bathroom with a listening device and a GPS chip, which was how he kept such close tabs on me. He seemed to be wobbling in and out of consciousness as he spoke, and occasionally what he said sounded more like the ravings of a fevered mind than the lucid thoughts of a coherent one.

At the conclusion of a particularly long rant, he seemed to gather himself, and focus clearly on me. "Everything I've told you is true, Tom. Believe me when I tell you that they will kill you without thinking twice.

The minute you stood up in the courtroom and that idiot Judge Klay put you on this case, your life was over."

Then he bit down, swallowed hard, and said, "Get
out of here. They'll be all over this place in minutes."
Seconds later, he collapsed.

THIRTY-FOUR

I LEAPT FROM the car and hurried to the downed man's side. The light from the open car door lit him poorly, but well enough to confirm what I feared. Beta's eyes and mouth were open, and he wasn't breathing.

They'll be all over this place in minutes. The harsh reality of my predicament forced me back to the car. I closed Beta's door, then jumped into the driver's seat, and sped away.

Although unable to leave the injured man despite what he had done to me, I had no problem leaving his dead body. The help he needed now was way out of my hands.

If Beta was right, and they were on the way, I was betting they would be coming from the Cactus Curt's area, from the north. So I continued south, on the county road.

I knew they had a description of the car, and the license plate number, so I also knew that one unlucky, random glance from a cop in a passing cruiser, and I was screwed.

I began to look for a place to ditch the car. But I was in such desolate country that I decided to get closer to Scottsdale. If I left the car here, it would be the only car parked in a ten-mile radius, and I'd have to walk for hours before I came across a living soul.

I was afraid of checking into a motel, no matter how remote. All I needed was for somebody to have put my picture on the news, and suddenly a Days Inn night clerk is getting interviewed on cable news by a shrill woman with hair like a blond helmet while a police helicopter broadcasts an aerial shot of me desperately running across the arroyos of central Arizona.

I needed to stop being so paranoid. I turned on the radio in an effort to return to reality. Even if the Foundation was as dangerous and powerful as Beta described, it had limits. It was a covert commando group—not a major law enforcement arm with direct ties to statewide media. Even if the plan was to get a manhunt started, it was going to take time to publicize. They couldn't just snap their fingers and put me on CNN.

It was a few minutes before eleven o'clock—less than five hours after we'd escaped back at the restaurant. And the driver of the SUV must have been seriously hurt, or else that car never would have spun out of control as it did. Dealing with that had to have taken some time.

The advertisements for KNWS, AM 740, called it a twenty-four-hour news station. In reality, though, from about eight P.M. to six A.M. it ran call-in shows for people who liked to telephone radio stations and gripe. The shows were hosted by people who liked to gripe more than the callers. But at the top of the hour, even at night, the station actually did broadcast news. I tuned it in, just to be sure that I was in the clear. In the few minutes left before eleven o'clock, the host of the show gave what I thought was a foolishly simplistic argument to vote for Governor Hamilton in the special election for senator—something about how we in Arizona more than anyone else in the nation needed a strong leader who would protect us in Washington, like Hamilton was personally protecting us from terrorists like Juan Gomez.

When that claptrap finally ended, at exactly eleven o'clock, I heard something else that I wasn't expecting.

"This is Neville Jordan, with news on the hour. Our top story: Local criminal defense attorney Thomas Carpenter, whose unconventional tactics in the Juan Gomez trial have garnered him national media attention this past week, is now wanted himself by authorities on charges of arson and murder. Mr. Carpenter, who is described by police as armed and dangerous, is a suspect in the shooting deaths of two men earlier today, and in the fire that claimed the life of his father, former Assistant District Attorney Henley Carpenter.

"Tom Carpenter was last seen north of Scottsdale, and the fugitive is believed to be traveling south in a white four-door Chevrolet Impala, with an Arizona license plate number ending in 347. Anyone with any information on the whereabouts of Carpenter may call this toll-free special hotline set up by the state police—"

I shut it off. While undoubtedly better than Beta's, my situation was growing considerably darker with every passing moment. Although I had a pocket full of cash and a loaded weapon in my possession, I was soaked in blood, had a headache from an earlier pistol-whipping, and a relatively fresh gunshot wound to the hand. I was wanted for three murders and an act of arson that I didn't commit, and my status as a fugitive was being broadcast all over the state. The car I was driving, besides having no rear window, was literally dripping with the blood of two victims of a gunfight. And its description, along with mine, was in the hands of every law enforcement agency in the Southwest.

And on top of it all, I was fleeing from the three most important people in the world to me, including my beloved Amy.

I had to think. I pulled down a small, unlit side road, turned off the car, and just sat there in the silence.

About a half hour later, I got an idea. But my head and my hand were throbbing so much it was tough to concentrate. I decided I'd better think it through some more.

And then I woke up.

It was three-fifteen in the morning.

The sleep had done nothing to ease the pain in my head, and my hand was considerably worse. It was stiff, and the makeshift bandage had dried and stuck to the wound.

The good news was that my plan had not been compromised by my inability to stay conscious. It was still inky dark, and I had time to do what I wanted.

I started the car, and pulled back onto the county road. I decided to stay off the interstate—it was only about forty-five minutes to Scottsdale, which was my destination.

At four A.M. sharp, I drove Beta's Chevy into the parking garage down the street from Cliff's office. It was one of those structures that required payment in a machine that generated a ticket which you placed in your windshield.

In hopes that it might buy me a little extra time before the car was discovered, I paid for several hours, and placed the ticket on the dashboard as instructed. I parked the car in a corner on the third tier, backing in to make the blown-out window less obvious, and to hide the rear license plate. In Arizona, we don't require front ones.

Then I exited the car, opened the trunk, and withdrew the solitary blue folder lying there. I closed the trunk, and walked to the enclosed stairwell located next to the elevator. My plan was to contact Cliff as he headed for work, and enlist his aid. All I wanted him to do was to confirm my suspicion that Beta was working alone, and that if I didn't go back to the trial, Amy and Erica and Henley would be okay.

If I was right, then I'd try to go underground, and live out my life as a fugitive. I certainly had enough cash to make a go of it for a while.

But if I was wrong, and somehow Amy and Erica's lives depended on my going into that courtroom, then I was going in.

I was ambivalent about the plan, because technically, even if all he did was contact Amy and Erica and make sure they were on their way, Cliff would be aiding and abetting a felon. I didn't like the idea of asking him to do that.

While I worked on that problem, I decided to sit in the stairwell and look through the papers that Beta had left for me in the car trunk. Although I had no intention of going into that courtroom again, I was curious about what he wanted so badly for me to read and to say at the trial.

An hour later, I had finished reading Beta's folder of material, and my plan had changed completely.

THIRTY-FIVE

I HAD PROPPED the stairwell door ajar and was watching as Cliff pulled into the parking garage at six forty-five. He was the fifteenth driver to enter the garage that morning. Sixteenth, if you counted me.

He normally parked on the second tier because a row of spaces on that level that was always open early in the morning was the closest to the exit. I kept my eye on the elevator, and when he emerged, I opened the door fully, caught his eye, and then retreated back into the stairwell. A second later, he opened the door and joined me.

He looked me up and down, eyes wide, mouth open. I could only imagine what he was thinking as I stood there before him in my blood-soaked clothing, head split open, hand wrapped in dried, blood-blackened paper towels. "Dude" was all he could manage.

"Before you say anything else, I'm a fugitive." He kept staring at me. "Just so you know."

Cliff continued to stare. "I listened to the radio on

the way in," he said. "Apparently you're going to be arrested for killing your father."

"Yeah."

"Well, you did a pretty bad job of that, my friend. I watched Henley drive off into the sunset with Amy and Erica yesterday afternoon, after they got their flat tire fixed. He looked pretty alive to me."

I closed my eyes, and literally sighed with relief. "You have no idea how happy I am that you told me that."

Cliff nodded. "So how about that hand? And your head? You thinking about maybe a trip to the hospital sometime soon?"

"Probably," I replied. "But I wonder if I could talk you into taking a personal day and helping me run an errand first."

Cliff insisted that he go across the street and get us coffee and something to eat. He said that I was not going to be any good as a fugitive if I went into shock. I told him that I thought he was being a little overdramatic, but gladly accepted the breakfast when it came.

Cliff was reluctant to let me drive, but when I explained what Beta had told me, and that he needed to read through the material that Beta had left for me, he acceded. "I texted Iris," he said. "She texted back to be careful. I think that means try not to get any more windows shot out," he said, as we pulled out of the garage.

We ran into rush-hour traffic, and crawled all the way into Phoenix. By the time we reached the courthouse, it was nearly eight A.M. I knew that Sarge would be there already, so I parked close to the building. "You finished reading?" I asked.

"I'm glad I got that coffee" was all Cliff said.

After I explained what I hoped would happen, I

reached into my pocket and pulled out the wads of bills Amy had given me on Friday. "I'd like to hire you to take over the Gomez case for me," I said.

Cliff looked at the money in my outstretched hand. Then he said, "That bump on your head must be pretty bad for you to be offering me money. And in case you got amnesia, too, I'm a real estate lawyer, not a criminal attorney. I can't defend Juan Gomez."

"You read what was in the folder," I replied. "And you've heard the news. I step into that building, I'm under arrest. There's no way I can stay on the case. But what Beta told me has to get into that trial."

"I'm not going to help you commit suicide," Cliff insisted.

"You know what would be suicide? Trying to run away. Look at me." I turned in the seat to face my friend. "Where am I going to hide, looking like this? And what do I know about staying underground? I'd be found in about fifteen minutes. My best chance is to get in there under my own power, and tell my story to somebody who's going to believe it."

Cliff wasn't convinced. "Why don't I just go to the press with this?"

"You saw Beta's files," I responded. "You saw who was on the list. How are you going to fight them? They completely control the major media outlets. Three days ago, they almost murdered my father, and yesterday, they almost killed me. But turn on the TV, listen to the radio, and I'm the one running away from murder charges. Who do you think people are going to believe? My best friend, the Navajo with the politically radical wife, or one of their politicians or military experts, who flies in on his star-spangled cape and tells the world that the documents you produced are all forgeries, and that the real ones prove the exact opposite of what you say?"

When I finished my rant, Cliff just stared at me. "I'll go get Sarge," he said. "But I hate this."

"Yeah," I replied. "And you haven't even been shot."

Sarge was still listening to Cliff as they crossed the street. Cliff must have been speaking softly, because Sarge was leaning down to keep his ear close to Cliff. I opened the door as they approached, but Sarge waved me back in and shut my door as he passed it. Then he went around to the passenger side, and Cliff got in the backseat.

The big court officer seemed to take up most of the interior of the car. He shifted to get a better look at me, shook his head, and said, "Are you sure you want to do this, Tommy? Because I can walk out of this car like this never happened. But if we go in there, that's it. You're locked up."

What I'd told Cliff about how long I'd last underground was true, but it wasn't the only reason I had to do this. "This is for Henley, and Amy and Erica. And Dale," I added. "I'm sure."

Sarge inhaled deeply. Then he let it out, nodding slightly. "Okay. Here's how it's going to go. You're going to pull into the garage beneath the building, where we unload the prison vans. I'll get out, and come around to your door. Then you get out, and I'll take you in. I'll be standing behind you and to the side, with my hand on your elbow. Cliff, you walk directly in front of him."

Cliff's job never brought him within fifteen miles of the courthouse. He asked, "Are we going right into a prison cell? Are reporters there? What's going to happen?"

Sarge was brusque. "The reporters are kept out of this area. Once we're in the building, you take the elevator up to the courtroom—it's on the first floor. I'll be taking Tommy to the holding cell up there, but we'll use the stairs."

So I started up the car, and drove down to the entrance at the back. Sarge's partner, Mike, was at the garage door, smoking a cigarette as we pulled up. His face registered surprise as he saw Sarge emerge from the passenger seat, but when Sarge leaned in and whispered something to him, Mike dropped the cigarette, and walked straight into the building. Ten seconds later the garage opened, and I drove in.

After the door closed, Sarge came to the driver's side of the car, and nodded to me. I opened my door at the same time that Cliff did. I held my hands in front of me, and Sarge placed me in handcuffs, carefully avoiding contact with the injury to my left hand. As he snapped the restraints in place, he said, "Thomas Carpenter, I'm taking you into temporary custody, pending your formal arrest by state police." Cliff moved in front of me, holding the blue folder, and the three of us, in tight formation, walked from the car through the courthouse doors.

Despite the fact that I'd done nothing wrong, being restrained like that was humiliating, and frightening. I had voluntarily surrendered myself into a system that I no longer trusted. Doubt churned within me.

As we reached the end of the entrance hallway, Sarge said to Cliff, "You take a left here, and go up the elevator to one. The courtroom is about halfway down the hall." Then Sarge turned to the right, and took me up the back stairs that led to the holding cell behind the courtroom's back entrances. He unlocked the barred door, and I stepped inside.

The cell itself wasn't particularly unpleasant, but it

seemed much smaller now that I was standing inside of it, instead of talking to a client from the outside. It was only about four feet deep and seven feet wide, with a small bench running along the back. The bare walls were painted white, and the floor was gray.

On the other side of the hall, about five feet down, was the doorway that led into the courtroom from behind the witness stand. It was the doorway judges and juries used when they entered and exited. I remember specifically looking at that door, and thinking that Cliff was on the other side, standing at the defense table, probably thinking similar thoughts to the ones I was having only a week ago, when I was desperately trying to formulate an opening statement with no preparation.

Sarge locked the door, and then said, "Stick your hands through the bars so I can get those cuffs off." I did as he said, and after he turned the little key in each of the cuffs and released me, he pressed something into my right hand. I flashed back to the days he used to sneak me Reese's Pieces, but what he had given me was not candy. "I don't know everything that's going on," he said. "And I don't have time for you to tell me. But something isn't right around here, and I'm not just talking about you getting locked up. For what it's worth . . . be careful, Tommy."

I looked through the bars as the beefy man with the flattop haircut walked across the hall, through the door, and into the courtroom.

Then I looked down into my right hand.

He had given me a cell phone.

THIRTY-SIX

I WASN'T THE most experienced prisoner in the world, but I knew that having a phone was against the rules, so I slid it into my pocket until I was sure that I could use it without being discovered.

That turned out to be a good move, because a lot of traffic developed in the hallway shortly after Sarge went into the courtroom. First, he and Mike came back out of the courtroom, and passed by me on their way to Judge Lomax's chambers. Then I saw Judge Lomax's clerk walk by carrying a box of four disposable coffee cups and a bag of doughnuts.

About five minutes later, I heard a lot of commotion to my left, and then Mike was walking the jurors down the hall to the courtroom door, where they all filed in after him.

Maybe ten minutes later, Sarge, the clerk, and the judge all walked to the doorway. Sarge went through first. I heard him bellow, "Court! All rise!" and then the clerk and the judge disappeared into the courtroom. The door closed behind them, and I was by myself.

I got the phone out of my pocket to call Amy. I wanted to be sure that she had managed to get to safety with Erica and Henley. But when I snapped open the cell phone, I saw that the signal was terribly weak. I didn't have much choice, though, so I dialed anyway.

My hearing difficulties don't affect me in phone use as much as in face-to-face conversation. The receiver is right up against my ear, eliminating many of the background noise issues that can interfere with my ability to hear clearly.

But when cell reception is sketchy, the static can create more problems for me than for the normal guy. I knew there was going to be trouble as soon as I heard the ring tone on the other end of the line. It was broken up, both by silences, and occasionally by white noise. It was going to be hard to have any significant discussion, but all I needed was to know they were okay.

As soon as the phone was picked up, the connection was immediately cut, and I was left listening to a sputtering dial tone. I hit the redial button, hoping that Amy wasn't rejecting the call simply because she didn't recognize the phone number on her caller ID.

Once again, the ring tone was interrupted by silences and static, and then it was disconnected.

I tried to call back, but what little signal had existed had disappeared entirely. According to the display on the phone, I had no service at all.

I slid the phone back into my pants pocket, and leaned against the bars. Even though the courtroom was just on the other side of the opposite hallway wall, I couldn't hear a thing. I would later learn about what went on when I was provided with the following transcript of the proceedings:

THE CLERK: This is the matter of Arizona versus Juan Abdullah Gomez, Docket Number 4201. The defendant is present, Your Honor, as is the jury and the assistant district attorney. However, Attorney Carpenter is not in the courtroom. Attorney Clifford Redhorse has filed a Notice of Appearance on behalf of the defendant, Your Honor, and Mr. Redhorse is present.

THE COURT: Thank you, Mr. Clerk. Ladies and gentlemen of the jury, before we begin, I'd like to make a special effort to ensure that you have carefully and scrupulously followed the instructions I have given to you regarding contact with news reports of any kind regarding this case. That is newspaper, Internet, radio, television, anything. If any of you have not followed my instructions, and have not protected yourself against any such media communications, please raise your hand. Let the record reflect that none of the jurors has raised their hand.

Mr. Redhorse?

ATTORNEY REDHORSE: Yes, Your Honor?

THE COURT: The court has been advised of the situation with Attorney Carpenter. Are you prepared to proceed?

This made sense. Sarge would have filled the judge in on what had happened to me, so that he wouldn't have had to ask Cliff about it in front of the jury, and possibly prejudice the jury against Gomez, because his lawyer had suddenly killed three people, burned down a house, and become a fugitive.

ATTORNEY REDHORSE: Yes, Your Honor—

THE DEFENDANT: I ain't prepared to proceed, Your Honor.

THE COURT: Mr. Gomez.

THE DEFENDANT: Yes, sir. I don't know this man. I want Mr. Carpenter back as my lawyer.

THE COURT: Mr. Carpenter is not available at this time, and has made arrangements for Mr. Redhorse to represent you in his stead.

THE DEFENDANT: I understand that, Your Honor, but this is bullshit. No offense. I mean, why can't I have Thomas Carpenter? He's the only lawyer ever did anything for me. I don't know nothing about Mr. Redcliff.

ATTORNEY REDHORSE: Redhorse.

THE DEFENDANT: Redhorse. Sorry.

THE COURT: I'm sorry, Mr. Gomez. For reasons that are not relevant to your case, Mr. Carpenter has been unavoidably detained. In the interests of justice, the court has determined that it is best to continue with the trial, with Mr. Redhorse as your attorney. Naturally, you are under no obligation to accept Mr. Redhorse as your lawyer, but if you refuse him, you will be forced to represent yourself. And I strongly advise you, Mr. Gomez, to accept Mr. Redhorse as your representative. The charges in this case are far too serious to attempt to defend yourself. Further, as you noted, Mr. Carpenter has done an excellent job on your behalf to this point, and it seems to me that his choice of a replacement attorney would command at least enough respect to see how Mr. Redhorse does, before rejecting his efforts entirely.

THE DEFENDANT: All right, Judge. But I still think this is bullshit.

THE COURT: The record will reflect that the defendant objects to the continuation of this trial in the absence of Attorney Carpenter, and objects to the court's ruling that Mr. Redhorse will represent the defendant in his stead.

Now if my memory is correct, I believe Captain Francona was on the stand...Yes, Attorney Redhorse?

ATTORNEY REDHORSE: I'm sorry to interrupt, Your Honor, but due to the unusual circumstances which arose over this past weekend, the defense will not be further cross-examining Captain Francona. Instead, with the court's permission, the defense would like to call a witness out of order.

A.D.A. VARICK: Objection.

THE COURT: Noting Mr. Varick's objection, can you elaborate, Mr. Redhorse, regarding this witness?

Cliff wisely asked to have the next part of the discussion at sidebar, out of the jury's hearing.

While that was going on inside the courtroom, I was on the other side of the wall, sitting on the bench in my cell, thinking about what I had read in the folder that Beta—or U.S. Army First Lieutenant Joshua Meadows, which I discovered was his real name—had left in the trunk of the car.

First, it cleared up the minor confusion I suffered when he mumbled those warnings to me in his sleep about being "white." The word he had actually used was "wipe." And although that kind of miscommunication often served as a minor amusement for me and my friends, in this case, it was far more sinister.

Because what Lieutenant Meadows had said, in his fevered, half-dream state, was, "Watch out, Tom—don't let them *wipe* you." And, "They'll *wipe* you if they can." And from one of Meadows's entries, the definition of *wipe* was unambiguous.

We entered the settlement without detection, established area responsibilities, and assumed Omega formation—all entrances and exits from the area manned with heavily armed personnel. Full wipe without incident. Target eliminated: Tariq el-Haraan. Collateral damage: thirteen unaffiliated—eleven men, two women. All cremated immediately. All evidence of habitation wiped as well. Area declared clean at 0500 and team returned to base.

It shouldn't have been as chilling as it was. After all, they had attempted to murder my father, and then me. But somehow, the cold, written report of the murders of thirteen innocent people, in order to "eliminate the target"—presumably a terrorist—seemed more monstrous, more evil.

But much more important than that, the time I had to reflect on the true nature of what the Foundation was doing forged within me an iron resolve to resist them. I understood that it was very likely going to be a suicide mission, but Amy and Erica and my father were safe. There was no more leverage that could be used against me. Everything I believed in was being attacked by an amoral and ruthless gang of outlaws, and I was not going to turn away from them.

Just then, Sarge came through the door, with the key to the cell in his hand. "Judge Lomax is letting you testify," he said, flatly.

I knew that Sarge knew I was in danger. And I think that if he'd been making the choices, he would have forced me to stay in that car that morning, and to drive off, saving myself from the grim fate that he now saw bearing down on me.

But there was a line of tanks rolling into my country, and it was time to stand up to them.

THIRTY-SEVEN

SARGE UNLOCKED the cell door, and led me by the elbow into the courtroom. The jury was the first to see me, and even I could hear the gasp. Then the gallery started to make enough noise for Sarge to stop my march to the stand and glare them back into silence.

It was hard to blame them.

Everyone in the room saw the blood-spattered condition of my T-shirt and pants. The injury to my head was big, bright, and ugly, and the two other cuts to my face from the fire were still far from healed. The crusted, gory paper towels that had adhered to my damaged hand served as the final horror-movie touch.

Of course, what made my condition so dramatic—beyond the obvious—was that on every day of the previous week, I had come into the court in a suit and tie, showered and shaved and looking like what everyone imagined a lawyer should look like.

That Monday morning, I looked like somebody had spent the weekend trying to kill me.

I stepped up onto the platform that served as the

witness stand. It was a unique experience for me—whenever I had been in a courtroom before this, I was the one asking the questions, not answering them.

I was behind a standard wooden lectern, about four feet tall, the top of which was a small platform on which the speaker could rest a book or papers, or simply his hands. There was a microphone on a gooseneck extending toward my mouth.

Cliff was sitting uneasily at the defense table, leaning on it with both hands, staring down at its surface. He looked like he was going to be sick.

Gomez sat next to Cliff, staring at me, intently. I couldn't imagine what he was thinking as this latest chapter in his own personal nightmare unfolded.

The faces in the gallery were a mix. I saw mostly shock, but there were a few smirks, as if I had somehow deserved this, or as if the real Tom Carpenter had finally been revealed to the jury.

The Judicial Broadcasting System's camera operator was at his post, filming everything, while murmuring something into his headset. His head was turned so I couldn't read his lips. Preston Varick was in his seat, alternating between glaring aggressively at me, and occasionally turning back to look into the gallery in the direction of Governor Hamilton.

And the jury was in a total state of confusion. They obviously had no idea what to think.

That was hardly a surprise.

Judge Lomax tried his best to defuse the situation.

"Ladies and gentlemen of the jury, when you and I stood at the beginning of the trial, in silent acknowledgment of the solemn responsibility that we were undertaking, I think that it's safe to say that none of us expected events to develop as they have over this past week.

"However, humanity being what it is, even the best legal minds cannot anticipate every situation that might present itself in the course of a criminal trial.

"That being said, there have been occasions in the past where an attorney, for any number of reasons, must become a witness in a case in which he is involved. This does not reflect in any way, positively or negatively, on the attorney. Nor does it reflect, in any way, positively or negatively, on his client.

"In this case, such a situation has arisen. Circumstances have dictated that Attorney Carpenter become a witness at this trial. Accordingly, he will no longer be representing Mr. Gomez. That duty has fallen to Mr. Redhorse.

"One further word. In no way are you to sympathize with Mr. Carpenter on account of his injuries, nor should you hold Mr. Carpenter's appearance against him, or against the defendant. It is urgent that he testify in this case immediately, which is why he has not yet had time to have his injuries properly addressed. How he came to be in his current condition is not relevant to this trial."

I could have quibbled with that last statement, but all in all, I thought that Judge Lomax was making the best of a very bad situation.

The clerk came over to me with a Bible. I gingerly put my gunshot hand with the hideous-looking bandage on it, raised my right hand, and swore to tell the truth. Then Cliff stood up, and asked the first question he'd ever uttered in a criminal trial.

The first time I tried a case, I was flat awful. I was defending a young man in Mesa District Court who had been accused of assault and battery—specifically, of breaking a young woman's nose in a bar fight. The defense was mistaken identity—a plausible one, as it was admitted by all that the bar was crowded, and that many different people on the scene, including the victim, were intoxicated. My client, Max Oesteroost, swore convincingly that the only reason he was anywhere near the fight was to attempt to break up the ruckus.

There were only three witnesses at the trial: the victim, the bartender, and Max. My questioning of each was a master class in hesitation, stammering, and overall insecurity.

I was trying so hard to ask my questions correctly, and I was so concerned that my client was factually guilty and that the truth might accidentally pop up in the middle of my question, that I could barely put two words together.

Although it is true that there are many complicated and difficult rules of evidence to contend with in criminal trials, the simple fact is that in general, the effective questioning of a witness shouldn't be that hard. The whole point of the trial, especially in a criminal case, is to give the jury the facts they need to use to decide whether the defendant is guilty.

But I could see that Cliff was terrified. Why wouldn't he be? He was deathly afraid of public speaking, and he was making his first courtroom appearance ever in the middle of the biggest murder trial in Arizona history, on national television. And oh, yeah, he wasn't even a criminal lawyer. If lives hadn't been hanging in the balance, I would have found it damn funny.

Cliff may have been scared to death, but he was game. We'd spent as much time as we could preparing. If you could call hurriedly reading through and jotting down questions about some of the most inflammatory material in history "preparing."

"Would you state your name and your occupation for the record, please?"

"My name is Thomas Carpenter. I am a criminal defense attorney. Until very recently, I was the defendant's attorney in this trial."

"Thank you. And can you tell us what happened to you after the trial was recessed this past Friday?"

"Yes. As I was driving home, I received a phone call from a man who told me that he was going to kill my father because I'd brought forward evidence that Esteban Cruz was *not* the person who detonated the Denver Tunnel Bomb."

There was an audible gasp from my left, and I turned around to see the bank teller, Juror Number 14, holding her hand in front of her mouth.

"My dad lives with me up on Payson's Ridge," I explained. "He's been partially paralyzed since he suffered a stroke four years ago."

Cliff looked like he was getting a little more relaxed. "What did you do when you got this threat?"

"I raced home to find the house on fire. Luckily, I was able to get my father out of there before he got hurt. Well, actually, I injured his shoulder as I was carrying him down the basement stairs, but considering everything, we got away in pretty good shape. Except for a few scratches and burns."

Varick stood up. "Your Honor, I object. This has absolutely no relevance to the case against Mr. Gomez."

Judge Lomax turned to Cliff. "Mr. Redhorse?" Suddenly, the sweat was back on Cliff's forehead. Obviously, Varick was correct, if you looked simply at the incident on Friday as an isolated event. Technically, an attempt to intimidate me had no bearing on whether Juan Gomez planned the Denver Tunnel Bombing. The only way to show that the threat against my father had any relevance to the Gomez trial was to put it into the context of the entire set of facts which we had learned from Beta—Joshua Meadows.

Unfortunately, that kind of argument is a lot easier to make when you're writing it down, with unlimited time. Cliff was standing there, on the spot, wondering what to say.

Judge Lomax spoke again. "Mr. Redhorse? Can you establish relevance?"

Cliff cleared his throat. "I think so, Your Honor. I mean, yes, Your Honor. It's just that, um, there's a lot of facts that need to be, um, Mr. Carpenter needs to testify to. When he does, then, uh, then it will be relevant. I mean it's relevant now. It will just be, I mean, you know, Your Honor will be able to tell that it's relevant. After that."

All I can say on Cliff's behalf is that speaking in court, especially your first time, is much harder than they make it look on television.

Judge Lomax didn't seem to hold my friend's inexperience against him, though. "For the moment, I am going to overrule the objection, and allow a limited amount of further inquiry on the topic. But if relevance is not established very soon, I will entertain another objection and I will strike the testimony."

A more experienced litigator would have heard the judge's words as a warning to get right to the main course, and forget about the appetizer and the soup. But Cliff was so committed to the strategy that we had discussed—a chronological description of everything that had happened to me over the weekend—that he plunged forward as if there had been no objection at all.

"Um, did anything significant happen to you on Sunday morning?"

It was not exactly the smoothest transition in the

world, but I think it's safe to say that we were way past worrying about style points by this time.

"Yes. I was on my way to the store, when I was attacked by at least two men in a car. They cut me off, one of them jumped into my car, threatened to shoot me, and hit me in the face with a pistol, which is when I received this injury to my forehead."

"And did you escape?"

"Yes. I managed to get away, but then, later that evening, I was attacked again, this time by at least three individuals, one of whom shot me in the hand." I raised up my injury and its disgusting mess of bandages.

I was shortcutting most of what had happened, hoping that Cliff would take the hint that everything now hinged upon getting to what Lieutenant Meadows had written in his folder. I wasn't looking directly at Judge Lomax, but I was getting a strong sense that he was running out of patience.

"I see," Cliff said. He cleared his throat. "And after that second attack, did you hear anything of interest on the radio?"

Varick had been given the perfect opening, and he took it. "Your Honor! The radio? Not only is the defense leading the witness, it hasn't even taken the first step in establishing how these fantastical tales of assaults and shootings and fires have any relevance whatsoever to the case at bar. And now we're about to hear testimony as to a radio broadcast? I renew my objection."

To his credit, Judge Lomax did not immediately act. Instead, he turned to Cliff. "Counselor? How is this relevant?"

"As I mentioned before, Your Honor, there is a lot of information that ties this all together. The radio, for instance, is how Tom—Mr. Carpenter—learned that the conspiracy extended to him directly. That's when he found out that even though he saved his father, he was being accused of killing him, as well as two other people."

To Cliff, and me, it made perfect sense. But without any kind of context, it sounded like my Navajo friend might have accidentally walked into the wrong courtroom.

It was obvious that Judge Lomax was going to shut us down, and I couldn't let that happen. The only way Meadows's information was going to get to the public was through this trial. And I didn't know any other way than through my testimony. If the judge sustained the objection, Juan Gomez wasn't the only person in the courtroom who was going to be executed for murder. I spoke up. "Your Honor, if I might address this issue—"

But the judge cut me off. "Mr. Carpenter, please. You are a witness, and no longer the defendant's attorney. The testimony is obviously irrelevant. The objection is sustained."

THIRTY-EIGHT

CLIFF WAS AT a loss. He stood there, looking at me.

For my part, I was trying to think of a way to convince Judge Lomax that he was wrong. Of course, as a witness, I had no business speaking directly to the judge at all. Yet if all that needed to be said was merely a key word or two, I would have gladly just blurted them out.

But the entire thing was so twisted. Where would I even begin my explanation? With Joshua Meadows, a man who had officially died as a member of the U.S. Army in Afghanistan five years ago? *Your Honor, at the beginning of this trial, I was accosted at gunpoint in the men's room by a man who told me I needed to represent Juan Gomez without incident until he secretly fed me information, through a hidden earpiece, regarding Esteban Cruz.*

And would it be any better if I began my remarks by talking about Landry? *Your Honor, this all began when a sociopath in the state police in a vast conspiracy with any number of other state and federal officials attempted to intimidate me, and then attempted to murder both my father and me by burning down our house. The last time I saw him I managed to throw him through the windshield of my car.*

I'd lived through it all, and yet I couldn't think of a way to make it sound like I wasn't mentally ill.

Judge Lomax interrupted my thoughts. "Mr. Redhorse? Do you have any further questions for this witness?"

Poor Cliff. He was already overwhelmed, and now the clock was ticking down the final seconds. He looked completely flummoxed, although, as always, undeniably sharp. From his five-hundred-dollar suit, right down to the turquoise-and-silver wedding ring that Iris had picked out for him. The ring that was on the hand that was nervously tapping. Tapping on the blue folder that Joshua Meadows had left in the car for me.

I cleared my throat, loudly. It probably sounded like a silly ploy to get Cliff to look at me, but I didn't care, because that's exactly what it was. When he did, I continued my cartoonlike prompting. I tilted my head down, clownishly lowering my gaze directly to the blue folder.

Cliff may not have been a litigator, but he was no fool. He saw what I wanted him to see, picked up the folder, and hesitated.

Unlike what Hollywood would have you believe, the typical friendship between men in the real world does not include a shared history of summer camp secret signal class, upon which they can draw to communicate silently at those critical moments when all is on the line. So there was nothing I could do for Cliff from my perch on the witness stand. He was flying solo but losing altitude, and he wore the expression of a man desperate enough to pull one of the shiny levers in the cockpit without the first idea of what was going to happen.

Cliff's actual words were "Your Honor, I'd like to offer the contents of this folder into evidence."

Unfortunately, that request was not going to have any effect on the flight path of our particular plane. Varick, now smug, shot to his feet and confidently objected.

Judge Lomax was well aware that Varick's objection had to be sustained. But by now, the judge also realized that while Cliff was hopelessly out of his league, Cliff and I both thought there was something terribly important to get in front of the jury. Rather than simply ruling on the objection, the judge chose to do a little piloting of his own.

"Mr. Redhorse, as you know, in order for me to admit any documents into evidence, you'll need to lay a foundation for their admissibility. Before we get to that, however, have you shown this material to Mr. Varick?"

"No, Your Honor," Cliff said. "But I can show it to him now." He handed the folder over to Varick. "I only received these papers this morning, so I haven't had a chance to make copies."

While Cliff spoke, Varick looked down at the documents, and underwent a frightening metamorphosis.

When he first opened the folder, the stocky prosecutor had smirked openly, as if to assure whoever might be watching that the contents were manifestly unimportant.

But after reading only the top portion of the first page, he flipped it over swiftly, and began scanning the second one. By the time he'd reached the third page, his expression had transformed itself into a fierce scowl. And after skimming through the rest of the folder quickly, he slapped it shut, turned to Cliff, and barked loudly, "Where did you get this nonsense? Do you realize that this folder is full of very dangerous lies that could seriously compromise national security?"

I hadn't expected that reaction, and neither, obviously, had Cliff. But happily, Judge Lomax was on the bench, not Judge Klay. He knew that just because one lawyer gets angry, the other lawyer isn't wrong. "May I see the documents, please?" he requested.

That was not what Preston Varick wanted to hear. He didn't want this stuff anywhere near becoming public information. "Your Honor—" he began.

"Is there a problem, Mr. Varick?" Judge Lomax interrupted.

"Quite frankly, yes, Judge," Varick responded. "This folder's contents are prejudicial, to say the least. It seems to me that they are so one-sided, and false, may I remind you, that to have the court even read them would risk prejudicing the court's opinion of the facts of this case."

I had never heard anything quite like that before in my professional life. Preston Varick was essentially saying that Judge Lomax couldn't so much as look at the folder and remain impartial.

Judge Lomax saw it for what it was—a desperate move. "Mr. Varick. I assure you that I will be able to continue to perform my duties without prejudice, regardless of what is contained in that folder. But putting that aside for one minute, and without waiving your objections to the foundation issues that may face Mr. Redhorse, do you have any other objections to the documents themselves?"

It took a second for Varick to process the fact that at least for the short term, he had managed to keep the information out of Judge Lomax's hands. He relaxed his grip on the folder slightly, so that now it didn't look quite so much like he was trying to strangle it.

"Yes, Your Honor, I do. From what I can tell, these papers are principally the writings of a third party, although there are some copies of forms, as well. In any case, the contents of the folder are entirely hearsay. Out-of-court statements—in this case, written statements—made by a person who is not testifying. The defense is trying to introduce them to prove what is contained in the documents. That is textbook hearsay. And it is inadmissible."

Cliff looked at me with an apologetic expression on his face. He had absolutely nothing to say.

It wasn't that Cliff was entirely ignorant of what Varick was talking about. Every lawyer takes evidence in law school—it's a required course. And in order to pass the bar exam in the state of Arizona, candidates for admission must prove some familiarity with the rules of evidence.

But that doesn't mean that real estate lawyers like Cliff, who haven't given the hearsay rule so much as a friendly nod over the past decade, could be expected to argue, off the cuff, at a murder trial, about the admissibility of handwritten documents by a non-witness. The rule and its seemingly infinite exceptions presented some of the most treacherous terrain for those of us who spend our lives trying to climb the mountain of jurisprudence. The excited utterance rule, the business record exception, past recollection recorded, present sense impressions, statements against interest, prior sworn testimony, fresh complaint, medical records—the list goes on and on.

And there Cliff stood, bearing neither shield nor weapon, in the very center of the arena, facing off with a seasoned and armored gladiator. It was going to be a slaughter. I watched, frozen, wishing desperately that we had gone to summer camp together.

Judge Lomax was tired of waiting. "Mr. Redhorse?"

But my friend Cliff wasn't going to go down without a fight. Over the next several minutes he gave a stammering, impassioned, but quite futile, plea for justice, conspicuously light on specifics with respect to the hearsay rule.

While Cliff was speaking, a serious-looking young woman entered the courtroom from the double doors at the back of the gallery. She walked right down the center aisle, and handed the governor a folded slip of paper. Then she continued over to A.D.A. Varick, and handed him another.

By that time, Governor Hamilton had read his note, stood, and walked out of the courtroom. The messenger followed him. The governor had clearly decided that whatever was on that paper was more interesting than a bunch of nerds dickering about hearsay.

When Cliff was done, Judge Lomax turned to me, and asked, "What happened to this Lieutenant Meadows?"

"I'm sorry to say that he was shot and killed in my presence late last night," I answered.

That certainly woke up the gallery. Reporters started scribbling furiously.

"In your presence?" Preston was on his feet again. He had relinquished his death grip on the blue folder, and was now holding the note he had just received. "May I remind the court that many of the difficulties being faced by the defense team this morning stem from their own actions. Mr. Carpenter and his friend, Mr. Redhorse, are struggling to get around the hearsay rule, but the reason they can't is because they cannot produce the alleged writer of these documents. That is no surprise, however, as I have just been handed a note which informs me that the only Army lieutenant in the past thirty-five years who was named Joshua Meadows died in Afghanistan, five years ago.

"More to the point—I have also just been informed that we all should assume that everything Mr. Carpenter says is a lie. That oath he swore on the Bible means nothing to him. That is because he himself is a godless terrorist. An enemy of this country. An enemy of America. He is already wanted for murder and for arson, and I have just been informed that he has been plotting with known terrorists to make large-scale biochemical attacks on targets within the U.S.

"This man has been declared an enemy combatant, Your Honor. United States marshals are on their way to take him into custody in a secret location, where he will be aggressively interrogated until he gives up the location of these future attacks. Until that time, he should be considered most dangerous, and he should be removed from this courtroom immediately."

THIRTY-NINE

I REMEMBER thinking how absurd Varick sounded at that moment, but then the words of Juan Gomez came back to me. *When they call you an enemy combatant, it doesn't matter if they're right or if they're wrong. They do whatever they want. They drowned me . . . And I confessed to everything . . . And I didn't do nothing wrong.*

Before Varick announced that I was to be hauled off to a secret prison, I had been wrongly accused of multiple felonies, and I faced a life without Amy and my family. I thought it was as bad as it could get. I was mistaken.

And as if the specter of imminent torture weren't quite enough, while Preston made his vile little speech, the door at the back of the courtroom and the doors on each side of the courtroom opened, and three uniformed individuals entered.

Each of the three was dressed in a dark blue police uniform covered by a light jacket. Each of the three positioned himself in front of the door he had just used to enter the courtroom. And each of the three was immediately recognizable.

Because they were Kappa, Gamma, and the third, short man, who had ambushed me at Cactus Curt's Steakhouse.

Suddenly, in the sweepstakes to control my future, immediate execution was giving secret imprisonment and torture a run for its money.

I needed to get a plan. Quick.

But it didn't seem like anyone else in the courtroom had noticed the three hit men's entrance. Instead, the prosecutor's latest message had really fired up the crowd. The entire room seemed to burst into conversation at once. Sarge instantly rose from his seat, and Judge Lomax hit the bench with his gavel. "Ladies and gentlemen. If there is one more outburst like that, I will clear this court."

The threat worked like a charm. Nobody wanted to leave now. Heck—one of the lawyers looked like he'd been mauled by a pack of wild animals, and the other one was calling him a godless terrorist.

"Mr. Varick." Judge Lomax spoke quietly, obviously in an effort to release some of the energy from the room. "Kindly contain your remarks to the evidentiary issue at hand. Mr. Carpenter's status should be no part of the jury's considerations in this case."

"I apologize, Your Honor." Preston didn't look contrite in the least. "But the defendant chose to put Mr. Carpenter on the witness stand, and whether the witness likes it or not, he's wanted for three murders, including that of his father. He's a dangerous man, and the jury is entitled to know—"

Cliff couldn't stand it anymore, and bolted up from his chair. "He just told you he *saved* his father's life!"

Preston shot back, "We only have his word for it,

sir. I, personally, have no idea what happened to Mr. Carpenter's father this weekend."

Simultaneously, three things then happened. Cliff said, "Well, I do," I pulled down the collar of my bloody shirt, exposing the burn on my neck, saying, "How do you think I got this?" and Judge Lomax hit the bench again with the gavel.

But Preston was not to be sidetracked. "Your Honor, I demand that this terrorist be taken from the court-room immediately. Not only is he a distraction in this case, but he is a danger to you, to everyone in the court-room, and to our entire country." The A.D.A. stabbed a finger in the direction of Baldy, who stood at the back of the room, then at the two other goons standing at the side courtroom doors. "These men have the author-ity to seize him, Your Honor."

Despite the apparently imminent threat I posed, Judge Lomax managed to remain calm. "Mr. Prosecutor, until I am presented with an official document that says to the contrary, Mr. Carpenter is currently in the custody of the Superior Court of the State of Arizona. No one will seize him, or anyone else in this room, without my express consent. I assume full responsibil-ity for him, as well as for the safety of him, and of any-one else here."

"That document you mentioned will be coming to you any minute, Judge," Preston replied.

Judge Lomax nodded. "Fine. In the interim, I'll see both lawyers at sidebar, immediately, on the question of the hearsay objection."

Less than a minute passed before Varick and Cliff walked back to their posts behind their respective ta-bles. Gomez passed a note to Cliff, who took a deep breath, and wrote one back.

"I have heard from both parties on the issue of the

admissibility of the writings produced by the defense," Judge Lomax told the enthralled room. "The documents are hearsay, and the defendant has satisfied none of the exceptions to the rule prohibiting hearsay from being admissible. Accordingly, the prosecution's objection is sustained. The contents of the folder will not be made available to the jury."

Of course, the judge was right. The legal system believed that it was okay to believe the dying accusation of a murder victim, but that it was not okay to believe anything else that he or she might offer as an exit line. As I stood there, watching the last chance to save my life vanish thanks to that absurdly arbitrary distinction, a parade of hypothetical final statements came to mind, each as likely to be true as an accusation of murder. "I always loved you." "The key to the safe-deposit box is in my sock drawer." "I never said that Cousin Louie went to college." "The money wasn't lost—I stole it." "The only crime I ever committed was breaking a taillight, fifty years ago."

The only crime I ever committed was breaking a taillight, fifty years ago.

And just then, I got my plan.

FORTY

WHILE THE reporters wrote furiously, the judge looked at Cliff. "Mr. Redhorse. Is there anything further from this witness?"

"Um, if I could just have a moment, Your Honor." Cliff looked down at the papers on the table before him. He was obviously stalling. Then he looked up. "Your Honor, just before he died, Lieutenant Meadows told Mr. Carpenter that he was a member—"

But Preston Varick was too quick, and started speaking over Cliff almost as soon as he opened his mouth. "Objection, Your Honor. Mr. Redhorse may not make speeches in an effort to ignore the rules of evidence and sidestep the authority of this court."

There was no reason to leave Cliff twisting in the breeze, and I jumped in. "Your Honor, the statements made to me by Lieutenant Meadows—and it was Lieutenant Meadows; he did not die in Afghanistan—were dramatic admissions of several serious felonies by Meadows, and are admissible as statements against interest."

The sad case of Charles Jackson and his father, Henry, had taught me that while the judicial system was not willing to accept what you said on your death-bed as true unless it was an accusation against your killer, it was perfectly willing to accept as true *anything* you said, *whenever* you said it, if you knew that what you were saying could get you into legal trouble, or could lose you money.

Cliff took a deep breath and let it out. He looked as relieved as I'd ever seen him, with the possible exception of the day two years earlier when he and Iris received the news that the lump in her breast was benign.

I turned to Judge Lomax, who was considering what I had just said. He looked first at me, and then at Cliff, but he said nothing. Then he faced the assistant district attorney, and asked, "Mr. Varick, what is the state's position on this?"

In the typical situation, the prosecutor would request a voir dire—a sort of dry run of the questions and answers that the defense was proposing to put into evidence. The examination would take place outside the presence of the jury, giving the judge a chance to make his ruling without exposing the jury to potentially inappropriate evidence.

But this was far from a typical situation. Even though the jury wouldn't hear it, Preston couldn't afford to allow a voir dire. Because then the courtroom full of people would learn about all of the things that Varick was desperate to keep in that blue folder.

"The state's position is that the defense hasn't offered anything new to the argument," Varick began. "This is just Attorney Carpenter's last desperate effort to deflect attention away from his own desperate situation. Perhaps he is hoping to make some kind of deal. I don't know, Your Honor. But for the purposes of this case, he has no business marching in here and saying that he was told some supposedly relevant things by this mystery man, who so conveniently gets murdered right in front of his eyes. How gullible does he think we are? This court should summarily reject any testimony this enemy of the United States might offer, on grounds that it is an obvious fabrication, made up at the eleventh hour, in hopes of either confusing the jury, or somehow tricking them into acquitting this other terrorist, Juan Abdullah Gomez."

By the time he was finished, Varick was breathing rather heavily. The judge let him catch his breath before asking, "Putting aside for a moment the state's characterizations of Mr. Carpenter and Mr. Gomez, what is your position on the evidentiary issue? It is argued that since the statements are against Mr. Meadows's interests, they are admissible. Do you contest that, Mr. Varick?"

"Absolutely, Your Honor," the prosecutor spat back. "I absolutely contest it. As I said before, the defense has made no showing that the statements were against anyone's interest."

Judge Lomax wasn't biting. "Except, of course, for Mr. Carpenter's assertion that they were."

"That's correct. The only thing this court has is the word of an accused murderer, an enemy combatant of the United States."

I couldn't tell if Varick thought that was getting him anywhere. He was sounding a little shrill, at least to me. I snuck a peak at the jury, and I couldn't read anything there except intense interest. I would have bet you *two* stacks of pancakes that at least one of them had already started writing a book.

"Is that your only argument, sir?" The judge was obviously getting tired of that speech.

"No, sir. I find it completely contrary to any notion of justice that the only reason the person who allegedly said all of these ridiculous things cannot testify himself is because this witness murdered him. I don't believe that the defense should be allowed to benefit from its own misdeeds."

Cliff saw through the argument. "Your Honor, Mr. Carpenter is not the defendant, nor is he aligned with the defendant any longer. By this court's own ruling, he had to step down as the defendant's attorney because he had to become a witness. Therefore, even if Mr. Carpenter had done something to Lieutenant Meadows, which he did not, it wasn't the defendant's act. If the defendant benefits by having this testimony come in, so be it. But it wasn't because of any wrongdoing by the defendant, Mr. Gomez."

I made a mental note to discuss with Cliff his possible future as a trial lawyer.

"The evidence is admissible," said Judge Lomax. "Mr. Redhorse, please continue."

"Mr. Carpenter, can you tell us when you first met Lieutenant Joshua Meadows?"

As I began to describe my encounter with Meadows in the bathroom the day I got Judge Klay thrown off the case, I noticed that the television camera operator got a puzzled look on his face. He held his hand up to press the earpiece of his headset tighter, and then he whispered, "Right now?" A moment or two later he mouthed, "Okay," and then he reached behind the camera, and the little red light blinked off.

Then he detached the headset, hooked it over a handle at the rear of the camera, and walked straight past the bald sentinel standing at the back doors of the courtroom.

I was a little disappointed that this information

wasn't going to get to the public in real time, but that wasn't going to make much of a difference. The information was coming, whether over live television or not.

And then my gaze returned to Baldy as he stood at the back doors. The rest of the courtroom's attention was on me, as I continued my story. That gave Baldy the perfect opportunity to deliver a final message to me. Very deliberately, he unbuttoned the light jacket he was wearing, and pulled it open.

Underneath, I could see what looked like a harness of some kind. But what the harness contained was unmistakable. Up the left side of his body ran a large weapon—what I recognized as a sawed-off shotgun. And on the right side, a handgun. Then he met my gaze, and slowly looked to the door on his right, and then the one to his left, implying that the men standing at those exits were similarly armed.

We entered the settlement without detection, established area responsibilities, and assumed Omega formation—all entrances and exits from the area manned with heavily armed personnel.

That's when I realized that the camera operator hadn't left the room merely because his bosses didn't want him to broadcast live what I had to say.

It was because Phoenix Superior Courtroom Number 1-B was about to be wiped.

FORTY-ONE

IT WAS AS IF I were being given one last chance. I could stop talking, and spare everyone in the room. Or I could keep testifying, and he'd kill them all. I sensed that the line I couldn't cross involved anything beyond the information I had learned regarding the death of Esteban Cruz.

I had no desire to be a martyr, or to martyr anyone else. But if the three assassins in the room, and whatever number of their teammates that might have been stationed out in the hallway, managed to get away with murdering us all, and manipulating the crime scene to make it look like the act of a foreign terrorist, we would have died for no reason at all.

On the other hand, I couldn't just walk away. I had no doubt that I would never get another opportunity like this. These people were cunning, and completely without morals. As soon as I was taken into custody I would be killed, without hesitation. And Cliff would die, too. They would see that there was no way this information got out.

So I was faced with two options. I could keep talking—I was up to the point in the story where Meadows gave me the earpiece—and hope that when the Kappa and Gamma gang started shooting, someone might make it out alive to tell the real story. Or I could succumb to the pressure, sacrifice myself, and hope that another opportunity would present itself to someone else in the future, but soon enough so that this madness could be stopped before more innocent lives were lost.

Cliff asked me another question, and as I answered, I looked at my friend of the past seven years, and at his fancy suit, and at the beautiful wedding ring that I envied so much.

And suddenly, thanks to Amy, the woman I would now never have a chance to spend my life with, and thanks also to my mother's gay brother, my favorite amateur magician, Uncle Louis, there was a third option.

Before Louis returned to Florida, he showed me that in almost every one of his tricks, he was able to distract or misdirect me, either with a joke or with some meaningless movement, so that I wasn't paying attention to the hand that pulled off the trick.

During the months immediately following Uncle Louis's one-weekend engagement in my life, I enthusiastically took up the art of prestidigitation.

I was atrocious.

But that wasn't going to stop me on that morning. I had a chance, and I had to take it. Pretending there was a gnat bothering me, I stopped talking for a minute, and waved my injured hand back and forth in front of my face. Then I continued for a few more sentences. And then I stopped again to wave futilely at the nonexistent insect.

The first time was the setup. The second was the

real misdirection. As I waved my bloodied, bandaged hand around in front of my face, I slipped my uninjured hand into my pocket, and withdrew Sarge's phone.

Then, I accidentally-on-purpose struck my wounded hand on the microphone that extended from the lectern toward my mouth.

I didn't have to fake the yelp of pain, nor my physical reaction. I hunched over, cradling my injured hand in front of me. Then I hid the cell phone behind the mass of paper towels around my left hand. As I stood back upright, I brought both of my hands up to the platform at the top of the witness stand, placed the phone there, and rested my hands on either side of it.

Then I apologized, surreptitiously pressed the redial button on the phone, and continued my testimony.

I couldn't pick the phone up, of course. So I simply leaned on the witness stand with my forearms, speaking loudly in the direction of the phone. I was hoping that there was a cell signal in the courtroom, that Amy would pick up the phone, that she would be able to hear me, and that if none of us made it out of the courtroom alive, she'd somehow be able to get the information I would reveal to the people who needed to know.

I realize that considering my situation, that was a lot of hoping. But at the moment, hope was the only commodity I had in any meaningful supply.

I finished my tale of cloak-and-dagger threats and counterthreats during the first days of the trial, and then moved on to the point where I rescued Henley from the fire. I briefly described my Sunday morning escape from Landry, and then detailed Meadows's phone call to me, the threats to Amy and Erica. At this point, gasps and murmurs were coming regularly from the jury box. While I hadn't reached the point in the narrative which was directly and obviously relevant to

Juan Gomez, the jurors were obviously astonished at the lengths to which these forces had been used to manipulate and intimidate me.

After about twenty minutes of my testimony, I got to where I was jumping off the balcony into the wagon on the street. I described how Meadows got me to safety and led me to his car. Cliff asked me, "Were you and Lieutenant Meadows able to escape?"

And then the doors behind Baldy opened, and once again everything changed.

Because walking through the back doors of the courtroom were the two people I least wanted to see at that moment in my life.

The first was Landry. His face was scratched and scraped up badly, and he had a thick bandage on his right hand. He walked with a bit of a limp, and every once in a while I thought I saw a grimace come across his face. But all in all, I have to say that for someone who had been propelled through a windshield toward a cliff in the middle of the high desert, he looked pretty good.

More important, though, was the second person who walked into the room. The woman whose hands had been restrained behind her back. The woman being gripped by Landry, and pulled into the courtroom by him, clearly against her will.

My beautiful Amy.

FORTY-TWO

LANDRY DIDN'T waste a second. As he came through the door, he made direct eye contact with me and mouthed the words "We've got your father and Erica, too." Apparently, he knew I could read lips.

And he knew, too, that the game was over.

There was no way I could continue. If I did, Landry would kill Amy instantly. And then his buddies would open fire on the rest of us.

There was a chance that by using the door behind me, I might escape. And I believed that depending on where the shooters focused their initial attack, there was a chance that a few of the jurors might make it out, too.

But that was assuming that the Foundation hadn't stationed someone in the hallway directly behind the door. Given the players and the stakes, I didn't think that was a particularly good assumption.

And I could no longer rely on the wild and desperate hope that Amy was listening by phone to everything going on in the courtroom, and somehow recording it for others so they would know what transpired here.

An image of the Chinese man standing in front of those tanks came to my mind as I watched Landry, mere seconds away from ending the life of the woman I loved. Had that man in Tiananmen Square planned to stare down a row of tanks when he woke up that morning? It sure didn't look like it—he was carrying a briefcase, for goodness' sakes.

And when he saw the tanks, and made his decision to act, was he thinking about the people he was leaving behind? Did he have a young wife, maybe a child? Or parents who needed him? Was he willing to sacrifice his life in order to make theirs better?

And would he have stood there, shoulders squared, so bravely defiant, if he had been told that to do so would result in the immediate death of his entire family?

I hesitated, and Cliff asked again, "Tom? Were you and Lieutenant Meadows able to escape?"

I was just inches from the line that I knew I couldn't cross. As soon as I began to repeat what Meadows had told me, the killing would start. I didn't know what to do. So I tried to stall.

"I, uh, well, obviously I escaped. Well, I got shot, of course, but I mean I got away. Lieutenant Meadows, um, that's another story."

I stopped again, and Cliff saw that something was wrong. "What happened to Lieutenant Meadows?"

Again, I hesitated. Landry had moved his left hand underneath his jacket. Amy was pressed against him, a look of pure terror stretched across her face.

"I can't answer that," I replied.

So many members of the jury did a double take that I could see the movement in my peripheral vision. Cliff stood at the defense table, looking down at a stack of papers next to a book in front of him.

And Landry was smiling again. His hand was still ominously hidden beneath the left side of his jacket, but he'd won, and he knew it.

Cliff lifted his head and pressed on. "Why can't you answer that question, Mr. Carpenter? Why can't you tell us what happened to Lieutenant Meadows?"

I felt like I was almost to the top of a very steep mountain, but I'd reached a point where it was too dangerous to continue climbing. Now I was desperately looking for a foothold I could use to turn around without plunging to my death.

"I can't tell you that because I'm afraid of what might happen."

I was praying that Cliff would back off. He was the only one who could possibly know what was at risk here, and if he didn't help me retreat, I was going to have to simply stop talking. But that could lead Judge Lomax to press the issue by examining the contents of the blue folder that A.D.A. Varick still held. I wasn't sure, but I believed that might provoke the attack as well.

But Cliff didn't back off. Instead, he walked us all right to the edge of the precipice. "Are you aware that everything you are saying is being broadcast all over the world?"

"Objection." Varick looked confused, but he certainly seemed to welcome the diversion. As far as he was concerned, the more time he spent engaging Judge Lomax, the less time I spent destroying the case against Juan Gomez.

I ignored him. I looked instead at the Judicial Broadcasting System television camera standing in the center of the room. No one was operating it, and the red light was not lit. "Actually," I answered, "I believe that the television signal went out several minutes ago."

Cliff went on. "I'm not talking about television. I'm talking about radio."

"Your Honor." Varick sounded a little like he was whining.

"Mr. Redhorse," the judge asked, "what is the point of this line of questioning?"

Cliff looked down again at the table before him, and then returned his gaze to the front of the courtroom. "Tom Carpenter has just recounted a systematic campaign of intimidation that has been mounted against him, almost from the minute he began his work on this case. From outright threats against him and his family, to listening and tracking devices planted in his house and car, to attempts on his life and on his family's. The reason I'm asking about the broadcast of his testimony this morning is to assure him that he does not need to feel intimidated any longer."

Judge Lomax turned to me. "Is Attorney Redhorse correct? Do you feel intimidated right now, Mr. Carpenter?"

One wrong step, and the whole room was going to erupt in gunfire. "Um, yes, Your Honor. I'm concerned . . . I'm feeling intimidated right now."

The judge nodded. "I see. Is there anything I can do to assure you that you need not fear testifying here this morning?"

I almost smiled. There was something truly noble in the way that he assumed that anyone speaking the truth in a courtroom in America had nothing to fear.

It was too bad that he was so dreadfully naive.

"Um, I don't think so, Your Honor" was the best I could do for a reply.

"That's why I was asking about the radio broadcast,

Your Honor," Cliff said. "I thought it might help Tom to know that everything he has said this morning has been broadcast live on my wife's Web site. She says that her listeners have heard it all, and are gathering outside the courthouse as we speak to witness whatever happens here today."

I couldn't tell if Cliff was bluffing. Unlike me, he was an excellent liar, and had fooled me countless times when playing cards. Henley was the only one who could keep up with him.

Cliff saw my hesitation, and upped the ante. He reached down to that part of the defense table that had taken up so much of his attention today, and held up a cell phone. "I've been trading text messages from Iris— my wife—all morning." Then he turned to face me. "The call you made to Amy was forwarded to Iris. That's how I know, Tom."

Relief flooded through me. My gamble had paid off. Thirty minutes ago, I had pressed the redial button on Sarge's cell phone, hoping that Amy would be able to tell the world what had happened. But instead, Iris had been the messenger.

So all was not lost. Whatever had been said this morning was out there, and whatever I would say from this point forward, at least until I was cut down by the assassins that lurked at every door of this room, would be heard.

Cliff cleared his throat. "And so I ask you again, Tom, what happened to Lieutenant Joshua Meadows last night, after you escaped the attack at Cactus Curt's Steakhouse?"

Now the question was whether I was willing to risk the lives of Amy, and Erica, and Henley, and Cliff, and everyone else in this room. It was one thing to be right.

It was quite another to play God with everyone you cared about in the world.

And just then, I knew that even if that anonymous Chinese man had been caring for his crippled father, or looking after his widowed sister-in-law and her daughter, he still would have stood up to those tanks.

Because he understood that the lives of everyone he loved were *already* in the balance. He knew that if the tanks weren't stopped then, it wouldn't make any difference—sooner or later they would be rolling into his front yard, and into the front yards of everyone that he held dear.

So I stood at that witness stand that Monday morning, and I decided to face down Landry, and his murderous thugs. Because I knew that if they weren't stopped, it would only be a matter of time before what had happened in Denver happened in Kansas City, or San Francisco, or Atlanta. Or Phoenix.

And there would come a time when Amy would be named the next enemy combatant. Or Cliff. Or Iris. Or, in a few years, Erica. And they would be the ones facing electric shock, or waterboarding, or whatever other nightmarish torture was being passed off as non-torture at that time.

So I reached down with my good hand and I picked up Sarge's cell phone and brought it close to my mouth, and I spoke loudly and clearly, because I wanted to be sure that Iris heard and broadcast every one of my words, in case they were my last.

"What happened to Lieutenant Meadows was that he was executed by a group called the Foundation. And the reason that is relevant to this trial is because the Foundation is a secret arm of the U.S. military. They were the people who planned the Denver Tunnel Bombing. And they framed Juan Gomez. Because they wanted to make the American people believe that we had been attacked by Muslim terrorists, so that certain elements of the government could capitalize on the fear of future attacks, and use that fear to consolidate their political power."

The room was dead silent. And then I saw Cliff's face, and I realized I had made a tragic mistake.

He had fooled me again.

What made Cliff such a terrific liar was that at the first sign of doubt, he would produce some piece of evidence which supported his lie. It was amazing how often he managed to sucker people into believing the craziest things—his mother was the first Native American chiropractor, he had all his baby teeth surgically removed as a child because of a rare disease, his given name was really Waldo.

And as the expression of fear came over him, I realized that's what his little speech about the text messages was. A bit of garnish to make his falsehood more palatable.

Landry leapt into action. "It's all bullshit!" he shouted, striding into the center of the courtroom with Amy in tow. "Prepare to execute full wipe."

And at his command, Gamma, Kappa, and the third hit man locked the doors they stood before, reached under their jackets, and pulled out their weapons. One held a gun to Sarge's head, and a second held one to Mike's. Then they pushed both officers to the ground, and handcuffed them.

Our bluff had been called.

FORTY-THREE

BEFORE THE occupants of the room could react, Baldy screamed, "Everybody stay in your seats, and shut up, right now!" He punctuated his message by firing a bullet into the ceiling. A few people screamed, but when the echoes of the gun blast died away, there was silence in the room, with the exception of some people moaning and crying.

Judge Lomax stood and shouted, "Officer! Put that weapon away. And release those court officers immediately!"

Gamma and Kappa stood over the prostrate court officers and looked back at the cop. The African American with the goatee was condescending. "Sorry, Judge. Just following orders."

Landry tossed Amy aside as if she were an old piece of clothing, withdrew a pistol from a holster, and marched to the center of the room. "You couldn't just let it go, could you, Tommy boy?" His sneer was made even uglier by the hideous scrapes and bruises all over his face. "You had to prove what a big man you were.

Well, congratulations, punk. You're a big man. You got all these people killed. Nice going."

I had to play out the hand. There was nothing else to do now. "There's no point in wiping the room, Landry. You heard what Cliff said. Millions of people know. Killing us won't make any difference."

"Your friend is lying." Landry's voice was hard, and the purple-blue vein in his forehead pulsed angrily. "You expect me to abandon this mission based on one lousy phone call to his psycho wife? When we're done here, I'll make my own phone call and she'll be gone in minutes. And if she manages to tell anybody before we get to her, who's gonna believe a crazy, left-wing nut job like her?"

"She's not the only one who knows," I insisted. "She's put everything I've said this morning out on the Internet. They heard every word."

Landry snorted. "Please." He turned to Baldy. "Take the back left, I got the back right. Kappa—"

Cliff interrupted him. "You hear that?"

Thanks to my particular infirmity, I didn't. But from the look on Landry's face, he did. And so did the others. "Shit!" the cop spat out, spinning in place. "Where's that coming from?"

I didn't know what they were talking about, but it was clear that I was the only one in the dark. Every person in the room besides me was listening intently to something which was apparently emanating from outside the courtroom.

And then I did hear something. Very faintly, at first, but growing steadily louder, until I could make out that it was some kind of chant. A chorus of voices.

Landry had pulled out his cell phone, and was cursing at his inability to get whoever he was calling to respond.

I still couldn't make out what the distant voices were saying. And then, when it got loud enough for me to make it out, I knew that we were saved. Because what I heard was voices, chanting, in rhythm, "We heard every word! We heard every word! We heard every word!"

Apparently, Cliff hadn't been bluffing.

"Goddammit, where's that coming from?" Landry demanded, of no one in particular.

By now, Kappa was speaking to someone on his cell phone. After a few seconds, he hung up, and rushed to Landry. "We gotta go," he urged, hurriedly. "Word got out. This gang just stormed the front doors. They're armed, and they're in the hallways, with the press. They all know. The order is to exfiltrate. Now."

Landry swung toward him. "Hold Omega positions."

Then there was a banging on the rear door, and a muffled shout from the hallway beyond. The bald guy unlocked the doors and three more paramilitary men came in, weapons drawn, and locked the door behind themselves. The three must have been stationed at the end of the hallway to keep people from straying into the wipe zone. One of them said to Landry, "Alpha, sir, containment is breached. Orders from HQ are to get out. Now."

I could see the rage in the cop's eyes. He *wanted* to shoot us all. But in the end, he obeyed his superiors. "Jesus Christ!" he barked. "All right. Go!"

The three new men and Baldy came up the center aisle, raced past me, and pushed through the back door.

The sound of the mob grew louder as the other two thugs followed quickly behind the bald guy. Landry came last, pistol in hand, staring me down all the way. He passed through the gate in the railing separating the gallery from the front of the courtroom, and when he reached Varick, he took the blue folder off the prosecutor's table. Then he walked slowly and directly toward me, the folder in one hand, his pistol in the other.

When he reached the witness stand, he stopped. "You think you did something important here, don't you, Tommy? Well, you know what, little man? All you did is make it harder for us to keep you safe. Think about that the next time some freakin' Muslim lunatic blows up a building in an American city."

It was supposed to be his dramatic exit line, but as he moved to pass by me and leave the courtroom, I got down from the witness stand and blocked his way. "Give me the folder," I demanded. "Josh Meadows died so that would become public."

Landry smirked. "Josh Meadows died in Afghanistan. Beta died because he betrayed his command. Now get out of my way." He lifted his left arm—the one with the gun—as if to sweep me aside, and stepped forward.

But I didn't budge.

"Josh Meadows died to save the Constitution," I said, grabbing the folder with my injured hand. As strange as it sounds, the pain that tore through me did not deter me—for some reason, it made me more resolute.

But Paul Landry did not release the documents. "You had your little moment in the sun, Tommy boy," he sneered. "Don't push it." And with that, he yanked down on the folder, as if to snatch it back from my grip.

But I did not let go, nor did I move.

He said nothing, but I knew what he was thinking. At the instant he began to lift his left arm to point his gun at me, I grabbed onto the pistol with my right hand, holding it so that it was aimed down at the ground.

Now Landry and I were eye to eye, each sharing a

grip on the blue folder with one pair of hands, and on Landry's weapon with the other.

I glanced quickly over the cop's shoulder and saw Amy. She had her back to another woman in the gallery, who was clearly trying to release Amy from whatever restraints were keeping her hands behind her.

I don't know how long Landry and I stood like that, straining against each other for control. By all rights, with the night I'd had, Landry should have been able to overpower me. Maybe he had been weakened by his trip through the windshield of the VW. Maybe I had finally gotten used to the tidal waves of adrenaline that were fueling me that morning.

Or maybe it was something else. Maybe the power of my hope for the future was greater than the power of his fear from the past.

But for whatever reason, every time he exerted force against one of my hands or arms, I countered with force that was at least equal. We were frozen against each other. Deadlocked. But I didn't know how long I could hold him like that.

And then Amy was finally free of her restraints, and was heading through the crowd toward us. If Landry pulled away from me, he'd kill me, and then her.

"Stay back, Amy!" I shouted. But she kept coming.

"This isn't going to end well, punk," the rogue cop wheezed. He was working hard.

It felt like I was perspiring, especially across my forehead. I learned later that the cut above my eye had reopened, and I was bleeding again. But my will was suddenly as strong as the arms that had chopped wood for my father for fifteen years. I wasn't going to back down—not one inch. To emphasize that, I even leaned forward a bit, and spoke quietly, but confidently. "Not for you, anyway."

As if on cue, a tremendous pounding on the door sounded. The chanting continued, louder than ever, in the hallway. The mob was moments from rushing in. Amy was less than ten seconds away.

"Let go of the folder, Landry."

We were literally nose to nose. Blood was now pouring down my face, yet I did not yield. But the man known as Alpha had one last dirty trick. One final, nasty move to win, whatever the cost.

With a vicious grunt, he snapped his head back, and brought his forehead straight down toward the bridge of my nose.

But just as he had read my face when I lied to him in the Volkswagen, I had read his, and I was ready.

At the moment Landry's head began to come toward mine, I shifted to the right, moving the top of my left shoulder to exactly where my face had been.

So it was Landry's nose that made the sickening *crunch* as it made contact with my long-ago healed collarbone.

And then everything happened at once.

The injured cop screamed in agony, releasing his grip on both the folder and the gun and covering his bloodied and broken nose with both hands.

There was a tremendous crash from the back of the courtroom, as the double doors there burst open. And then dozens of Navajos led by David and Jack West poured into the room, followed by scores of reporters and cameras.

I heard a *bang* behind me, and when I turned I saw that Landry had run away and slammed the door behind him.

And then Amy was in my arms, and we were surrounded by a swarm of armed Native Americans, all asking if I was okay.

It turns out I wasn't the only one standing in front of the tanks that morning.

When order was finally restored, Judge Lomax naturally recessed the Gomez trial for the rest of the day. I was escorted by police officers—the kind who don't threaten the lives of the people they're supposed to protect—to a hospital where I was treated for my wounds, and then placed in protective custody for the night. On the next day, which would turn out to be the final day of the Juan Gomez trial, I testified as to what Joshua Meadows told me before he died, and I was allowed to read into the record a portion of the notes he had left behind.

As everybody knows by now, the Foundation was the brainchild of a couple of men—Undersecretary of Defense Newton, and a career army officer named Burton. It was conceived as a top-secret unit after September 11, and it was dedicated to keeping America safe from terrorists, whatever the cost.

All soldiers who joined the Foundation had to allow the army to inform their family that they were dead, and had to give up all hope of ever seeing or contacting their families again. All believed they were sacrificing their lives in order to ensure that their country was never attacked the way that it was on September 11. They were trained to follow any order, without question, including orders to commit illegal acts, even murder.

But the patriotic fervor which led to the Foundation's formation was soon warped into a formidable underground political movement. Over several years, carefully screened people who wielded power in every branch of government all over the country were approached to join the clandestine group. Judges, senators, governors, and law enforcement officials came together to secretly create an organization so strong that when its existence finally became public knowledge, there would be nothing to stop it from controlling the country.

The Foundation grew and thrived during the early aftermath of 9/11. Highly placed people developed strategies for increasing government control over the population, such as warrantless wiretapping and the elimination of habeas corpus. The further the country drifted toward authoritarian rule, the stronger the Foundation grew. New members were recruited to run for government positions on platforms touting national security above all else.

But then, the Iraq War and a variety of scandals began to drain the country's energy and attention away from the fear of future terrorist attacks. The Foundation was still years from putting into place all of the pieces needed to stage what would, in effect, be a bloodless coup. Certain members of the Foundation were even threatened with losing their positions in the elected government; others came under pressure to resign for perceived failures.

It was decided that in order for the Foundation to continue to grow and thrive, the country needed to refocus on the fear of an enemy attack. So plans were drawn up to create one.

Lieutenant Meadows was in charge of planning and executing a terrorist act within the U.S., and framing a Muslim U.S. citizen for the crime. And when you've got access to state-of-the-art technology, developing incriminating video- and audiotapes is just a laptop computer away. When the "perpetrator" was discovered,

Americans would come to realize that it was vitally important to give up more of their liberty in order to become safe from any future attack.

Because in that environment, the Foundation would flourish.

And that is how the Denver Tunnel Bombing plot was hatched.

I am still dumbstruck at how the leaders of an organization conceived to protect American citizens from attack would come to the conclusion that the best way to do that was to attack American citizens.

In any event, the Denver plan was a stunning triumph. One hundred thirteen people died. The country was plunged into panic, and the rampant fear led to increased power among Foundation members already in government.

It was, in fact, that power that led Juan Gomez to be tried in Arizona. Everyone knew he was guilty, and thanks to his status as an enemy combatant, he didn't need to be tried at all, but it was decided that a public spectacle in the home state of one of the Foundation's rising stars, Atlee Hamilton, would help propel him to victory in his upcoming special election for the senate. Judge Klay was already a trusted member of the Foundation, as was Landry—it was a perfect fit.

It was just coincidence that I shot off my mouth when I did. That got Landry to put his second-in-command—Meadows, code-named Beta—into action, to coerce me into ensuring that nothing got in the way of a guilty verdict.

But what Landry didn't know was that the mass murder of scores of Americans had been too much for Meadows, and it had finally broken his loyalty to the Foundation. Meadows came to the conclusion that he had to blow the whistle on the organization, but the group was far too controlled to let one of its members stray far from supervision, so it was near impossible to rat out the traitors. In fact, Meadows assumed that he was going to be killed in his effort to get the truth out. What he didn't intend to do was die in vain.

Enter Tom Carpenter, on a noisy silver platter.

One very high-profile trial, one act of arson, three bouts of hand-to-hand combat including a pistol-whipping, a three-story-high dive, a gunshot wound, and countless physical and psychological injuries later, the charges against Juan Abdullah Gomez were dropped, and the Foundation was exposed.

But as for me, I gathered up my father, Amy, and Erica, and we fled.

Because I had become terrified of Landry, and everyone like him.

Because I had become terrified of domineering politicians and government officials who would do or say anything to increase their stronghold on power.

Because I had become terrified of my country.

EPILOGUE

Four years later

WITH THE HELP of some friends of Cliff and Iris, Amy and I found temporary shelter out of the country, and we stayed there for over a year, recovering.

When we both felt a little more confident about bringing Henley and Erica back into the U.S., we bought a place together high in the woods near a mountain lake in Virginia. Don't try to find it, please. We value our privacy.

By the time we settled into our new home, Amy and I had decided to get married. And exactly three years ago today, Amy and I exchanged vows under a tall oak in our new backyard. Cliff and Iris were our witnesses. Erica was the bridesmaid. Henley was the best man.

I have looked back on what I wrote after the Gomez trial, and I am happy to report that I am less angry now. I have rebuilt much of my life, thanks largely to the love of Amy, Erica, and Henley, and the newest additions to our family, twins named Chloe and Will. Our home is not fancy, but it is comfortable, and features a woodstove for Henley with an extra-large hearth for safety.

There are plenty of dead trees for me to chop into firewood with my new ax.

Amy insisted that I put a small table and a chair out at this end of the yard so she can keep an eye on me when I'm working. But occasionally I find myself using the furniture for my own purposes. Such as now, as I write this while enjoying the mountain air.

Despite my personal recovery from the trauma of four years ago, I am still more cynical than I wish to be. I know that members of the Foundation still hold office in our government. They weren't all unmasked in the investigation following the Gomez trial. And junior Senator Atlee Hamilton pulled enough strings to turn the evidence of his involvement in the Foundation into mere rumors circulated by his political opponents. So I find myself quite skeptical these days when I hear our nation's leaders speak.

Maybe that isn't such a bad thing. Maybe power's corruption is always just a seductive whisper away. Maybe it is inevitable that bad people will try to take what isn't theirs from good people, and maybe brave men and women must stand guard against tyranny forever. For peace surely isn't the product of cowardice—it is the offspring of truth and courage.

Whatever the case, I sincerely hope that there will never be another time in this country when I feel the need to stand in front of a row of oncoming tanks—literally or figuratively. That was really terrifying.

Yet despite what happened during those late-spring days four years ago, I have reclaimed much of my optimism, and my sense of wonder at the world. I can confidently say that if there are evildoers amongst us, there are also angels. I should know—I share a home with five of them. And together, we live happily—one pancake breakfast, one Stevie Wonder song, one sunset, one bedtime prayer, at a time.

Sometimes, when I get distracted by petty things and I forget just how good my life is, I read Dale's last letter to me. I suspect my brother would be surprised that I carry it with me always, and read it often, but that's just because he was always such a humble person.

Greetings Captain Rootbeard. If you are reading this, then I must be dead.

I know that if I got a letter from you with that kind of an opening message, I'd be very angry. But if anger is what you're feeling right now, I hope that will change soon. Because the truth of the matter is, as I write this, I feel very good—very lucky. My life was overflowing with people and events that I cherished. And you can be sure that if you received this letter, it is because I died doing exactly what I love.

I know I don't have to ask this, but I'm a husband and a father, so I'll ask anyway. Since I'm not going to be there anymore, can you please look after Amy, and help her with our baby, when it's born? I get a lot of comfort knowing you're there for them, no matter what happens.

And when enough time has passed, make sure you tell the little one about the time I fell off the boat. It'll say all you need to about me, and it'll get a laugh, too. I really hope the kid grows up laughing a lot.

There's a corporal in my unit who has a very interesting religious philosophy. He believes that before souls are born, they all attend a kind of eternally ongoing, cosmic social mixer. And the idea of the event is for the souls to choose each other for companionship when they ultimately inhabit human bodies on earth. Whether as family members, or spouses, or teammates, or whatever.

I don't know whether the corporal is right, of course. But on the off chance that he is, I wanted to make sure that I got a chance to tell you how truly grateful I am that out of a universe of souls, you chose me.
Dale

I've always valued my brother's opinion, but he definitely turned that last thing upside down. I'm the one who will always be grateful for his presence in my life. Any implication in Dale's letter that I am somehow special is simply wrong. I am only a flawed lawyer, working in a flawed legal system, living in a flawed country, run by flawed politicians. I have been criticized for undervaluing my contribution in the Juan Gomez matter. But I contend that it was only the most bizarre set of coincidences that propelled me into temporary notoriety, not anything extraordinary about myself.

The fact is, the headline-grabbing events of that tumultuous week don't hold the smallest flickering candle to the dozens of truly special moments I now am blessed with every day. Amy still teases me about that—she thinks I attach way too much importance to occurrences that everyone else in the world would see as mundane.

Like right now. My heart-stoppingly beautiful wife is watching from the kitchen window as Erica, Chloe, and Will emerge from the house, giggling, hand-in-hand-in-hand. Amy laughingly tells them to remind me that it's time for me to come inside.

Thanks to her grandfather, Erica has recently become enamored of the music of Diana Ross and the

Supremes. And she sees it as her solemn, sisterly duty to impart everything she learns to her little siblings. So now the youngest blue-eyed soul trio in music history stands before me, belting out an exuberant, if undisciplined, rendition of "Stop in the Name of Love."

My soul is so filled with joy that I sit here like a grinning fool, wondering how I could be so lucky to have this life.

Amy would say that what just happened was nothing more than three kids running across the yard, rather ineffectively calling their father in to dinner.

But with all due respect, I disagree.

Because I know the voice of God when I hear it.

ABOUT THE AUTHOR

ED GAFFNEY took ten years of work as a criminal lawyer, added an overactive imagination, and came up with a new career as a novelist.

He lives west of Boston with his wife, *New York Times* bestselling author Suzanne Brockmann.

Ed is shamelessly proud of their two children, Melanie, who is also a writer, and Jason, who is a stage actor. *Enemy Combatant* is Ed's fourth novel, and he is currently at work on his fifth.

THE SUSPENSE WILL KILL YOU....

VICTOR GISCHLER

GUN MONKEYS	$6.99/$10.99
THE PISTOL POETS	$6.99/$10.99
SUICIDE SQUEEZE	$6.99/$9.99
SHOTGUN OPERA	$6.99/$9.99

ASA LARSSON

SUN STORM
$12.00/$15.00

THE BLOOD SPILT
$12.00/$15.00

MORAG JOSS

FUNERAL MUSIC	$6.99/NCR
FEARFUL SYMMETRY	$6.99/NCR
FRUITFUL BODIES	$6.99/NCR
HALF-BROKEN THINGS	$13.00/NCR
PUCCINI'S GHOSTS	$13.00/NCR

CODY MCFADYEN

SHADOW MAN
$6.99/$8.99

THE FACE OF DEATH
$24.00/$30.00

STEPHEN BOOTH

BLIND TO THE BONES
$7.50/NCR

ONE LAST BREATH
$7.50/NCR

THE DEAD PLACE
$7.50/NCR

LISA GARDNER

THE PERFECT HUSBAND	$7.99/$11.99
THE OTHER DAUGHTER	$7.99/$11.99
THE THIRD VICTIM	$7.99/$10.99
THE NEXT ACCIDENT	$7.99/$11.99
THE SURVIVORS CLUB	$7.99/$11.99
THE KILLING HOUR	$7.99/$11.99
ALONE	$7.99/$10.99
GONE	$7.99/$10.99
HIDE	$25.00/$30.00

Ask for these titles wherever books are sold, or visit us online at _www.bantamdell.com_ for ordering information.